Billy Hopkins  ...ed:

'Hopkins, lik... ...rtlessly simplistic pro... ...uthor' *Manchester Ev...*

'Rich in anecdote, the story exudes a heartfelt quality, making it a delight to read. Billy comes across as very human – making mistakes, thinking creatively and caring for his family' *Historical Novels Review*

'Heart-warming fictional memoirs of a wartime childhood. Nostalgic and sad, but with pages of gentle humour too' *Bolton Evening News*

'A very enjoyable read' *Bradford Telegraph and Argus*

'Thanks to the former Liverpool school-teacher's uncluttered writing style, *Going Places* flows beautifully' *Liverpool Echo*

'A cracking yarn' *Warrington Guardian*

'This is well-written nostalgia for those of us old enough to remember' *South Wales Argus*

'Nostalgic, funny and romantic, *High Hopes* is a vivid and funny evocation of northern life after the Second World War. The author's work has been compared to that of Frank McCourt (*Angela's Ashes*) and Roddy Doyle (*Paddy Clarke Ha Ha Ha*)' *Lancashire Life*

'His many fans will soon be chortling as he relates adventure after adventure. I can't wait for more of his escapades' *Northern Echo*

'This story of a family dealing with their dreams, new challenges and heartaches, is sure to capture the imagination' *Huddersfield Daily Examiner*

'A good read' *Times Educational Supplement*

Billy Hopkins has legions of fans throughout the world:

'Congratulations on an excellent book. I laughed and cried, it was so delightfully warm and funny' Mrs Anne Greenhalgh, Sorrento, W. Australia

'I just finished your book, in tears. It just got better as I went. So much for the image of the cold, distant Englishman – you just blew that away. You write very well, with honesty, and with a lot of human passion. Thank you for a terrific book' Robert Stever, MD, Seattle, USA

'This rags to riches tale, set in my own lifetime, recalls wartime boyhood, is packed with nostalgia, filled with laughter and is often tinged with pain. As a tale it is compelling and difficult to put down' Robin Hull, Professor of General Practice

'Read it faster than many books I've read all year . . . Makes you laugh – makes you cry' Kathleen Quinlan, infants teacher, Blackpool

'Many thanks for reviving "old times"' Ron West, Burlington, USA

'It took me just a day to read and I feel as if I have a long-lost friend' Anne Gardner, Australia

'I feel I must write to thank you for the pleasure I got reading your books. How true to life, as it were, they all are!' Mrs Margaret Roberts, Keighley, Yorkshire

'Thanks for your wonderful and nostalgic books which have given me the most enjoyment I've had for a very long time. Please, please, keep writing' Harry Pemberton, Auckland, New Zealand

'Every chapter grips with events and places, people and circumstances described with drama and authentic realism' Brian McGuinness, Professor of Primary Health Care, University of Keele

'It's more than just a story, it's a history lesson as well' Simon Abram, Cheshire

'Highly entertaining . . . Recalls memories of a Manchester I knew' Dan Murphy, retired teacher

'I half read my mother's copy of *Our Kid* when the team was playing in Italy. Enjoyed it so much I thought I'd better order my own copy' Brian Kidd, Deputy Team Manager, Manchester United

'*Our Kid* . . . was the funniest book I have ever read – it had me laughing out loud, it was so great. You sure have the gift of writing' Isobel Fox, Doncaster, Yorkshire

'Everyone will enjoy *High Hopes* . . . The book reflects the exuberance of youth in those early days of post-war Britain. Thank you for providing such a good read and for bringing so much pleasure to all who enjoy tales of Manchester' Bernard Lawson, MBE, Retired Private Secretary to the Lord Mayor of Manchester

'A little masterpiece' Dr Darragh Little, GP and writer, Limerick, Ireland

'I truly feel that *Kate's Story* is what I would describe as a classic masterpiece' Amy Carter, Author, Lancashire

'I have lived in the States for the last thirty-five years but was born in Manchester. [Your books] brought back so many memories of places I knew. Thank you for all the pleasure [they] gave me' Marilyn Gresty, USA

'Congratulations on the best series of books I have ever read' Alan Townley, Manchester

'Just to let you know how much I have enjoyed reading *Going Places*. The good humour, sincerity, narrative power and "old-fashioned" values of this book are qualities I particularly appreciated' Dr Gabriel A. Sivian, Jerusalem, Israel

'Your books are of great interest to all ages' Mrs Patricia Hall, Eastbourne

'My congratulations on the freshness of your memory, the richness and generosity of your values, and the liveliness and sincerity of your creative touches' Dr Con Casey, Retired Head of Education, Hopwood Hall

Also by Billy Hopkins

Our Kid
High Hopes
Kate's Story
Going Places

ANYTHING GOES

Billy Hopkins

headline

First published in 2005
by HEADLINE BOOK PUBLISHING

First published in paperback in 2005
by HEADLINE BOOK PUBLISHING

1

ISBN 0 7553 2055 7

Typeset in Baskerville by Avon DataSet Ltd,
Bidford-on-Avon, Warwickshire

Printed and bound in Great Britain by Clays Ltd, St Ives plc

Headline's policy is to use papers that are natural,
renewable and recyclable products and made from wood
grown in sustainable forests. The logging and manufacturing
processes are expected to conform to the environmental
regulations of the country of origin.

HEADLINE BOOK PUBLISHING
A division of Hodder Headline
338 Euston Road
London NW1 3BH

www.headline.co.uk
www.hodderheadline.com

DEDICATION

I dedicate this book to the many readers who have
encouraged me with their letters and e-mails.
Undoubtedly, an author's greatest reward lies
in the knowledge that his work has given pleasure
to someone somewhere.

Acknowledgements

For some time, readers have been asking for a sequel to GOING PLACES.

So here it is: Book Number Five in the Billy Hopkins saga.

The book is a work of fiction in that the names of places and persons have been changed though the incidents are inspired by true events. As with the first four books in the series, a generous measure of poetic licence has been employed in the hope of making the story interesting. If you enjoy reading this story as much as I enjoyed writing it, I shall be content.

I owe a debt of gratitude to my children, Stephen, Catherine, Peter, Laurence, Paul and Joseph, all of whom wrote their own mini-memoirs to jog my memory in the writing of this latest episode. Their reminiscences about flower power, the hippie generation and family life in general were invaluable. A special thanks goes to my son Paul for his photography and for building my website (www.billysbooks.info). I am also indebted to Mr David Newton for background information about geriatric nursing homes, the heartbreak and the occasional humour.

But my greatest thanks must go to my wife, Clare, for her unfailing help at every stage along the way. Without that constant and daily support, I doubt if I could have produced a single book, let alone five.

In the world of publishing, I wish to thank all those who have made my books possible. At the Blake Friedmann Literary Agency: Isobel Dixon and support staff, in particular David Eddy. At Headline Book Publishing: Publishing Director Marion Donaldson, for her professionalism; Kate Burke for keeping me in touch; Justinia Baird-Murray, Debbie Clements and Andrew Wadsworth, whose attractive cover designs for my books have been an important factor in their success; and backroom staff in sales, in particular Press Officer Helena Towers, who organized and escorted me so efficiently on book-signing tours, and Marketing Executive Beatrice Denison for her imaginative ideas in book promotion. And finally, copy editor Jane Heller and proofreader Alice Wood for their thoughtful and judicious work on the text.

I believe what really happens in history is this: the old man is always wrong; and the young people are always wrong about what is wrong with him. The practical form it takes is this: that, while the old man may stand by some stupid custom, the young man always attacks it with some theory that turns out to be equally stupid.

G. K. Chesterton

Insanity is hereditary. You get it from your kids. (Anon.)

Britain in the Sixties

Mention the sixties and what does it bring to mind? For some it was an age of violence; they remember the Vietnam War, protest marches and student sit-ins, the Cuba crisis which brought the world to the brink of nuclear war; the assassination of President John Kennedy (most of us remember exactly what we were doing when the news came through) and later his brother Robert and the black leader, Martin Luther King. Others associate the decade with great technical advances, like space exploration and the first men in space, Yuri Gagarin, John Glenn and Neil Armstrong, the first man to walk on the moon. Or maybe they think of it as the time when authority and traditional values were thrown into the melting pot, and the young believed that to change the world, all they needed was music, drugs or simply love.

Bob Dylan sang 'For The Times They Are A-Changing' and this title seemed to sum up neatly the decade that became known as the 'Swinging Sixties'. A sentiment confirmed by President Kennedy when he told the American people: 'The old era is ending. We stand today on the edge of a new frontier, the frontier of the 1960s . . .'

We British were certainly ready for change. We'd had enough of hard times: depression in the thirties, suffering in the forties, austerity in the fifties. Television was black and white and so were the lives of most people. Then towards the end of the fifties, things began to look up, so much so that Harold Macmillan could tell us: 'You've never had it so good.' Pursuit of pleasure and a hedonistic lifestyle became the new ideals. And there was no need to wait. It was a case of enjoy it today, pay for it tomorrow.

On this optimistic note and with their new-found wealth, people embarked on a spending spree to buy the things that would make life easier: washing machines, fridges, inside lavatories with modern bathroom suites, and central heating. More important, however, was the fundamental shift in people's attitudes and expectations. They were no longer willing to put up with obsolete restrictions, for they had developed greater expectations of what life could offer. Parliament responded with a programme of liberalization with capital punishment abolished, divorce made easier, homosexuality decriminalized, abortion legalized, and the laws on censorship relaxed. After an acrimonious trial, the mass publication of the unexpurgated version of D.H. Lawrence's *Lady Chatterley's Lover* by Penguin Books seemed to act as a catalyst. Many of the older generation feared that it heralded the opening of the floodgates of immorality and the dreaded 'permissive' society. Other public bodies took their lead from the trial and adopted a more tolerant attitude towards books, plays and films. Even the staid BBC, long regarded as the upholder of traditional values, became more permissive, prompting some wag to remark that Auntie Beeb hadn't merely hitched up her petticoats, she'd taken them off altogether.

It wasn't long before there appeared pressure groups determined to stem the headlong rush into immorality and licentiousness. There were people like Mary Whitehouse who saw television as a pernicious influence; she described one BBC programme as 'anti-authority, anti-religious, anti-patriotism, and pro-dirt'. She was a voice crying in the wilderness because irreverence was in the air and poking fun at the establishment had become a national pastime. Conventional morality and traditional institutions were debunked from every quarter: in television programmes like *That Was The Week That Was (TW3)*, and towards the end of the decade *Monty Python's Flying Circus*; in satirical magazines like *Private Eye* and *Oz*; and in stage shows like

Beyond the Fringe. No aspect of the establishment escaped the acid wit of the debunkers, whether the target was the Church, royalty, the BBC, the Conservative Party, patriotism, the war, or the class structure. It became more important to be against something than to be for it. Even in the fifties this had become evident. When Marlon Brando in *The Wild One* was asked what he was rebelling against, he asked, 'Whaddaya got?'

For the young, the sixties was a time of bliss and omnipotence. The sky was the limit and there was no difficulty they couldn't overcome. They had more money in their pockets than their parents had ever dreamed of and there soon developed a culture of youth with its own distinctive values, along with the inevitable get-rich-quick merchants intent on relieving them of their cash. Britain's young claimed to be the trendsetters in clothes and music for the rest of the world; London was hip, 'the swinging city'. And while London may have had the latest fashion gear with its King's Road and its 'switched-on' Carnaby Street, when it came to pop music, the north of England reigned supreme. Manchester had Herman's Hermits and the Hollies; Newcastle, the Animals; Birmingham, the Moody Blues. It was Liverpool, though, that claimed first place because it could boast not only the Beatles (more famous than Jesus Christ Himself, according to John Lennon) but also Cilla Black, the Searchers, Gerry and the Pacemakers, Billy J. Kramer, and a host of others.

An essential characteristic of this youth culture was its anti-authority attitude and rejection of adult norms and mores, what they scornfully called 'the rat race'. Youth saw the 'oldies' as wrong about all the important issues, like war and peace, sex and religion. The one thing the young were adamant about was that they didn't, under any circumstances, want to be like their parents. 'We hope we die before we get old,' said some. The sixties became a titanic struggle between young and old, amounting at times to something

3

like trench warfare. The past was gone and anything that smacked of former times was contemptible and to be despised. When it came to clothes, fashion designers did not lead the trend but followed it. And what the new clientele demanded was garish modes of dress, not only as a way of asserting their individuality but also as a way of 'winding up' the adults around them. Men grew their hair long and women wore skimpy skirts.

'We grew our hair shoulder-length and dressed in the craziest outfits we could find,' said one young man. 'Anything to annoy our parents.'

'Doing one's thing' became the 'in philosophy' whether it meant attending love-ins and rock festivals, getting high on pot, dropping acid, joining a hippy commune, or experimenting with transcendental meditation and oriental mysticism. Youth had its models, like Mick Jagger of the Rolling Stones who was admired because of his brazen defiance of cultural convention in drugs, clothes, hair, sex and manners. When, following a leading article in *The Times*, he won his release from prison after being convicted of drug possession, the younger generation saw it as a victory over authority. Overnight he became their hero and knight in shining armour.

But nowhere was the youthful rebellion more evident than in the matter of attitudes to sex. The contraceptive pill which became available in 1961 changed the whole moral landscape, inspiring the poet Philip Larkin to lament the fact that he'd been just too late for the start of sexual intercourse in 1963. The Pill was not only simple and safe to use, it was available on the NHS. The sexual freedom this brought about prompted one assize court justice to observe that many of the young people who came before him appeared to attach as much importance to sexual intercourse as they did to buying an ice lolly. The kiss of the forties and fifties had become the sexual intercourse of the sixties.

Older people saw all this happening under their noses

4

and, while they were in favour of moving with the times, things were going too far, too fast. Reasonable change, yes, but this was more than they'd bargained for. Had the sluice gates been finally opened, they wondered, threatening fundamental moral values and the British way of life? The result was much friction between the generations though it would be wrong to believe that the young were entirely hedonistic and self-seeking. Many took a moral stance against war, especially that in Vietnam, and in various ways expressed their concern at the destruction of the environment. It is also true to say that while many young people manifested their dissatisfaction with things to which they were opposed by taking part in demonstrations, rallies, sit-ins, and the like, the great majority unnoticed by the media went on to pursue their careers in the normal way.

And while it had become infra dig to express patriotic sentiments (many cinemas and theatres, for example, had ceased playing the National Anthem at the end of a performance), there was a brief resurgence of national pride when England achieved success in various sporting fields. In 1961, Lester Piggott rode his thousandth winner and in the same year at Wimbledon, Angela Mortimer became the first British woman to win the singles since 1914 when she beat Christine Truman. In swimming, Anita Lonsbrough won Britain's first Olympic gold medal since 1924; and in 1968, Tony Jacklin became the first British golfer to win a US tournament. In 1968, Matt Busby's Manchester United, rebuilt since the 1958 Munich tragedy, won the European Cup. But the most spectacular sporting event of the decade was the 1966 World Cup final when England, captained by Bobby Moore, beat Germany 4–2.

This was the society to which Billy Hopkins returned with his wife Laura and their young family after five years in East Africa where Billy had worked as Education Officer for the Kenya Government. They had left their home town, Manchester, to start a new life in Kenya but when the country was granted independence in 1963, the pull back to their roots proved too strong. But it was a very different Britain they were coming back to. How would they cope with the culture shock and how would they readjust to their mother country, which had undergone such a major social upheaval during their absence abroad?

Chapter One

'What's all that white stuff?' young John asked. 'Has someone spilt piles of talcum powder everywhere?'

'That's called snow, stupid,' his brother Mark replied. Mark was eight, two years older than John, but even he had only the vaguest memories of snow whereas John who'd been born in Kenya had never seen the stuff before.

It was December 1963 and Billy Hopkins with his wife and four children had landed at Heathrow. Billy had visited Britain two years earlier but that had been in spring when the weather had been mild. Now when the air stewardess opened the aeroplane doors, they were met by an icy blast that took their breath away.

'It's like walking into a gigantic freezer,' Laura exclaimed, holding the two youngest closer to her.

Billy took one look at the frost and the snow.

'You know,' he gasped, 'I'd completely forgotten how cold the English winter could be. What do you say we book return tickets straight back to Nairobi on the next available flight? And look at the sky, so dull and grey; it's only three o'clock and the lights are switched on everywhere. Everything looks so dull and washed-out like one of those old sepia photographs.'

'You're right,' Laura said cheerfully. 'After the dazzling Kenya sunshine, it does look totally miserable. And I absolutely love it.'

They wrapped up as well as they could given their tropical outfits. Blue with cold they took the transit bus to the terminal where they collected their luggage from the carousel. No problems getting through Customs and Immigration, a poker-faced officer giving them hardly a second glance as he chalked their suitcases. It was warm inside the airport building but the moment they stepped outside to board the coach for Victoria, the winter weather chilled them to the bone and within seconds the shivering and the teeth-chattering began again, lasting all the way into the city centre. The two youngest clung to their mother partly because of the freezing temperature but more because of the suicidal speed and madcap manoeuvres of the bus driver as he fought his tortuous way through the heavy London traffic.

'The world seems to be whirling madly about our ears,' Laura said, clutching Mark and John as the coach skidded round a hairpin bend.

'Reminds me of one of those Mack Sennett silent movies with the action speeded up.' Billy grimaced, tightening his grip on young Lucy's shoulder to prevent her being thrown into the aisle.

'Hey, Dad, maybe we'll get to see the Keystone Kops,' Matthew called out gleefully. At least one of the family was enjoying the hair-raising journey.

'This is definitely the most dangerous part of the trip so far,' Billy said as the coach swerved to avoid a collision with a pantechnicon. 'We'll either be wiped out in one momentous pile-up or freeze to death in this arctic weather.'

'Talking of freezing,' Laura said, 'first chance we get, we buy warmer clothes for everyone.'

'I'm not sure I want anything for myself,' Billy said. 'Remember I mothballed many winter suits in your parents' loft when we went abroad. I can wear those when we get back to Manchester.'

Laura laughed. 'Don't be silly. They're all out of date now. Why, some of them go back to your student days. You're a real hoarder, Billy. Never want to throw anything away in case it comes in handy at some distant date in the future. If we've got the money, we should buy new for everyone.'

'Oh, great, Mum!' Lucy exclaimed. 'Can we go to Carnaby Street and get the latest gear?'

'And how, young madam, do you know about Carnaby Street and the latest gear, may I ask?' Laura said.

'I saw it in a teenage magazine, Mum.'

'You're much too young to be reading such rubbish,' Billy said.

'Oh, Dad. I'm not a baby. I'll be eleven in a few weeks' time.'

'And I'll be a teenager in a few months,' Matthew said proudly.

'A teenager!' Billy exclaimed. 'How do you make that out?'

'I'll be thir*teen* next birthday.'

'Sorry, sorry,' Billy laughed. 'I didn't realize I had such grown-up fashion-conscious kids.'

'Anyway,' Laura said, 'we shan't be doing any shopping in Carnaby Street. We'll be buying sensible clothing at Marks and Spencer. We'll have none of this talk about latest gear.'

'I think we can do better than Marks and Sparks now we've got a little money,' Billy said. 'A visit to Chelsea or Oxford Street might be on the cards. And no, I don't mean Mary Quant's,' he added, eyeing the two eldest.

From Victoria, they took a cab that gave them a ride that was madder and more dangerous than that of the bus, if that were possible. The family stared intrigued at the unfolding spectacle. Here was a different scene from the area round the airport. Preparations for Christmas were evident everywhere. The streets were necklaced in bright decorations, and festoons of twinkling coloured lights were reflected in the murky waters of the Thames. London was swinging. Gaily painted Mini-Coopers overflowing with happy-go-lucky youngsters who waved gaily as they whizzed past, and policeman on the beat seemed to be there more as props for tourists' photos than upholders of the law. Laura and the children gazed open-mouthed at the bizarre hairstyles and outlandish dress of both male and female pedestrians: bowler-hatted City gents rubbing shoulders with long-haired cavaliers; and despite the cold weather, mini-skirted models mingling with smartly groomed girls in short PVC raincoats, one or two with Union Jack motifs. From innumerable cafés, there wafted the aroma of roasted coffee beans and mulled wine. There was little chance for Billy to enjoy the scene, however, for his attention was monopolized by their cab driver who had views on everything under the sun and seemed determined to let Billy hear them. He slid back his dividing window and looked round at the family.

'You lot look suntanned for this time of the year. Been on holiday?'

'No,' Billy said. 'Just got back from Kenya. We've been out there for five years.'

The driver gave a whistle of surprise. 'Five years, eh! What were you doing out there?'

'I was teaching in an African secondary school.'

'I'll bet that was a job and a half, eh. Kenya! Isn't that where Kenyatta's the boss?'

'That's right. The country's recently got its independence. Kenyatta's the new President.'

'Wasn't this Kenyatta geezer head of a bunch of terrorists? The Moo-Moo or something.'

'You mean the Mau Mau.'

'That's what I said. Typical of this country of ours. Next thing you know, this Kenyatta thug will be having dinner with the Queen at Buckingham Palace. We're always doing it. First we put the terrorists in prison then release 'em, make 'em presidents, then wine 'em and dine 'em. Like what they did with that fellah Bishop Maracas in Cyprus and Necrummy in Ghana.'

'You mean Makarios and Nkrumah?'

'Yeah. That's what I said. I tell you this country's going to pot. Earlier this year our Minister of War was caught with his trousers down sleeping with a high-class hooker, Christine Keeler. The other week they gave her nine months in Holloway. I'd have given her nine years if it'd been left to me. Not many women can say they brought down the government, the way she did. But all them big politicians are at it.'

10

'You think so?'

'I know so. Take that Lord Astor geezer. He said at the trial that he hadn't touched Mandy Rice-Davies. Now she was a stunner and no mistake. Brought the house down when she giggled and said, "Well, he would say that, wouldn't he?" I tell you, the country's gone sex mad. Had to stop a couple doing it in the back of my cab the other night. Could have lost my licence for running a mobile brothel. And now Macmillan's resigned. Says it was prostate trouble but more like prostitute trouble, if you ask me. I reckon it was all due to the scandal; couldn't stand the heat in the kitchen. And now we have that chinless wonder, Douglas-Home, as Prime Minister. Says he doesn't know how to add up and does his sums using matchsticks. Wouldn't be surprised, though, if he was like the rest of 'em, unable to keep his flies zipped up.'

'I'm sure you're right,' Billy said, thinking it was best to agree with this firebrand character.

'And there's another thing . . .' the cab driver said, turning his head to catch Billy's eye.

But Billy didn't hear what this other thing was for they had reached their destination, the Royal Court in Emperor's Gate, Kensington, a small but elegant private hotel.

'My, my,' Laura exclaimed. 'Haven't *we* gone up in the world!'

'And why not?' Billy said vehemently. 'I think we've earned it. Before we went abroad, we lived from one month to the next always waiting for pay day. Now, after five years of hard saving, it's time to start spending some of it.'

Early next day, they visited Harvey Nichols in Knights-bridge where Laura bought a beautiful brown woollen coat with mink collar whilst Lucy chose a blue Mary Quant midi coat trimmed with fur. The males of the family were equipped with more traditional suits, Billy having turned down the frilly shirt, the colourful waistcoat and the hipster trousers suggested by the obliging assistant. He rounded off his outfit with a heavy black Crombie and a smart trilby.

11

'Now you look like a business tycoon,' Laura said, looking him up and down appreciatively.

In the afternoon, they took a taxi to the Scala Theatre to see a performance of *Peter Pan* starring the film stars Anne Heywood, Jane Asher and John Gregson. For them this was indeed the high life after their spell living in a small African township fifty miles from Nairobi. The kids were agog at the wonders of the technological wizardry that enabled Wendy to fly through the air with such ease and grace. At five o'clock they emerged from the theatre mesmerized by what they had seen on stage.

Lucy in particular was moved by the play. She said, 'Thank you for taking us, Dad. Watching Wendy and the others fly like that was the most wonderful thing I've ever seen in my whole life.'

'Fine,' Billy said, 'as long as you don't try it at home.'

They had travelled to the theatre by taxi but by popular demand opted to return by underground. It'll be an experience, they thought.

It was a mistake because they were caught in the rush hour and had to stand most of the way back. At Oxford Street a massive throng boarded the train and it became like the photographs of a Tokyo bullet train they had seen in *Picture Post* where platform porters physically crammed people into the train. Young John came close to being suffocated down amongst the legs of the jostling crowd and was only saved when Billy, with skilful use of the chin and much elbow-jabbing of his-fellow sardines, hoisted him up to give him air. They had learned their lesson early and thenceforth travelled everywhere by taxi.

They spent the next three days strolling open-mouthed around London, taking in the sights – Buckingham Palace, Westminster, Trafalgar Square, Piccadilly Circus. Every place they visited had an association either with a song or with the game of Monopoly which they'd played on Saturday evenings in Kenya.

'Look, Dad. It's Mayfair! Best on the set. Rent here's a massive four hundred pounds. And over there is Park Lane, three hundred and fifty pounds.'

As they strolled about the famous landmarks, they found themselves singing unforgettable ditties like 'Goodbye Piccadilly, farewell Leicester Square . . .' or reciting lines from A.A. Milne about changing guards at Buckingham Palace and how Alice was marrying one of the guards.

Soon it was time to return to their beloved Manchester. 'The Athens of the north' Billy called it. How they'd missed the place in the last five years! Shopping on bustling Market Street on a Saturday afternoon; joining the throngs flocking to watch the Derby match between Manchester United and City; rowing on Heaton Park lake or visiting the beautiful gardens at Fletcher Moss.

At Euston, they were taken aback by the bewildering array of magazines on display in W. H. Smith's – *Woman, Woman's Own, John Bull, Practical Householder* – the list seemed endless. There were many books on the shelves that hadn't been there when they'd left in 1958: *Lolita, Lady Chatterley's Lover, Tropic of Cancer*. Billy noticed, too, the way the eye of his soon-to-be-a-teenager son was drawn to the girly magazines, *Reveille* and *Playboy*, on the top shelf.

'Matthew's growing up,' he whispered to Laura. 'Here's a magazine more in your line,' he said to Matthew, tapping him on the shoulder and pointing to the *Boy's Own Paper*.

'Thanks a lot, Dad,' Matthew grinned. '*Boy's Own Paper*! I didn't know it was still around.'

For the journey, they bought a wide selection of children's comics: *Comic Cuts, Film Fun, The Dandy* and *The Beano* for the young ones, *The Eagle, The Rover* for Matthew, and *Girl, Girl's Crystal* and *School Friend* for Lucy. Laura selected *Woman* and *Woman's Own*. Billy bought twenty Kensitas tipped and a copy of *Punch* and *The Times*.

'It's so refreshing to read a newspaper on the day of its

publication instead of one a fortnight old,' he remarked. 'But I don't know if I can afford to go on smoking here in Britain despite the wonderful prizes the tobacco companies offer for smoking yourself to death. In the gift catalogue I picked up, it tells me that for a Dansette record player I'd need five thousand coupons, for a table tennis or badminton set, six thousand though even if you get them, you'll be too sick to play. And look at the big prize! Wow! Cough, cough. If I smoke a few hundred packs more, I can get a Stowaway bicycle for sixteen thousand five hundred coupons. It says collapsible in forty seconds but it's not clear whether it means you or the bike.'

'I suppose for twenty thousand coupons,' Laura laughed, 'you'd earn an iron lung.'

'Or an invalid bed,' he chuckled. 'But at two and eight for twenty, who can afford to go on smoking?'

'So when will you be giving up again?' Laura smiled.

'Mañana.'

The four-hour journey back to Manchester passed quickly and the four young ones were soon absorbed in the comics which they devoured like addicts deprived of their fix. Billy wondered if he'd done the right thing bringing them back to England. In the short time he'd stayed on his previous visit, he'd been shocked by the materialism, the selfishness, and the 'I'm all right, Jack' attitude he'd found everywhere. As far as he could see, the man in the street's chief preoccupation had appeared to be what was on telly last night, the perpetual quiz shows and the fortunes that some clerk or shop girl had won or narrowly missed winning. How different life in Kenya was! It was sunshine and the outdoor life for his kids. There they had played in the treehouse in their spacious garden and it was freedom and fresh air all the way. Sure, there was drunkenness and shenanigans in the Country Club but nevertheless there was a strong community spirit and people truly cared for each other. Especially so among the Africans. Whole villages would make tremendous sacrifices to give their children an education and to help a neighbour.

14

People were more concerned with basic survival than keeping up with the Joneses and competing with each other. They'd miss their servants, not so much for the work they had performed though that had been considerable, but for the people themselves. A bond of genuine affection had grown up between them and they were regarded as close as family members. Then there was the sport, the glorious holidays at the coast, swimming and surfing in the Indian Ocean, and the drink in the bar afterwards. No drink on earth could taste as good as that. To think they had left all that behind in order to exchange it for this cold, grey English climate. He was having misgivings already. Had he been stupid giving up that wonderful lifestyle? It would have been so easy to have accepted an extension of his contract as his good friends and neighbours, the Sherwoods, had done. His mind was filled with doubt as to whether they'd made the right, the sensible decision. But then, he thought, more important than how *he* felt, how did his family feel? And most important, how did Laura feel about it? He gazed across at her and his concerns melted away. Her magazines remained unread on her knee as she gazed out at the passing scene, her first sight of the English countryside after so many years. She had a smile on her face and he had never seen her look so happy. That smile said it all.

A few miles beyond Watford, she took both of Billy's hands in her own and with tears sparkling in her eyes said softly, 'It's such bliss to see an English landscape again, Billy, even though it's shrouded in snow at the moment. I've missed dear old England so much. I can't begin to tell you how pleased I am to be back. This is where we all belong. Home.'

'If that's the way you feel, Laura, then so do I,' he murmured. 'Now we can make a fresh start and start life anew. There's so much to be done when we've settled back. First, I need to find a job, then a house. Your folks are kind offering to put us up but, as you know, I'm never comfortable in someone else's home and I hope it's not for too long.

We'll waste no time in looking for a house of our own in one of those so-called leafy suburbs of Manchester.'

'Are you sure we can afford it?'

'Of course we can. We're a lot better off now than when we left. After the house business is fixed, next thing is try to get the kids into decent schools.'

'It'll be like a dream come true.'

'It would be wonderful to see them all do well with decent careers one day, maybe the professions, if they've got the brains. That should please your father. He was always going on about the top professions, law, medicine, accountancy.'

'Fine, Billy, but I do hope you don't have ideas of pushing them into jobs against their will. Or, worse, trying to achieve your own ambitions through them.'

'Nothing like that, Laura. They can do and be whatever they like, even follow in my own father's footsteps and become market porters if that's what they want to do. But I'm sure they'll feel more fulfilled as people if they go for jobs that are of service to others and make full use of whatever talents God has blessed them with.'

Chapter Two

It was a joyous homecoming when they finally arrived at London Road Station (re-named Piccadilly) and were met by Laura's father, Duncan, and Billy's two old school chums, Titch and Oscar. There was lots of laughter, hugging, hand-shaking and back-slapping the moment they emerged from the train.

'It's been such a long time,' Duncan enthused. 'So good to see you all again. And look at those bairns, so grown up. They were mere babes when you left. And young John there wasn't even born.'

The 'bairns', Matthew, Lucy, Mark, and John, glowed on hearing these words. Duncan couldn't have picked a more pleasing way to greet them.

'As I told you in my letters', Duncan said, 'you'll be staying with us in Regina Park until you fix up your own accommodation. We have plenty of room now that old Auntie and Grandma have passed away and the younger end of the family has flown the nest.'

'Everyone still doing well, I hope?' Billy said.

'Yes, everyone's fine,' Duncan said. 'We'll have time to catch up on everyone's news later.'

'I can hardly wait to see them all again,' Laura said.

It was arranged for Laura and the children to go with Duncan in his Daimler while Oscar, Titch and Billy brought up the rear with the luggage in a taxi. An elderly black porter collected their suitcases from the luggage van and piled them up on a big trolley. As he loaded them into the taxi, Billy slipped him half a crown and unthinkingly said in Swahili, '*Asante sana, mzee.*' (Thank you very much, old chap.)

The porter took the coin and stared at Billy suspiciously as if he'd exposed himself.

'Yeah, yeah,' he said in a thick Manchester accent. 'I don't know what that mumbo-jumbo was all about, but thanks a lot, mate.'

'You can drop all that big white bwana stuff,' Oscar guffawed. 'You're back home now. This is mucky Manchester, not tropical Africa.'

'Oops, sorry.' Billy laughed. 'Force of habit.'

Billy was pleased that his old pals had made the effort to meet him and his family at the station. They'd been his friends ever since they had passed their 'scholarship' at the age of eleven and attended the same grammar school, Damian College.

'You all look so disgustingly healthy,' Titch exclaimed as they climbed into the cab.

'Especially revolting to be so suntanned,' added Oscar, 'while we've been suffering in the bleak mid-winter here.'

'Don't fret,' Billy replied. 'It shouldn't take us too long to lose our tans. Then we'll look as wan and sickly as the rest of you.'

'I see you haven't lost your acerbic wit,' said Titch, 'but you *have* lost your Manchester accent and no mistake. You've acquired a plummy BBC announcer's voice.'

'Sorry again, Titch,' Billy said. 'That's what comes of mixing with public school characters in Kenya. But I'm not the only one with a BBC voice. You and Oscar have both got one as well.'

'How do you mean?'

'You both put me in mind of Wilfred Pickles.'

'Wilfred Pickles was a Yorkshireman but we'll overlook that detail,' Oscar said graciously.

'Thanks a lot, Hoppy.' Titch grinned, digging him in the ribs. 'Welcome back. A few weeks back home and you'll soon be sounding like the rest of us.'

'So what's new with you both?' Billy asked.

'Well, I'm still teaching English in a grammar school,' Oscar answered. 'I share an apartment with my flatmate, Derek.'

'As for me,' Titch said, 'I'm still teaching in a crummy school in Moss Side. One achievement, though, was that I managed to get an advanced Education Diploma from the University of Manchester.'

Billy patted his friend on the back. 'Congratulations, Titch. It must have been tough studying in the evening after a hard day at school. I know that none of us is Lord Chesterfield when it comes to correspondence but I seem to remember you writing to tell me that you were thinking of getting hitched. What happened there?'

'Sorry, Hoppy, I should've told you. As you know, I've spent most of my life drifting around aimlessly like the *Marie Celeste*. Then Elaine came on the scene. We've been married for two years now.'

'He forgot to say that Elaine was waiting for her new prescription spectacles when she met him,' Oscar said with a grin.

'Ignore him,' Titch said. 'He must have his little joke. Elaine's eyesight's perfect. She's a little taller than me though. But I always wanted a girl I could look up to.'

'Considering your pigmy stature,' Oscar pointed out, 'that wouldn't be difficult.'

'Better than being a beanpole like you,' Titch retorted.

'He forgot to add,' continued Oscar, 'that Elaine's ten years younger. Our Titch here is a cradle-snatcher.'

Billy laughed. 'You two are as crazy as ever. Where did you meet Elaine, Titch?'

'She teaches botany and biology at my school. It was a case of love at first sight.'

'Who could resist such a combination of subjects?' Oscar said languidly. 'The birds and the bees. It's what life's all about.'

'I find it hard to take all this in!' Billy exclaimed. 'Our

little Titch married! Who'd have thought it? Why, it means everyone in the old gang is now married, except for you, of course, Oscar.'

'And there's not much fear of that,' Oscar replied, 'unless this government changes the marriage laws, and the way things are going in this country, anything could happen.'

Billy laughed. 'Both of you are just the same. It's good to know that some things in this world never change.'

'Oh, but they do,' Titch gushed. 'The one thing I've not got round to telling you yet is that Elaine and I are now the proud parents of twin baby boys, born a year ago.'

'Will wonders never cease?' Billy said. 'Typical Titch. So lazy he has his kids two at a time. You and Elaine must be very happy.'

'Happy, yes. But broke. Always broke. We totter from one month's end to the other, just about keeping our heads above water. Teachers' salaries in this country are still as lousy as ever. I've been teaching fourteen years and I earn only nine hundred and fifty pounds a year, about half that of a plumber or a bricklayer. That's something I wanted to talk to you about, Billy. You seem to have done all right working abroad, and Elaine and I are thinking about doing something similar. Emigrating to Canada in fact. They're crying out for teachers over there and the salaries offered are much better with a higher standard of living. What do you think?'

'Sorry, Titch. Can't advise you there. Don't know a thing about Canada.'

'If I remember you, Hoppy,' Oscar said, 'that never stopped you venturing an opinion. What do you say we organise a booze-up in town? We can all bring wives and friends.'

'Give me a few days to settle in,' Billy said, 'and you're on.'

Chapter Three

Laura's mother, Louise, gave them a rapturous welcome when they met.

It was as if the Mackenzies had brought the New Year celebrations forward by a couple of weeks in their honour. First there was a beautiful leg of lamb with the usual trimmings and a wide selection of vegetables. But when Duncan brought down his twelve-year-old malt from the top cupboard, Billy knew that their homecoming was indeed a special occasion. Billy noted, though, that Duncan's carefully measured tots were still the same, being considerably smaller than the generous drams he was accustomed to in the bar of the Marangu Country Club in East Africa.

After dinner, Laura and her mother talked nineteen to the dozen, catching up on news of the rest of the family – Laura's younger sisters Jenny and Katie and brother Hughie. Jenny lived in Edinburgh with her husband Hamish Dinwiddie and their two young daughters. Hamish, always considered the successful son-in-law and Billy's erstwhile rival, was now more successful than ever having been promoted to the rank of Senior Actuary in his company. The news left a bitter taste in Billy's mouth until he remembered that Hamish had never got further than Scotland whilst he had feasted his eyes on the Indian Ocean, Mount Kenya and Kilimanjaro. Hughie and Katie were working in the same hospital in Staffordshire; Hughie was a houseman and Katie an SRN.

Later in the evening as the exchange of news began to slow down, Louise said, 'It's a long time since we heard you on the piano, Laura. Will you play something for us?'

'I'm not sure I can remember how, Mammy, but I'll have a go.'

Laura renewed her acquaintance with the piano by playing a Mozart sonata and then, accompanied by her mother, sang Haydn's 'My Mother Bids Me Bind My Hair'. It was a song that Billy hadn't heard for many years and hearing music like this brought back many happy memories of the 'Edwardian' musical evenings they had enjoyed at the Mackenzies', oh so long ago. After the musical interlude, the young Hopkinses could hardly wait to escape to the drawing room. The big attraction was the eighteen-inch television and it wasn't long before the four of them were glued to the set. There had been no television service in Kenya and they were anxious to make up for lost time.

Duncan seized the opportunity to turn to the subject dearest to his heart, Manchester United, and he was soon singing the praises of the team Matt Busby was rebuilding after the Munich disaster.

'Mark my words,' he said, 'we have a champion in that young Bobby Charlton whom God spared five years ago. The day will come when we'll be contenders for the European Cup again, you'll see.'

Meanwhile, Laura and her mother, both crossword enthusiasts, had turned their attention to the back page of the *Daily Telegraph* and were soon engrossed in unravelling the enigmatic verbal clues set by some recondite compiler. It was a skill Billy had never been able to get his head round and he maintained that it required a twisted mind and a warped imagination to solve them.

'Nonsense,' Laura said. 'What you need is intuition and lateral thinking.'

'How do you mean?' he asked.

'For example, give me a five-letter word in answer to this clue: "It's the wailway for Mark".'

'No idea,' he said. 'It's gibberish. What's the answer?'

'Twain.'

'How do you make that out?'

'Twain is the American writer. It's saying "train" with a lisp.'

'If that's lateral thinking,' he replied, 'I prefer to think in straight lines. As I said earlier, it requires a warped mind.'

'Sour grapes,' she smiled.

Billy looked round at the domestic scene – the kids immersed in television, Laura and Louise puzzling over the crossword puzzle, Duncan going on about football – and he had an eerie sense of déjà vu, as if they'd never been away. Gosh, it's good to be back, he said to himself.

'We've missed you all so much,' Louise said warmly as they prepared to retire. 'It's so good to have you all back safe and sound and I do hope you're going to be comfortable here. We've given you the two bedrooms at the top of the house so that you can be together as a family.'

'Anyway,' Duncan said, 'there's no need to tell you you're welcome to stay with us as long as you like.'

'It's kind of you to make such a generous offer, Duncan,' Billy said, 'and don't think we're not grateful when I say that our main aim now is to get into our own house as soon as poss. We're anxious to be independent once again.'

'You'll need a pretty penny if you're thinking of buying,' Duncan told him. 'Property values in this country have gone through the roof. In my opinion, houses are over-priced and can't go up much higher. A modern three-bedroomed semi in Withington or Didsbury can cost you up to two and a half or even three thousand pounds. It's crazy.'

'Hopefully, my compensation should take care of that,' Billy replied. 'I'm hoping to receive in the region of three thousand. Admittedly paid over a period of five years but it'll help us to get on our feet. Also a small pension for life of which I can commute a quarter.'

Duncan whistled quietly. He was impressed.

'You were very lucky, Billy, to receive such a large sum of money to come back with,' he said. 'Out like a pauper and back like a prince.'

'That's a bit of an overstatement, Duncan,' Billy laughed. 'As for being lucky, the lump sum which civil servants jokingly refer to as "lumpers" or "the golden handshake" is for loss of the permanent and pensionable post I had with HMOCS, Her Majesty's Overseas Civil Service. But, yes, you're quite right, things are looking up. Tomorrow I'm due to pick up a new Morris Oxford station wagon from Cockshoots on Bridge Street. The only thing I need now is a job but there's such a shortage of teachers everywhere, there shouldn't be a problem.'

Later that evening as they were unpacking upstairs, they overheard Duncan talking on the hall telephone to Jenny in Edinburgh.

'Oh, yes, Jenny, we collected them from the station all right. They're all looking so suntanned and bonny, simply bursting with health. They seem to have prospered too, so well dressed and Billy's due to collect a new station wagon tomorrow. I think you'll be surprised when you see them.'

This was meat and drink to Billy, especially since he knew that Duncan's glowing report would soon be relayed to Hamish. For so long the Hopkinses had been regarded as the poor relations, with Billy struggling to make his way while Hamish, Mr Moneybags himself, had prospered.

Maybe I'm not among the also-rans, after all, he thought.

Chapter Four

The following day, Billy visited Cockshoots, the agent for Morris cars. He'd ordered and paid for the car in Nairobi and now all that remained was to complete the formalities. There it stood in the showroom window, a spanking new estate car gleaming in its two-tone beige livery and as he tried sitting at the wheel to get the feel of it, there was that rich smell of new leather. Luxury indeed. Like a dream come true and he could hardly believe his fortune in being the owner of such a magnificent vehicle. Billy signed the various documents confirming the accessories he had opted for, a Blaupunkt automatic radio, the tinted window, walnut fascia. Finally he arranged for it to be delivered later that afternoon to the Mackenzie home in Regina Park. He came away with a light step, happily humming 'We're in the money', a tune he hadn't sung since a kid delivering firewood on a Saturday morning in Cheetham Hill. Strange to think that it was only a stone's throw to Honeypot Street where he and his pal Henry Sykes had chopped and bundled up the wood in the backyard of their terraced house. A short distance measured in feet and inches but an aeon measured in time.

As he walked up Bridge Street thinking these thoughts, he was surprised to see a familiar figure on the other side of the road. Could it be? It was! His brother Les striding purposefully downhill on his way into town. Billy was overjoyed to see him after such a long time.

'It's certainly a small world!' Billy exclaimed after crossing the street. 'I was going to contact you in the next day or two but fate has anticipated me. Quite a coincidence bumping into you like this.'

'I work near here at the Alligator Rainwear,' Les explained. 'I'm on my way back after an early lunch.'

After fraternal, and somewhat inhibited bear hugs, they exchanged their news. Les had his home in Pendleton where he lived with his wife Annette and their two young children, a girl and a boy. Les was also a Labour councillor on Salford City Council, and he wasted no time in imparting this piece of information.

'Congratulations,' Billy said, shaking him warmly by the hand. 'You *have* moved up in the world.' Then he added, 'But only two kids! You've got some way to go to catch up with me in that department.'

'Give us time,' Les grinned. 'We'll soon draw level. But what are you doing in this part of town? I thought you were staying with your in-laws in the leafy Regina Park suburbs.'

'Making final arrangements to pick up a new car,' Billy said nonchalantly, examining his fingernails. How he enjoyed needling Les and watching him squirm. Brotherly rivalry was still alive and kicking.

'A new car, eh!' Les said sourly. 'Bought, I suppose, on the profits made from grinding the faces of the poor in Kenya.'

'Not really, Les. I took early retirement and paid for it from compensation for loss of office. If anyone helped me foot the bill, I suppose it would be you, as a British taxpayer.'

'Typical Tory trick,' Les said, 'exploiting the workers to fill the pockets of the colonialists. Anyway, perhaps we can drive up together in this posh motor car of yours to see the old folk.'

'Sure thing, Les. Mam and Dad did write telling me they'd moved from Gardenia Court and giving their new address but I've no idea where it is.'

'They've moved into an old people's bungalow on the Langley Estate up Middleton way.'

'Thank God for that,' Billy said. 'That tenement block they lived in was always so congested with people living on top of one another. Everyone tried so hard to keep their homes neat and tidy but it was a thankless task and it was impossible to do much about the assortment of pongs in the stairwell. I can still smell 'em. Someone was always cooking sauerkraut and cabbage. Either that or the couple in the top apartment had died a few weeks earlier. We could go later today if you like. Cockshoots have promised to deliver the car early this afternoon.'

'It'll be best if we meet somewhere and go together as you'll never find it on your own. It's a bit off the beaten track.'

It was four o'clock when Billy picked up Les later that day and it was already dark. The damp mist that descended didn't help matters and Billy was feeling nervous about his first drive in his new car. Without Les, he'd never have found Langley Estate; it seemed to be located at the back of beyond. There was building going on everywhere and many of the roads were neither named nor made up. It was a relief to pull up at last in front of one of a row of bungalows in Martindale Crescent. It was Mam who answered the door after Les had given several sharp rat-a-tats with the metal door knocker. She had the rent book in her hand and she looked up uncomprehendingly at the two male figures silhouetted on the threshold.

'It's your sons come to see you,' Les said loudly, 'not the rent man. Aren't you going to ask us in?'

It took a moment or two for the penny to drop.

'Tommy, Tommy,' she yelled. 'It's our two lads. Les and our Billy home from Africa! Come quick! Come in, lads. Eeh, it's good to see you.'

Tommy came to the door adjusting his braces and fastening his belt.

'Well, I never!' he exclaimed. 'Our Billy back from the jungle! I was beginning to think we'd never see you again. Welcome back, Billy! By gum, you look like a fine figure of a man.'

'That means he thinks you've put on weight,' Les laughed.

'Thanks for interpreting, Les,' Billy said.

'Anyroad, it looks good on you,' Mam said. 'You were always too thin and a few extra pounds will keep out the cold.'

After much hugging and hand-shaking, Mam made a brew and the four of them, mugs of tea in hand, sat before the blazing coal fire, the only source of heat in the room. Billy looked closely at both his parents and experienced something of a shock. They were now well into their seventies and he hadn't seen them for a few years. In his head he had carried round a static picture of them at a younger age but now he saw how time had taken its toll. But then it had for all of them, he supposed.

Mam showed him around the bungalow while Les talked to Dad who seemed reluctant to wander too far from the fire. The accommodation consisted of one living room, a bedroom, a kitchen, and a bathroom. That was it. Billy's first impression was that the place was functional, clinical and lifeless. What's more, away from the fire, it was freezing cold, especially in the bedroom. He made a mental note to come back soon to improve matters with thicker wall insulation.

'I'll say one thing for it, Mam,' Billy said, 'it's compact. Everything's convenient and to hand. But how are you? Have you been keeping well since your visit to us in Kenya?'

'Not so bad, not so bad. The usual aches and pains that come with old age. I don't find it so easy getting around any more. I've thought of asking the Corporation to put in one of them lift chairs I've seen advertised.'

'But you live in a bungalow,' Billy chuckled. 'Those are meant for stairs.'

'Doesn't matter. It'd be handy for getting me round from room to room. Apart from that, my eyesight's beginning to go. The lights keep flickering on and off and I think I need stronger glasses. The doctor says it may be cataracts that's troubling me. But apart from that, it's this place we're living in that gets me down.'

28

'Well, Mam,' he said, trying to be cheerful, 'you must be feeling happy to be away from the Gardenia Court tenement and to have your own little place. How long were you living there?'

'The town hall rehoused us there in nineteen forty-one after we were bombed out during the war. How many years is that?'

'That makes twenty-two years,' Billy said. 'Surely it's got to be better living here in this bungalow.'

'I hate it here,' she said vehemently. 'It's a dump. An absolute dump. We've left one dump to come to a super dump. And it's that cold, it's like Russia up here.'

Russia! Billy thought. This from his mam who, apart from her brief visit to Kenya, had never got further than a visit to Walsingham in Norfolk to visit Our Lady's shrine with the Union of Catholic Mothers.

'Well, it's certainly smaller than Gardenia Court and there's less to clean,' he said, looking for positive points. But Mam wouldn't be swayed once she made her mind up.

'These bungalows were built in a factory like them pre-fabs we had after the war. And there are that many rules and regulations. Who wants to live in a place where you have to ask the rent man, "Please may I keep a cat or a dog? Please may I hang a picture on one of these composition walls?" It's not home when you're not allowed to do homely things.'

'Not that Mam takes too much notice of these rules and regulations,' Les grinned, 'as you'll notice from the pictures she got me to hang up for her.' Then he tried to sound an optimistic note. 'At least it's not as cold this year as it was last. Then we had blizzards and the whole country came to a grinding halt. According to the BBC, it was the coldest winter since nineteen forty-seven and that was saying something.'

'Nineteen forty-seven is a year I shall remember as long as I live,' Billy said. 'I was at college and we nearly froze to death without heat. At least you have a good fire, Mam.'

No use. She wasn't to be consoled.

'I've never lived in such a freezing place. It's like an icebox. It's worst in the bedroom which has an outside wall which gets all the bitter weather. As for the district, sometimes I think we're living in the middle of a building site. Nothing but big lorries unloading bricks, and tractors digging up the place. There's mud everywhere. And the shops are miles away.'

'How do you go on for shopping then?' Billy asked.

'Your two sisters, Flo and Polly, come up on Friday afternoons to do my big shopping. During the week, I go myself for little items. No use sending Dad, he always forgets what he's gone for once he gets to the shops. The doctor says he's suffering from magnesia. I sent him last week for corn flakes and he came back with corn plasters. Only yesterday I asked him to go to the shops for a pound of tomatoes and ten pounds of potatoes.'

'Don't tell me,' Billy laughed.

'Yes, you've guessed it. He returned with a pound of potatoes and ten pounds of tomatoes. We'll be living on tomatoes for days.'

'Things could be worse, I suppose,' Billy said.

'Maybe you're right but I don't see how. We miss our old friends – we don't know a soul round here. Sometimes I feel as if I don't belong anywhere.'

'I know the feeling only too well,' Billy commiserated.

'How do you mean?' Mam asked. 'You're staying in a big posh house with your in-laws in Regina Park.'

'True, Mam. It was nice of the Mackenzies to put us up but already after only one day, I'm missing having our own home. My little family seems to have merged into their household and we've lost our privacy. I'm like Dad in that respect, not comfortable in someone else's house, having to ask permission if you want to make a cup of coffee or switch on the television. The sooner we get our own place, the better.'

'You can't be as bad as Dad. He won't even take his cap off

when we visit someone. It's the same if anyone comes to see us, he keeps throwing out big hints for them to go by asking them what time their last bus is.'

'How are you getting on with your next-door neighbour nowadays?' Les asked.

'Mrs Binks? Don't talk to me about 'er next door. She's a right funniosity. Interferin' old busybody. I can't take to her. A real curtain-twitcher. Never misses a trick. And always telling me what I should and shouldn't do.'

At that moment, there was a knock at the front door.

'Talk of the devil,' Mam said, making her way to the door. 'I'll bet that's her. She'll have seen you and our Billy arrive and will want to know what's going on. Always shoving her nose in where it's not wanted.'

Mam opened the door and they heard 'er next door say in a plaintive, sing-song voice, 'I notice you've got your two sons here. You should ask 'em while they're here to fix that hole in the fence.'

'Listen,' Mam said in that severe tone the family knew only too well, 'don't you be telling me what I should and shouldn't do. My sons are here to see us not to be fixing holes in fences. You should get the rent man to do it.'

'Now look, you,' the neighbour whined, 'no need to take offence. I was only suggesting.'

'Well, don't,' Mam said. 'And another thing, don't you *you* me, you!' With that she slammed the door. 'See what I mean, the bloody nosey-parker,' she said when she came back. 'Not that it'll do any good asking the rent man to do anything. It's a waste of breath. Gardenia Court was no garden of Eden but we do miss it. It was the worst move we've ever made coming up here.'

'I can see you're not happy,' Billy said. 'I wish there was some way we could help. Maybe we could do something about that outside bedroom wall. I'll look into it. And another thing, I think we should get you a telephone in case of emergency.'

'I've never used a telephone in my life and I wouldn't know what to do with it.'

'I'm sure we can soon teach you. We've got to try and do something to make life more comfortable for you. Les and I hate to see you so unhappy.'

'Your dad feels the same,' she said. 'He's seventy-eight this year and he thinks he should still be going into work in Smithfield fruit market. At his age, I ask you! He also misses his pub and playing crib with his cronies.'

'Isn't there a pub round here for him?' Billy said. 'Les and I thought we might take him out for a drink.'

At the mention of trigger words like 'drink' and 'pub', Dad pricked up his ears and shot into the bedroom to put on his 'going-to-the-pub' outfit.

'Listen, you two,' Mam whispered when he was out of the room. 'I wish you'd try to do something to get this idea of going back to work out of his head. Sometimes I think he may be losing his mind. He's worked like a dog all his life but he's like an old carthorse and can't think of anything but going back to the market. Last week he was up at half past two to catch the all-night bus into Manchester to do some portering. He went out in the pouring rain but couldn't find any work when he got there. All his old customers are either dead or retired.'

'Look, Mam,' Les said, 'don't think I'm interfering but maybe it's best to leave him alone. Going into work means a lot to him and perhaps he's trying to supplement his pension with a few bob. I think going down to the market to do a bit of portering at the age of seventy-eight takes a lot of guts.'

'Les,' Mam said irritably, 'you're talking through your hat, so don't be so obstroculous. Your dad's worked like a donkey for sixty years in the market and it's about time he recognized that he's getting too old to be pulling great loads of fruit and vegetables about the place. On his way back last week, he fainted on the bus and had to be brought back by a copper. That scared the wits out of me. I thought he was done for.'

'We'll see what we can do,' Billy said, 'but you know how stubborn he can be.'

Two minutes later, Dad was back, dressed in his old raincoat and cloth cap.

'Are we going or what?' he asked impatiently.

'Right, Dad, you're on,' Billy said.

'It's only ten minutes' walk from here,' Dad said.

'We're not walking, Dad. We're going by car.'

'Going by car! You mean by taxi? That'd be bloody stupid 'cos it's only round the corner.'

'No, Dad. We're going by car. MY car.' Billy had waited five long years to say that.

Outside the front door, Dad gazed at the car with its gleaming, streamlined contours.

'Whose is that?' he asked.

'It's mine, Dad,' Billy said proudly, puffing out his chest.

'Where the hell have you got that from? You've not pinched it, our Billy, have you? I hope you're not in trouble with the law or anything.'

'No,' said Les, grinning. 'He's bought it out of his ill-gotten profits from the African slave trade. Must have cost him a thousand pounds.'

'Don't let him drink too much,' Mam called. 'He can't take it the way he used to. And remember what I asked you.'

As they set off, Billy showed off the various accessories to his dad: the Blaupunkt radio, the heater, the walnut fascia dashboard, the windscreen washers, the shag pile carpets. He offered him a cigarette from his silver case and handed him the electronic lighter.

'What's this? A cigarette lighter?'

'No, Dad. The manual calls it a cigar lighter.'

'By gum, you've done well, our Billy,' Dad said admiringly.

In the pub, while Billy and Les were getting the drinks in, they could hear Dad telling the couple sitting at the same table, 'See that fellah over there? The one in the black Crombie overcoat. That's my son, Billy. He's a millionaire.

Just come back from Africa, he's been learning the Zulu warriors to read and write. Has a spanking new car with a German wireless and a cigar lighter.'

The couple looked over at Billy deferentially.

Billy and Les returned with two pints of mild and a shandy for Billy because he was driving.

'You're being very abstemious, Billy,' Les said. 'Your halo must be tight round your head.'

'As you know, Les, I'm no Holy Joe,' Billy replied, 'but I've vowed to stick to shandy whenever I'm driving. People tell me that while I've been abroad, the authorities here have clamped down on drinking and driving.'

'Too true, Billy,' Les said. 'If you go over the limit you could land up in jail. I'm on the road safety sub-committee and I can tell you, driving over the limit is not only stupid, it's bloody dangerous. Anyway, Dad,' Les said, turning his attention to the old man, 'get that down you. A pint of the best mild in the place for the best dad.'

'Thanks, son,' he said. 'You know I've never been one for the bevy. It was the market and all that heavy work that got me into the habit. It was the way we sweated, you see. I hate the stuff and I wouldn't give you a penny a bucket for it.' He picked up his pint and downed it in one draught, his Adam's apple going up and down like the lift in Lewis's store. Billy and Les exchanged glances. Same old Dad! Another thing that hadn't changed.

'It's a nice pub you've got here,' Les remarked, looking round the lounge. 'You'll soon make friends if you come down regularly to the vault and join in a game of crib.'

'Nah, I don't make new friends easily at my age. Besides, I can't afford to drink on the old age pension.'

Mam will be glad to hear that, Billy thought. In his time, Dad must have drunk several breweries dry.

'What do they call this pub then, Dad?' Billy asked.

'The New Broom.'

'A new broom sweeps clean, as they say,' Billy remarked.

'I suppose the idea is that people can make a fresh start in this new modern estate.'

'Perhaps you're right but they've got to finish putting the bloody place up first. At the moment it's like living in the Sahara Desert miles from anywhere. Anyroad, a broom's for sweeping up all the rubbish and that's what the Town Hall thinks we are, Manchester's rubbish. Overspill, they call us, and they've dumped us up here on this estate.'

'You'll settle in, given time,' Billy said, though he didn't believe what he was saying.

Then Dad adopted a conspiratorial tone. 'Don't tell your mother this but I've decided to go back to work. I reckon I can still pull a cart as well as the next man. And after sixty years working as a market porter, I'm used to getting up early in the morning. You see, you've to get down there at the crack of dawn before the work's all gone.'

'But Dad,' Billy protested, 'you're getting on in years. Portering's work for a young man, isn't it?'

'Aye. But the young men expect big pay for the simplest of jobs. I can do the same job for half what they charge.'

Les shook his head. 'Dad, you've worked hard all your life. Isn't it time you took things easy?'

'To tell you the truth, I don't know what to do with myself half the time. What would you have me do? Sit around all day watching stupid television programmes or sitting on a park bench going quietly mad with a lot of other old fogies? I may as well be in my coffin. Besides, we could do with a little extra money; the pension I get is an insult.'

'I'm sure the family would be willing to organize a regular collection to help out,' Billy said.

'I won't accept no bloody charity from no one,' Dad said angrily. 'That's the one thing I don't want. Every night, I ask God to keep me from being a burden to my kids. You've got your own families to think of. As long as I have my health and strength, I can still work and provide.' Then out of the blue, he asked a strange question. 'Are you still teaching in Longsight, Billy?'

'No, Dad. I've just come back from Africa, remember.'

'That's right, I was forgetting. During the war our Jim went to Africa a few times on the *Renown*. You didn't see anything of him when you were out there, did you?'

'How could I, Dad? Jim was killed in the merchant navy in nineteen forty-three.'

A look of bewilderment crossed Dad's face. 'Our Jim? Killed?' Then his mind drifted off again. 'But just the same. You never know. You might have bumped into him on your travels.'

They drank two more pints each and then it was time to get Dad home. He'd have stayed till they chucked him out if they'd let him.

Later, as Billy drove Les home, he said, 'I hadn't realized how much Mam and Dad have aged in the last couple of years, especially Dad. I think his memory's going.'

'Going?' Les exclaimed. 'It's already gone.'

Chapter Five

For children, Christmas is Christmas no matter where they are when it comes. With mounting impatience they wait for the big event with its prescribed procedures and evocative smells: the mince pies, the Christmas pudding, the smell of Dad's cigar, the parties and the silly paper hats, the cracker-pulling and the corny jokes and riddles, the nocturnal visit from Father Christmas with his big bag of goodies even if, as in the case of the three older Hopkins children, they know full well the goodies were bought the week before by Mum and Dad from a store on Market Street and stuffed into their stockings by Dad on Christmas Eve. For the children, the joy was the same no matter where it was celebrated. Not so for their parents. For Billy and Laura, this particular Christmas was different and one they had looked forward to and dreamed about for so long. There had been Christmases abroad in Kenya of course, where they had tried to celebrate them with the usual customs – a tree, mistletoe and holly or the nearest thing to them that they could find in the African bush, Christmas cards with robins and reindeers, stagecoaches and snowmen, rubicund town criers and the three wise men following the star of Bethlehem. Somehow it had never seemed the same in the bright tropical sunshine. But that was all behind them.

A few days before Christmas, Billy and Laura took the children into town on a shopping expedition. For John in particular it was an exciting time for he still believed in Santa Claus and the three older children had been warned strictly not to give the game away.

'Let him enjoy the fantasy as long as possible,' Billy declared. 'He'll have the rest of his life to deal with reality.'

A visit to Father Christmas in his grotto at Lewis's store was an essential part of the ritual and John came away glowing with pleasure and clutching a huge Christmas stocking filled with all kinds of sweets, Rowntree's Smarties, Cadbury's Buttons, Bassett's Jelly Babies and Liquorice All Sorts, plus sundry knick-knacks and puzzles.

'I asked Santa for a fort with lots of soldiers,' he said breathlessly, 'and he told me that he would see what he could do.'

A short walk from Lewis's brought them to Wiles's Emporium, a toy store which was every child's dream come true since it offered a vast selection of gifts for young people of every age. The air buzzed with the excited voices of children as they jostled with one another along the crowded aisles. The Hopkins family pushed their way through the doors and entered an Aladdin's Cave, a wonderland of treasures like something out of the *Arabian Nights*. On the ground floor they found toys classified according to gender. For girls, dolls galore, prams, doll's houses, nurses' outfits, miniature kitchens, an endless array of playthings which would equip them for a life of domesticity. For boys, a collection more in keeping with the perceived male role: military paraphernalia, guns, tanks, uniforms and a host of handyman tools which would afford useful training for them as future husbands and workers. The basement sections catered for amusement, entertainment, and leisure activities: art and construction kits, cameras, 8 mm cine projectors, and a wealth of games of every description: draughts, ludo, snakes and ladders, quoits, rings, hoop-la, bagatelle. Children shoved and wriggled their way through the store, open-mouthed and spoilt for choice.

Not so for Matthew. For him, there was no hesitation for he knew exactly what he was looking for. He made a beeline for the science section and chose a Meccano set plus a magnificent box of basic apparatus entitled 'The Young

Scientist: 50 Experiments Every Young Person Can Safely Conduct At Home'. It included a chemistry set with optional refills, and as an extra bonus the equipment contained parts and instructions to build a steam engine. 'Just like Newcomen's' it proclaimed on the lid.

Lucy, too, wasted no time in making up her mind and it didn't take her long to find what she was looking for: an art kit entitled 'The Leonardo Painting Outfit', containing all the materials, paints, brushes, palette, and even smock and beret, that 'The Young Artist' would require to turn out a masterpiece.

'Tell me, Billy,' Laura smiled. 'How come our two oldest kids have selected gifts that reflect precisely your ambitions for them?'

'Search me,' he replied, his face the picture of innocence. 'Nothing to do with me. You saw how they made up their own minds. But they can only develop their talents if they have the materials to hand. Could Boyle have discovered his law without a laboratory? Could da Vinci have created the Mona Lisa without palette, paint and brushes?'

Mark's choices were less ambitious if not less expensive than his older siblings'. He opted for a conjurer's outfit, which promised that the skills he would acquire would enable him to deceive his audiences by 'proving that the hand's quicker than the eye', a ventriloquist's dummy in the form of a shabbily dressed tramp with movable facial parts, along with 'full instructions on how to throw your voice', plus a jumbo jigsaw puzzle depicting the Tower of London.

'Judging from his choices,' Billy grinned, 'I'd say he's destined for a career in law. With such skills in prestidigitation, and voice projection, plus a picture of the Tower, he'll make the ideal barrister.'

John had already made his selection with Santa in the grotto. He soon tracked down a 'Build Your Own Castle' Lego kit, together with two boxes of lead soldiers. Billy wrote the name of the product down for him so that he could specify that particular make when he wrote his letter to Father Christmas in Lapland.

When everything was settled, Billy went to the cashier's office, paid the bill and arranged for delivery a couple of days later. Hiding the presents until Christmas Eve would not be easy as it wasn't their own home but they had a number of cubbyholes in mind, which they were sure would be secure.

One evening at about eight thirty, Billy and his family were watching television. John had been put to bed at his usual time of eight o'clock. Everyone was absorbed in watching yet another episode of the exploits of Ben Cartwright and Little Joe in *Bonanza* when Billy had a sudden presentiment.

He went to the foot of the stairs and called up.

'John, are you still awake?'

'Yes, Dad.'

'What are you doing up there?'

'Nothing. Just lying here, Dad.'

'You're not rooting through our things, are you?'

'No, Dad. Honest.'

'Are you sure?'

'Yes, Dad.'

'Make sure you don't. OK?'

'OK, Dad.'

It's truly amazing, Billy reflected, how kids reply to an accusation. When asked what they were doing at the time the offence was committed, they always answer with a simple 'Nothing' as if that settles it once and for all. An adult feels he has to add all kinds of justifications. 'I didn't do it. I couldn't have 'cos I was somewhere else at the time. I have an alibi.' Let there be a rumpus upstairs and the sound of crashing furniture but it's useless to ask, 'What are you doing up there?' because the answer is invariably the same: 'Nothing.' Mark was particularly adept at quibbling when confronted with a misdemeanour. 'Did you slam the kitchen door?' 'Not me! I didn't slam the *kitchen* door.' (It was probably the lounge door.) 'Did you punch John?' 'Not me! I didn't *punch* him!' (He probably slapped him.) Any charge levelled at Mark had to be couched in precise, specific language if there was to be a successful prosecution. Apart from this, it was probably a complete waste of time to ask, 'What were you doing?' as most children with any nous have developed the art of prevarication.

Billy returned to the lounge and to the programme. Adam, Hoss and Little Joe were riding desperately across the sprawling Ponderosa ranch to rescue their father Ben from the bad guys and the story was reaching its climax when little John popped his head round the door.

'What are you doing out of bed, John?' Laura asked anxiously. 'You should be fast asleep.'

'I came to tell you I'm not going to ask Father Christmas for that fort and the soldiers.'

'Why not?' Billy asked though he thought he knew the answer already.

'I don't need them now.'

'How do you make that out?' Laura inquired, puzzled.

'I've found a fort and two boxes of soldiers at the back of your wardrobe. They're the exact same make as those in Wiles's.'

'Oh, no!' The Hopkins family sighed collectively.

'He must have brought them early as he has so many deliveries to make,' Billy said quickly in an attempt to preserve the Santa Claus myth.

'Mark says there is no Father Christmas and you are the one who buys them and leaves them in our bedroom.'

'I told you not to tell 'em that I told you,' Mark protested.

'Don't believe everything Mark says,' Lucy said, trying to put things right with her young brother. 'There *is* a Father Christmas and he has a big round of deliveries to make. He was making sure you got yours in time.'

It was no use. The seeds of doubt had been sown and from

that day the scales fell from John's eyes. He collected his presents along with the others on Christmas morning and though he felt joy on seeing his toys, somehow the element of surprise and fascination had been lost. So as not to lose the sense of wonderment altogether, they had to supplement his gifts that year with a toy zoo and a selection of animals.

On Christmas Eve they set off for midnight Mass with Duncan and Louise Mackenzie at St Joseph's Church on Plymouth Grove. Laura was uncertain about taking the children but Billy reckoned it was an essential experience for them and part of the Christmas ritual.

'We'll soon have them tucked up in bed after Mass,' he said. 'I'd love Matthew and Lucy to hear the choir and the carols and there is something special about the atmosphere of midnight Mass. There's the smell of soap, perfume and incense and I can't explain it but somehow people look brighter and happier at a late-night service.'

'We'll have to make sure they're well wrapped up,' Laura said, 'especially John. He's not stopped shivering since we landed at Heathrow.'

'Give him time. He'll get used to it.'

Everything came up to their expectations. In church, people did look brighter, even radiant, in the light of a hundred candles. The choir sang wonderfully and at the end of the service, the rafters rang when the congregation lifted their voices in the '*Adeste Fidelis*'. Then it was on with gloves and mufflers for the walk back. Billy carried John through the snow beneath the twinkling frosty stars. It was one of those profound experiences that would remain with them all, adults and children alike.

Despite the late night, everyone was up early on Christmas morning. The four children, or five if Billy were included in this category, were soon preoccupied exploring, experimenting and playing with their new toys. Matthew, with Billy's unsolicited help, was engrossed in operating his steam engine

42

and building a Meccano workshop; Lucy, suitably attired as an artist in smock and beret, was absorbed in painting a Christmas scene; Mark wandered around the house giving ventriloquist performances, trying out his conjuring tricks on any family member willing to participate and, in between acts, fitting the occasional piece into his jigsaw puzzle; and John, with appropriate sound effects and military commands, was engrossed in defending his fort against marauding armies while a menagerie of zoo animals looked on.

There followed the usual Christmas turkey dinner complete with plum pudding and exciting anticipation of who would find the sixpence, though hoping it would not be John in case he swallowed it. It was not perhaps as big a celebration as used to be the case in the Hopkins family. There weren't as many people for a start and it was not in the Scottish tradition to splash out at Christmas, the big celebration being reserved for Hogmanay. Duncan, though, made a concession in honour of his English guests by buying an evergreen tree complete with lights and baubles from Lewis's (it cost five pounds, he told everyone several times) and there was an exchange of the presents which had been left underneath the tree. For the sake of the children, or so he said, he agreed to paper hats and crackers with everyone reading out the corny jokes they found (of the 'When's a door not a door? When it's ajar' variety). And for the adults there was Bristol Cream sherry before dinner, and after the meal a carefully measured tot of Duncan's malt, but only for the men since the ladies were not expected to aspire to such an exalted tipple. Billy could have sworn it was the same bottle of malt from which Duncan had distributed his largesse at their farewell party five years previously.

The afternoon was spent as every Christmas Day afternoon had been spent for as long as Billy and Laura could remember, listening to the address of the reigning monarch to the Commonwealth, which had become as much a part of the Christmas tradition as turkey and mince pies ever since

George V had initiated the ritual in 1932. The inevitable snooze followed for the men while the ladies tackled the mammoth seasonal crossword in the newspaper.

Later in the evening, Billy took the youngest pair up to bed.

'Come one, you two. You've had a busy day. Now it's time for some shut-eye,' he said, though he knew that after the day's excitement they wouldn't settle down so easily.

'Come on, Dad, tell us a story,' John pleaded, in an effort to prolong the day.

'Oh, very well, but I'm not sure I'm any good at telling stories.'

'We'll soon tell you if it's no good,' Mark said.

'OK, then. Once upon a time, a long, long time ago . . .' Billy began.

'How long ago?' Mark asked. 'Fifty, a hundred, a thousand years?'

'Say a hundred.'

'Then you don't need two "longs", one "long" would be enough, surely,' Mark commented.

'OK. A long time ago, there lived in the forest a poor woodcutter and his wife.'

'Didn't they have any children? In these stories, they usually have one or two.'

'In my story, they have no children,' Billy answered.

'I suppose if they were poor, they couldn't afford any,' Mark said.

'Shut up, Mark, and let Dad tell the story,' John cried, exasperated.

'OK. I wanted to be sure about this woodcutter before the tale began.'

'Now, one day, the woodcutter was chopping down a tree when a little voice inside the trunk of the tree piped up, "Please don't chop me down." '

'I'll bet his wife was a ventriloquist and was playing a trick,' Mark said. 'Maybe it was her favourite tree and she didn't want to lose it.'

'No, it was not a ventriloquist. It was a fairy inside the tree.'

'What was she doing in there? What kind of tree was it? Was it a hollow tree?'

'Shut *up*!' John snapped. 'I want to hear the story.'

Billy soldiered on with his tale, ignoring Mark's interrogation. 'The fairy said, "If you will agree not to chop me down, I shall grant you three wishes." The woodcutter felt sorry for the fairy and so he left the tree alone. When he got home, he sat down at the table and his wife gave him his supper of a crust of dry bread.'

'Is that all they could afford?' Mark said. 'They lived in a forest. Didn't they have a vegetable garden like we had in Kenya so he could have some potatoes or beans or something?'

'No, they didn't,' Billy said impatiently. 'They had no money for seeds.'

'But, Dad—'

'I want to hear what happened!' John wailed.

'The woodcutter looked at the piece of stale bread and said, "I wish this was a great big sausage." And lo and behold, it was! A beautiful big sausage. His wife was amazed.

' "How did that happen?" she gasped. "How did you change the bread into a sausage?"

'The woodcutter told her about the fairy in the tree and how she had granted him three wishes.

' "You stupid man!" his wife shrieked. "Fancy wasting a wish on a sausage when you could have asked for a kingdom, a palace, precious jewels, a crock of gold. You are the most stupid man in the world."

' "I didn't think," the woodcutter answered humbly.

'But the old woman kept yelling at him, calling him all kinds of bad names until the woodcutter lost his temper and shouted back at her.

' "Be quiet, woman, going on and on at me about it. I wish the stupid sausage were hanging from your nose!"

'And bingo! It was!'

45

John was shocked. 'What happened next?'

'What do you think happened?' Billy asked. 'The old man had only one wish left.'

'He had to use the wish to get the sausage off her nose,' John said.

'That's right,' Billy said. 'So in the end he'd wasted all three wishes.'

'If that had been me,' Mark protested, 'I'd have left the sausage hanging on her nose. She was the cause of it all, so it served her right. The woodcutter could have wished to be king in a castle with a beautiful princess.'

The story finished, Billy tucked the two boys in and went downstairs to join the rest of the family.

'You know, Laura,' he said, 'if Mark, that son of ours, doesn't become a barrister, I'll eat my hat.'

Christmas for the Hopkins family that year was not like the get-togethers of old, what Mam called a family 'conflagration', when everyone crammed into the little flat in Gardenia Court to exchange not only presents but the latest family gossip. For a start, the various branches of the family liked to celebrate Christmas Day with their own kids in their own homes and in their own way. And then again, if they'd all tried to squash into the small bungalow, it would have been standing room only. In addition, Mam and Dad were getting too old to put up with the whole family descending on them all at once and they were happy, not to say relieved, when their eldest daughter Flo invited them to share Christmas dinner with them and their grown-up children.

On Boxing Day, however, the family arranged to pay brief visits on a staggered basis to wish them all the best and to exchange gifts.

'Whatever you do,' Mam pleaded, 'don't give your father any spirits. He can't take it the way he used to and there's no telling what he'll do if he gets whisky inside him.'

But her pleas were in vain for somehow he got hold of

half a bottle of Bell's and with that rolling around his brain he slobbered over Billy's children, much to their dismay and, in the case of Lucy, horror. What was worse was that he insisted on giving each one of them a 'beardie' by rasping their cheeks with his stubbly beard. That was enough for Lucy and she spent the rest of the visit sitting sulkily in the car until it was time to go home.

'That was awful,' she repeated ad nauseam all the way back to Regina Park.

Chapter Six

New Year's Day at the Mackenzies' was a different affair. To the Scottish way of thinking, Hogmanay was reckoned to be a more important festival than Christmas and it was a true gathering of the clan for the occasion. Hamish and Jenny came down with their two young daughters, Portia and Rosalind, from Edinburgh, and Hughie arrived with younger sister Katie from Stoke.

The dinner was the usual sumptuous affair with Duncan carving the leg of pork with the precision of a Harley Street surgeon. It was a splendid repast with entertainment provided by yet more funny paper hats, a new box of crackers and by Hamish and Jenny who, seated opposite each other, seized the opportunity to start a row over money. Billy, Hamish's long-time rival for the position of Duncan's favourite son-in-law, relished the squabbling. Perhaps he should have been horrified and embarrassed by the display of marital strife but, on the contrary, he found it most diverting and the highlight of the evening. The signal for the opening round of the battle was given by Jenny when she observed, 'I like your Christmas tree, Daddy. How much did it cost?'

'As you can see it's an evergreen type and it cost five pounds.'

'We bought *our* Christmas tree from Woolworth's for one pound, ten shillings,' said Jenny, looking round the company. 'It's the artificial type that folds up like an umbrella.'

Hamish frowned his disapproval.

'You see how he pulls a sulky face as soon as I mention the subject of money,' Jenny said.

'I don't believe in throwing money about on a tree each year,' Hamish protested, throwing her a deadly glare. 'An artificial one does the job adequately and it means we can use the same one from one year to the next, so saving money.'

'That's the story of my life,' Jenny sighed, rolling her eyes and scanning the table in an attempt to recruit support for her cause. 'Always saving money, a penny here and a penny there.'

That eye-rolling routine, thought Billy, is a sure sign of marital disaster.

'You two always seem to enjoy squabbling,' Duncan laughed.

'Don't worry, Daddy,' Jenny said, grimacing. 'We thrive on confrontation. We'd find life dull without the occasional spat.'

'Anyway, Jenny,' Louise chipped in, trying to keep the peace, 'you sent us a lovely Christmas card this year.'

'Glad you liked it,' Jenny said, 'cos Hamish bought the cards as a job lot last January when there was a sale on and he's been keeping them all year. He'd rub out the signatures on the cards we received and re-use them if he had the chance. He even buys Christmas wrapping paper and tinsel in January.'

'I don't hold with waste. Not like someone I know,' Hamish retorted, accompanying his response with a raucous throat-clearing as if he had a bone lodged in his tonsils, 'who insists on having two of everything and spends a fortune on cakes and biscuits.'

'Talking of biscuits,' Louise said, looking round the company and attempting once more to defuse the situation, 'my favourite biscuit has always been the Garibaldi. What about you?'

'We used to call them "squashed flies" when I was a kid,' Billy observed, supporting her by introducing a little levity into the discussion.

'We learned about Garibaldi at school,' said Katie. 'Wasn't he the great Italian patriot?'

'The very one,' Billy said. 'He was always a favourite question in the School Certificate.'

The conversation was descending into the absurd and Duncan thought it was time to change the subject.

'So, Jenny, how are you finding life in Edinburgh?' he asked.

'We find the people of Edinburgh are—'

'A lot friendlier than the Glaswegians,' Hamish cut across her.

'What do you put that down to?' Billy asked.

'Well,' Jenny began, 'I think maybe it's because there are—'

'Fewer pubs and not so many alcoholics,' said Hamish.

'Look, Hamish,' Jenny snapped. 'Would you mind not finishing my sentences for me! I can think for myself, you know.'

'You always forget what you're going to say, my dear. Maybe if you didn't drink so much . . .' he said, looking pointedly at Jenny's glass as she refilled it with Beaujolais.

'Sure, I have the occasional drink,' she rejoined, 'and who can blame me, being married to someone like you? Silas Marner was a spendthrift by comparison.'

'Have you forgotten, my dear, that this Silas Marner you speak of bought you a lovely gift for our tenth wedding anniversary last year?'

'How could I forget, Hamish dear. A tin wedding anniversary. So I got a set of tin pans. And with those he now expects me to be a culinary goddess and turn out cordon bleu meals.'

'There's nothing wrong with having high standards,' he replied.

'That's the trouble with you, Hamish. Your standards are too high.'

'They can't be that high, my dear,' he smirked. 'After all, I married you.'

Jenny looked at him. 'That's because my standards are too low, dear.'

Up to now, Billy had been enjoying the verbal skirmishes but things seemed to be turning nasty.

'So how are things at the hospital, Hughie,' he asked cheerily, 'now you're a fully qualified doctor? How many lives have you saved today?'

'Saved? That's a laugh, Billy. More like how many have I snuffed out.'

'You surely can't mean that,' Duncan said.

'Oh, but I do. As a houseman I put in a seventy-hour week and I'm always tired and that can be dangerous. But what's worse, I feel hopelessly inadequate. As you know, I'm a beginner and new to hospital work. In medical school, we learned how the body works, how it can go wrong and how we can fix it. But knowing all about rare diseases is pretty useless when you're faced with reality on the ward. I've been thrown in at the deep end without the skills that matter, like how to set up a heart monitor, how to insert a catheter, or how to fill in a medical form.'

'So what do you do when faced with a life or death situation?' asked Billy aghast.

'He shouts for one of us nurses,' Katie laughed, 'or asks if there's a doctor in the house.'

'It's no laughing matter, I can tell you,' Hughie said. 'It's pretty frightening when you're called to an emergency and everyone says, "Ah, we're all right now, here's the doctor." My big worry is that I might do something wrong and make things worse, even kill someone.'

'Wasn't it George Bernard Shaw who said that doctors simply bury their mistakes?' Hamish looked at Duncan for appreciation of his wit. 'That way we never hear about them.'

'This is not a good subject to be discussing at Hogmanay, surely,' Louise said brightly. 'We should be talking about cheerful things. What about you, Laura and Billy? What are your plans now you're home again?'

'Billy and I have talked it over and there are two parts to our plans, Mammy. The first thing we need to do,' Laura said, addressing the company, 'is to buy a house, one with at least four bedrooms.'

'Do you have a particular district in mind?' Duncan asked.

'We were thinking of something in the Withington/ Didsbury area, Daddy.'

Duncan pursed his lips and gave an involuntary whistle. 'You've picked the most expensive area of Manchester. I hope you're not both getting out of your depth. An ordinary semi-detached there could set you back anything from three to four thousand pounds.'

'What's a teacher's salary nowadays?' asked Hamish, stroking his knife on the table and smiling maliciously at Billy.

'I believe it's around nine hundred maximum,' Billy answered.

'That means you'll be buying a house five or six times your annual salary.' Hamish smiled, once again looking towards Duncan for approval but the latter studiously avoided his eye.

'We should be able to put down a substantial deposit,' Billy said equably. 'Not only that, I have eight months' paid leave accumulated and that gives me plenty of time to find a better-paid job. That's the second part of our plan, Louise.'

'My own house in Edinburgh,' Hamish said, preening himself, 'is now worth in the region of six thousand pounds, but of course,' he added, darting a sidelong glance at Billy, 'I have the income to pay for it.'

'We all know what a bigshot you are. The last of the big spenders,' Jenny scoffed, indulging once more in her eye-rolling, followed by a shake of the head, implying incredulity and the unspoken question: how in heaven's name did I come to marry this moron?

'That's something you know all about, my dear,' Hamish said, giving full rein to his clearing of the bronchial tubes. 'Spending.'

Uh-oh, Billy thought. Here we go again.

'Talking of Spender,' he said, interrupting once more, 'Stephen Spender has long been one of my favourite poets. How did that verse go again? Something about nude giant girls, I seem to remember.'

'Wasn't it also something about their having no secrets,' said Hughie, 'if my memory serves me right.'

'Trust Hughie and Billy to be acquainted with pornographic poetry,' Laura laughed.

'Not at all. It's modern verse,' said Billy.

Once again the conversation was taking a surreal turn and Louise felt it was time to act.

'If everyone's finished, shall we go into the lounge? We could hold one of our little "at homes" like we used to. I'm so looking forward to hearing young Portia and Rosalind do their party pieces.'

The term 'at home' sounded alarm bells in Billy's head. A Mackenzie 'at home' usually involved being pressed or blackmailed into performing something, especially if you protested that you were talentless. This cut no ice with Duncan who kept his eyes skinned for any hint of hidden aptitudes, even if it were no more than the ability to make animal noises, wiggle your ears or twitch your nostrils.

In the lounge, everyone settled around the Bechstein. Like old times, Billy thought. Laura and Louise began the proceedings with a lively rendering of a duet, Schubert's 'Marche Militaire', followed by Duncan's party piece 'The Laird of Cockpen'. Next, Hughie recited 'The Highwayman'. Katie ducked out of her turn neatly.

'Last time I performed,' she said, 'I did so from under the piano, you may remember. Somehow I don't think I'd fit under there today.'

It looked as if everyone was going to be called on in turn just as they had been years ago when Billy had caused a furore with his version of Al Jolson's 'Mammy'. He doubted he'd be able to sing it with the same amount of verve as the pipes had become a little rusty since then. Not only that, he no longer had the nerve. He racked his brains for a suitable throat disease: tonsillitis, mumps, quinsy, or even his old stand-by, polypi on the larynx, but he knew he'd never get away with it as he'd talked normally at the dinner table and they could see there was nothing wrong with his voice. It was Hamish, of all people, who saved his bacon.

'I think we should leave the entertainment to the children,' he declared.

'Good idea,' Billy said enthusiastically. 'Let's see what the young 'uns can do. Maybe Matthew will play the piano even if it's only chopsticks.'

Matthew looked daggers at him. He knew what was going on. His dad was asking him to pull his chestnuts out of the fire.

'Sorry, Dad,' Matthew said. 'I'm not ready to play yet. It's years since I touched a piano. I'll play chopsticks if you've got the music,' he added with a grin.

'Maybe you should be a comedian,' Billy said.

'We didn't have a piano in Kenya,' Laura explained.

'Very well,' Hamish said triumphantly. 'We shall have to rely on *my* two daughters for entertainment, that's all.'

The two girls stepped forward and opened their music cases, smirking as they did so.

'What would you like us to play, Daddy?' Portia simpered.

'Let's hear that little Haydn rondo,' Hamish crowed, smiling smugly at the company, unable to keep the note of self-satisfaction out of his voice.

'That's too hard,' Rosalind pouted as she slotted her flute together. 'I prefer the Mozart minuet.'

'Oh, all right,' Hamish said.

Stuck-up turkey cock, Billy thought.

'Interesting instruments, violin and flute, you've chosen for them,' Laura observed.

'I'd have preferred the cello and the oboe,' Jenny said, darting a hostile glare at her husband, 'but they were too expensive. Hamish bought these secondhand at an auction.'

By this time the two performers were ready and the air was suddenly rent by the screech of their instruments as they squirmed their way through the piece. Billy could have sworn the bust of Mozart on the piano grimaced.

They stopped abruptly in mid-performance.

'You played a wrong note there,' Portia snorted. 'You're hopeless.'

'I *did not*,' Rosalind retorted. 'It was you. You got the time wrong. You should learn to count, dopey.'

'That's it. I refuse to play with her,' Portia snapped back. 'She always blames me whenever it goes wrong.'

Hamish now stepped forward. 'Come along, girls. No bickering. Everyone's waiting.' He sounded desperate.

'Oh, all right,' Rosalind said, tossing her head, 'but if you hear something weird, you'll know who it is.'

The duo started up again and once more the air was filled with squawking and squeaking as the two girls struggled through the minuet.

There was applause when they had finished.

'I think they were brave in performing like that before an audience,' Billy said, clapping enthusiastically. He remembered his own terror when he'd been called on years before.

'I'm sure they'll improve,' Jenny said with a disdainful look at Hamish, 'when we fork out the money for proper lessons.'

'At least they got up and tried,' Laura said. Then turning to her own daughter, she asked, 'What about giving us one of your poems, Lucy?'

'The family reputation's at stake,' Billy added.

'I think I still know the words of "I remember" by Thomas Hood,' Lucy said. Courageously she stepped forward and in a clear voice recited her poem.

> *I remember, I remember,*
> *The house where I was born,*
> *The little window where the sun*
> *Came peeping in at morn.*

'Well done, Lucy,' Billy called when she had finished. 'You restored the family honour.'

'Where did she find that upper-class accent?' Duncan asked when the applause had died away.

'The result of mixing with so many public school people in Kenya,' Laura said.

'I dare say they'll lose their plummy accents soon enough here in Manchester,' Billy added.

'Well, I suppose that concludes the entertainment for the evening,' Duncan said, looking pointedly at Billy, 'unless . . .'

Uh-oh, thought Billy.

Then a little voice said, 'I'd like to do something now.'

All eyes turned to the speaker. It was young Mark. He produced his ventriloquist's dummy from behind his back.

'I've been rehearsing with my dummy since Christmas Day. He's called Harry the Hobo.'

Mark stepped forward and with his wooden doll on his knee went into his act.

'What is your name, my friend?' he asked.

'You know my name very well,' the dummy answered, his mouth opening and shutting as Mark operated the controls, ' 'cos you're the one who gave it to me and the one who's doing the talking. I'm Harry the Hobo.'

'You're a tramp then?'

'I don't know why you call me a tramp,' Harry said, ' 'cos I can't even walk with these funny legs they've given me.'

'But you're a beggar, aren't you?' Mark asked him.

'I am. Today I asked a man for a bite. So he bit me. I wasn't always a tramp though. At school I was clever. The teacher asked me to use the word "seldom" in a sentence. So I said, "A man had three horses but then he had to seldom." '

Mark continued his performance with a stream of corny jokes in this vein until he finally said, 'Say goodbye to everyone, Harry.'

'Goodbye, everyone. And if you see me in the street, don't forget to give me a shilling.'

The assembled company broke into spontaneous applause

56

when Mark stood up and bowed. Billy and Laura were as surprised as anyone there because they'd had no inkling that Mark had been preparing an act.

'He's worth a guinea a box,' Duncan enthused. 'He should be on the stage.'

'Sweeping it,' brother Matthew laughed, 'or maybe he could do his ventriloquism on radio.'

'You mean television, surely,' Hughie said.

'No, I don't,' Matthew chuckled. 'I mean radio where listeners won't be able to see his lips moving.'

'Give him a chance. He's only just started,' Lucy protested.

'Well done, our Mark,' Billy said, patting him on the back, 'and here's a shilling for your hobo friend.'

'Thank you to all the children for their magnificent performances,' Duncan proclaimed. 'There's a wealth of talent in the family waiting to be developed.'

Too true, Billy said to himself. When we were abroad, there was little opportunity to develop musical aptitudes. We must try to make up for that now that we're home again.

'And now,' Duncan said, looking round the company but, or so it seemed to Billy, concentrating his gaze in his direction, 'what about something else from the adults?'

Oh no, Billy thought.

Laura came to the rescue. 'I've an idea. Why don't we get the men to sing "The Gendarmes' Duet"? I've got the music right here.'

She opened the piano stool and selected the Offenbach score. Standing round the piano, the men took up their parts: Hughie and Billy sang bass, and Duncan and Hamish baritone, with Laura playing the accompaniment. With a great deal of tomfoolery and merriment, everyone sang out at the top of their voices.

We're public guardians, bold yet wary
And of ourselves, we take good care . . .

The song served to relieve earlier tensions and everyone became more relaxed. It was a perfect and amicable way of rounding off the social part of the evening.

Since it was Hogmanay, the young ones were allowed to stay up to see in the New Year. Duncan switched on the television to catch the last hour of the *White Heather Club* presented by Andy Stewart and the music of Jimmy Shand. As the sound of Big Ben chimed out the old year, there was a good deal of hugging, including Hamish and Jenny who seemed to have agreed on an armistice. The whole family joined hands and with great gusto sang:

> *Should auld acquaintance be forgot*
> *And never brought to mind?*
> *We'll tak a cup o'kindness yet,*
> *For auld lang syne*

At the beginning of the second verse everyone crossed hands for the singing of:

> *And there's a hand, my trusty fiere!*
> *And gie's a hand o' thine*
> *We'll tak a cup o' kindness yet,*
> *For auld lang syne*

Because of his dark hair, Hughie went out of the house, rang the bell and, as was the custom, came back in carrying a piece of coal. Duncan distributed the usual carefully measured drams of malt for the men, Bristol Cream for the ladies, and Coke for the children.

'Welcome to nineteen sixty-four,' Duncan said, raising his glass. 'A guid New Year to ane and a' and mony may ye hae. Here's tae us; wha's like us? Gey few, and they're a' deid.'

As Billy joined in this strange toast, he felt a warm glow of happiness pass through him and it wasn't entirely because of the whisky. How I've missed occasions like this during our time abroad, he reflected. At the same time he couldn't help but feel a pang of sorrow when he thought about his own parents' unhappy predicament in their old people's bungalow up there in Langley.

Later when Billy and Laura were alone, he told her how much he had enjoyed the festivities with her family.

'What a wonderful time we had,' he said, 'but it's a pity Hamish and Jenny aren't happier. I shouldn't think their marriage will last if they keep up that perpetual squabbling.'

'You're wrong, Billy. In their own strange way, they are happy. Jenny's told me several times that she prefers a life of cut-and-thrust to one that's smooth and unexciting. They're like Richard Burton and Elizabeth Taylor in that play about Virginia Woolf, the one where they bounce insulting remarks off each other.'

'As my mam would put it,' he said, 'there's nowt so queer as folk.'

Chapter Seven

If there was one activity that Billy's friends enjoyed, it was meeting up in a pub. For a number of years since leaving college, the 'gang' had been in the habit of getting together to catch up on each other's news and enjoy one another's company and conversation. They also enjoyed the drink though none of them was seriously addicted. The activity they loved best was word-fencing, exchanging repartees, and honing their best epigrams to needle sharpness. Getting a word in, though, was never easy. While one of them was giving forth and the others seemed to be listening with grim concentration, what their minds were focused on was not the bon mots of the current speaker but what they were going to say as soon as he'd stopped. They were adept at dissembling and giving the appearance of paying close attention when what they were really doing was running through their own stockpile of stories, awaiting their chance to nip in as soon as the guffaws provoked by the last anecdote began to subside. It required perfect timing and the most effective device was to dovetail the previous contribution with a logical connection such as, 'Speaking of the theatre, did you ever hear the one about the actress and the commercial traveller?' It was essential to keep an up-to-date mental checklist of which stories had been retailed and to which group. Otherwise there was a danger of the company reacting with, 'We've heard it!' It could result in humiliation and loss of face, and ruin the evening.

Oscar, who saw himself as a cross somewhere between Noel Coward and Oscar Wilde, was the most skilful at these ploys but he was by no means the only player. There was fierce rivalry to produce the wittiest quip or the most barbed comment, especially if they felt one of their crowd was in danger of becoming too serious or too pretentious and needed taking down a peg.

Early in the New Year, Titch kept his promise and organized a night out for the gang. Laura hadn't been too keen on leaving the kids at first, especially John.

'I'm worried about him,' she told Billy. 'He seems so listless and just wants to sit by the fire.'

'I think he's just finding it hard to adjust to our English winter after the tropical sunshine,' Billy said. 'A break will do you good. I'm sure your folk are perfectly able to look after the young 'uns.'

The Pineapple was a small comfortable public house not far from the Granada Television studios and was a convenient meeting place for everybody. Titch and his young wife Elaine got there first in order to reserve seats in the lounge, known as 'the best room', and to greet everybody on their arrival. Billy and Laura came next.

'We started coming to this new pub about a year ago,' Titch told them as they hung up their coats. 'The Sawyer's Arms has got so popular,' he said with a laugh, 'that nobody goes there any more. So we've made this pub our rendezvous instead. It doesn't get too busy, there's always a good fire in the grate, and if you ask her nicely, Doris, the barmaid, will lay on sandwiches around nine o'clock. Incidentally,' he added, hardly able to contain himself, 'I've got something to tell you. I'll let you have it later when the rest get here. I think you'll be surprised.'

'Almost as much as I am,' Elaine said, giving an enigmatic Mona Lisa smile though it could have been merely indigestion.

'I'm intrigued,' Billy said, 'but we've got some news for you as well. Maybe not as exciting as yours but I think things are beginning to move for us.'

Nobby and Olly arrived together with their wives, Prudence and Cordelia. Oscar, with his soul mate Derek, came last.

It wasn't long before the ale and the conversation flowed freely though Billy found that no one wanted to hear about their African experiences.

'We get enough of Africa on the telly,' Olly said. 'We see repeats of *White Hunter* and, since the Lancaster House Conference, we don't seem to hear about anything else. It's Kenyatta said this and Kenyatta said that. Next thing you know, we'll make him Lord Jomo and give him a seat in the House of Lords.'

'You'll have to write up your experiences in a book,' Nobby said.

'Who knows? Maybe I will one day,' Billy replied.

'That'll be the day,' Laura remarked. 'It takes him all his time to answer his mail and pay the bills.'

Titch went through to the bar to order a round to be paid from the kitty that had been organized.

'So, how have you found England now you're back?' Olly asked. 'Has it changed as much as the media would have us believe?'

'We've certainly found it changed,' Billy replied. 'After the rural simplicity of Kenya, life here seems somehow more hectic, and more materialistic. Despite, and maybe because of, the welfare state, there appears to be less community spirit than there used to be and too many people trying to get something for nothing. "What's in it for me?" seems to be the prevalent attitude.'

Titch came back from the bar in a state of high excitement.

'You're not going to believe who's in the back room,' he gushed.

'Pray, tell us, do,' Oscar drawled, inserting a black Russian cigarette into his holder.

'Only Pat Phoenix and Violet Carson! Along with a lot of other celebrities.'

'And who are all these people when they're at home?' Billy asked. 'Friends of yours, are they? Are we supposed to know them?'

'Know them! Know them! They're world famous. They play Elsie Tanner and Ena Sharples in *Coronation Street*, that's all!'

'Very well,' Billy said. 'You go into the back room and tell these two ladies and their friends that Billy Hopkins and his wife, Laura, are in the lounge.'

'You've got a lot of catching up to do, Billy,' Titch said, 'about England and the way it's changed since you've been away.'

'You can say that again,' Billy replied. 'Anyway, let's hear this exciting news you've got for us. I think you're going to wet yourself if you wait any longer.'

'Elaine and I are going to Canada. It's all fixed up. I've been appointed to a job in a high school in Grande Prairie.'

'Congratulations,' said Oscar, taking a pull at his cigarette. 'But where in heaven's name is Grande Prairie? Sounds like one of those one-horse towns in a Hollywood Western.'

'Nothing of the sort,' Titch said. 'It's a thriving little town in Alberta and I'm to be head of English. We fly to Montreal at the end of this month.'

'What in heaven's name possessed you?' Nobby asked. 'What's the big attraction in Canada?'

'Almost double my present salary. That's what. It's our big chance to put some cash in the bank and,' he said, glancing in his wife's direction, 'there's a job for Elaine, if she wants it, in the primary department. Billy and Laura made their little pile by working abroad. Why shouldn't we do the same?'

'That's fine, Titch,' Laura said, 'but how does Elaine feel about all this?'

'I wasn't so keen at first,' Elaine replied, 'but Titch has persuaded me and now, I suppose, I'm all for it, if it allows us to build up a little capital. We're both tired of the penny-pinching existence here, living from hand to mouth each month. Salaries in this country are hopeless. The only thing that worries me is my parents who are getting on in years and I don't like leaving them.'

'But it's not forever,' Titch added, putting his arm round her reassuringly. 'We'll be back in a couple of years with money in our pocket like Billy and Laura there.'

'Still, Canada is different from Africa,' Billy said taking a sip of his shandy.

Oscar said, 'Speaking of the maple leaf country, somebody somewhere has said that Canada is like that vichyssoise soup you sometimes get as a starter in the better restaurant.'

'Vichyssoise soup?' Titch said. 'What's that? I'm not with you.'

'It's cold, half French, thick and difficult to stir.'

'And I read somewhere only last week,' said Olly, not to be left out when it came to a show of knowledge and a display of sparkling wit, 'that Canada was in a unique position with a glorious opportunity to adopt the best features of three countries: French culture, American technology, and English government. And look what it ended up with: French government, American culture and British technology.'

'Very funny, I'm sure, ha, ha ha,' said Titch scornfully.

'And I've heard,' Oscar added, determined not to be outshone by Olly, 'that it's a gloomy region without culture where the year is divided up into one day and one night. For half the year, the people hibernate in their gloomy houses and when spring comes they go mad careering across the country like lunatics released from an asylum.'

'It's so cold,' Nobby laughed, 'that when you pour a cup of tea, it freezes before it reaches the cup and people's piss turns to little ice cubes.'

'Thanks for all these encouraging observations,' Titch said. 'But have you forgotten that Canada has half the Niagara Falls in its territory?'

'And didn't the great Oscar Wilde remark', Oscar said haughtily, 'that Niagara is simply a vast unnecessary amount of water going the wrong way and then falling over unnecessary rocks.'

'The only thing I know about Canada,' said Olly's wife,

Cordelia, 'is that it's useful in supplying me with my fur hat.'

'And my fur gloves,' added Prudence.

'Remind me not to send you lot a postcard when we get there and are piling up the loot,' Titch grinned.

'Apart from all this Canada business,' Gertrude said, smiling cattily and addressing Elaine, 'how do you find life being married to an old man like Titch there?'

'Steady on,' Titch said. 'Less of the old man. There's only ten years difference, not fifty.'

'I find it's fine,' Elaine answered, smiling back at Gertrude. 'It's so wonderful to come to meetings like tonight's and find that I'm the youngest woman there by at least a decade. Who needs a facelift when I'm already years younger than the crowd Titch goes around with? Not only that, I'm married to a man who is less likely to trade me in for a younger model because, to him, I'm already one.'

Touché, Billy thought.

'Well said, my dear,' Titch said, kissing her on the forehead. 'But what about you, Hoppy? Didn't you say you had some news to impart? It's your turn to have the mickey taken.'

Billy wondered whether he should submit himself to the same ridicule that had been meted out to Titch. His friends were a cynical lot who enjoyed nothing better than shooting down one's ideas and dreams. Then he thought, what the heck? It's all in fun.

'My news is not as definite as Titch's,' he said. 'It's more in the nature of hope than accomplished fact.'

'Cut the preamble, Hoppy,' Olly said. 'Let's hear it so we can prepare to shoot you down.'

'OK,' Billy said. 'Sharpen your arrows and prepare your barbed shafts. First of all, Laura and I have found our dream house in Didsbury.'

The assembled company lifted their noses with their fingers to signify snootiness and upmarket snobbery.

'By 'eck, we 'ave gone up in't world,' Titch scoffed. 'I

won't ask you how much you're going to pay for this piece of real estate.'

'That's fine, Titch, as I don't want to say. It's too embarrassing.'

'OK, Hoppy, I understand. So come on, tell us. How much? Over three thousand?'

Billy smiled but said nothing.

'Can't be over four K? People like us don't pay more than four thousand for a house. Or do we?'

Billy continued to smile.

'Aw, come on, Hoppy. Don't keep us in suspense. How much? Can't be over five! Tell you what, Hoppy. If you don't speak, we'll know it's over five.'

Billy remained silent. Then he said, 'You don't want to know.'

'We do! We do!' Titch pleaded. 'That's why we're asking.'

'Mrs Cohen, the owner, is asking five thousand two hundred and fifty but we should be able to bargain and knock that down to five thousand.'

The gang gasped. Titch whistled incredulously.

'Billy, you're a bloated plutocrat,' Olly exclaimed. 'Why, only a few moments ago you were the one telling us that society had become too materialistic. And now here you are with a flash car and thinking about buying a mansion in Didsbury.'

'Wanting a nice house and owning a car are not materialistic in my book,' Billy retorted. 'A materialist is somebody who is obsessed by wealth and possessions to the exclusion of everything else. Acquiring things becomes the be-all and end-all of such a person's existence. As the great Oscar put it, he knows the price of everything and the value of nothing. I pray to God I never become like that.'

'Apart from all that, it's pretty difficult to be materialistic with four children to feed and educate,' Laura laughed.

'As far as I'm concerned,' Titch grinned, 'a materialist is anyone who's richer than me. And that means nearly everybody.'

'Aside from this talk about materialism and all that, what about the mortgage you'll be taking on?' Nobby said. 'You'll still be paying off the mortgage when you're a hundred.'

'As to the final figure you agree on,' Oscar chuckled, 'if you can knock your vendors down by two hundred and fifty, you're a better man than I am, Gunga Din.'

'Have you forgotten that I spent my childhood in Manchester's Cheetham Hill district?' Billy grinned. 'I learned a trick or two in my fire-lighting days.'

'Even so, that's still on the high side,' said Olly, doing rapid calculations on his fingers. 'You'll have a great millstone round your neck for the next twenty-five years.'

'But worth it for a beautiful house,' Laura countered.

Oscar grinned. 'For five thousand pounds, I should expect Buckingham Palace. What's this house got that makes it so special? Gold taps and solid marble?'

'Not exactly,' Laura answered, 'but it sounds like our ideal home. The estate agent describes it as Edwardian.'

'Ah, but does he say which Edward?' Oscar said haughtily. 'Sixth or seventh? Besides, you shouldn't believe everything in an estate agent's blurb. They're well known for their euphemisms and their mendacity. Even the term "estate agent" conjures up a picture of rolling acres of parkland dotted with trees surrounding a stately home.'

'I don't know what it is,' Billy laughed, looking round at them all, 'but whenever one mentions estate agents, it's like waving a red rag to a bull; it's the signal for everyone to bring out their corniest comments. I had this many years ago from my own family when we bought our first home in Regina Park. Anyway, the ad described it as elegant and gracious, prestigious and select, with a landscaped garden.'

Billy knew he was leaving himself open with these feed lines and giving his friends yet another chance to demonstrate their brilliance. He was not disappointed.

Olly was first. 'Elegant and gracious mean old and a nightmare to maintain.'

It was Oscar's turn with, 'Prestigious and select is estate-agent speak for expensive and over-priced.'

Titch had the last word. 'Garden rockery and landscaped garden equals rubble left behind by the builders.'

'OK, OK,' Billy said. 'You've had your fun but Laura and I like the sound of the house and we'll let you know how we get on.'

'Fine,' said Olly. 'I hope you can afford it.'

'That leads me to my second piece of news,' Billy said. 'I've applied for a job as senior lecturer in a Catholic women's training college and I've been invited to attend for an interview.'

There was a long silence as the gang took in this piece of news. They seemed to stare into their drinks for an unconscionably long time.

'Did I hear you right?' Nobby said at last. 'Did you say you've applied for the post of senile lecherer?'

'Very droll, I'm sure,' Billy replied.

'If such a college were to appoint a man to the staff, I'd be a safer bet,' Oscar laughed.

'You did say "women's training college"!' exclaimed Olly incredulously.

'Not only a women's training college but a Catholic convent college,' Billy said.

'What in heaven's name made you apply for a job like that?' Titch asked. 'What's wrong with a job in an ordinary school?'

'For a start, it's more money. Next, it's in higher education and that's why I worked all those years for extra qualifications. It's time they paid off. Finally, with the demand for more and better qualified teachers, the training colleges are crying out for well-qualified staff.'

'But nuns won't even contemplate having a man on the premises, yet alone on the staff,' Olly spluttered.

'*Tempora mutantur*,' Oscar said loftily. 'Times change.'

'If you were appointed, Hoppy, it'd be like giving a drunk a job in a brewery,' Nobby observed.

'You speak for yourself,' Billy laughed. 'Things have moved on. This is the swinging sixties.'

'I was a convent girl,' Elaine said, 'and boys were always considered a species apart and we were warned every day not even to speak to them.'

'And at my convent,' Gertrude giggled, 'we were told to beware of bright patent shoes in case they reflected our knickers. Modesty was the most highly prized virtue. It was a strict regime. We once got a new teacher, a Miss Dexter, who was very much with it, wore high heels, had shapely legs and all that. Naturally we all had a crush on her. One day she came to school wearing an elegant silk dress. She was an inspiration, a vision with a slim, beautiful figure.'

'Sounds intriguing,' Laura said. 'What happened next?'

'Sister Agatha, the head, was not so keen on her as a role model and soon took the wind out of her sails. On one occasion Miss Dexter appeared with a suggestion of lipstick but later that day it was gone. She was seen coming out of the head's room in tears. She was too attractive and too modern, you see.'

'I went to a convent teacher training college,' Laura said, 'and I can confirm much of what Elaine and Gertrude are saying. There were strict rules of dress. For example, we had to wear black during the week and were never allowed to wear any dress which displayed elbows or collarbone.'

'I must say that those parts of the anatomy never struck me as erotic,' Nobby remarked lasciviously. 'Perhaps I've been missing something.'

'At weekends though,' Laura continued, 'we were permitted to wear our own dresses and were allowed out on Saturday afternoons on the strict understanding that we were back by nine o'clock.'

'Sounds more like a reformatory than a training college,' Olly observed. 'Were you permitted to have boyfriends?'

'Yes, though it was frowned on. Boyfriends were never allowed to set foot on the premises and had to say goodnight at the main gate. Apart from the usual tradesmen, the only man allowed was an octogenarian gardener,' Laura laughed.

'And I'll bet he'd been castrated,' Oscar said.

'If all this is true, what chance do you stand, Hoppy?' Titch asked.

'I repeat,' Billy said, 'this is the swinging sixties. There's a new atmosphere abroad. Even the nuns have got to get with it if they're to avoid empty colleges. And my philosophy is "Nothing ventured, nothing gained".'

Oscar had to have the last word. 'You stand as much chance of getting the job as I have of becoming the Arch-bishop of Canterbury.'

'Yes, Your Grace,' Billy laughed.

Chapter Eight

The week after the meeting in the pub, Billy went to St Helens to attend Sherdley Park College for his interview. He associated St Helens with Pilkington's, the world-famous glass manufacturer, but that was pretty much all he knew about the place. So in preparation he went to the library to find out more. St Helens, he discovered, was a well-established Lancashire town, not far from Liverpool, which had prospered in the nineteenth century because of its coalfield and its canals and railway systems. As well as being one of the largest glass manufacturing centres in Britain, it was well known for its association with nearby Rainhill where the locomotive trials for George Stephenson's 'Rocket' had been held in the early part of the nineteenth century.

On the morning that he caught the train at Central Station, he was tired. He'd hardly slept the night before despite the Persomnia tablet he had taken. He'd tried counting sheep jumping over a stile but for some inexplicable reason the fourth sheep always refused to jump and he finished up more wide awake than ever, worrying about that recalcitrant ewe that he'd had to hoist over in the end. Typical, he thought, as the train pulled out of the station, here I am feeling sleepy when I should be bright and alert. Ridiculous. A teacher with seventeen years' experience and I'm as nervous as a newly qualified rookie. The trouble is, he thought, I've no experience in higher education teaching young adults. And this job I'm in for involves not only that but training the next generation of teachers as well. This was altogether a different proposition. He'd played out the interview in his mind and he could imagine all manner of awkward questions, like 'What attracts you to working in a college of young females?' And he could see himself blushing with embarrassment. Why *did* he want to work with young ladies? He didn't really know himself.

After a thirty-minute journey, he emerged at Lea Green Station from where it was but a short walk to the college. At the entrance he pulled on the long chain which rang a bell somewhere deep in the bowels of the building. Eventually the fortress-like door was opened by a young pretty nun who gave her name as Sister Anna.

Sister Anna will carry the banner, Billy thought, irreverently recalling a bawdy saying from his adolescent days.

She led him along a maze of corridors, past numerous statues of saints, mainly female and mainly nuns: Teresa of Avila, Therese of Lisieux, Catherine of Siena. There was a strong smell of floor polish and beeswax and he could hear the strains of plainchant being sung in a remote part of the college.

Sister Anna showed him first the cloakroom, which surprised Billy as he'd never imagined there'd be a gents' toilet in a convent. Next, she led him to a little waiting room where he found three other candidates, two ladies and one man, waiting to be interviewed. They smiled and nodded in his direction but it was difficult to tell if their rictus expressions were meant to be friendly, hostile or simply a sign of nerves. The two ladies continued their conversation with each other.

'I've been teaching in the convent high school in nearby Rainford for over twelve years now,' said one, 'and I think I'm ready to move into higher education. I should so love it if I were selected. The Principal, Sister Benedict, suggested to me personally that I should apply.'

'I wish you every success,' said the other. 'I'm sure you'll enjoy it if they appoint you. I know I've loved my work training Catholic teachers in Lincoln.'

The male candidate raised his eyes heavenward and exchanged glances with Billy.

'I'm going to pay a visit to the cloakroom,' he said, getting up from his chair.

'I'll join you,' Billy said.

In the gents' they lit up fags.

'I'm Gerry Flynn,' said the man. 'Here for the job in philosophy of education.'

'Billy Hopkins. Sociology of education. Glad to know you.'

'I'm already a lecturer in education at a polytechnic in Hull and I'm hoping to move up a grade to senior lecturer here but this appointment is probably a fix, a put-up job,' Flynn proclaimed. 'Did you hear those ladies? Both convent types.'

'You never know,' Billy said. 'Perhaps the authorities are looking for a change.' His words sounded hollow.

'I've been through this kind of thing before,' the other retorted. 'We're "makeweights" to give the impression that selection is fair and above board. Some authorities, and it looks like this may be one, advertise nationally and appoint locally, usually an inside candidate. Still, we can claim our travel expenses.'

Negative thoughts whirled round Billy's head. A put-up job – an inside candidate. Why bother to invite us for interview if it's already been fixed?

Half an hour later, Billy found himself in the interviewing room.

The jitters were upon him now; his heart fluttering, his stomach churning, and his legs had turned to jelly. So much was riding on the outcome of this interview: his hopes for the future, his career prospects, his family's prosperity, the house and the mortgage.

He hoped his nervousness wasn't obvious to the committee. Large breaths, in and out, that's the answer, he told himself as he sat down in the chair facing the panel.

Sister Benedict, the Principal of the college, introduced the committee: Sisters Peter and Paul, the Head and Deputy Head of Education; George Winters, Chief Education Officer; and a Professor Hodgett from Keele University.

73

Sister Benedict, Peter and Paul! Females with men's Christian names? What sort of place is this? Billy wondered. It gave an oxymoronic ring to their titles, a male sister. Come to think of it, why not Brother Mary and Father Catherine? Must stop thinking like this, he told himself.

The Principal proceeded to go through Billy's qualifications though they took his word for it that he really did have them. In seventeen years in education, no one had ever demanded to see evidence of his various certificates and degrees. A con man would have no difficulty in bluffing his way into an educational position.

There followed a series of questions about his experience. Had he ever taught in higher education? (Bloody obvious he hadn't if they'd only take a look at the application form he'd completed so painstakingly.) Had he ever taught in a single sex establishment, in particular young ladies between the ages of 18 and 21? (No, he hadn't. Also patently obvious if they'd only glance at the form.)

The two nuns from the Education Department then concentrated their questions on his personal background and his family. Was he a *practising* Catholic? How long had he been married and was he still living with his wife? They seemed impressed by his four children and especially that one of them was a daughter. So you'll know all about teaching young ladies! A remark which caused a ripple of polite laughter round the company.

'If you're appointed,' the Principal said, 'you'll be the first male lecturer we have ever employed. I should perhaps point out, too, that the appointment is for a period of three years with the possibility after that time of permanent status. I trust this is acceptable.'

'Yes, Sister, I should be glad to agree to those terms.' What else could he say? He'd be happy to be offered the job on any terms.

Sisters Peter and Paul smiled and nodded in unison,

reminding Billy of the nodding dogs he had seen on the rear ledges of motor cars.

The first male lecturer to work in this all-female college! Would a medal be struck to mark the momentous event? He felt like David Livingstone when he discovered the Victoria Falls.

The professor went on to explain how the new B.Ed degree would be inaugurated within the coming year and how there'd be a great need for well-qualified staff to teach it. It means, he said, that new teachers of the future would be able to add the letters B.Ed after their name. Billy wondered how that would go down with the young ladies when they suffixed BED to their titles.

The professor asked him about the subjects he could teach. Billy told him that he had studied sociology of education under Professor Niblett and Frances Stevens of the University of Leeds. The professor smiled and nodded his approval.

'I hope also,' Billy said, 'to begin work for a masters in education when I find a suitable field of research.'

'I feel sure a subject will occur to you in this college,' said Sister Peter, nodding vigorously, 'that is, *if* we appoint you, of course,' she added hurriedly.

George Winters, the Chief Education Officer, was more interested in Billy's experiences in Kenya.

Billy became animated as he explained how he felt about education in the former colony.

'Much of what we taught was irrelevant. At times I felt I was foisting an alien culture on an unsuspecting people.'

Winters nodded enthusiastically and, leaning forward, looked at Billy intently.

'I'm inclined to agree with you,' he said warmly. 'Give me some examples.'

Billy was on a roll.

'I strongly believe that different political systems suit different people and I've often felt that it's wrong and even dangerous to attempt to transplant any kind of "ism" or ideology abroad, whether it be republicanism, socialism, fascism, communism, or even egalitarianism. In the field of government, we were pushing democratic government on to them when their own tribal system was pyramidal in structure, from the ordinary peasant to the headman of the village and upwards to the tribal chief. The notion of "one man, one vote" was alien to their practice. It used to be said that it was a case of one man, one vote, once! What many African politicians find difficult to understand about parliamentary democracy is why, once they have achieved power, they should be compelled to hand it over to another person because of an election. For them, power means wealth and a chance to feather their own nest. And take the subjects we were teaching. In music competitions, we were often required to teach English folk songs about plough boys and maypoles, which meant nothing to them. My colleague teaching maths found a similar difficulty. His arithmetic syllabus contained problems about baths filling and emptying when our students had never seen a bath. In English literature, the Overseas Cambridge School Certificate included many highbrow works, such fatuous choices as *Moby Dick* for students who had never seen the sea, nineteenth-century English essayists like Hazlitt, Belloc, Macaulay and the rest. Admirable classics for British students but largely irrelevant and inappropriate in the Africa context. I felt strongly that we should have spent more time trying to promote an understanding of their own or similar cultures.'

Winters became excited. 'Yes, yes,' he said, slapping the desk. 'But which books would *you* have substituted?'

'I would have preferred books like Elspeth Huxley's *Red Strangers*, Alan Paton's *Cry, the Beloved Country* or Arthur Grimble's *A Pattern of Islands.* I think our students would have related better to books like those.'

'What about Shakespeare?' Winters asked.

'Shakespeare, I think, was the exception to the rule. There

was something about the plays that made a direct appeal to African students.'

'How do you explain that?' the Chief Education Officer inquired.

'I think the basic raw emotions expressed in Shakespeare were truly understood and appreciated by the students. Emotions like jealousy, anger, ambition, greed. They loved plays like *Macbeth* and *Hamlet*, though sometimes they put their own interpretation on them.'

'I must say I've found this discussion fascinating,' Sister Benedict said, 'as I am sure we all have.'

The two nuns at her side did their nodding dogs routine.

'Now I'm afraid I must bring the interview to a close,' the Principal continued. 'In preparation for the B.Ed degree, we shall be recruiting many new members of staff and so we have many more interviews to conduct. We have been most impressed, Mr Hopkins, and we'll be in touch as soon as we're able to reach a firm decision. You should know within a month or so. Thank you for attending.'

What else could he say but, 'Thank you. I enjoyed the interview very much.'

He was pleased with his performance and he left the college hopeful although his future was still as uncertain as when he had arrived. There was nothing to do but wait.

Chapter Nine

A week after the interview, Billy drove Laura across to Didsbury to take a look at the house they were interested in buying. Although it was situated on a main road, the house itself was set well back in what the estate agents had described as a mature garden. The gang would have had fun with that, Billy thought, and no doubt would have redefined it as tired-looking and overgrown with weeds but in fact the garden was well tended and well stocked with a variety of bushes and shrubs: rhododendrons, laurel, forsythia, and foxglove. Billy and Laura fell in love with the house as soon as they saw it.

It was a large semi-detached, genuinely Edwardian having been built at the turn of the century, a period of building noted for its fine, solid workmanship. The front of the house contained a long porch and a solid oak door with a fancy brass knocker, which they employed to announce their presence. Mrs Rachel Cohen, the owner, opened the door, revealing a large hall with its own oak fireplace and a warm welcoming fire.

'Mr and Mrs Hopkins? I've been expecting you,' she said, holding out her hand. 'I'm so glad you were able to make it.'

The house had six bedrooms. 'A bedroom each,' Laura had remarked when she saw the estate agent's description.

'I hope you don't mean we're to have separate bedrooms as well as the kids,' Billy had chuckled.

Mrs Cohen gave them a brief history of the house. 'It was built about nineteen hundred and two and previous occupants have been mainly business people but we've had one former celebrated resident in Miles Benison, a writer who died in mysterious circumstances around nineteen twenty-eight, I believe. Can't say I've ever read anything he's written.'

'What about your immediate neighbours?' Laura asked. 'What are they like?'

'Living next door is a medical practitioner, Dr Gillespie, and his wife. We have always got on well with them. We've found them kind and considerate. They have one son aged about twelve or thirteen. We hear him practising his trumpet in the cellar from time to time. But not too loudly,' she added quickly.

She took them on a tour of the house beginning with the large attic bedrooms on the third floor.

'Perfect study and bedroom for Matthew,' Billy observed.

'We're not leaving it to democratic choice then,' Laura said.

'No fear. The kids would never stop squabbling.'

In their mind's eye, they allocated the various rooms. The large front bedroom they chose for themselves, and the smaller bedroom with the veranda seemed perfect for Lucy, while the two back rooms were right for the two youngest, Mark and John.

'And this is the bathroom with its separate shower cubicle,' Mrs Cohen announced proudly, opening the door. 'There is a separate WC on this floor and a second one downstairs adjoining the kitchen.'

The ground floor consisted of two large lounges with inglenook fireplaces and huge bay windows. Already in their mind's eye they could see the family gatherings they could hold there. Next they were shown the enormous farmhouse kitchen and had there been any lingering doubt in their minds up to this point, for Laura it was now completely dispelled. Her eyes shone and her face lit up when she saw it and imagined herself in it conjuring up delightful dishes for her family. She squeezed Billy's hand to communicate her enthusiasm and he sensed that he daren't even think about not buying it. The kitchen may have won Laura over but for

Billy, the spacious cellars were the clincher. Not only big but dry and recently painted in bright emulsion. He could see himself down there pursuing all sorts of practical hobbies, like wood-turning or furniture-making, not that he had ever indulged in these activities. But he could dream.

'There is also a dummy cellar under the main lounge,' Mrs Cohen explained. 'Only four feet standing room but useful for storing things, like wine if you're that way inclined.'

'I notice there are no windows or doors to it,' Billy observed. 'How do you get into it?'

'The only access is through the hole in the brickwork. It's big enough to allow a man to crawl in to carry out repairs if need be. As for a window, no need for one. There's an air duct that comes out in the garden so that the air can circulate freely down there.' She smiled wistfully when she mentioned the air duct. 'I used to call down the air pipe when I was in the garden if I wanted my husband Hymie to come up for one reason or another. My voice would carry into the cellar.'

As they inspected the cellars, for Billy the memories of the cellars in Honeypot Street came flooding back. There was the time his dad had belted him and shoved him down there for losing his pincers; there were the war years when he'd sat with his family during the air raids, cowering in terror night after night. But that was all in the past. Now he could look forward to putting a basement like this to more creative uses. And what a contrast this house was to the homes he had known before marriage! The Collyhurst tenement where he'd been born, the Red Bank house in Honeypot Street where he'd played as a boy with his pal Henry Sykes, and the unspeakable block of flats where he had spent his adolescence. He'd come a long way since those days. Then his thoughts went out to his mam and dad so unhappy in their state-of-the-art iceberg of a bungalow on that new housing estate. I must try to do something to make life more comfortable for them, he vowed, though precisely what, he couldn't at that moment imagine.

'It's a lovely house, Mrs Cohen,' Laura remarked. 'but as we've been walking about, I couldn't help noticing those little ceramic tubes attached to each doorpost. What are they?'

Mrs Cohen smiled mysteriously. 'They are mezuzahs.'

'Mezuzahs? I'm not with you,' Billy said. 'What are they for?'

'Mezuzahs are signs of a Jewish home. In each tube there is a little parchment with verses from Deuteronomy and we believe they bring a blessing and good luck to the house where they are installed.'

'We have a belief like that in the Catholic church,' Laura said. 'We sometimes have holy water fonts but only at the front door not on every doorpost. They, too, are supposed to bring good luck to the house when we bless ourselves on leaving.'

'We have a similar practice,' Mrs Cohen said. 'We kiss the mezuzah by touching it first with the fingertips which we then bring to the lips. My rabbi son tells us we must always say, "May God protect my going out and coming in, now and forever." If you decide to buy the house, I'd advise you to leave the mezuzahs in place for they bring good fortune and, who knows, maybe bad luck if you remove them. Some people regard the mezuzah as a talisman to ward off evil.'

'Have they brought *you* good luck?' Billy asked.

'They certainly have,' Mrs Cohen said warmly. 'Like you, Hymie and I had four children and they've all been succesful. Harold, my eldest, is a solicitor with his own practice – he will be handling the sale of the house; Sadie is a surgeon at the Manchester Royal; Mildred has her own dress shop on King Street in Manchester; and Reuben is a rabbi in Prestwich. It was Reuben who insisted that we have them on every room doorpost, except the bathroom.'

'I'm sure we'll leave the mezuzahs in position if we buy the house,' Laura said.

'I'll be sorry to leave this house,' Mrs Cohen sighed, 'but all my children have left. Hymie died a year ago and it's too big for one person. I'll be taking a little apartment near my daughters.'

They had reached the front door and as Billy and Laura were about to leave, Mrs Cohen said, 'I hope you buy the house. It's ideal for a family like yours. We've been happy here and I'm sure you will be too.'

'Thank you for the tour and your help and advice, Mrs Cohen,' Laura replied. 'You have been most helpful.'

They shook hands and said goodbye, promising to be in touch if they decided to proceed.

A short distance away was the Nag's Head, which would probably be their local if they bought the house and so they thought it might be a good place to repair to talk things over and to sample the brew.

The pub's décor was equine with lots of horseshoes, brasses and reproductions of Stubbs's paintings adorning the walls. They settled down in the lounge and Billy went into the bar to get the drinks. The clientele were in keeping with the upmarket aura of the establishment because propping up the bar were a number of drinkers who could have been part of the décor: ladies in tailored Harris tweed costumes, men in Norfolk jackets and deerstalker hats, bow ties, and accents to match. One man sported a monocle. As Billy waited to be served, he caught a smattering of their conversation.

'Don't know what the world's coming to,' a military-looking barfly snorted. 'Manchester's going to pot, I tell you. Latest thing I hear is they're going to close down the grammar schools and switch over to those damn comprehensive dumps. As for our city council sitting up there in Albert Square! They're all bladdy communists.'

'A bad business, Rodney,' his companion rasped. 'A case of the proles taking over. This government won't be happy till we're all equal and in the gutter together.'

The speaker looked over to catch Billy's eye as if seeking agreement but Billy felt it wiser to avoid getting involved. Instead he asked the landlord about the horseshoes and the brasses.

'We've a thriving riding school nearby,' the landlord told him.

'How different all this is from Ancoats and Collyhurst,' he said to Laura when he returned with the drinks. 'If we end up here we shall certainly be going up in the world. Who knows? Maybe we can fix up for Lucy to have riding lessons. Then she'd be like royalty – like Princess Anne.'

Laura said, 'Somehow, Billy, I can't see us joining the horse-riding set. It's just not our scene. The big question for us is can we buy that house, which I absolutely love. Can we afford it? It's a steep price.'

'I think we could raise a deposit of one thousand two hundred and fifty pounds,' he said, 'leaving a mortgage of around four thousand which is manageable, provided I nail down a well-paid job.'

'It's a case of prayers to St Joseph, patron saint of homes and families,' she said as she sipped her port and lemon.

'Might be better appealing to St Matthew, patron saint of finances, or maybe St Jude for desperate cases. I hope you noticed that there's a lot needs doing. Apart from the cellar, it's in need of decoration and modernization. Did you notice that it has no central heating and the electric wiring looked old and out-of-date. I think Wylex plugs have long been superseded.'

'Given time, Billy, we can overcome those problems and lick it into shape.'

'Then there's the traffic on the main road. Do you think you can live with that, Laura?'

'Live with it? I love it!' she exclaimed. 'After living for so long in the African bush, it's nice to hear signs of civilized life.'

'You mean the wailing sirens of ambulances and police cars,' Billy grinned.

'Those especially. They mean we're right in the middle of things, where it's all happening. Oh, Billy, do you think we can do it?'

'We can have a damned good try.'

'Then let's go for it!'

Chapter Ten

The following week, Billy made an offer of £5,000 but the Cohen family wasn't having any. In many ways it was like a game of poker with high stakes. He wasn't sure how far he could press his luck trying for a reduction without blowing the deal. On the other hand, the Cohens couldn't be sure what price to stick out for without losing the sale. Then he suggested £5,100 but the least they'd accept was £5,150. At least it was a hundred pounds off, he thought.

Once the figure was agreed, Billy got down to work. He moved fast and soon had a four per cent, twenty-five-year mortgage arranged with the Teacher's Assurance Company, a reputable institution with a firm financial background and a good name in the teaching profession. Given Billy's qualifications and experience, the TAC had complete confidence in his prospects of landing a well-paid job. For this house purchase, he was taking no chances and there would be no fly-by-night finance companies involved as there had been the last time he'd arranged a mortgage back in 1951 when the managing director of the mortgage company had misappropriated the funds. Billy put down a deposit of £1,150 pounds, leaving a balance of £4,000. It was a fairly hefty debt and he'd need a substantial salary to cover the monthly payments, such as would be attached to the post of senior lecturer he had applied for. It was taking a risk but he was optimistic about his chances of getting the training college job.

With Duncan's contacts in the legal world and Mrs Cohen's son, Harold, handling the conveyancing, things made rapid progress and within the month they had exchanged contracts. Came the day he returned from the solicitor's office with the key of the house and they found themselves the proud possessors of a new home and a frighteningly large mortgage.

The kids were bubbling with excitement as they ran through the house and the cellars exploring the nooks and crannies, each staking a claim to a particular part of the house, only to find that their parents had already done the allocating. Matthew loved his little suite of two rooms at the top of the house, Lucy adored her bedroom with its own balcony overlooking the main road. As for the two youngest, Mark and John could hardly contain their glee when they realized they were to have their own separate rooms.

'Keep your greedy eyes off the cellar,' Billy announced before the kids could lay a claim. 'That's reserved as my workshop.'

'What about the dummy cellar, Dad?' Matthew asked.

'It's all yours,' Billy said, 'You can share it amongst you though I don't know what use it'll be as there's no light in there and you'll have to crawl on all fours to move about.'

'Perfect as a secret den,' Matthew replied.

The next few weeks were occupied in buying basic furniture though this had to be mainly second-hand selections from the miscellaneous columns in the local newspaper as most of their capital was needed for modernization and improvements. There was one item, however, that had the highest priority and could in no circumstances be omitted. A piano. They found a second-hand Broadwood in superb condition at Forsyth Brothers on Deansgate. Laura's eyes glowed with joy when it was delivered to the house.

Soon there was an army of workmen traipsing through the house, rewiring and installing central heating from top to bottom. Chaos reigned both upstairs and downstairs as they went to work. Floorboards were up everywhere and it wasn't long before the house echoed with the sound of workmen calling instructions to each other. From the cellar could be heard subterranean voices giving technical, esoteric commands like, 'Ernie, pass down a Yorkshire elbow and the bending spring. Where's the boss white? Check that thermostat! No, not the moleskin! The moles, you cuckoo!' All double Dutch to Billy and his family. Upstairs, the orders from the other team were equally mysterious. 'Pull that earth flex through, Alf! And get some grommets on that pattress! Run them spur wires to the ceiling rose in the bedroom. What have you done with the strippers?' The work proceeded smoothly if noisily until the two teams clashed somewhere in the middle of the house when each accused the other of responsibility for a hot water pipe being located next to a live flex.

'I've had it up to here with these clowns,' the foreman plumber declared.

It took all of Billy's diplomatic skills to prevent one team from walking out on the job.

In the interests of economy, the family did its own painting and decorating. Though it seemed a trifle risky, they allowed the kids to take responsibility for decorating their own bedrooms, 'pads' they called them. They went about the task gleefully and it wasn't long before the territorial imperative, each staking a claim to his own private world, asserted itself in dazzling colours and garish posters, like Matthew's Fidel Castro and Lucy's Beatles.

'Who was this Fidel Castro, Matthew?'

'I dunno, Dad. I just know it's the in thing to have his silhouette on your wall.'

On every door appeared warning notices: 'Enter this room at your peril' and 'Keep Out! This means you!' Even young John joined in by painting his room bright pink but halfway through the job he ran out of energy.

'Don't worry, John,' Matthew said. 'I'll help you as soon as I've finished my own room. Are you sure you want pink?'

'Pink walls and a green ceiling but I want to do it myself.'

But it was no use. For the rest of the day, he could do nothing but rest in one of the second-hand fireside chairs.

'He looks pale and seems listless and tires so easily,' Laura said. 'I think we should take him to the doctor. He's too listless for a six year old.'

Laura had a point for they had found that when out shopping, John demanded to be carried. 'My legs feel wobbly,' he complained.

Billy persisted in putting it down to difficulty in adjusting to the English climate. It was February and still bitterly cold. 'He'll perk up when spring and the warm weather comes,' he said.

In the kitchen, Billy put up new kitchen wall cabinets using a hand drill, which caused blisters and sores on the palms of his hands.

'Why not let me do some painting for a change?' he complained. 'It's a lot easier on the hands.'

'I'll attend to the painting, if you don't mind, Billy,' Laura replied. 'You know only too well that you get more paint on the carpets and the furniture than on the woodwork. It would cost us a fortune in white spirit.'

No use arguing, Billy thought, as he attached another cupboard to the wall.

'One day, some bright entrepreneur will bring out an electric drill that we amateur carpenters can afford.'

It may have been the hammering and the drilling that caused it or it may have been simply coincidence but as they were busy working, they were treated to a visit from little furry creatures. Mice! Two of them came from behind a skirting board and scurried across the kitchen. Laura leapt onto a chair and screamed.

'Billy! For heaven's sake, get rid of them! That's the one thing that terrifies me! Mice!'

'That's two things, Laura, 'cos they're a pair. Probably husband and wife, in which case we can expect visits from their prolific progeny.'

'Never mind all that clever alliteration, Billy. I cannot work in a kitchen where there's vermin.'

'We could set a mousetrap, I suppose, but they don't always work. Mice soon get wise to them and they simply nick the piece of cheese. The long-term answer is a cat.'

'Oh, good!' exclaimed Matthew who'd overheard. 'And maybe we could get a dog as well, Dad, while we're at it.'

'Nothing doing,' Billy answered. 'I've nothing against dogs even though I was once bitten by one and I've been wary ever since. But a dog needs to be taken for walkies every day and that will probably be left to me. Cats are more relaxed and refined. In our family tradition, it's always been a cat. The last one we had was called Socrates and he was cultured and wise.'

'I'll go along with the cat idea,' Laura said warmly. 'Anything to be rid of the mice.'

'Leave it to me, Laura. It shall be done according to thy word.'

'Don't be blasphemous,' she laughed, going back to painting the doorposts. She hadn't got far when she was faced with a dilemma.

'What shall we do about the mezuzahs?' she asked. 'Mrs Cohen claimed they brought a blessing and good fortune on the house. What do you think, Billy?'

If he wasn't allowed to paint, at least he could make decisions as to decoration strategy.

'Let's remove 'em,' he said. 'They contain Old Testament verses and are symbols for a Jewish home.'

'I'm not so sure,' Laura said. 'Mrs Cohen warned us not to remove them in case they brought bad luck.'

'I don't believe in all that mumbo-jumbo, Laura. If we were Jewish, perhaps there might be some point in leaving them up but since we're Catholic, none of it applies. I don't know what the parish priest would say when we invite him to bless the house. I say, take 'em down, stop up the holes with filler and paint over the traces.'

'I hope you're right.'

'If you're worried, we'll keep them together in a box in the cellar and then at least we've not thrown them out.'

The mezuzahs were fastened to the posts by long thin nails and it took considerable effort to remove them with pincers. Billy opened one of the tubes and removed a tiny roll of parchment on which were written two Hebrew texts.

'These are the verses from Deuteronomy that Mrs Cohen spoke about,' he said. 'I'll put the scroll back in the tube.'

'I hope you know what you're doing,' Laura said.

'If you're worried, we can put them back some time but for us, holy water fonts would be more appropriate.'

Chapter Eleven

The following week, they took John to the doctor. His condition had become worse and he was constantly exhausted, wanting to do nothing but sit before the fire.

They had recently registered with Dr Travers who lived and practised close by. They told the GP their story and filled in their background details. The doctor conducted a thorough examination, checking John's heart, lungs and blood pressure.

'It's not easy to make a thorough diagnosis here in my surgery,' he said finally, 'and I think we should organize a visit to Booth Hall Hospital where they can carry out a whole battery of tests to determine the cause of this fatigue. Mr Hugh Jolly there is one of the finest paediatricians in Britain, one might even say in the world.'

Jolly! Hardly a suitable name, Billy thought, considering the way we're feeling at the moment.

'Normally it means a wait of six weeks to see him,' the GP continued, 'but I think we may be able to expedite matters in your case.'

Hospital? A battery of tests? Paediatrican? What did it all mean? And why did he need to expedite matters?

'Is it something serious?' Laura asked anxiously.

'Hard to say,' the doctor replied. 'Let's leave it till after the visit to the hospital.'

'It's not leukaemia, is it?' she asked, now deeply worried.

'We can't rule anything out until we get the results of the tests,' he replied evenly. 'My advice to you is to stay calm and wait until the experts have taken a look.'

A few days later, the doctor phoned to say he had managed to fix up an appointment for the following week.

It was for nine o'clock and so it meant an early start. They drove over to the Mackenzies and left the three oldest children with them, promising to be back by lunchtime since it was only a matter of a few straightforward tests.

'Don't worry,' Laura's mother, Louise, replied. 'The bairns'll be all right with us until you get back.'

Although Billy was not familiar with the district of Blackley, it didn't take him long to find Booth Hall. They drove along Rochdale Road past Mount Carmel Church opposite Boggart Hole Clough Park, turned right up Charlestown Road and found the hospital at the top of a steep hill. They arrived early in plenty of time. John was nervous and was even paler than usual.

'What are they going to do to me?' he inquired anxiously. 'How long do we have to stay here?'

'Don't worry, John,' Laura told him, giving him a hug. 'You're here for a little while so the doctors can find out why you're so tired.'

They didn't have to wait long and, unusually for the NHS, punctually at nine o'clock a nurse showed them into Mr Jolly's surgery where they described John's symptoms: his lack of energy, loss of appetite, and shortness of breath after walking a short distance.

The consultant listened patiently, checking with the GP's notes from time to time.

'Since you have come recently from a tropical climate,' he said at last, 'it's no easy matter to pinpoint the cause of your little boy's lethargy. It could be anything, perhaps something he's picked up in Africa, like malaria, bilharzia or even encephalitis or sleeping sickness though that last one is a remote possibility. We shall only know when we have the results of the various tests we're going to carry out today.'

The morning was spent going from one department to another, interspersed with long periods of waiting between each. John clung to Laura like a limpet as he was poked, prodded and punctured as if he were a pincushion. They took his blood pressure, temperature, pulse, followed by samples of his blood and urine. Gently they felt his stomach, his groin, the sides of his neck, and under his armpits.

'I don't like it here. I want to go home,' John repeated over and over again. 'Please, Mum, make them stop pricking me with those needles.'

Billy and Laura could only look on helplessly.

'Don't cry, John. It'll soon be over and then we can all go home,' Billy said comfortingly.

The routine continued into the afternoon until there was a final meeting with Mr Jolly.

'What's the prognosis?' Billy asked nervously. 'Is there anything we can do at home to help matters?'

'I'm afraid it's impossible to say at this stage,' he said slowly. 'The samples we have taken will be analysed in our laboratory and we should know something definite in a day or two. Meanwhile, I'm afraid we must keep John here in hospital until we get to the bottom of the trouble.'

For Billy and Laura, this last piece of news was like a thump in the chest. They were stunned.

'Keep him in hospital? Surely not,' Laura stammered. 'I mean, it's not that serious, is it?'

'Your son is one sick little boy,' he replied. 'We have no choice but to keep him until we find out exactly what's wrong.'

Billy and Laura had turned white with worry and John had done the same, sensing now that something wasn't right.

'Please, Mum. Don't make me stay here. Please! I want to go home.'

'It won't be for long,' Billy said with a reassurance he did not feel. 'It's only until they make you better.'

John clung even more tightly to Laura. 'I feel better now, Mum,' he pleaded. 'Honestly. I do. Please let me come home with you.'

'You'll soon be home again,' she said, 'and we'll come to see you every day. You'll be out again before you know where you are.'

But nothing would console him and as they gave him a final hug, he wept piteously and called out over and over again, 'Please, Mum, don't leave me here.' His pleas were still resounding in their minds long after they had waved goodbye. As he stood watching them through the window of the ward, he made a forlorn figure, bewildered and unable to understand what was happening to him. Only a few months previously he had been happy in the sunshine playing in the garden of his home in Kenya. Then he had been transported to this country with its ice and snow and now his mum and dad were being taken away from him. Was it something serious *he'd* done? If so, what was it exactly that he'd done wrong?

When they reached the car, Laura broke down and the tears she'd been holding back all day came in a flood.

'It's leukaemia, I'm sure of it,' she sobbed, her shoulders shaking as she tried to control her weeping. 'The doctors are afraid to tell us the truth.'

'You can't know that,' a distraught Billy said. 'You mustn't jump to conclusions. We must wait till we get the results.'

'It's because we took down those mezuzahs,' she wept. 'Mrs Cohen warned us that it would bring bad luck if we did so.'

'I can't believe that nonsense,' Billy declared. 'That's just superstition. John's sickness is physical and I'd rather be guided by what the doctors tell us than a lot of old wives' tales.'

He put the key in the ignition to start the car. The engine along with the Blaupunkt radio burst into life in time to catch Ken Dodd singing 'Tears'.

They hardly slept that night, worrying. The other kids were affected too and there was a sombre atmosphere about the house. Meals were eaten in silence and sadness. Gone was the laughter, the joking, the noisy horseplay. As if John had already died.

'Things don't seem the same without him,' Lucy said sorrowfully. 'Will he be home soon?'

'I wish we knew the answer to that,' Laura sighed.

Next day at the hospital, they found John had been isolated in a room of his own and Billy and Laura were required to wear mask and gown. Not a condition to inspire confidence.

'What's the reason for this?' Billy asked the ward sister.

'Until we're sure what's wrong with John, it's best to take precautions. Better safe than sorry.'

'Then we still don't know what's wrong?' Laura said.

'The one thing we're sure of,' she replied, 'is that he's severely anaemic, which explains his tiredness and his lack of energy. We should have the full results of the blood tests in a day or two when the laboratory gives us their report.'

Throughout the visit, John clung to Laura for dear life, as if afraid she might suddenly melt away in his grasp.

'Please take me home with you,' he pleaded. 'I'll be good, honest, if you'll take me out of here. Can't you stay with me? You were gone a long time.'

'I wish I could, John, but they won't let me. We have to wait until you're better and then we can take you home. Your room is waiting for you and Matthew has been painting it for you.'

'I'm better now, Mum. Honest. I think I can go home now.'

Turning to Billy, Laura said, 'I wish they'd let me stay with him. It seems ridiculous that they restrict us to a two-hour visit when he's such a little boy. Surely a parent should be allowed to stay.'

Visiting time seemed to fly by and when the final bell rang and the ward sister called, 'Would visitors prepare to leave now, please,' John's sobs became more urgent and Laura found it almost impossible to extricate herself from his grip.

'We'll be back tomorrow, John. Don't worry and you be good for the nurses.'

'You'll be too long!' John wailed repeatedly. 'You'll be too long!'

His cries were still ringing in their ears as they walked away down the long corridor that led to the car park.

Chapter Twelve

That evening, Billy had a long-standing arrangement with his male cronies to have a farewell drink at the Pineapple for Titch who would soon be departing for Canada. Billy hardly felt in the mood for meeting his friends but since it might be a long time before he saw his bosom pal again, he felt it incumbent on him to attend.

Throughout the evening, Billy was lost in thought, worrying about John and the outcome of the tests. There was the usual jocularity and comments from his friends about Canada and the funny things that might happen to Titch and his wife but Billy was unable to join in. He decided not to spoil the party by burdening them with his worries about his son. Since he was driving, he drank no more than two halves of lemonade shandy despite the entreaties of his friends to 'have one for the road' and he felt relieved when the evening finally came to a close around ten thirty. Outside the pub, there was much hand-shaking and back-slapping with promises to stay in touch as everyone prepared to go their different ways. Titch said he'd find a cab but Billy felt that the least he could do for his closest friend was to drive him home to his house in Whalley Range.

On the way, Billy recounted his deep anxiety about John and how they were awaiting the results of the hospital tests, how he was worried out of his mind, how Laura was distraught with grief. He went on to tell him about the mezuzahs and how Laura believed that removing them from the doorposts might have brought them bad luck.

'But I don't buy any of that hocus-pocus,' Billy said as they drove along Alexandra Road. 'I'm a practical, down-to-earth sort of bloke. In real life that's not the way things work.'

'I agree entirely with you,' Titch was saying when it happened.

As they crossed over the minor junction at Raby Street, there was suddenly the most almighty bang at the back of the car and they found themselves spinning round and round, out of control. When they finally came to a stop, the engine was still running but they were now facing the opposite direction. There followed a moment when time seemed to stand still. Then on the other side of the road they saw a Ford Consul literally wrapped around a lamp post.

'My God!' Billy exclaimed. 'We've been hit by that car over there!'

Before they could fully take in the enormity of what had happened, a man emerged from the Ford and ran for all he was worth down Raby Street.

'What the devil's going on?' Billy yelled. 'That bloke has done a runner and left us to face the music! What are we going to do, Titch?'

'We're going to get the hell out of here, that's what we're going to do!' Titch replied. 'Otherwise we're going to be left holding the baby. They'll smell drink on us and they'll put two and two together and make five.'

'But I drank only a couple of shandies.'

'Doesn't matter, Hoppy. They'll jump to the wrong conclusion and blame you. Apart from that, he gave us one helluva swipe when he hit us and I think I've hurt my leg.'

'I'm so sorry, Titch. I hope it's not serious.'

'I'll survive, I think,' he gasped.

'It's a good job there was no other traffic about,' Billy said. 'Otherwise it could have been nasty. Someone might've been killed.'

'Let's go before the police arrive on the scene,' Titch insisted. 'No one's been seriously injured and, judging by

97

the way that bloke took off, he could be chosen for the next Olympics.'

Billy turned the car down Raby Street thinking they might catch the culprit but he'd disappeared down some back alley. Billy's car had been damaged, however, for as he drove along, there was a high-pitched whine and grating noise from the rear axle as if the car were in mortal pain. They reached Titch's home safely and an anguished Elaine made a pot of tea after examining Titch's knee, which had received a bad knock though not severe enough to warrant a visit to the hospital.

'This is something we could have done without,' she exclaimed, 'when we're about to emigrate. We're due to fly to Canada early next week.'

'I'll be OK,' Titch said, grinning ruefully. 'Nothing to worry about. It'll take more than a bump on the knee to stop us going.'

'What about the legal position?' a worried Billy wondered aloud. 'Isn't it an offence to leave the scene of an accident? Won't I be accused of being a hit-and-run driver?'

'But *you* didn't hit anybody,' Titch protested. 'You were the one that was hit. I may be wrong but I think you're only bound in law to remain at the scene if someone's been injured. Otherwise you must report the accident within twenty-four hours.'

'Then we'll go to the police station together tomorrow and give a full report,' Billy said.

Laura was frantic when she heard what had happened. 'Thank God nobody was seriously injured,' she said. 'You were lucky to come out of it alive. That other man must have been drunk or crazy to drive across a main road like that.'

'True,' Billy said, 'and he's made an awful mess of our nice new car, I'm afraid.'

'Never mind about that,' she said, taking his hands in her own and embracing him. 'I'm just glad to have you back in one piece. We can always repair the car. But you know, Billy. . . .'

He knew what was coming. 'Before you say it, I don't think this latest event has anything to do with mezuzahs and taking them down.'

'I'm not so sure,' she said. 'All this is too much of a coincidence. First, John into hospital with a life-threatening illness. Now you in this accident. And all within the space of a week since you removed those mezuzahs. I know it's far-fetched but suppose there *is* a connection? Lately we seem to have been dogged by bad luck.'

'As you know, Laura, in my logical universe, things don't happen because of black magic and occult connections; cause and effect have a physical basis and a rational explanation.'

'I'm sure you're right, Billy, but I prefer not take any more chances. You never know, there might be more bad luck waiting in the wings.'

'For example?'

'Well, we're waiting to hear about the training college job. If you don't get it, we'll be in Queer Street. We'll be left with a whacking great mortgage and you'll have to go out job-hunting all over again. Let's not press our luck. Put the mezuzahs back on the doorposts.'

'I'm not sure where we put them,' he stalled. 'Besides, I wouldn't know which mezuzah went on which doorpost.'

'They're in a shoebox in the cellar. And I don't think it'll matter if they don't go back exactly where they were before. Please humour me and put them back.'

'Very well, though it's against my better judgement.'

Next morning, Billy and Titch reported the car accident to Moss Side police station. The duty sergeant wrote down the details on his accident report form after requiring Billy to present his driving licence and insurance certificate. Finally the officer looked up from his papers.

'We received reports of this accident from several wit- nesses,' he said. 'They told us that a light-brown Morris Oxford station wagon had been the cause and for a while we were convinced that the driver of that vehicle was responsible. We were ready to issue a warrant for his, your, arrest. However, we heard later this morning that yours wasn't the only car involved in a collision. The Ford Consul which hit you had been stolen from outside a pub and had already written off two other vehicles on Wilmslow Road and Princess Parkway before he crashed into you.'

'How did he manage to do that?' Billy asked.

'He was probably drunk and he simply drove across two major roads without stopping. He probably has neither driving licence nor insurance cover. He'll be for it when we catch him.'

It was a relief for Billy to know that he was not to be prosecuted for leaving the scene of the accident but he was left with a severely damaged car and the hassle of claiming on the insurance. It was a good job he'd taken out comprehensive cover because his car was deemed a write-off by the garage that assessed the damage.

'The back axle's buggered and the chassis has been twisted,' the examiner decreed, pursing his lips in the way all car mechanics do. 'It's up to head office but I would say it'll cost too much to repair. Probably cheaper to get a new car.'

Billy's heart sank when he heard this. Pride goes before a fall, he thought. Serves me right for showing off. I just hope my insurance will cover all the bills.

Chapter Thirteen

That afternoon, Laura and Billy's mam went to Booth Hall to visit John. To occupy the long days, Mam took him a jigsaw puzzle in the vain hope that it would help him forget his misery. Assisted and advised by his other three kids, Billy spent the afternoon replacing the mezuzahs on the doorposts throughout the house.

'I've forgotten how they were positioned,' he said to Laura as she was about to depart. 'Do you think it matters?'

'Let's not take any chances,' she replied. 'If I remember rightly, they were placed at an angle slanting inward towards the room.'

'I don't suppose you calculated the exact angle,' he grinned. 'I mean, do I need a protractor or anything?'

'Put them back and stop trying to be funny,' she said as she went out through the front door to catch the 42 bus.

The three kids left in his charge helped by handing him the nails and the hammer as he called for them.

'That doesn't look right,' Matthew said when Billy had tacked up the first mezuzah. 'I'm sure the angle was about forty-five degrees.'

'Pass up the hammer,' Billy said impatiently, 'and forget the trigonometry.'

An hour later, Billy had the mezuzahs back in place. A load of codswallop, he said to himself, as if little bits of parchment stuck on doorposts can affect life outcomes. Why, it's idolatry; we may as well put our trust in totem poles.

When the chore was finished, Billy had one other task to complete before Laura got back. Taking Lucy with him for a second opinion, he drove out in a hired car to an address in

Cheadle Hulme and collected a beautiful sealpoint Siamese cat with a long pedigree. But her beauty was incidental as Billy hadn't bought her to exhibit at cat shows. She was needed to do a job of work because the mice population in the kitchen was threatening to explode to Malthusian proportions. The cat had just grown out of the kitten stage, and was house-trained but young enough to adapt to a new life. It was meant as a surprise and he hoped Laura would approve.

Towards six o'clock, Laura came back from the hospital. She looked tired but she was smiling and she looked happy for the first time in weeks. The family gathered round to greet her.

'It looks as if you've had some good news,' Billy said, hardly daring to ask any further.

'Good news from the hospital!' she exclaimed.

'Hurray! John's coming home!' Lucy cried.

'No, no. Not yet. Not for some time. But it's not leukaemia and that's the good news.'

'Tell us the details,' Billy said, overwhelmed with joy.

'Not leukaemia,' she repeated. 'They've found kidney stones in his ureter. Still serious but not as bad as we thought. He's anaemic and he'll have to have an operation, which means he'll have to stay in hospital for some time yet. Maybe five or six weeks but then he'll be all right. I can't tell you how relieved I am.'

'I suppose you're going to put the good news down to replacement of the mezuzahs, Laura.'

'Not entirely, Billy. You see, every day on the way back from the hospital, as I've changed buses in Albert Square, I've called in at the Little Gem, you know St Mary's in Mulberry Street, to say a prayer and light a candle at Our Lady's altar.'

'That's called taking a belt and braces approach, Laura, making doubly sure!'

'No matter what, Billy, it's a cause for celebration.'

'We have another cause for celebration,' Billy told her. 'Today, Lucy and I collected a Siamese cat.'

Laura was beside herself with joy when she saw it. 'She's so refined and what beautiful blue eyes!' she exclaimed. 'And so graceful. What an elegant way she walks! John will simply love her when he comes home.'

'Now you know where we get the expression the catwalk,' he said. 'But she's got to earn her keep. Her presence and her scent should be enough to frighten off every mouse for miles around.'

'But if the mice do a bunk, where will they go?' Mark asked.

'Probably next door to the Gillespies,' Matthew chuckled.

Laura said, 'I think we should give our new cat a name which reflects its aristocratic appearance.'

'What about Samantha?' Lucy suggested. 'That has an upper-class sound.'

'Perfect!' Billy said. 'A blend of the boy's name Samuel and the girl's name Anthea. Definitely has a superior ring to it.'

And so the latest addition to the family was awarded her sobriquet.

At dinner that night, they opened the bottle of wine they'd been saving to celebrate good news from the hospital. Laura was euphoric now that she knew she'd soon have all her family around her once more. And the arrival of Samantha was forever afterwards associated with the occasion.

It would be an exaggeration to say that, after putting the mezuzahs back in their rightful places, there was a dramatic improvement in their affairs but, and it may have been Billy's imagination, things gradually began to fall in place.

A month later, after John had built up his strength, he underwent an operation for the removal of stones and part of a kidney. After that, his recovery was rapid. As the weeks went by, the colour returned to his cheeks and the juvenile energy he'd lost since returning to England came back. It was a day of jubilation when Billy and Laura along with the other children went to collect him. For John it was

Christmas all over again as he exchanged his hospital garb for the new suit they'd bought for him in London, oh so long ago. On the drive back, John sat with a quiet smile on his face, unable to take it in. And when he saw his own room painted in the bright pink and green he'd requested, his face lit up and his joy knew no bounds. Not until, that is, he was introduced to Samantha. It was love at first sight. The two of them hit it off immediately. For weeks afterwards, John could be seen stroking her fur, talking to her and giving her details of his stay in Booth Hall. And judging by the way she rubbed her head under his chin and purred contentedly, Samantha understood every word. Often she would jump on his shoulder like Long John Silver's parrot and occasionally even onto his head. At mealtimes, she sat daintily and patiently waiting for scraps of meat to be thrown to her.

'You're training that cat in bad habits,' Laura said. 'She's got her own food dish.'

'I don't think she's fully accepted the notion yet that she's a cat,' Billy chuckled. 'She considers herself as one of the family and claims equality.'

'I think she considers herself superior to us humans,' Lucy said.

As for the mice, they disappeared overnight from the Hopkins household. There was a rumour in the district that the Gillespies had been complaining of a sudden plague of the rodents but there was no way they could prove that the mice belonged to Billy's family.

On the subject of the car accident, a week after the incident Billy's insurance company contacted him to tell him that his comprehensive policy fully covered all eventualities. Though the Morris Oxford was a write-off, he was authorized to replace it with a new car exactly like the old one, complete with Blaupunkt radio, cigar lighter and other accessories. Meanwhile he was given a courtesy car to get him around. Billy could hardly believe his good fortune.

That was not the end of the good news. Finding schools for the kids had been a worry and a problem ever since their return to Manchester but even that was solved when they managed to find places at the schools of their choice. Mark and John were accepted at St Cuthbert's, the local primary school, which was within walking distance, while Lucy and Matthew took and passed Manchester's eleven-plus and thirteen-plus grammar school entrance exams and were accepted at Laura and Billy's alma maters, the Fallowfield Convent and Damian College.

For the two oldest children, this involved new school uniforms. The youngest pair went to Laura's mother and the rest of the family made the trip into town to Wippell's on King Street to be kitted out. What memories the visit brought back for the two proud parents who had been measured at the same shop twenty-five years previously!

Matthew was the first to emerge from the changing room. He looked splendid in his royal-blue blazer with the college emblem on the pocket, and the metal badge on the cap. Billy's heart skipped a beat when he saw him and the hair on the back of his neck stood on end. He felt as if he were looking back on an image of himself a quarter of a century earlier.

'Well, what do you think?' Matthew asked, viewing himself in the long mirror. 'Don't you think the blazer's too big? More suitable for Billy Bunter?'

'You look handsome,' Laura replied. 'The blazer doesn't look too big at all. Just right, in fact. We need the larger sizes for the two of you because you're both growing so fast. We can't afford a new blazer every six months.'

'I've the strangest sensation of having played this scene before,' Billy exclaimed. 'This could be nineteen thirty-nine instead of nineteen sixty-four. Same uniform, same cap badge, same motto.'

'What exactly does *Astra Castra, Numen Lumen* mean, Dad?' Matthew asked, examining the badge.

'I think it means "The stars, my camp, God my lamp," but I think some boys had an unofficial version.'

'What was that, Dad?'

'I think you'd best wait till you get to the school where one of the senior boys is bound to tell you but it was something about new men being loo men.'

At that moment, Lucy popped her head out of her changing room and said, 'Are you ready for this? I'll never forgive you if you laugh.'

She stepped out into the shop and Billy and Laura gasped in admiration. Laura's eyes went big, and tears sparkled in her eyes. She opened her mouth to speak, but the words wouldn't come.

'Do you think it fits?' Lucy asked doubtfully.

'It fits as the leaves do a tree. Perfect,' Billy said. 'And so it ought, considering how much it cost.'

She was resplendent in the light-brown blazer complete with emblem on the pocket but what was distinctive about her uniform was the headgear – a straw hat like the ones worn at snooty public schools.

'Superb!' was Laura's comment when she finally found her voice. 'You look so posh and seeing you dressed in my old school uniform like this takes me back to my own school-days. I hope you're as happy at the convent, Lucy, as I was.'

'You look beautiful,' Billy added, 'and I love the straw boater; it suits you to a T.'

'I don't think the nuns at the school like them to be to called boaters, Billy,' Laura said. 'They reckon it smacks of Maidenhead and Gaiety girls. But I do think, Lucy, that the hat would look even smarter if you had your hair cut short.'

'But long hair is the fashion nowadays, Mum. Pop stars like Sandy Shaw and Kathy Kirby wear it long. Besides, I want to be like my friends.'

'Well, *you're* not Sandy Shaw or Kathy Kirby,' Laura retorted.

Throughout these exchanges, Matthew had been studying his sister carefully, waiting his opportunity.

'I think the hat makes you look like a fishmonger,' he scoffed.

'And your cap,' she retorted, not to be outdone, 'makes you look like a jockey or one of those Victorian cricketers you see in old photographs.'

'OK. Enough of the squabbling,' Billy warned. 'I think you both look snazzy and there's an end to it.'

Uniforms apart, Billy was delighted that his children had found schools so quickly and he thought his cup was full to the brim. But with the next piece of news, it was overflowing. A week after the visit to the tailor's, Sherdley Park College of Education wrote to tell him that his application for the post of Senior Lecturer in Education had been successful. Would he be free to start at the beginning of the next academic year, in September? Would he! His letter of acceptance was in the next post.

'Now aren't you glad you put the mezuzahs back and I lit candles at the Little Gem?' Laura said, with a told-you-so smile.

'I suppose so,' he said grudgingly.

'How else do you explain the abundance of good fortune we've been having lately?'

'Coincidence,' Billy said. 'Mere coincidence.'

'Then why do you touch the mezuzah and bless yourself at the font every time you leave the house?' she asked. 'You'll be sending God mixed messages.'

'Best not tempt providence,' he grinned.

'Now who's employing belt and braces insurance!' Laura laughed.

'Simply hedging my bets.'

'I'll never understand you,' Laura said, giving him an old-fashioned look.

Chapter Fourteen

When the painting and decorating of the house was finished, Billy invited his family across for a house-warming party. They came together on the 42 bus which set them down not far from the house. Billy was so glad to see them standing there when he opened the front door. Everyone was there except Sam and his wife, May, who lived in Belfast. There were his sisters Flo and Polly with their husbands, Barry and Steve, and his brother, Les, with his wife, Annette. And of course Mam and Dad in their best clothes; Mam was wearing her imitation mother-of-pearl brooch in honour of the occasion.

'I like your house,' Steve exclaimed, looking up at the large bay windows and the front bedroom verandah. 'You did well finding it so quickly.'

'That's right,' Barry said. 'It's not often that houses like this come on the market.'

Before anyone would enter, they had to examine the plants and flowers in the 'mature' garden.

'You've got some beautiful things here,' Polly enthused. 'I hope you'll let us have some cuttings to take back.'

'By all means. Help yourself,' Billy said.

They lingered overlong in the garden as if too shy to enter the house.

'That's a lovely chiming doorbell you've got,' Flo remarked. 'It seemed to go on forever echoing through the house. Did it come as part of the building?' '

'No, we bought that at a DIY shop in Didsbury. We've been doing lots of refurbishing and decorating.'

'Sounded like an ice-cream van to me,' Les added. 'Thinking of going into the trade, are you?'

Les had to have his little joke but Billy was used to his cracks, they were like water off a duck's back.

'Anyway, you're all welcome. We're only sorry we haven't invited you before now but what with one thing and another – young John in hospital, my trouble with the car accident and all the repairs and decorating – this is the first chance we've had.'

'Don't worry about it, Billy,' Flo, his big sister, said warmly. 'We know you've had your hands full. I think I speak for all when I say we're only too glad that things have turned out right for you at the finish.'

'Thanks for that, our Flo,' Billy said. 'Anyroad, don't stand at the door. Come in and make yourselves at home.'

'You make sure you wipe your feet, Tommy,' Mam said, giving Dad a nudge. 'And you can take your cap off for a start.'

'No, Kate,' he said. 'My cap stays where it is. I don't feel right taking it off in someone else's house. It's disrespectful. Besides, we're not stopping long, are we?'

'You daft ha'porth,' she said. 'Anyone would think you were Jewish the way you keep your head covered. You don't want anyone to see your bald head. That's it, isn't it?'

Despite Mam's protests, Tommy's cap stayed on his head throughout the visit.

'And another thing, Tommy,' she said. 'Don't show us up. When you go to the toilet in this house, be careful not to dribble on the floor. Anyroad, I've brought a cloth to wipe up round the lavatory bowl in case you miss.'

Laura came forward and gave everyone a warm greeting and after the usual formalities of hand-shaking and cheek-kissing, she escorted them on a tour of the house. Matthew and Lucy had been allowed to stay up to join in the fun but Mark and John had been put to bed, which had caused a certain amount of friction.

'That's not fair,' Mark had protested. 'I'm eight and a half and old enough to stay up.'

'And I'm old enough as well,' added John. 'I'm six and a half. So why aren't we allowed to come to the party?'

'You'll have to wait till you're grown up like Lucy and me before you're allowed to attend adult parties,' Matthew retorted.

The air was filled with a good deal of 'oohing' and 'ahhing' as the visitors went from room to room examining and commenting on the various features and amenities.

'You've done well for yourself, Billy,' Steve commented. 'This is the kind of house that most people can only dream about. So your hard work studying for degrees and all of that has paid off in the end.'

'I like the spaciousness,' Barry added. 'You feel that there's plenty of elbow room and everyone can do their own thing without falling over each other.'

Mark and John, who were still feeling hard done to at missing all the fun, were considerably bucked up by all the attention they received as crowds of relatives gathered round their beds. Their aggrieved feelings were soothed even more when their Aunts Flo and Polly pushed a shilling into their hands 'to buy themselves a few toffees'.

Finally Laura showed them the bathroom facilities. They were most impressed by the two toilets – one upstairs and one downstairs.

'You've come a long way since the Honeypot Street days,' Polly said. 'There we had just the one and that was out in the yard.'

'And Billy, weren't the previous owners of your house Jewish?' Flo said. 'That means it's bound to be a good house as they're usually very good judges of property.'

'Eeh bah gum, they knew how to live all right,' Mam remarked. 'This house reminds me of the place where I worked in service in Macclesfield years ago. They had a hallway like yours, as big as a station waiting room. A whole family could have lived there. I never thought I'd see the day when a son of mine would own a mansion like this.'

'He doesn't own it,' Les observed wryly. 'He's got a whacking great debt round his neck and the real owner is the mortgage company.'

'It will be ours in twenty-five years' time,' Billy said defiantly.

'That's if you're not in debtor's prison by then,' Les said.

'So, if we dare to ask, how much did you pay for this chateau?' Steve smiled.

'Just over five grand.'

Billy's mam and dad were dumbstruck.

'I always knew our Billy would join the toffs,' Dad commented. 'First a car, now a castle.'

'Eeh, lad,' Mam gasped. 'You've overstepped the mark this time. What happens if you don't pay?'

'They take the house away from us, I suppose.'

'That'll mean the workhouse. You'll be like your old Grandma McGuinness years ago.' Mam looked worried.

'It means oakum picking,' Les laughed, sounding hopeful. 'But, don't worry. We'll come and visit you once a month. It's one of the corporal works of mercy to visit the imprisoned.'

'We should get by,' Billy said. 'I've just heard that I've been appointed to a well-paid job as senior lecturer. The salary should be enough to cover the mortgage.' Then he added, 'And maybe enough for food if we're careful.'

Billy outlined the arrangements for the evening. He was to escort the family over to his local, the Nag's Head, for a jar or two. Laura would remain behind and, with the help of Matthew and Lucy, prepare corned beef and pickle sandwiches for their return.

The news was greeted with all-round approval, especially by Dad who was never comfortable visiting someone else's house unless it was of the public kind.

'I've also got a crate of Boddington's ale in for afterwards,' Billy said, 'in case you're still thirsty after your visit to the pub.'

* * *

Over in the Nag's Head, the family settled down in the lounge, having first established a kitty to pay for the drinks. A waiter took everyone's order and went across to the bar to collect the drinks while the family gazed in awe at the décor.

'This is a bloody snooty place if ever there was one,' Dad remarked loudly, looking around him. 'Nowt but bloody horsey stuff everywhere. What's the name of the landlord here? Lester Piggott or Gordon Richards?'

'Did you ever hear that one about the fellah who thought he was a horse?' Les called out. 'He did nothing but neigh and whinny all day long. His wife used to feed him with a nosebag of Quaker Oats for breakfast. It got so bad they took him away in the yellow van. So his wife rang up the hospital. "How is he?" she asked. "He's in a stable condition," they said.'

The family burst out laughing.

'That's a good 'un!' Dad roared.

'Talking of horses,' Barry said, joining in the fun. 'I had a bet on a horse at Epsom last week. It came in at ten to one.'

'You must have had a tidy packet coming to you,' Steve commented.

'Not really. You see the race started at eleven o'clock and my horse didn't come in till ten to one.'

More guffaws from the Hopkins family, with one or two spectators on the periphery grinning their appreciation.

Imperceptibly, though, a number of drinkers of the Harris tweed variety were beginning to drift out of the lounge into the public bar. From the corner of his eye, Billy noticed the quiet exodus. Unaware, the family blithely continued their boisterous joke-swapping.

A red-faced military-looking man exchanged one or two sneering remarks with a companion at the bar.

'The proles have arrived,' Billy heard him mutter.

'Damned bad show,' his companion replied. 'They're everywhere.'

Billy seemed to be the only one in his group aware of

112

the remarks. The only one to feel ill at ease.

The waiter arrived with the order and for a short time there was nothing but the hum of quiet conversation as everyone got down to the serious business of downing their drinks. That didn't last long, though, and it was soon time for the next round. While they waited for it to arrive, Dad couldn't resist another observation about the pub and its pretentious setting.

'These brasses, horseshoes and leather saddles remind me of them stables under the arches in Dantzig Street in Collyhurst that I used to know when I worked as a lad in the market. And when I look at all these pictures on the walls, I can even smell the horseshit.'

The two men at the bar were now shaking their heads in disbelief and muttering remarks to the effect that they didn't know what the world was coming to.

Billy's embarrassment was further intensified when his sister Flo suggested a sing-song.

'Anyone know any horsey songs?' she asked.

'What about "Horsey, keep your tail up"?' Polly cried, launching into the melody. The rest of the family joined in with gusto.

'Horsey, keep your tail up! Keep your tail up!'

Billy sang with the rest but he had one eye on the two critics who had lowered their heads and were now in earnest conversation with the pub landlord.

The family had got some way into their second choice, 'Horsey, horsey, don't you stop', when the landlord strode determinedly across the lounge and ordered them to desist.

'Sorry, you'll have to stop that singing.' he proclaimed. 'I don't have a licence for music.'

'Good God!' the red-faced barfly declared, looking around the room for support. 'Call that caterwauling "music"? I've heard better alley cats at two o'clock in the morning, what!'

'Come on, I suggest we leave,' a red-faced Billy said. 'We're obviously not appreciated here.'

'I'm sure you're right,' Steve added. 'Hardly the right atmosphere for a knees-up.'

'If that's Billy's local,' Les said as they went through the revolving door, 'he can stick it. Give me my own pub in Openshaw where the natives are friendly.'

'My local?' Billy said ruefully. 'You mean *was* my local. After tonight, I don't think they'll let me back in.'

They strolled back to Billy's house where a mountain of corned beef and pickle sandwiches awaited their attention, and for afters there was hot apple pie smothered with custard, and of course the *spécialité de la maison*, Mackenzie nutty nibbles. They sat round the table, tucked paper napkins into their collars and got down to dispatching the grub.

'You shouldn't have bothered, love,' Mam said to Laura, tucking in. 'But anyroad, you've done us right proud,'

'Here, here,' everyone chorused.

For a while, conversation stopped as they concentrated on the feast. When it was all gone, it was into the front room for bottled beer and entertainment.

'I shall be recording this for posterity on my new Ferrograph tape recorder,' Billy told them. 'So I insist on the highest standards.'

'Eeh. A recording machine,' Mam said. 'Isn't it marvellous what they can do nowadays?'

When it came to enjoying themselves, the Hopkins family had no inhibitions. Over the years they had developed a routine that was closely adhered to. It began with a medley of old songs, of the kind they'd been forbidden to sing in the pub, initially happy and optimistic but gradually becoming sad and sentimental as the evening wore on and the drink took effect. Tonight was no exception and it wasn't long before the citizens of Didsbury and the streets beyond were treated to: 'I've got a lovely bunch of coconuts', 'Tea for Two', 'Spread a Little Happiness', progressing to 'I'll Take You Home Again, Kathleen', 'Roses of Picardy', and then

114

'Danny Boy' which always brought Mam to tears as it brought back memories of her brother Danny who'd been killed in the Great War. Encouraged by Dad who exhorted her throughout her performance 'to go higher', Mam gave her soulful rendering of Harry Lauder's 'Keep right on to the end of the road' and no Hopkins party would have been complete without Les singing the 'Goodbye' song from *The White Horse Inn* which involved everyone waving their handkerchiefs, including an enthusiastic Matthew and Lucy though it took some considerable time for them to locate their hankies.

'I don't know why I have to sing this song every time,' Les complained good-naturedly, 'especially since no one's going anywhere.'

That means they're staying, Billy thought ruefully.

History was made that night when another song was added to the ritual: Flanders and Swann's 'Hippopotamus Song' in honour of Billy's time in Africa.

'Come on, our Billy. Give us Mud!' they called.

Accompanied by Laura on the piano, Billy treated the company to his interpretation, everyone joining in the chorus: 'Mud! Mud! Glorious mud. Nothing quite like it for cooling the blood.' Forever afterwards, the song, along with Les's 'Goodbye', became a fixed feature of family festivities.

After the singing, it was time for Dad's speech.

'I'd like to say,' Dad began, 'how proud we are of our Billy. He's done well for hisself. I always knew he'd make his fortune in Africa and it was me what encouraged him all along to go and make something of himself.'

'You did nothing of the sort,' Mam snapped, starting the sniping routine that invariably accompanied his speeches and was part of the tradition. 'You said he'd be eaten by tigers and that any babies they had over there would be black.'

'Anyroad,' he continued, ignoring her, 'I'm glad to see him and his missus and kids living in this lovely palace and

115

good luck to him. This is what comes of having a good education. It was me what told him to get off to that there college in London and become a teacher.'

'You're a bloody liar, Tommy. You were the one who tried to stop him. You wanted him to take a rubbish job at the Wallworks on Red Bank. All the other kids in the family could have gone to college but for you. You were too fond of the bevy.'

'I always did my best to bring up my family proper. To see them well fed and to encourage them to be honest and always tell the truth. I've set them a good example. I've worked in the market for seventy years and I've never done a dishonest thing in my life and I could have stolen thousands.'

'What about that stuff you swiped from Deakins' stall at the end of the Great War in nineteen eighteen?'

'We was hungry and I had no choice. I had to feed the kids.'

'Doesn't matter,' Mam proclaimed. 'You'll burn in hell one day for it.'

'Then so will you and Flo and Polly because you ate it with me. Anyroad, I don't mind going to hell because that's where all my pals'll be. They'll be there playing crib.'

'You'd better be careful what you're saying,' Billy laughed. 'Remember it's all being recorded on my machine.'

'I don't give a bugger,' Dad said. 'They can send me to Strangeways for all I care but that grub I stole from the black marketeers in nineteen eighteen was well worth it.'

After his speech, he felt the call of nature and he wandered into the kitchen where he met Laura clearing up.

'Excuse, me, love,' he said, 'but where's your back?'

'My back?' Laura asked, puzzled. 'Sorry, Mr Hopkins, I don't understand.'

'You know. The gents. Your privy. Your urinal.'

'Oh, if you mean the toilet,' Laura replied, 'there's one upstairs but I think that's occupied at the moment. There's another cloakroom outside the kitchen door.'

116

'Thank you very much, love,' he said and he stepped outside.

It was a good half hour before anyone noticed his absence.

'Where's Dad?' Mam asked anxiously. 'It's not like him to be missing the fun.'

'Last time I saw him,' Laura said, 'he was looking for the toilet and I told him there was a cloakroom downstairs.'

'He can't surely be still in there. I'll take a look,' Les said. He stepped outside the kitchen and knocked on the toilet door.

'What're you doing in there, Dad? Making your will, or what?'

No answer. Les opened the door. 'There's no one there,' he called back to the rest of the company. 'Maybe he's gone into the garden.'

Everyone rushed outside to check. They drew a blank. He wasn't to be seen.

'I'll take a look upstairs,' Billy said. 'Perhaps he's gone to the toilet up there.'

No use. Not there either. The company was becoming concerned. 'Where the devil could he have got to?' they asked.

'He's gone wandering off again,' Mam said, now out of her mind with worry. 'He can't have gone far but just the same he'll be lost 'cos he won't have a clue where he is. We'll have to find him, otherwise he'll freeze to death in this weather.'

'Perhaps he's gone back to the pub,' Steve suggested. 'I'll go over and check.'

With conversation subdued, the company waited around nervously for Steve to return.

Ten minutes later, he was back. One look at his face and they knew the news was bad.

'No sign of him,' he said. 'I spoke to the Colonel Blimps in the lounge there and they said he had definitely not been back. They never forgot a face, they said, and he had a face they'd remember as long as they lived.'

Things had become serious. The gathering, which only half an hour earlier had been so happy-go-lucky singing their ditties, now looked despondent and shell-shocked, not knowing what to do for the best. Flo's husband, Barry, stepped forward with a possible plan of action.

'When we had a situation like this in the army, we tackled it methodically. Dad is on foot and so he can't be too far away. I suggest we go out in pairs, each little search party taking a particular area, fanning out from the house. Then we report back in twenty minutes whether or not we have any news. Billy, do you have an A to Z map of the streets around here?'

Billy rummaged through his desk and produced one. Barry organized the pairs: Les and Annette, Billy and Laura, Polly and Steve, and Flo and himself. Mam agreed to stay behind to look after the house and the children and also to be there in case Dad found his way back. Each pair took an area and set off to scour the streets, asking passers-by if they had seen an old man in a flat cap wandering round the streets and looking lost.

Twenty minutes later, everyone was back. No news. Nothing to report. No sign of Dad. He'd disappeared into thin air.

'Perhaps he's been kidnapped for a ransom,' Matthew suggested.

'You've been reading too many American comic books,' Billy said. 'Who would want my dad as a hostage? They couldn't ask much for him.'

'There's nothing for it but to phone the police,' Barry said, 'and report him as a missing person.'

'I'll go over and do it,' Billy said. 'Meanwhile, I think you should continue with the search parties.'

Though Billy had drunk no more than his usual shandies, a faint whiff of hops might make a policeman suspicious if he were stopped and so he deemed it wiser to go on foot rather than drive. At the station, Billy told his story of how his dad had wandered off. The desk sergeant was sympathetic and understanding.

'Sorry to hear about it, sir,' he said, 'but we don't consider a person missing until they've been lost for a period of at least twenty-four hours. Your father may simply have gone for a stroll round the district.'

Billy had difficulty controlling his temper.

'Look,' he said irritably, 'my dad's an old man with a tendency to meander both in body and mind. Under no circumstances would he wander off from a party by himself. He doesn't know the district for a start and he won't have the first notion of where he's going. Not only that, it's turning chilly and he could easily die of hypothermia. Can't you send out a constable to look for him?'

'Not a chance,' the sergeant replied. 'We're short-staffed and I couldn't spare a man to go out on what's probably a wild goose chase. It's a big area and he could be anywhere. The best thing I can do is take down some details and complete a form. I'll ask my constables to keep an eye open for him.'

Exasperated, Billy supplied the officer with his dad's personal details. Name, age, date of birth, address, phone number (if any), distinguishing marks, clothes he was wearing. The details seemed endless. The policeman painstakingly wrote them out on his form. We're losing valuable time, Billy thought.

Thirty minutes later, he left the station, frustrated and angry, with a carbon copy of the report in his hand, in case he didn't know what his own father looked like. On the way back, he passed Fog Lane Park. Then an idea struck him. Could Dad have wandered into the park? A remote possibility maybe but worth a try. Billy strode through the gates and across the deserted fields.

'Dad! Dad!' he bellowed into the darkness. 'Are you there? It's your son, Billy!'

To his amazement and utter relief, there was an answering call from somewhere in the distance. Remote and indistinct but there was no doubt about it, it was Dad's voice. Still calling, Billy ran in the direction of the voice.

'Where are you, Dad?'

'Over here, Billy lad. By the bowling green.'

Billy made a sharp left turn and there he was, sitting on a park bench. Still wearing his cap of course.

'What in God's name are you doing here, Dad?'

'By heck, Billy, you've got a bloody big garden. I still haven't found your back though, so I had to do it behind them bushes. Anyroad, I sat down here on this bench. I'm waiting for the next bus to take me to the market. I have to be at work by four o'clock, you know.'

There was rejoicing and indescribable relief when Billy got back with Dad.

'You can't be trusted no more,' Mam told him. 'I'll have to put a chain on you to stop you wandering off. I think you're having your second childhood.'

'Maybe you should buy him a big playpen,' Les suggested, 'and put him in there with a few toys.'

'Good Lord, have you seen the time?' Polly exclaimed. 'It's one o'clock in the morning. We've got Steve's aged parents babysitting for us and we told them we'd be back by eleven. They'll be worried out of their minds, wondering what's happened to us.'

The rest of the visitors were in a similar situation.

'How are we going to get home?' Flo asked. 'There'll be no buses at this time.'

'We can phone for a taxi,' suggested Barry.

'More like two or three taxis,' Steve said. 'There's eight of us altogether.'

'Leave it to me,' Billy said. 'There's a few taxi firms round here. We're bound to find one with a cab free.'

For the next half hour, Billy phoned every firm in the district and some beyond. To no avail. A taxi at that time in the morning wasn't to be had for love nor money.

'I don't know what we're going to do,' Mam said. 'We're stuck.'

All eyes, including Laura's, now turned to Billy.

'I suppose everyone could stay the night here,' she said slowly. 'You could bed down here on couches and we've got a couple of air mattresses somewhere.'

Les's wife, Annette, who'd been fairly quiet most of the evening now spoke up. 'Impossible,' she said. 'My parents will be waiting to go home. We'll have to get back even if we have to walk all the way.'

Now everyone's eyes were boring into Billy's.

'Alternatively . . .' Laura began, 'if we asked Billy nicely, I'm sure we could persuade him to . . .'

'No, no,' Billy protested. 'I can't drive everyone home. I've had a couple of drinks myself and it wouldn't be wise. Not only that, I'd never fit everyone into the car. Including me, it would make nine. Can't be done.'

The eyes continued to stare at him. Pleadingly.

'You've drunk only shandies,' Laura said sweetly, 'and that was some time ago. You've also eaten a fair amount and so there's nothing to worry about.'

'Oh, bugger it,' he said at last. 'We can give it a go, I suppose. But it'll mean driving all round north Manchester.'

The troubled expressions around him now turned to smiles, like the sun coming out from behind a dark cloud.

Around that time, the popular press had been devoting endless column inches to intriguing questions involving challenges as to how much of a particular commodity could be fitted into a given space. Knotty problems, like how many people could ride on a bike or be accommodated in a telephone box. Or how many elephants would fit into a Mini? Now Billy was faced with a similar conundrum. How many adults could he get into a Morris Oxford estate car? It took some working out but in the end he managed it. The answer was nine.

Steve, Barry and Les squeezed into the back section; Mam, Dad, Flo on the rear seat; Polly, Annette, and Billy on the bench seat at the front. Billy found he could only reach the steering wheel by stretching out both arms to his left to their fullest extent. He started the engine and carefully drove along Wilmslow Road towards town. He hoped and prayed there were no traffic policemen about.

'Right,' he said as he sailed past the White Lion at Withingon, 'I'll drive over to Cheetham Hill Road first, then up to Langley Estate in Middleton, and finally to Salford. I trust that meets with everyone's approval.'

There was a general murmur of acceptance. Not that they had any choice.

Then a thin little voice piped up from the back. It was Dad.

'Doesn't this taxi driver sound like our Billy?' he said.

There was a roar of laughter and Mam said, 'It *is* our Billy, you daft bugger!'

Very funny, Billy thought, and he joined in the merriment but deep down he was uneasy for he suspected that Dad's confusion was the symptom of a deeper malaise.

Chapter Fifteen

One Sunday afternoon a couple of weeks after the house-warming party, Billy was following his usual routine. Sunday was always a busy day for him. He began by attending nine o'clock Mass with the family, following it with a cholesterol-producing breakfast of bacon, eggs, sausage, tomato, marmalade and toast. This normally took him to eleven o'clock, leaving the rest of the day to wade through the *Sunday Times*, described as a 'quality' broadsheet, mainly because it contained no pin-ups and avoided sensationalism in its reporting. On this particular Sunday, he had settled into his favourite armchair in the lounge but he was behind in his personal schedule as he'd only just finished reading what was described as the 'serious news' section and already it was two o'clock.

It's a funny thing the way we fathers become obsessed with 'the news', he mused, as if it's the most important thing in our lives. My own dad was the same. He used to read the *Daily Dispatch* and the *Evening Chronicle* from cover to cover every day of his life. Whenever the news was on the wireless, being read by someone with a curious name like Alvar Liddell or Bruce Belfrage, everyone in the house had to stay silent and creep around on tiptoe. Woe betide anyone who spoke or made a rude noise when it was being broadcast. Maybe we dads think we're going to be consulted by the Prime Minister or the Foreign Secretary one day. It would be: 'Look, we've got a problem in the Far East. You keep up with current affairs and we were wondering if you could help us out and tell us what to do about Indo-China.'

It was amazing that on the day you wanted to relax, the

Sunday paper came along with pages and pages of stuff they hadn't been able to cram into the weekday editions. Billy still had the Arts, Sports, and Travel sections to plough through, not to mention the colour supplement. Most of the big news, about top-level conferences and wars, he'd heard earlier on the radio and the TV which left the remaining spaces to be filled with the trivia that editors felt he simply had to know about. That ancient Egyptians had been taught how to build pyramids by aliens from outer space. That an in-depth (and expensive) market research into life in Oxford had concluded that the city had a good university and a strong sense of history. That the award of MBEs to the Beatles had sparked the return of a record number of medals in protest. That a new type of industrial accident was prevalent as a result of young men's long hair being entangled in moving machinery. That Enid Blyton's books had been banned in Cape Town libraries 'because the children portrayed in them were impertinent to their parents'.

These reports had had the usual soporific effect, when he was jolted from his afternoon nap by the ringing of the telephone.

The sound of a telephone still makes me jump out of my skin, he reflected, but I soon calm down for it's never for me, so let one of the kids answer it. Lucy and her new friends take up to eighty per cent of the calls, Matthew fifteen per cent and Laura and I are left with the five per cent crumbs. I'm only the stooge who pays the bills and so I don't count. I provide a free service for all the kids in the neighbourhood who want to discuss the relative merits of the Beatles and the Beach Boys or to find out where the next party's to be held. Furthermore, once they take possession, they stay on it for hours and Lucy is convinced she has monopoly rights. If the call is short, say fifteen minutes, they sprawl in the armchair with feet on the telephone table. For longer sessions, Lucy stretches out full length on the hall carpet. Occasionally, if I'm quick enough,

I'm permitted to nip in between calls to phone somebody but that's a big concession. One of these days, I shall have a pay box installed. That should give 'em something to think about.

'It's for you, Dad,' Lucy said, popping her head round the door.

'For me? Are you sure? Who is it?'

'Don't know, Dad. He didn't say.'

Billy put the newspaper down and picked up the phone in the hall.

'Hello,' he said brusquely, irritated at being disturbed on a Sunday afternoon.

'Billy, it's me,' the voice replied.

'Me? Who's me?' Billy grumbled.

'Surely you recognize the voice.'

'Wait a minute,' Billy spluttered. 'But . . . but . . . it can't be. Titch! It *is* Titch, isn't it?'

'It's me all right, Billy.'

'Where on earth are you? You're supposed to be in Canada.'

'I'm here at home at my mother's in Rusholme. Oscar is with me. I need your help and advice. Can you come over here? Please, Billy. It's urgent.'

'Say no more, Titch. I'm on my way.'

Billy explained to Laura that Titch had returned home to Manchester and was asking for his assistance. Laura was equally bewildered.

'I can't tell you any more, Laura. I'll drive across to see him. Speak to you later.'

Billy found Titch and Oscar sitting in the front room of the little terraced house on Walmer Street. Billy was shocked at Titch's appearance; he looked pale and drawn, grief-stricken. Billy's heart went out to his friend and he embraced him. Titch's voice sounded flat and broken when he finally spoke.

'It's Elaine,' he said.

Billy's heart skipped a beat and he feared the worst. 'She's not . . .?' He let the unfinished question hover in mid-air.

'She's left me.'

'I don't understand,' Billy said. 'How do you mean? Left you?'

'She's walked out on him,' Oscar snapped. 'Dumped him. That's what she's done. Leaving him with the kids.'

'Good Lord!' Billy exclaimed. 'Young Elaine! It's unbelievable. Tell me what happened.'

'We flew out from Manchester to Montreal as planned with the twins. We had a comfortable flight out and the passenger in the next seat was most helpful with the twins. He couldn't do enough for us, went out of his way to be friendly. He said his name was Archie Sutton and he worked for a national forestry company. He was based in England but his job involved travelling across the world providing advice and expertise on conservation. You may remember that Elaine's special subject was botany and so they had a lot in common and much to talk about.'

'He sounds like a great bloke,' Billy said.

'Exactly what we thought,' Titch said ruefully. 'When we reached Montreal, we found that by coincidence he was booked into the same hotel. We were due to stay for a few days waiting for finalization of our onward passage to Grande Prairie; he was awaiting fresh orders before flying on to Winnipeg. So that first day we agreed to have dinner together after we'd put the kids to bed and he kindly offered to show us around the city as he knew it well.'

'That was a bit of luck,' Billy remarked.

'Bad luck, as you'll see in a moment,' Oscar snorted. 'Let Titch finish his story.'

'On the second day,' Titch continued, 'he escorted us around the old section of the city and it was there I happened to spot a notice advertising a circus. Just right for the kids, I thought. However, Elaine, being a botany teacher, was keen to visit the Montreal Botanical Gardens, which are world

126

famous. As we had only a couple of days left, Archie offered to take Elaine to the gardens in the morning for two or three hours while I took the boys to the circus. Fine, I thought. An admirable arrangement.'

Billy could hardly bring himself to ask, 'So what happened next?'

'The circus finished later than expected and I returned with the twins to our hotel. I was surprised to find that Elaine was not yet back. Imagine the wild, crazy ideas which ran around my head. She came back a few hours later and told me she'd fallen in love with Archie, that she was going to leave me and return to England with him.'

'Good grief!' Billy gasped. 'I'm so sorry, Titch. What did you do?'

'What could I do? It was a bombshell. It was no use arguing, her mind was made up. She'd never loved me, she said. All our plans for the twins, for teaching in Grande Prairie, for our future together collapsed.'

'If I had that bastard Archie here, I'd throttle him with my bare hands,' Oscar exclaimed.

'It's beyond belief,' Billy said, shaking his head, 'that Elaine should've decided to throw up everything like that without any thought of the consequences.'

'Exactly what I thought,' Titch murmured. 'I was at a loss to understand it. I always thought Elaine was happy being married to me. At one point I thought that maybe this guy had drugged her or hypnotized her because it was so unlike her.'

'I doubt if it was anything like that,' Billy said. 'If anything, I think it would be the shock and anxiety about starting a new life in a new country, which must have been traumatic for both of you. Perhaps it was a breakdown resulting from exhaustion. From what you've told me, looking after the twins with their relentless demands must have taken a lot out of her. And if I remember rightly, when we met in the pub she said something about being worried about her aged parents here in Britain.'

'Anyway, I didn't want to take up the job in Grande Prairie without her,' Titch said sadly. 'There was nothing left for me to do but cancel our plans and return home with the kids. Now I have to start all over again, find a new job and somewhere to live.'

'Where's Elaine and this guy now?' Billy asked.

'She's staying with her parents in Liverpool and, as far as I know, he'll be staying in London before flying off somewhere else.'

'That's where we come in,' Oscar interrupted. 'Titch wants us to visit Elaine to see if we can't talk some sense into her.'

'I'd be willing to give whatever help I can,' Billy said slowly, 'though it does sound as if she's made up her mind. But what about him? What does he intend to do?'

'That's the big question,' Titch said. 'If we could make him see the error of his ways, he might decide that discretion was the better part of valour. I know that between overseas visits he usually stays at the Airways Hotel near Heathrow. But before we tackle our friend Archie, maybe you could talk to Elaine first. She thought highly of you, Billy, and I'm sure she'll listen to you.'

'OK Titch,' Billy said, placing a hand on his shoulder. 'Give us the details and Oscar and I'll see what we can do.'

On Monday morning, Billy rang Elaine and arranged for Oscar and himself to go over to see her. She seemed anxious to talk the matter over with someone and was more than willing to meet. That afternoon, the two friends drove over to Aigburth to her parents' home.

'I'm going to let you do most of the talking,' Oscar said, as they drove along the East Lancs road. 'You're the married man and the one with experience. I'm afraid I might say the wrong thing and make matters worse.'

Elaine looked anxious and strained when they met her. Her mother seemed equally tense and worried out of her mind as she showed them into their front room.

'I'm going to leave the three of you to it,' she said, 'but I do hope you can help Elaine to sort out the mess she appears to have got herself into.'

After she had gone, Billy took out his cigarettes and offered them all round. They lit up and looked at each other for what seemed a long time, wondering who would make a start.

It was Elaine who spoke first.

'I suppose Titch has sent you to ask me to come back,' she said, drawing nervously on her cigarette. Her hands were trembling.

'Nothing like that,' Billy said softly. 'We've come mainly to find out what's been going on and what you intend to do.'

'It's no use asking me to go back because I don't love Titch any more. I don't think I've ever really loved him. There's a ten-year age gap between us and we've never really hit it off.'

'Hit it off ?' Billy said. 'What does that mean?'

'Life with Titch is so dull. Every night's the same. We watch TV. We go to bed. He kisses me on the forehead as if he were my long-lost uncle. We don't talk; we don't seem to connect. He never tells me what sort of day he's had and when I do inquire, he says, "Don't ask," or simply grunts.'

'I'm surprised to hear you say that about the age gap,' Billy said, tapping his cigarette in an ashtray. 'When we all met in the Pineapple you said you liked being younger as it gave you an advantage over other women.'

'I had to say that to answer that bitchy woman, Gertrude, didn't I? But the truth is I find Titch too quiet and withdrawn, always so damned calm, never raises his voice, never gets excited about anything. I like people to say what they think, show a bit of enthusiasm, express their feelings.'

'We're not all built the same, Elaine. Maybe Titch is all for the quiet life. Nothing wrong with that.'

'I know it's not easy with the twins to go out enjoying

ourselves,' she said, lighting up another cigarette, 'but surely we could arrange a babysitter once in a while. I miss out on having a good time and Titch is so unimaginative. For my birthday he bought me a new vacuum cleaner, for goodness sake. If only he were more romantic, took me out to dinner, or to the theatre, made a fuss of me.'

The thought flashed through Billy's mind that many of Elaine's accusations could equally be levelled at him for he rarely took Laura out to dinner or to the theatre. And for her last birthday he'd bought her a Kenwood food mixer. *Maybe I should start watching my step in case Laura decides to ditch* me *for a more romantic type.*

'Very well,' Billy said. 'I get the message. What are we to tell Titch? That it's all over?'

'Tell him that I'm staying with Archie,' she said. 'He's the very opposite of Titch. He's handsome, younger and knows how to relax and have a good time. With us, it was a case of love at first sight.'

Billy had heard enough. It was time to put Elaine straight about one or two things but he had to choose his words carefully.

'I can well understand your feelings, Elaine. You're not the only one to have been tempted. A few years ago, when I was studying in Leeds, I too was severely tested and I came close to giving in. Then I realized how much was at stake and how much I was risking. If I'd yielded, I could've lost everything that was dear to me: wife, family, home, happiness. Marriage is something precious that you have to work at and spend time nurturing, not something to be abandoned lightly at the first sign of trouble. We've come here today to ask you to think carefully before you do anything rash and lose everything. Remember the vows you made at your marriage? You promised to love and cherish each other, until parted by death and not until somebody younger, richer or better-looking came along.

'You say you've fallen in love but I think you've got it

mixed up with passion. It's not the same as true love. This love at first sight thing you spoke of is like a kind of insanity that flares up, burns fiercely, then fizzles out. What then? What's left? Real love is stronger than that and will survive whatever trials life throws at you. It's then that two persons become as one, bound together by a bond that is unbreakable. If what you have with this Archie fellow is simply a passing fancy, you'll have thrown up everything for something false. Imagine the misery that'll follow. At the moment, what I'm saying may seem meaningless and irrelevant to your situation, but there'll come a time when it'll make sense to you. I must tell you, Elaine,' and Billy's voice became solemn, 'that if you decide to throw in your lot with this man, you'll have sacrificed everything that was worthwhile in your life.'

'What do you mean by that?' Elaine wept. 'Titch can't keep the twins. I nearly lost my life giving birth to them.'

'I don't know the answer to that,' Billy said, 'but since you're the one who walked out, a court may regard you as the guilty partner and decide in Titch's favour. But none of this need be. Titch'd be overjoyed to welcome you back if you so decide. I'm sure you can persuade him to be less neglectful, to liven himself up and start paying more attention to you and your needs. Oscar and I are leaving now but it's entirely up to you. Titch is waiting to hear from you.'

On the way back, Oscar gazed at Billy in awe.

'That last speech you made could be the subject of next Sunday's sermon at the Holy Name,' he said. 'You went to town on the marital vows stuff. I had no idea you were so traditional in your views about marriage.'

'As a matter of fact, neither did I until I started speaking but I meant every word.'

'Most unusual for the swinging sixties, Billy. God help your kids if ever *they* go astray.'

On the drive back Billy reflected on what Elaine had said about Titch being neglectful, not wanting to go out anywhere.

131

Her description of life with Titch had hit Billy on a tender spot. What if Laura began having ideas of ditching me? he thought with dismay. It's unthinkable! On impulse, he drew the car in at a florist's shop on Wilmslow Road and bought a bouquet of a dozen roses. Further on at Platt Lane, he stopped at the Coq d'Or restaurant and reserved a table for two for the following Saturday night.

At home, he presented the flowers to Laura with a kiss.

'Red roses for a beautiful lady,' he murmured, 'and I've booked a table for the two of us for Saturday.'

'What's this all about, Billy? It's not my birthday nor our anniversary. What's going on? You've been up to something, haven't you? Have you been having an affair?'

'Me? An affair? That's crazy. The very idea! I've bought you flowers and dinner to show how much I appreciate you and how much I love you. It's Elaine who's been having the affair and I've been chosen for the task of sorting things out.'

Later that evening, Billy and Oscar reported back to Titch and told him what Elaine had said. Titch looked traumatized as he heard about Elaine's accusation that he'd been neglectful.

'I never thought,' he murmured.

'Exactly,' Oscar said.

It was then a matter of waiting to see what Elaine's next step would be. Meanwhile, Titch had confirmed that Archie would be staying at the Airways Hotel for a few days before his next trip abroad. Oscar and Billy made plans to visit him to see if they could bring home to him the consequences of his actions.

The following day, they took the sleeper to Euston, booked themselves in the Holiday Inn close to Heathrow, and walked over to the Airways Hotel. They were both apprehensive about the confrontation, Oscar having to fortify himself with a couple of whiskies.

'How should we play it?' he asked.

'By ear,' Billy replied. 'Let's see how it goes.'

The clerk at the reception desk of the hotel rang through to Archie's room.

'There are two gentlemen here in reception to see you,' the clerk said.

'OK, I'll be right down,' Archie said.

Billy and Oscar took a seat on the sofa close to the desk.

Archie appeared five minutes later. He was smartly dressed and Billy's first impression was of a handsome, dark-haired young man about twenty-five years of age. He smiled nervously when he saw them. Billy stood up and held out his hand. Oscar remained seated, his features impassive.

'Archie Sutton?' Billy asked in a kindly tone

'That's me,' he said suspiciously, reluctantly taking Billy's hand. 'What can I do for you?'

'My name's Hopkins,' Billy said gently, 'and this is Tony Wilde. You can call me Billy.'

Oscar gave him a curt nod.

'We are friends of Titch and Elaine whom you met on the flight out to Montreal recently. Maybe you can guess why we're here.'

'No, I can't,' he snapped.

'Titch has asked us to meet you to find out your intentions with regard to Elaine.'

'I don't see how it's any of your business,' he retorted angrily. 'It's between Elaine and me.'

'Look, Archie,' Billy said softly, 'no need to take it the wrong way. We're here on a peace mission to find out what you have in mind. You and Elaine are both young, good-looking people. In many ways what happened was under-standable.'

Billy maintained a friendly approach, smiling encouragingly and speaking calmly though inside he was burning up.

'It was like this, Billy,' Archie said, regaining his composure. 'Titch and Elaine and I became good friends on the flight out. I saw that they had their hands full with their kids and I did my best to help them.'

'That's one way of putting it, I suppose,' Oscar sneered, scowling at him.

'Titch did tell us how helpful you were,' Billy said, throwing Oscar a warning look. 'I can see how you and Elaine were attracted to each other. You're both young and were bound to have a lot in common.'

Heartened by Billy's words, Archie opened up.

'Thank you, Billy. I can see that you appreciate what happened. I got to know the pair well but as time went on, I couldn't help noticing how cold and distant Titch was with Elaine. He acted almost as if she weren't there.'

'I can see your point of view,' Billy said, maintaining his composed approach. 'It was inevitable, I suppose, that you should be attracted to each other.'

'When Elaine said she was interested in looking round the Montreal Botanical Gardens, I volunteered to show her since I know Montreal well and it's in my line of work. Titch said he'd take the twins to the circus as the kids weren't interested in botany.'

All the time Archie was speaking, Oscar was squirming in his chair with frustration. Any moment now, Billy thought, the dam will break.

'So what happened next?' Billy asked.

'As we walked around inspecting the exhibits, I held her hand so that she wouldn't get lost in the crowds. Then I don't know what happened. Our eyes met and that was it. Fatal attraction or something. You know the rest.'

'So what are your plans now?' Billy lit another cigarette, his tenth of the day. I'm smoking far too much, he thought, I must give up this filthy habit.

'It depends on how Elaine feels about it but if she wants me, I'm here for her.'

Time to stop being Mister Nice Guy, Billy thought.

'You know of course that if you pursue this line, you'll be

responsible for looking after her children as well. You'll have to find a permanent home for them all. That'll mean a mortgage and the household bills that go with it. It'll be goodbye to the free and easy lifestyle you're used to.'

Archie looked unhappy and shuffled uncomfortably.

Oscar, who'd been drumming his fingers on the arm of his chair in pent-up anger, now flared up.

'My friend Billy here has been too easy with you,' he rasped, 'but I've no patience with the likes of you. I see your little game: acting the part of the solicitous fellow passenger as you pick your victims. You spot a nice-looking young lady like Elaine who's at her most vulnerable having left her home and family behind, get her away from her husband and kids for a few hours, lay on the charm, and she's an easy tumble.'

'It was nothing like that,' Archie protested.

Oscar leant forward menacingly. He was bristling with anger. 'Well, I've got news for you, sunshine,' he muttered through clenched teeth. 'If you make any attempt to contact Elaine again, you're for it. If you show your face anywhere in Manchester, we've got friends in Moss Side who know how to deal with your type. They'll swat you like a fly.' He slapped the table loudly to emphasize his point. 'Be warned, matey,' he continued. 'Make so much as a move to communicate and we're coming for you. I've only to make a few phone calls.'

Billy and Oscar prepared to leave.

'If I were you I should listen to him,' Billy said ominously. 'There's no telling what he'll do.'

Archie Sutton looked shaken.

They strode out of the hotel leaving a worried man behind.

'What the hell happened back there?' Billy asked when they were clear of the hotel. 'We seemed to fall automatically into the roles of good cop/bad cop.'

'Search me,' Oscar replied. 'We were like a couple of Al

Capone heavies in the roaring twenties. You softened him up, lifted his chin back, as it were, and then I socked him. Perhaps we should take it up professionally. Maybe the Kray twins could use us.'

A fortnight later, Elaine went back to Titch. They decided against returning to Canada. Instead, they bought a house in the Chorlton-cum-Hardy district, and Titch began looking for another job. At first things were strained but, in time, the wounds healed. Titch realized how remiss he'd been and tried hard to turn over a new leaf, to be more thoughtful and romantic. Elaine was young and not ready for an ultra-quiet domestic existence. At least once a week they arranged a babysitter and Titch took her somewhere, to dinner, to the theatre, or simply to visit friends. The rift between them was not mended overnight but gradually settled down to a more content and satisfying marriage.

Billy was secretly glad that his friend was back and, in helping to sort out Titch's problem, he learned a valuable lesson himself: that marriage was something you had to work at, to keep it romantic with flowers, candle-lit dinners, surprise presents, and all of that. And, most important, never to take things for granted.

Chapter Sixteen

By the late summer of 1964, the Hopkins family were beginning to feel settled. It had been a busy seven months and, after their five idyllic years in East Africa, Billy and Laura felt that, in so many ways, they had come down to earth with a bump. But for all the worry about John's grave illness, Billy's dad's bizarre behaviour, which looked as if it might be advanced signs of senility, and adjusting to a new house and lifestyle, they felt they had landed on their feet.

When the sun shone, Laura spent her time tending the garden and had produced the most beautiful array of flowers from roses and geraniums to petunias and marigolds. John, who still had to take things carefully, worked alongside her. He had started his own little patch of garden in which he'd nurtured his own selection of flowers: Virginia stock, snapdragon and sweet peas. He weeded, watered and watched their progress every day and at mealtimes gave the family an itemized report.

'The snapdragon are doing fine but I'm worried about the sweet peas; they're looking a bit sick.'

'Boring! Boring!' Mark declared. 'Do you think we want to hear every lousy detail each time a flower grows another half inch?'

'Not as boring as your stupid tricks,' John retorted. 'As for your lousy ventriloquist act, we can see your lips move. And what a barmy-looking dummy Harry the Hobo is with his dingly-dangly legs in those stupid black shoes.'

Matthew made a new friend when he found that the young boy living next door, the trumpet-playing Desmond Gillespie, attended Damian College, although being a year older, he would be in the form above. And it hadn't taken the others long to form new friendships either. Lucy met Mary Feeney one day at St Cuthbert's when the parents had got talking after Mass. Mary attended Fallowfield Convent High School and she promised to show Lucy round on the first day of term. Mark and John had also found companions – Brian, known as Spud Murphy and his younger brother Charlie – when they'd joined in a game of football at Fog Lane Park.

For the older children, Billy had fixed up swimming lessons at Stretford Baths under the tutelage of Jack Winne, an excellent teacher but a rough diamond and a hard taskmaster. Regular weekly instruction involved driving them over to Chester Road every Saturday and the occasional Sunday morning.

'I missed out on swimming when I was a kid,' Billy explained to Laura. 'At Damian College, the lessons and the practice were always after school at the Victoria Baths in High Street, Chorlton-on-Medlock. For us day pupils that would've meant getting home at six or seven o'clock every night, which wasn't on if we were going to do our homework as well.'

'But why didn't you learn to swim at St Chad's like your brothers?' she asked.

'At St Chad's Elementary School, the swimming instructor Mr Hincks taught pupils from Standard Five upward, and as I left after Standard Four when I passed the scholarship, I somehow slipped through the net. But I'm determined our own kids won't do the same. Swimming is a skill everyone should learn.'

Matthew and Lucy took to swimming like the proverbial ducks and within a few weeks were gliding with smooth strokes along the length of the baths. Mark on the other hand was more like a cat than a duck and was not at all keen on getting his face wet. Jack Winne stood for no nonsense and would have none of that water wings rubbish that Billy suggested. He simply lowered Mark in at the shallow end and ordered him to start doing the doggy paddle.

'Swim, swim, you silly sausage!' he commanded in a sergeant-major voice that echoed round the baths.

Mark was faced with desperate choices: he could argue (as he usually did), he could drown, or he could swim. He decided on the latter. Within three months, he too was moving easily through the water.

Swimming wasn't the only thing on the agenda.

Matthew wanted to take up the piano again. For years he'd nursed an ambition to, as he put it, 'tinkle the ivories' once more. Before going to East Africa, he'd impressed people both young and old by his bravura rendering of Chopin's 'Revolutionary' in the style of Paderewski. Only later did he disabuse them by demonstrating how his virtuoso performance was produced by pumping furiously on the foot pedals of their Aeolian Pianola.

Billy made a few inquiries amongst his musical friends and arranged for tuition with Dora Gilson of the Northern College of Music. Her fees were high and Billy wondered if he'd bitten off more than he could chew but then he thought, what the heck were we saving for all that time we were abroad? He decided to throw caution to the wind and book a course of lessons.

'As a youngster I always wanted to play the piano properly,' he told Laura, 'but there were no piano teachers within ten miles of Collyhurst and Red Bank and even if there had been, we wouldn't have been able to afford them. And another factor which was just as important, I suppose, was that we didn't have a piano.'

'I certainly go along with the idea of piano lessons,' Laura declared. 'In the Mackenzie family we all had to learn to play an instrument. But, at the same time, I can't help feeling, Billy, that you're trying to achieve your own life ambitions through your children, trying to produce miniature versions of yourself. First swimming, now music.'

'So, what's wrong with that?' he asked.

Lucy decided she didn't want to get into competition with Matthew and, after seeing a programme on television which featured a performance by Yehudi Menuhin and Stephen Grappelli playing 'Tea for Two', she made up her mind that the violin was to be her instrument.

'I can see myself playing at the Albert Hall before an audience of thousands,' she said. 'Matthew'll be green with envy and I'll see that the whole family, except Matthew of course, gets complimentary tickets.'

Billy bought a second-hand violin advertised in the *Evening News*, picked out a local teacher and Lucy went for lessons. After her first session, she came home and went to her room, set up the music stand and began.

Billy was watching the news on the BBC when the first waves of sound rent the air and vibrated through the house, rattling windowpanes and ornaments. From somewhere in the vicinity of the alley at the back of the house, there came an earpiercing yowl in response. Billy rushed to the window and looked out.

'I'll kill that blooming ginger moggie if I get my hands on it,' he yelled. 'He thinks Lucy's violin is Samantha on heat. Make sure all the doors and windows are closed to stop her getting out. I mean Samantha, not Lucy.'

For the next few weeks, the family was patient. They put up with the noise for as long as was humanly possible, though they made her practise in the back coal cellar and everyone inserted wax plugs in their ears. But when the screeches that she produced merged with the piercing note of Desmond Gillespie's trumpet, the discord became too much.

'Let's be honest,' Billy said. 'The yowling sounds she produces can only be beaten by the racket made by Hamish's kids, Portia and Rosalind, at the New Year party.'

'She could get a job in a pub,' Matthew said. 'If she played at closing time, instead of "Time, gentlemen, please", she could empty the place in two minutes flat.'

That was enough for Lucy. She gave it up pronto and

concentrated on drawing and painting, at which she'd manifested definite talent.

'Perhaps she's going to be an artist,' Laura observed.

'Hope not,' Billy said. 'There's no money in that. Most artists spend their lives starving in garrets unless she's another Andy Warhol and can persuade a gullible public that paintings of cans of beans constitute art. Maybe if she gets a job in an art gallery or teaching art in a school, she might survive. At least the money would be steady and there'd be a pension at the end.'

As for Mark and John, they contented themselves with the recorder and penny whistles taught by Laura at home. The sounds they produced were simple but harmonious.

Chapter Seventeen

The first day of term came round and the whole family was a jangle of nerves as everyone, except Laura who'd opted for the roles of mother and housewife, would be starting at a new school or college. How would they cope with the new demands that'd be made upon them? How well would they survive in the new environments? How would they get on with their new companions and colleagues? These were the questions uppermost in their minds on that first day.

For Laura, who had the almost impossible task of getting everyone out on time, it was a madhouse as she strove to meet the hundred and one calls on her services. Her first duty was making up sandwiches for Billy, Matthew and Lucy.

'I don't want meat paste sandwiches,' Lucy announced.

'And I hate cheese and tomato sandwiches,' Matthew proclaimed. 'The sandwiches end up all soggy.'

'Whatever you do,' Billy added, 'don't give me Marmite. I'd prefer to eat rat poison.'

'You'll all get what you're given,' Laura declared. 'And I do hope I haven't got to do this every morning,' she added, as she spread the various fillings on the umpteenth slice of bread.

'I should think not,' Billy said as he rummaged through the heap of clothes on the sideboard. 'It's only until we find out what our lunch arrangements are. Laura, did you see where I left my briefcase? Only it has my college notes.'

'I haven't a clue,' she said. 'I thought you got all your stuff prepared last night. I don't know where you put things. I can't follow you round all the time.'

'Mum, have you seen my PE kit?' Matthew called.

'Surely you don't need it on your first day!'

'It says in the letter to new pupils that we have to bring it for inspection on the first day or we'll be in big trouble with Brother Adrian, the PE master.'

'Well, I don't know where it is. I haven't got eyes in the back of my head. Look after your own things, Matthew. Billy, your briefcase is in the lounge where you left it last night.'

'Is this all we have for breakfast, Mum?' Lucy complained as she sat down at the table.

'This isn't the Ritz, you know,' Laura snapped 'Porridge or corn flakes. Like it or lump it.'

'Mum,' John whined. 'Can't eat this porridge. There's a lump in it.'

'Well, chew it, then.'

'I'm the only one not moaning about something,' Mark said unctuously. 'But I've got to have a clean shirt and a tie, the school said.'

'In the airing cupboard. I've got to iron it yet. I've got only one pair of hands. I'll do it as soon as I've finished these sandwiches.'

'Aw, Mum. I'll be late,' Mark whinged.

The family sat down to a hurried breakfast with the exception of Lucy who preferred to eat her corn flakes standing up, and Laura who got down to the business of ironing Mark's shirt.

'I think I'll be the laughing stock when I get to school,' Lucy pouted. 'First my blazer's too big; it was made for Hattie Jacques or some fatty like that, you could almost fit two of us in it. And my hair looks an absolute mess. You shouldn't have made me cut it short, Mum. Everyone will point at me and snigger. No one wears their hair like this.'

'Except the mentally retarded,' Matthew called out.

'Tell him to shut up, Dad. He's always making cracks at me.'

It was bedlam with everyone shouting at once and to add to the confusion the doorbell rang.

'That's my friend, Mary Feeney, from down the road,'

Lucy said breathlessly. 'She's going to school with me to show me where to go and all that.'

Lucy abandoned the half-eaten corn flakes, grabbed her coat and satchel and fled through the front door.

'Lucy! Lucy!' Laura called after her. 'You've forgotten your sandwiches!'

Too late. She was gone.

'The way she shot out through that door,' Billy remarked, 'she and Mary Feeney will be halfway to school by now.'

Billy finished his toast and marmalade, swallowed his tea and collected up his things.

'Right, Matthew, if we're going to catch the bus together, we'd better make a move.'

'OK, Dad. I have to call for Des Gillespie next door; he's promised to show me round at the school.'

'Fine but let's go. We don't want to start off by being late. Remember I've got to catch the train to St Helens.'

Then turning his attention to the youngest, he said, 'Remember, Mark, to hold John's hand all the way to school.'

'Aw, do I have to, Dad? The other kids'll make fun of us and think we're a couple of sissies.'

'All the same,' Billy said, 'you make sure you look after him. I don't want him bullied as I was by the skenny-eyed kid in Collyhurst. He used to wait for me after school to steal my money and anything else I had on me.'

'Don't worry. I'll look after him, Dad.'

'Make sure you do, Mark. Now, John, what do you do if you meet a bully?'

'Get Mark to thump him for me.'

'What if Mark isn't there?'

'If the bully's smaller than me, I thump him myself.'

'What if he's bigger?'

'I run like mad.'

'What if he catches you?'

'I roll up into a little ball like a caterpillar until he's stopped thumping me.'

144

'Good lad. You'll get by, young 'un,' Billy grinned, giving him a hug.

Next he shook Mark's hand. 'I'm relying on you. You're his defender.'

'If we do meet a bully, Dad, I'll talk him out of it first. As you're always telling us, we'll remember what Churchill said: "Jaw-jaw is better than war-war." '

'True,' Billy said, 'and like Theodore Roosevelt once said, "Speak softly and carry a big stick and you will go far." Starting this Saturday morning, I'll give you and John boxing lessons. They didn't do me any harm when I was a kid. If ever you do meet a lout, you should be able to defend yourselves.' He gave Laura a peck on the cheek and said, 'I must say I felt a surge of pride when I saw the kids in their uniforms this morning.'

'So did I. It was like seeing ourselves twenty-five years ago.'

'See you later, Laura,' he said, opening the front door. 'Wish me luck. How do I look?'

'Smart and lecturer-like. I'm sure all your young student debutantes will fall for you.'

'Come off it!' Secretly he was pleased.

So saying, Billy and Matthew left the house, followed by Mark and John, leaving Laura to enjoy a quiet reflective cup of coffee.

Chapter Eighteen

September 1964 and Billy's first day at his new job. He arrived at college in plenty of time having decided to travel by train as it was less stressful than driving along the busy East Lancs road and it gave him an opportunity to get in some concentrated reading.

Despite his seventeen years' teaching, he was apprehensive. His experience up to that time consisted of eleven years in a mixed secondary modern, one year as head of English in a boys' school, five years in an African boys' boarding school. This thing he was embarking on was totally different. A college for young ladies aged eighteen to twenty-one and all training to be teachers. What gall he had in thinking he was the right person to take on such a responsible job! Who did he think he was? How could a kid from a Collyhurst tenement block claim to have the expertise to train the next generation of teachers? How long before he was found out? Would they unmask him on his first day and expose him as the fraud he was? Or would it be a more gradual process as he put his foot in it time and time again? And today, how would they receive him? Would they laugh at him or take him seriously? He'd soon find out.

At the main entrance, he yanked on the lavatory-like chain he remembered from his first visit when he'd come for interview and heard the bell ring somewhere in the nether regions of the college. The large oak door was eventually swung open by the same Sister Anna, the novice nun, who led him along a series of labyrinthine corridors until they reached a suite of offices and lecture rooms marked

'Education Department'. She flung the door open wide and with a flourish announced his arrival.

'Mr William Hopkins!' she proclaimed as if introducing him at a formal civic reception.

Sister Peter came forward, hands outstretched and a big smile on her face.

'Good morning, Mr Hopkins. So happy to see you here once again.'

Billy had had a couple of informal preliminary meetings with her and her deputy to decide on his part in the teaching programme.

'I hope you had a good journey here,' she said.

'No problem. It's a good train service from Manchester.'

He looked round the rest of the Education Department staff, and was happy to see Gerry Flynn there. So he'd been successful after all despite his suspicions that the interview was a fix. At least, Billy thought, I'll have one simpatico colleague with whom I can share confidences when the going gets rough or when people start to take themselves too seriously. The rest of the staff consisted mainly of nuns and middle-aged ladies but he noted that one or two of the sisters could have doubled for Ingrid Bergman or Audrey Hepburn. He wondered if any of the senior nuns might break out into a chorus of 'You'll Never Walk Alone'. I must stop thinking this nonsense, he told himself.

An elderly auxiliary nun wheeled in a trolley containing tea and chocolate biscuits on a silver platter. And when she began serving the tea in china crockery, Billy knew he'd entered a different world. His mind went back to his first staffroom at St Anselm's Secondary Modern where the mugs had been marked with one's name in Elastoplast and where Grumpy Grundy, the science teacher, had ruled the roost by commandeering the best armchair and the best cup, the only one not chipped.

As they drank their tea and Billy agonized over whether he should crook his little finger, Sister Peter introduced the other members of staff. He already knew Sister Paul, the Deputy Head of Education, but there were eight others beside himself.

'The college has five hundred students,' the nun explained, 'with seventy staff, of whom ten are in the Education Department. It is our job to service the students on all courses.'

Gerry Flynn caught Billy's eye at this point and arched a meaningful eyebrow. Billy maintained an impassive expression but with difficulty. He could see they'd have to watch their step surrounded by so many religious females.

'For the Teacher's Certificate,' the sister continued, 'students study for three years but this year we shall begin courses for a selected group leading to a four-year B.Ed. That's the reason we've recruited new staff. We now have almost a full complement to inaugurate the new degree. We're short of only one more specialist lecturer to teach History of Education. If you know of any suitable colleague who might be interested, please let me know. The post would be at lecturer grade.

'One final point I want to make and I'm sure that in many ways it's unnecessary but it's this. Our students are at an impressionable age and we must try to set a good example at all times in our behaviour and our deportment. For instance, if you smoke, I'd appreciate it if you'd confine it to the staffroom and not smoke in front of the students. It's a habit I'm trying to discourage, especially in view of the recent government health warnings.'

Billy's mind was concentrated on that part of her speech about needing another member of staff. His thoughts raced ahead. Titch! His friend back from Canada and without a job. He'd leap at the chance of working in a training college. The subject was right up his street and, even at lecturer grade, was a well-paid, prestigious job, which would no doubt please his wife Elaine.

When the sister had finished her introduction, Billy sought

an opportunity to speak to her and the deputy head privately about his friend. When they'd heard the details, they began their synchronized nodding and agreed to fix up an interview for Titch that week.

'If all is in order and all goes to plan,' Sister Peter enthused, 'we could employ him in the next fortnight or so. Our need is becoming desperate if we're to start the degree on time.'

An interview was arranged by telephone. Titch attended and got the job. Everything was falling nicely into place. Now, Billy thought, I have two confidantes working in the college.

Meanwhile, Sisters Peter and Paul took Billy to view his own private office. It was one of three rooms situated in St Joseph's Hall on the edge of the college grounds.

'These rooms were formerly used as guest rooms for visitors,' Sister Peter explained. 'That is why each of them has a washbasin and mirror, and of course you have your own telephone. The other rooms are reserved for Mr Flynn and the next male lecturer that we appoint. I hope you'll be comfortable here.'

Comfortable! That's putting it mildly, Billy thought. A shiver of delight ran down his spine when he saw his name in capital letters on the door: MR WILLIAM HOPKINS, SENIOR LECTURER IN EDUCATION.

Now he appreciated the full significance of the term 'territorial imperative' and the basic animal need to claim ownership of a place against all challengers. A dog might leave its mark on a tree by simply cocking its leg but for Billy nothing so athletic or so pungent was required. The title on the door said it all. It announced to the rest of the world that here was his own private domain to which he could retire to rejoice when things went well or to lick his wounds when they didn't.

'We're so happy to have you on the staff, Mr Hopkins,' the departmental head continued with a broad smile. 'Though your post is initially for three years, we feel confident that it will be confirmed as permanent when the period is up.

149

After that, you'll have security of tenure. In other words, if it's then your wish, you'll have a job for life here provided of course that everything works out satisfactorily. We haven't the slightest doubt that it will.'

I wonder what she means by 'works out satisfactorily', Billy asked himself. Probably means if I keep my nose clean and don't put my foot in it. Still, a three-year contract with the promise of permanence was something to rejoice about.

The room was spacious enough to hold seminar groups and there was a large window overlooking the college grounds. Billy sat at his desk and looked out at the manicured lawns and the lush, flower-filled gardens. Somewhere in the college a choir was singing and his joy was complete. What with the music, the statues and the paintings he'd seen about the place, he felt as if he were at the heart of medieval European culture. This was heavenly bliss, like coming up on the pools and getting married all on the same day. How did I come to get this wonderful, wonderful job? he asked himself. Fortune has certainly smiled on me.

Most of the morning was taken up with meetings, discussions, and planning. At lunchtime, Gerry Flynn and he walked to a nearby park to eat their sandwiches, share a flask of coffee, and to swap notes about how they saw their new jobs.

'I was told that our positions could be permanent,' Billy said as he unwrapped his lunch package, 'provided things work out satisfactorily. What does that mean, Gerry, "work out satisfactorily"?'

'It means, old son, that you and I will be granted tenure provided we don't make a cock-up of our teaching and we're not accused of moral turpitude.'

'What the heck is "moral turpitude"? I've often wondered.'

'It means fiddling your travel expenses or trying to have it off with one of the students.'

'Not a chance of that, Gerry. I'm an old married man with four kids.'

'Ah, but do the students know that?' He grinned lecherously.

'I shall make sure I keep them at arm's length,' Billy said, sipping his coffee. 'What about lecturing? I've got my first this afternoon. Any hints or wrinkles to pass on to a greenhorn like me?'

'You're hardly a greenhorn with all those years of teaching behind you. But a couple of tips I'd pass on would be about ways to capture and hold the students' attention.'

'I'm all ears.'

'Whenever you see that glazed look come into their eyes, it means their minds are switching off and they're away to the Land of Nod. The way to bring 'em back to the land of the living is to do one of two things. First of all, start to number your points. Say, "On the subject of juvenile delinquency, there are ninety-nine points I want to bring out. One . . ." Watch them wake up suddenly and start jotting them all down.'

'And the other way to capture their undivided attention?'

'It's to be used only in an emergency. Switch to the subject of sex and see how they sit up immediately.'

'Thanks, Gerry. I'll bear your advice in mind. Now there are five things I want to say to you about this.'

'Huh! Funny!'

After lunch, Sister Peter escorted Billy to a small lecture theatre where a group of second-year Certificate students was waiting. He was down to give a talk on the Socialization of Children. After a few preliminary words of welcome and introduction to the class, the nun turned to him and said, 'Well, Mr Hopkins, I'll leave you to it.'

He was on his own. A thousand and one butterflies fluttered in his stomach.

'Thank you, Sister,' he said, trying to sound confident as if he'd been giving lectures to young ladies all his life.

He turned to face his class and beheld thirty film starlets,

151

including a few young novice nuns straight out of *The Sound of Music*. All eyes were on him now and the students smiled at him encouragingly and waited for him to begin, their pens hovering at the ready. Billy returned their smile to show he, too, was friendly but he was so tense, it was more like a grimace than a smile. He had no notes with him but that wasn't a problem. He'd prepared this first lecture thoroughly by memorizing it word for word, intending to deliver it like a part in a play so as to give the impression that it was off the cuff. In many ways, he was like a kid showing off riding his bike down Honeypot Street and calling, 'Look, Mam, no hands!' but stage fright was upon him now. His hands were damp and his legs wobbly.

'Our study of education,' he began, his voice an octave higher than he'd intended, 'will be concerned with an examination of the factors which influence the socialization of children.'

To his utter amazement, they wrote it down as if God Himself had come down from Mount Sinai to address them and they were anxious not to miss a word. Not all of them though. One student was giving her total concentration to the garment she was knitting. Her lips wore an amused smile as if she found the whole business of note-taking beneath her. This was most disconcerting. Why wasn't she getting all this sublime erudition down on paper like the rest of 'em? He went on with the lecture and was relieved to see that the others continued scribbling for dear life, some of them tearing page after page from their notepads. Seeing this, he began to feel more sure of himself. Maybe this stuff's better than you thought, an inner voice whispered. After half an hour, some of the students had reams and reams filled up with his profound observations. Now he felt not merely confident but sagacious. He wondered how this process had come about. Was a lecturer appointed because he was wise or did he begin to feel wise only after he'd been appointed? But that tricoteuse student on the third row, the one with the rictus smile, was niggling him. She was going at it hammer and tongs. Knit one, purl one. Knit one, purl one. Why wasn't she getting *his pearls* of wisdom down in her notebook? He had to find out. He paused for a moment and looked at her.

'Why aren't you taking notes like the other students?' he asked her gently.

She looked up from her knitting. 'It's all right, Mr Hopkins.' She grinned condescendingly. 'My mother was at this college a few years back and I've got her notes.'

'We must be glad at least that it wasn't your grandmother,' he laughed. 'But things have moved on since your mother's day. You should be taking notes.'

She smiled and went on with her knitting, which rattled him even more. He was determined to make her forget, even drop, her knitting. But how?

He remembered what Gerry had told him. Time to put Plan A into action: numbering points.

'Turning now to the influence of the peer group in adolescence,' he said, 'there are three important points I want to stress. First, in the peer group the adolescent learns the values of his culture and sub-culture.'

Gerry had been right. It worked. Now his listeners were writing more furiously than ever. But not the knitter.

'Secondly, in the peer group the adolescent learns social skills.'

The deviant continued clicking her needles with dedicated concentration. Time for emergency Plan B, he thought.

'Thirdly, in the peer group, the adolescent learns new sex roles.'

The students' pens hovered in mid-air as they looked up from their notepads and gazed at Billy quizzically and with renewed interest. The knitter dropped not only a stitch but also her needles.

'Excuse me, Mr Hopkins,' she said. 'Did I hear you right? Did you say "they learn *new sex roles*"?'

153

'I did indeed.'

Her smile broadened and there was a twinkle in her eye as she looked round at her fellow students and asked mockingly, 'How do you spell that word "roles"?'

Billy blushed to the roots. 'Why, R-O-L-E-S of course,' he replied.

'Thank you, Mr Hopkins,' she said with that derisive smile of hers and went back to her knitting. 'Just wanted to be sure.'

'I think that might be an appropriate place to end,' he said. 'I shall expand on the points I've made in the next lecture.'

The students filed out of the room, nodding and smiling in appreciation. One or two complimented him with comments like, 'Thank you. I enjoyed that lecture,' and 'Most interesting.'

Billy collected his things and left the room. As he walked along the corridor on his way back to his office, he passed an adjoining classroom where the door had been left slightly ajar. A few students were waiting for their next lecturer and as he reached the doorway, he caught snippets of conversation.

'What did you think of the new guy?' said a voice.

'You mean Hopkins? A good lecturer. He certainly knows his stuff. Did you notice that he lectured without notes?'

'I certainly did. And he's not bad-looking either,' said another.

'He was OK, I suppose. Passable. Maybe a little overweight though.'

'His hair was thinning on top.'

'And he's going grey.'

'Maybe but I liked the streaks of silver in his hair,' a student with a husky voice remarked. 'Gives him a mature, distinguished look, I think. I quite fancy him.'

Billy bent down to tie his shoelaces. Slowly. Both shoes. This is like a Shakespeare play, he thought, where one of the characters listens from behind the arras.

Husky voice was speaking again. 'Did you see how he blushed with embarrassment when I asked him how to spell roles? He's shy. I like that in a man.'

'He's too old for us, Beryl. He must be about forty.'

'He may be too old for you youngsters,' Beryl said, 'but he's not too old for me. At twenty-five years of age, I reckon I'm within his orbit.'

'That may be so, Beryl, but I've heard on the grapevine that he's married with kids. So eyes off,' said the other student, effectively putting the kibosh on any romantic notions any of them might have been entertaining.

Billy stood up and hurried back to his study. So that was the impression he'd given! He thought he'd been teaching educational theory and that his audience had been learning about sociology but, despite their fervid note-taking, it looked as if they'd simply been giving him the once-over and at least one of them had been weighing him up as a likely prospect. Back in his room, he didn't know whether to laugh or lament.

He gazed at his reflection in the mirror over the wash-basin. The students' remarks had touched his vanity.

What was it that student said? Thinning hair? She was right. My hair *is* receding, I'm going bald. I could go for treatment, I suppose, to a hair-restoring clinic and maybe have some grafts. I wonder how it works and would it be expensive? And I can see the beginnings of crow's feet at the corners of my eyes. I'm getting old but not too old, I hope. I need to pull myself together and turn over a new leaf. 'A little overweight' that other student said. Funny thing that because I've spent half my youth being called 'Beanpole'. Now, at the age of thirty-six, they're probably calling me 'Fatty' or 'Fatso' behind my back. There's nothing for it. I'll have to go on a diet and get back to my natural weight. The thin man inside me is trying to get out and who am I to get in his way? And what about that student's remark about my hair turning grey? She was right. It *is* going grey. Maybe I should start dyeing my hair though another did say she liked the streaks of silver. Gave me a mature, distinguished look. A new me is what is required. I need to get fit and healthy. I'll get up early and start jogging every morning before coming to college. And what was it the Principal said this morning about smoking? We must set a good example, that was it.

I must give up the filthy habit. I'll start next Monday morning. Must find a foolproof method though. I've tried a thousand times before and it's never worked. It was like Mark Twain once said, 'Giving up is easy. I do it every week.' Just the same, I must have another go. Probably best to start on a long weekend when we have a Bank Holiday Monday, to give the new regime a chance to become firmly established.

And when I'm fit and healthy, what then? I need to occupy my spare time with worthwhile occupations. William Morris said somewhere that the well-rounded, educated individual has a practical skill as well as intellectual knowledge. I need to learn some rural craft, a new hobby, something that is a complete change from academic work. For example, making country wines from natural fruit as people used to do in olden days. Or furniture-making or wood-turning; they're skills that have always held out a fascination for me. The ability to turn out coffee tables, bowls, clocks, barometers, pepper mills in a variety of beautiful hardwoods, like yew, mahogany, rosewood. I've often wondered how it's done and if I can do it. Won't cost much to buy the tools and the wood and I can always sell the products. Should be a steady demand for that kind of thing. Seems a shame not to make use of the basement in our new home.

Billy looked at his watch. Four fifteen. For a first day, it had been pretty busy and he'd had a lot to absorb. In some ways it had been a turning point in his life and career. But now it was time to go home. He caught the four thirty train and settled down to read his book. After a little while he became conscious of someone staring at him. He looked up and recognized her immediately. It was the knitting student, and she was still at it, her needles going hammer and tongs, at the same time watching him with that knowing smile he had seen in the lecture theatre. He gave her a friendly nod in acknowledgement and returned to his book. What was she doing on the same train? Surely she wasn't following him. What a crazy arrogant thought! When they reached Central Station, he went over to her.

'Hello,' he said. 'I thought it was you I saw on the train. You're still knitting, I see. Do you live in Manchester?'

'Hello, Mr Hopkins. Yes, I'm a Mancunian and I live in Ladybarn. I'm a day student and so we may see each other regularly if by chance we find ourselves on the same train.'

'That would be nice. What's your name, by the way?'

'Beryl Benson. Sorry if you misunderstood when I said I had my mother's notes. I was paying attention and I enjoyed your lecture. I'm looking forward to the next.' There it was again. That amused, even mocking, smile.

'Glad to hear it, Beryl. See you next lecture.'

They parted company to catch their separate buses.

Chapter Nineteen

It was five fifteen when Billy reached home. As he stepped through the door he was met by the most delicious smell in the world. Laura's homemade soup! He went straight into the kitchen, kissed her and said, 'Glamorous ladies in Paris may have their Chanel Number Five with which to lure unwary males but there is no perfume in Paris or indeed in the world to equal the aroma of Laura's homemade potage.'

'You've obviously had a good day at college,' she said, digging him playfully in the ribs.

'Wonderful day, Laura. Treated like royalty. I think I've found my niche. Teaching Hollywood starlets who are all in love with me.'

'Dream on, Billy, dream on.'

'OK, Laura. Don't destroy my illusions on my first day. Where are the kids?'

'Where would you think, Billy? Watching television in the lounge. They made a beeline for it as soon as they came through the door. Straight in to watch *Thunderbirds* – after they'd had a round of bread and raspberry jam of course. But Lucy isn't home yet and I'm concerned about her. She should've got back by now.'

'Not to worry, Laura. No doubt she's gone to her friend's house after school.'

Billy went into the lounge to join the kids engrossed in their TV programme. He watched quietly for a while.

'A load of old rubbish,' he declared. 'Whoever heard of a snooty dowager like Lady Penelope in her pink Rolls-Royce with that daft-looking chauffeur Parker being an agent on a team of space travellers?'

'Shush, Dad,' they chorused. 'You're spoiling the programme.'

'Too many shushers in this house,' he declared. 'I'm the chief shusher around here. You lot are the shushees.'

'Shush, Dad. Please! It's nearly the end and Brains is about to rescue them all with a cunning plan.'

'OK. But dinnertime as soon as it's over.'

At five thirty, Lucy arrived home.

'You're late, Lucy,' Laura said. 'Where've you been?'

'Nowhere.'

Did you stay behind at school?' Billy asked. 'Talking to your teachers?'

'Not exactly.'

'At Mary Feeney's house?' Laura said.

'Not exactly.'

'Look, Lucy,' Billy said, irritated, 'you must have been at some exact place at some exact time doing some exact thing.'

'I haven't been doing anything,' Lucy snapped. 'I'm going upstairs to unpack my things. Talk to you later.'

Thunderbirds came to a triumphal conclusion with the usual victory of the goodies over the baddies. The children were about to get involved in the next programme when Laura called.

'Dinner in two minutes! I want to see clean hands at the table.'

Billy washed his hands in the bathroom and handed the soap to Matthew who passed it down the line to the two boys who had formed a queue at the washbasin. Lucy came last.

The family waited round the table until Lucy joined them.

Billy intoned the Grace Before Meals. 'Bless Us, O Lord, and these Thy gifts which we are about to receive from Thy bounty through Christ Our Lord.'

'Amen,' they all said.

Billy and Laura began ladling out the soup.

'Good nourishing Scottish broth,' Laura said, 'with new potatoes in it.'

'So tell us about your first day at school,' Billy said when everyone had settled down. 'Let's begin with the boys, two young 'uns first.'

Mark answered for both. 'I'm in Standard Three, that's Mrs Brennan's class, and John's in Standard One, Mrs Dearman's class. We did lots of tests all day to see what section we're going to be in. I'm in Section B for maths and Section A for English. We learned poetry and for homework I've got to memorize "The Vagabond" by Robert Louis Stevenson. Later in the afternoon, we started geography about China and after that history about King Alfred and the cakes.'

'Is that it?' Billy asked.

'I've been picked to play for the football team, and I learned my nine times table. Ask me what seven nines are?'

'OK,' Billy said. 'What are seven nines?'

'Sixty-three. Ask me another.'

'Well done! Nine nines?'

'Eighty-one. Another.'

'Eighteen nines,' said Billy.

'That's not fair. It's not in the tables.'

'A hundred and sixty-two', answered Matthew immediately.

'Huh, clever clogs,' Lucy scoffed.

'Oh, another thing,' Mark said. 'I forgot to tell you I was given lines for talking in class.'

'They should give tests for the gift of the gab,' Billy laughed. 'You'd be top. Did you remember to look after John on the way to school?'

'Yeah, but I didn't hold his hand like you said. Not all the way. The other kids were laughing at us and calling us namby-pambies.'

'Doesn't matter, ignore them. Or tell your teacher.'

'That'd make it worse, Dad. We'd be known as telltales and teacher's pets.'

'That's better than a black eye.'

Mark remained unconvinced.

'And what about you, John? What did you learn in school today, dear little boy of mine?' Billy sang.

'Not much, Dad. We said prayers in the hall first and then went to our classrooms and our teacher called the register. We had to say, "Present, Miss." After that we played with plasticine and I made a lot of animals like those in my toy zoo. After playtime, we did reading and Mrs Dearman said I was to go straight on to the Beacon Book Five 'cos I already know how to read. In the afternoon, we did counting with Cuisenaire rods and me and Charlie were made gerbil monitors.'

'What on earth's a gerbil monitor?' Billy asked.

'It's our job to look after our pet gerbil. He's called Jake and we've got to make sure he's fed, and his cage is clean.'

'How many monitors are there, John?' Laura asked.

'Lots and lots because everyone's a monitor of something.' John counted on his fingers. 'There's one for pens, pencils, books, library corner, giving out milk, collecting the bottles, and a monitor for each pet. We've got a hamster, a guinea pig, a mouse, and the gerbil. And Mrs Dearman says we may be able to bring him home some weekend. And I tried to tell Mrs Dearman a joke but she said she didn't have time to listen. Some of the kids are real sissies and were crying for their mothers but I didn't.'

'What did you do at playtime?' Billy asked.

'Me and Charlie Murphy played at *Emergency Ward Ten* with two girls from our class, Annie Degnan and Irene Reidy.'

'You and Charlie have soon found yourselves girlfriends,' Billy laughed. 'I suppose you were one of the doctors?'

'Yeah. I was Dr Dawson and Charlie was an ambulance driver. Agnes was a nurse and Eileen was the patient. And they're not our girlfriends, Dad.'

'Would you like to be a doctor when you grow up, John?'

'I wouldn't mind.'

'Why is that?'

'So I can get my own back and stick needles into people.'

161

While John was talking, Mark had helped himself to one of John's new potatoes, a particular favourite of his.

'And what about you, Matthew? How did you get on?'

'Not bad. I got to school OK with Des from next door. He's a year older than me and I thought we'd be in different forms but they've put me in Lower Four with him. That means I'm a year younger than everyone else.'

'Why have they done that?'

'I think it's because I got high scores on the entrance exam.'

Billy turned to Laura and said, 'I always said that the discipline and strict traditional education they were given in Kenya put them streets ahead.'

'Congratulations, Matthew,' Laura said. 'You must be proud and happy.'

'Not really, Mum. I'd rather be with my own age group. Already the others in the form are thumping me and pushing me around, calling me names. In school, it's best not to be too different from the others or they say you're stuck-up. They've already nicknamed me "Lightnin' Hopkins" because I could answer quickly in mental arithmetic. The only good thing is that I'm with Des and we can go to school together.'

'If Matt's so clever,' Lucy said, 'why can't he go to a boarding school for geniuses, like Eton or Harrow? Or anywhere far away from here.'

'Now, Lucy, don't be like that,' Laura said. 'Remember he's your brother. One day you will look up to him.'

'Only if he's at the top of a ladder.'

'So, Lucy, tell us about how you got on,' Billy said. 'How did you find your school on your first day?'

'I caught the ninety-six bus, got off, and there it was.'

'Very funny. But tell us, how was it?'

'OK, I suppose.'

'OK? What does that mean?' Laura asked.

'It was OK. What else can I say? It was my first day and I don't know anyone except Mary Feeney and another girl called Sally Simpson.'

'What about the subjects you're going to study?' Billy asked.

'I don't know yet. I've only been there one day, haven't I? I know there are nine and I can't remember the titles of them all. I only know that one of them is French. What is this? The third degree?'

'Fair enough,' Billy said, 'if you don't want to share your experiences with us. But why were you so late getting back tonight? Were you at Mary's house?'

Lucy looked extremely worried as she answered. 'No. Mary, Sally and me—'

'Mary, Sally and I,' Billy corrected.

'OK, Dad. Mary, Sally and I went to Didsbury railway station and we talked to the stationmaster there.' Lucy had turned pale and her hands were trembling.

'What on earth were you doing there?' Laura asked, now equally anxious. 'Something's worrying you. What is it?'

'He told us lots of ghost stories. One was about a ghost who appears on the tracks at night and howls, "The day is for the living and the night is for the dead." And he told us about banshees that weep and wail and float round houses where someone's going to die.'

'Tell her to shut up, Mum,' John said. 'She's scaring me.'

'I think that's enough for the time being, Lucy,' Billy said. 'I don't approve of your visiting Didsbury Station after school. I want you to make me a solemn promise here and now that you will not go back to that stationmaster with his frightening stories. Ghosts and banshees indeed! You can only do yourself harm listening to such rubbish.'

'I promise, Dad. Mary and I were terrified out of our wits. I think we'll have nightmares tonight.'

'Right. Enough of this nonsense. Who's for dessert?'

'What is it?' Mark and John chorused.

'Your favourite. Angel Delight. Butterscotch flavour. It's all ready in the fridge.'

The stationmaster's stories had a long-lasting effect on Lucy. For that first night and for many nights afterwards, she could only sleep after she'd checked out her room thoroughly by looking in the wardrobe, behind the curtains, and under the bed and then sleeping with the covers over her head. And for many a night, such was her fear that she could only find rest by creeping in next to her mother while Billy moved into her single bed.

But now there was no sound except the clinking of spoons on dessert dishes as they demolished the Angel Delight.

Finally, Laura said, 'I've listened to all your reports. Doesn't anyone want to know what sort of day I've had?'

'OK, what sort of day have you had, Mum?' Matthew asked.

'After you'd all gone, I had a visit from a Martian with eyes on stalks and later I had a date with my secret lover. After that I went to the bank and drew out all the money. I and my lover have booked a flight to South America for next week . . .'

No one appeared to be listening. Their attention was concentrated on their pudding.

'*I* was listening, Laura,' Billy said. 'But I envy you. You don't know how lucky you are being able to stay at home taking things easy while the rest of us are out there in the jungle struggling for survival.'

Laura glared at him. 'So you think I sit here taking it easy while you're at college putting on your act for your admiring debutantes, discussing great educational matters and the world's problems with your colleagues over cups of coffee in the staffroom, arranging the pens and the blotting paper on your desk. Back here I've a thousand and one things to attend to. First thing in the morning, you may remember, it's like a madhouse. I have to wake everybody up, get their breakfast, prepare sandwiches, make sure they're dressed properly, and see them off in good time for school. The rest of the day I spend making the beds, dusting, hoovering, washing, drying and ironing clothes, shopping, cooking, putting the bins out, weeding the garden, sending birthday cards and presents to our numerous relatives, arranging appointments with the plumber or the electrician for various repairs to be done. And when you and the kids get home, sorting out squabbles, putting sticking plaster on their cuts and wounds, preparing a meal for you all, dragging you away from the television for dinner, washing up, helping the kids with their homework and finally seeing them off to bed. And you call that taking things easy.'

'OK, Laura,' Billy said holding up his hands defensively. 'My only question is: what do you do in your spare time?'

He was too late to duck before the flying cushion hit him.

Chapter Twenty

'Smoking is a disgusting, filthy, unhealthy, abnormal, wasteful, nauseating, objectionable and anti-social habit,' Billy declared. 'I'm so glad I've given it up forever because at this moment I've never felt so fit and healthy; I'm a different man and I'm experiencing a new lease of life. A new dawn has broken. My eyes and my skin are clearer; my sense of taste and smell have come back. No more coughing and spluttering; no more halitosis; no more indigestion and acidity. I feel renewed and invigorated.'

It was early Saturday morning on a Bank Holiday weekend and Billy was having a late morning, lying in bed thinking aloud and ruminating about his future and his life in general.

'I didn't know you'd given up smoking,' said Laura who was lying next to him. 'When did you stop?'

'About an hour ago.'

She sighed. 'I'd better warn the family. Maybe I should take the children to my mother's for the next week or two.'

'Why do you say that, Laura? You know I'm always a shining example of sweetness and light.'

'Not when you've given up smoking, you're not. I know from bitter experience, Billy. The first day you're OK and elated at your success in having got through twenty-four hours without a cigarette. The second day, you're prickly and touchy. By the third day, you're a bear with a sore head and the family has to creep about on tiptoe. But the fourth day's OK because that's when you usually light up again, to everyone's relief.'

'I don't remember being like that. However, I must stop smoking. It's now a proven cause of lung cancer – a case of ashes to ashes, as someone said. Apart from that, it's

166

unnatural. My mam always said that if God had wanted us to smoke, He'd have given us noses pointing upwards like a chimney. This time it's going to be different though. I'm going to try a new method of self-hypnosis.'

'Have you ever thought of taking up a pipe, Billy? Somehow I think it makes a man look wise and mature. Like Sherlock Holmes, J.B. Priestley, or Bing Crosby.'

'If anything, Laura, pipe-smoking is more deadly. At least smoking a cigarette is intermittent but a pipe is continuous, and is much more potent.'

Laura laughed. 'I've never smoked but when I see someone puffing away on a cigarette or a pipe, I'm reminded of a baby on the bottle or a little kid sucking his thumb. Why do people smoke anyway? Beats me.'

'The easy answer is they like it and it soothes the nerves. Some say it helps them think. The real reason is that they can't help themselves, they're hooked.'

'You could give the same reasons for opium smoking. You know, I've always hated smoking. Smokers foul God's good air, burn the furniture, scatter ash and fag ends everywhere, they have nicotine-stained fingers, blackened teeth, and permanent halitosis.'

'OK, OK, Laura. Take it easy! No need to overdo it!'

'Sorry. I hope this latest effort does the trick, that's all.'

'I started smoking at the age of fifteen in the Damian College smoker's club when we all thought we were Humphrey Bogart or in the case of Oscar, Noel Coward. I've lost count of the methods I've experimented with. I've tried everything: cold turkey, dummy cigarettes, strong peppermints, chewing gum, coloured pills, even emetics. Nothing worked.'

'You haven't tried the Raleigh method though.'

'The Raleigh method. That's a new one on me.'

'It's what happened to Walter Raleigh when he appeared in public smoking a pipe. They chucked a bucket of water over him.'

'I think we'll give that one a miss. I could try following Titch's method. He says he never smokes before midday. When I asked him why, he said it's because he doesn't stop coughing till half past eleven. But if you've never smoked, Laura, you can't know how strong a vice it is. Even George the Sixth suffered badly from it. One man was told by his doctor that if he didn't pack it in, they'd have to amputate his leg. This bloke thought for a moment, then asked, "How high?" '

'So what's this miraculous new method you've discovered?'

'It's called psycho-integration and it trains the mind to form a completely new habit which excludes smoking. No will power, no pills, no drugs, no dummy cigarettes. Just mind training. Furthermore, I can go on smoking at the same time that I'm giving up.'

'You smoke as you're giving up? Sounds like a lunatic method to me. How does that work?'

'I take a fag out of the packet, put it in my mouth without lighting it and then put it back. Then I take it out again, put it to my lips, light it and as I'm about to take a puff, I put it down on the ashtray, and say "I am an abstainer" ten times and after that I can take a drag if I like. In this way, I'll learn to forget to smoke and gradually the habit will die away for good.'

'You've tried some strange methods, Billy, but this must be the weirdest.'

'It was pretty expensive and so it had better work. I simply have to keep saying "I am an abstainer" a thousand times a day as I do the exercises.'

'When you say you're an abstainer, Billy, I do hope it doesn't mean *everything*.'

'Not everything,' he laughed, 'but, starting this morning, I begin a fitness campaign. First a jog round the park, next I'm going on a fruit regime called the Hollywood Diet, so called because it's used by film stars and people like that.'

'I've seen the list you've given me and you need a Hollywood income because it's going to cost a fortune. Paw-

paw, mango, grapes, kiwi fruit, pineapple. Cheap enough if we were still living in the tropics but here they'll cost the earth. What are you doing all this for? As if I didn't know.'

'I'm doing it for your benefit, Laura. To make myself hale and hearty and so live a longer life. Then I can look after you when you're old and decrepit.'

'Thanks a lot, Billy,' she said, poking him playfully in the ribs. 'But we both know you're doing it simply to impress all those fawning young ladies at the college. And what was it Shakespeare had the cheek to say? "Vanity thy name is woman." He couldn't have been more wrong. And what about the grey hair you said your admirers had noticed? Will you be dyeing your hair?'

'I'm leaving the silver streaks. They make me look disting-uished.'

'You're nearly twice the age of those students of yours, Billy. Why, you could almost be their father!'

'Of all those students? I think that's a bit of an exaggeration, Laura. There's about five hundred of them.'

There was a knock at the door.

'It's John. Can I come in?'

'Yes, John,' Billy called. 'What can we do for you?'

Already fully dressed, John came into the room. 'Mrs Dearman let me bring Jake the gerbil home from school yesterday, Dad. Do you want to come and see him?'

'I certainly do want to see this wonderful creature, John. I'm about to go for a run round Fog Lane Park and as soon as I'm back, have had a shower, and finished breakfast I'll be in to inspect your friend Jake. Whatever you do, make sure Samantha is locked in the boiler room or she'll have Jake for breakfast in two seconds flat.'

'OK, Dad. Charlie Murphy's with me. We're building a huge fort out of Lego bricks. We'll wait for you in my bedroom.'

'You're looking smart this morning, John,' Billy remarked.

'Mum took me to the barber's yesterday, Dad,' he said looking guiltily towards Laura.

'Yes, I certainly did.' Laura chuckled. 'The shop was crowded and we had to wait over an hour for our turn. And then John embarrassed me in front of everyone. When the barber had finished the haircut, he asked if John was to have a shampoo. And what did you say, John?'

'I told him that the nit nurse at school said I wasn't to have a shampoo, that's all. What's wrong with that?'

'Never mind, John,' Billy laughed. 'I'll see you later.'

Dressed in his new tracksuit, Billy jogged the three-mile perimeter of Fog Lane Park, came back and, after a shower, ate a breakfast of pineapple. He made himself an instant coffee and was about to light his first cigarette of the day when he remembered he'd given up that morning. He took a fag from the packet, put it back, took it out again, lit it, raised it to his lips, then before he could inhale, placed it on the ashtray and went into his 'I-am-an-abstainer' routine.

'Billy, I've been thinking,' Laura said.

This statement usually prefaced some momentous decision she'd made and always made his heart skip a beat. Uh-oh, he thought, what now?

'I've been thinking,' she continued, 'that since you're going on a diet and will be losing weight, you won't need all those old suits you have hanging in the wardrobe. Most of them are hopelessly out of fashion anyway. I thought I might sort them out and take them to the Salvation Army.'

'Which suits did you have in mind, Laura?' he asked suspiciously. 'Styles have a way of coming back into fashion again after a few years.'

'Somehow I can't see corduroy trousers and drape suits coming back into vogue but some poor tramp might be glad of them. Then there are those safari suits. You won't be needing them again, surely?'

'You never know. Suppose I'm offered a big job some-where in Africa. What then?'

'You can buy them back again from the Salvation Army.

Anyway, I'll take them all to the cleaners this morning and then take them down to the depot.'

'Take them to the cleaners? It's me you'll be taking to the cleaners! You mean the clothes have to be in pristine condition and neatly pressed and ironed before Manchester's down-and-outs and meths drinkers will condescend to accept them? That's taking charity to extremes.'

'Think of the Brownie points you'll have earned when you reach the Pearly Gates.'

There was no answer to that so Billy went upstairs to view John's gerbil.

Chapter Twenty-One

Jake the gerbil was a beautiful golden colour with a long hairy tail. Its home, which John, with the help of his pal Charlie, had carried home from school was a medium-sized tank with a wire lid. Its bedding was wood shavings and shredded paper with a few well-chewed toilet roll tubes and little rocks scattered about. One or two gnawed twigs were evidence of the rodent's sharp teeth. In one corner was a small water bottle and in the other a metal box which served as sleeping quarters. At that moment, Jake the gerbil was curled up, enjoying a lie-in. Since he wasn't in the school classroom, perhaps he knew it was a long weekend and had grabbed the chance to catch up on some shut-eye.

John and Charlie stopped their Lego building and came over to show their pet.

Charlie, who was the same age as John, had a mop of untidy red hair, a cheeky face and a little snub nose.

'Your gerbil's a handsome fellow,' Billy said. 'He looks a little like a rat or a large mouse though.'

'Don't let him hear you say that, Dad. He's touchy. He's not a rat or a mouse. He's a Mongolian gerbil and he's proud of it.'

'Oops, sorry, sorry,' Billy whispered. 'Is that all he does? Sleep all day?'

'No, he sleeps during the day and gets lively later on, especially at night. You should see him jump over things.'

'Maybe you should enter him in the rodent's Olympics. Why the toilet roll tubes?'

It was Charlie who answered. 'He likes tunnelling, Mr Hopkins, and he plays at running through them as if they're underground tunnels. As you can see, he also likes chewing them to bits.'

'We must see if we can get him some new tubes. What does he usually eat?'

'He likes fruit and vegetables he can chew on, like apples or carrots,' Charlie said.

'Does he bite?'

'Only if he doesn't know you. He has to get used to your smell before he becomes your friend,' John said.

'He's all alone,' Billy said. 'That seems a shame. Doesn't he have a brother or a friend to play with?'

'No, Dad. Mrs Dearman says it'd be good if he had a friend and maybe, if we can raise the money, we'll buy another gerbil to keep him company.'

'You must look after him well here, John. First thing you must do is clean out his tank because it smells a bit. While he's asleep, you could gently move his nesting box out of the tank and give him new bedding. I'll go down to the kitchen and see if I can find him a carrot. I'll make doubly sure that Samantha is locked in the boiler room. She loves it in there where it's nice and warm.'

'Right, Dad.'

Five minutes later, Billy returned to the bedroom with a large juicy carrot only to find a distraught John and Charlie on hands and knees looking frantically under the bed.

'What happened, boys?' Billy asked.

'I lifted Jake's nesting box out of the tank,' John said, 'and suddenly he woke up and leapt out of my hands and ran off. He was too quick for me but he's got to be in this room somewhere.'

'I'm sure we'll find him.'

The three of them went down on all fours to search under the furniture. They looked under cushions, in the wardrobe, at the back of the desk, in the drawers, amongst the bedclothes. No good. There was no sign of the pet.

'Was the bedroom door open, John?'

173

'I think it was. Maybe he's got out of the room. He could be anywhere in the house. We'll never find him now!' John wailed.

Billy went out onto the landing and in a loud voice called out to the rest of the family who were in various parts of the house.

'OK, everybody! Wherever you are. We need your help. All hands to the pump! Jake the gerbil has escaped and is hiding somewhere in the house.'

They came running from all parts of the house. Matthew with his friend Des; Lucy with Mary Feeney and Sally Simpson; Mark with Spud Murphy, and finally Laura from the kitchen.

'I'd no idea there were so many people in the house!' Billy exclaimed. 'But this is an emergency. Let's spread out and into search parties and check rooms on this floor first; next, upstairs in the attic. Look everywhere and under everything. I offer a shilling to the first one who finds him.'

Family and friends went to work. For over an hour, they turned the house upside down. No use. No gerbil. There was nothing for it but to abandon the search and hope that the pet would turn up of its own accord.

'Mrs Dearman's going to be angry when I tell her we've lost Jake,' John wept. 'I'll lose my job as gerbil monitor. She'll put me on bottle collecting instead.'

'Somebody'll come across him, I'm sure,' Billy said, trying to console him though deep down he felt the animal might have got outside where there'd be no hope of finding him.

Then Mark, accompanied by Spud, strode into the kitchen.

'We've found him!' he announced. But if the news was good, why was Mark looking so miserable?

'He was in my satchel which I'd left on the chair in my room. It had an apple core inside it, left over from school on Friday. Jake found it and he must have been chewing on it when Spud accidentally sat on him. He's dead. I mean Jake, not Spud.'

'Sorry. Sorry,' Spud Murphy cried. 'How was I to know that the gerbil was in the satchel?'

John and Charlie started to howl.

'Mrs Dearman will never trust us again,' John cried.

'I'm sure she'll understand,' Laura said. 'When all's said and done, it was an accident.'

'At least he died happy,' Matthew grinned. 'For his last meal, he was eating his favourite fruit.'

'Does this mean we get the shilling?' Mark asked. 'After all, we found him, Spud and me, and you said nothing about finding him alive.'

These comments did nothing to console the two young guardians who had been charged with Jake's care. They continued to blubber.

'I'm sure Jake's now in gerbil heaven,' Billy said.

'I didn't know there was a separate heaven for gerbils,' Matthew said. 'Which part of the Bible is that to be found in?'

'Look, Matthew, this is no time to start a theological debate. The two young 'uns are upset and need solace, not your clever arguments.'

'I think we should say the Eternal Rest prayer for Jake,' John said.

'How do you know he was a Catholic?' Mark asked.

'He's bound to be,' John replied, 'because he went to a Catholic school.'

'Why not hold a funeral ceremony for Jake and bury him with all due honours?' Laura said.

'I've never heard anything so crazy,' Billy said. 'Maybe we should invite the priest and have a requiem Mass. Why leave it there? We could arrange to have a twenty-one gun salute as we lower the body into the grave.'

'No need to go over the top, Billy. I believe strongly that a funeral will help these two lads to come to terms with their loss.'

*   *   *

It was drizzling when Billy dug the hole for the interment in the garden. A foot should be enough, he said to himself. Anyway, that's all he's getting. The gerbil's corpse was wrapped in a winding sheet of first-aid bandage, then placed in a fancy eau-de-cologne box for a coffin. There was a good turnout for the obsequies and everyone wore black. Even next door's red setter, Lois, came to pay her respects.

To the humming of Handel's 'Dead March' by Matthew and Des, the cortège processed sadly to the graveside, big umbrellas up to protect them from the rain. Matthew, Des, Mark, and Spud acted as pall-bearers, the two chief mourners being Charlie and John. The four ladies, with heads covered, stood by, as was the custom, and watched from the graveside. Billy was not only gravedigger but funeral director as well. The dignity of the ritual was spoiled when Lois the dog began barking loudly in support.

'Sit, Lois!' Matthew commanded. 'Sit!'

As the pall-bearers lowered the coffin into the grave, Billy said a few words in praise of the deceased, before intoning the solemn words of entombment.

'Jake was a good gerbil and gave much joy to all who knew him. He was a one-off; they broke the mould when he died and we'll never see his like again. And so we commit Jake the gerbil's remains to the ground; earth to earth, ashes to ashes, dust to dust.'

Lastly, the chief mourners delivered a brief funeral oration over the grave. First, Charlie, then John.

'Goodbye, Jake. You were a good pal. Sorry my brother Spud sat on you. He didn't mean to.'

'Goodbye, Jake,' said John. 'You were one of my best pals. Always ready to play and you only bit me twice. I hope you're happy up there in gerbil heaven with loads of carrots, apples, and soil for digging. And I hope you have lots of other gerbil pals to keep you company.'

Next each mourner threw a handful of soil onto the coffin. Charlie and John completed the ceremony by placing a beautiful sepulchral vault built from Lego bricks in the form of a cross with Jake's name on it. With this final ceremony, the obsequies were well and truly completed.

After the funeral, the mourners retired to the dining room where Laura had prepared a snack of tongue and ham sandwiches; everyone tucked in heartily, talking as they munched away about what a fine gerbil Jake had been and how he'd be missed. Billy seized the opportunity to practise his smoking abstention course by constantly taking out a cigarette from the packet and replacing it. Finally he lit it, raised it to his lips and, without drawing on it, put it down on the ashtray and recited his incantations: 'I am an abstainer. I am an abstainer, I am an abstainer.' Then he picked up the cigarette, took a deep puff and heaved a sigh of contentment.

Lucy's friends, Mary and Sally, watched him fascinated.

Finally Mary whispered in Lucy's ear, 'I think your father's more upset by this gerbil's death than you realize, Lucy. What's he doing with that cigarette?'

'Not to worry,' Lucy replied. 'That's his way of giving up.'

The funeral party was disturbed by the furious yapping of Lois who had been left outside.

'We forgot about the poor dog,' Billy said. 'No doubt she can smell the ham sandwiches. We can't lock her out. After all, she was one of the mourners too.'

He opened the kitchen door and there sat Lois with Jake's coffin in her mouth. Her tail was wagging excitedly as if waiting for a reward for finding and digging up the recently buried treasure. As funeral director, Billy felt that arranging the burial had been demanding enough but he hadn't reckoned on the body being exhumed in such a macabre manner. There was nothing for it but to re-inter the corpse, this time in a hole three feet deep beyond the reach of Lois's paws.

Billy promised to write a letter of explanation to Mrs Dearman about the untimely demise of Jake and, by way of amends, to buy not one gerbil but two to take his place. In the afternoon, Billy and Laura took the two young lads over to Tib Street in the city centre to choose replacement gerbils. As they drove out of the garage, Billy was taken aback to see a familiar figure on the other side of the road. It was Beryl Benson, the student knitter. She gave them a friendly wave as they moved off.

'Who is that girl?' Laura asked suspiciously. 'I've seen her several times on our road. At first I thought she was watching the house, but I'm sure I must be mistaken.'

'That lady spoke to me and Charlie on Friday afternoon when we were playing in the garden,' John said.

In Billy's head, warning bells sounded.

'What did she want?' he asked.

'She said "What a lovely haircut" to me and she asked our names, that's all.'

'She's one of our student teachers,' Billy replied in answer to Laura's question. 'I believe she lives somewhere in the district.'

Deep down, he sensed trouble.

Chapter Twenty-Two

On the Sunday after the gerbil funeral, Billy arranged with his brother Les to visit their mam and dad to see what they could do to make life easier for the old folk. After Mass the family had the usual Sunday bacon-and-egg breakfast and Billy prepared to make the journey to Langley. To his surprise, Matthew and Mark said they'd like to go also to see if they could do anything to help. They collected the equipment and materials needed for the jobs they were planning: the steam wallpaper remover, decorating tools, new wallpaper and, most important, battens plus insulation fibreboard. They picked up Les in Albert Square and drove up to Langley.

As usual, it was Mam who opened the door. Dad sat huddled up at the fire staring into the glowing embers as if hoping to find the answer to life's riddles there. Each time Billy saw his dad he experienced a shock at how much he had deteriorated since the last visit. He looked terrible, more like a vagrant than the father he'd known, respected and, at times, feared. He was unshaven and dressed in his shabbiest clothes. There was a faraway look in his eyes as if his mind was in another world. Was this the father who, in former days, had been so proud and particular about his appearance?

'Well, Mam, how are things?' Billy asked.

'Not so bad, Billy. Dad's not been so good and the doctor's put him on tablets to keep him calm and help him sleep. One piece of good news is that I've made a new friend on the block. It's Mrs Reynolds who lives a few doors along. She's about my age and she's had a hard life like mine, so we've lots to talk about.'

'I'm so glad to hear that, Mam. The way Dad is at the moment, you need someone else to talk with. We've come here today to see if we can make things more comfortable for you both. I'm going to show you how to use the new telephone and we're going to tackle that cold outside bedroom wall which makes the place like an icebox. What would you like us to do first?'

'Make a cup of tea, of course. The things are in the cupboard. Then it'd be nice if you could give Dad a shave. He hasn't got around to doing it himself for a couple of days.'

'OK, that can be a job for Matthew and Mark,' Billy said.

'You mean us? Give Grandad a shave?' Matthew gasped.

'No, daftie. You and Mark make the tea.'

'Right, Dad. Leave it to us.'

Les said, 'I'll make a start in the bedroom and fix the battens to the wall; then we can tack on the fibreboard and after that paste on the wallpaper. That should make things warmer not only in the room but in the whole bungalow.'

'Are you sure the council will allow it?' Mam asked anxiously.

'No need to tell 'em,' Billy said. 'They won't be able to see it when we've finished. Meanwhile I'll get on with the job of giving Dad a shave.'

Billy went into the bathroom to collect Dad's gear: a shaving mug, a brush, a stick of soap, and an open cut-throat razor which he sharpened on the leather strop. Somehow, his father had never got round to using a safety razor. As for an electric razor, not a chance.

'I don't feel clean after using one of them bloody new-fangled things,' he was fond of saying. 'There's nowt like shaving soap and hot water to give you that tingly fresh feeling.'

Using the hot water in the mug, Billy worked up a lather which he brushed vigorously onto Dad's wrinkled face and chin. Manipulating the razor between the facial crevices and creases was no easy matter for he'd grown considerable stubble and it was obvious he hadn't shaved for several days. He'd let himself go. Most unlike him, Billy thought.

The shaving finished, Billy turned his attention to the new telephone, which had been installed by the GPO on Friday. It was a model specially designed for elderly and disabled people. It had the normal circular dial but in addition there was a square box with a large button which, when pressed, went straight through to the operator.

'Isn't it marvellous what they can do nowadays?' Mam remarked. 'But my eyesight's now so bad I can't see the numbers on the dial and I've never used a telephone in my life, so you'll have to show me what to do.'

Billy handed her the phone which she held as if it were a bomb that might explode in her face.

'I don't know which way round I have to hold it. Where do I speak and where do I listen?'

'No problem,' Billy said, showing her the correct way to hold the phone. On a piece of white card he wrote out in huge letters the phone numbers of his brothers and sisters, and his own, making sure that Mam could read them.

'Now, let's put it to the test,' he said. 'We'll phone our Flo. First, press the button and listen.'

She did so and was startled when a female operator asked, 'Number, please?' She looked at Billy anxiously. 'What do I do now?'

'Read off Flo's number. It's the top one.'

She recited the number to the operator and a few seconds later was rewarded by the sound of a phone ringing followed almost immediately by Flo's voice.

'Hello? Is that our Flo?' she yelled into the mouthpiece as if calling to someone several hundred yards distant.

There was a buzzing sound as Flo responded.

'I'm here with our Billy,' Mam bawled, 'and we're testing the telephone to make sure it's working. I think *I'm* being tested as well.'

Billy took the phone from her. 'You've passed your test with flying colours, Mam.' He gave Flo the return phone number but before he rang off, he said, 'This is a red letter day for Mam and Dad. They've entered the electronic age.'

'Not only can you phone your family,' he told Mam, 'you can ask the operator to put you through to all kinds of services. Time, weather, and even the dish-of-the-day recommendation. Let me show you.' He dialled the appropriate number, then handed the phone over to Mam. 'Listen. Here's today's recipe. Hungarian goulash.'

Mam listened carefully to the disembodied voice, commenting from time to time with remarks like, 'I see. I see. Now, that's interesting. I'll try that.' She finished by expressing her gratitude. 'Thank you very much, love. You've been very kind.'

These two tasks completed, it was time for Billy to join Les in his work on the bedroom wall. While they were thus occupied, Mam seized the opportunity to phone round the family to show off her new skill.

In the bedroom, Matthew and Mark were recruited to help with the mundane job of mixing the wallpaper paste while Billy and Les tackled the more skilful and delicate task (or so they claimed) of fixing the insulation board to the battens and, after that, the new wallpaper. While this was going on, Dad sat on the bed gazing out of the window.

'Did you see those kids go past the window?' he asked suddenly.

'Which kids, Dad?'

'Those kids. I've seen them there in the garden lots of times.'

'There are no kids, Dad,' Billy said.

'They're there now,' he said triumphantly. 'See for yourself.'

Everyone went to the window to take a look. All they could see were daffodils nodding in the breeze.

'They're flowers, Dad,' Les said.

'They may look like flowers now but I tell you, they keep

changing into young kids and back into flowers again. I'm not barmy, you know. I see them every day.'

They left the house around seven o'clock and Billy drove Les home. As they parted company, Billy remarked, 'I'm worried about Dad. These hallucinations of his are a bad sign. I think his condition's become much worse.'

'I'm sure you're right,' Les replied. 'At least they now have a telephone and Mam can reach us quickly if there's an emergency.'

Chapter Twenty-Three

It was Saturday morning and Billy was working at his wood-turning lathe in the basement. There was something hypnotic about a lump of wood whirling around on a lathe which induced a trance-like state and he found himself reflecting on the past year which seemed to have flashed by since they'd first moved into their new house. Everything, or nearly everything, has fallen into place, he thought. I feel so much fitter and healthier now that I've stopped smoking. Even now I don't understand how that self-hypnosis method worked because I've completely forgotten about smoking and I haven't even thought about having a cigarette since. As for the family, I'm so proud and happy at the way things are turning out.

As he worked at the lathe in the basement, he often paused and listened to the piano music floating down to him from the lounge above. Sometimes it was Laura playing Liszt's 'Liebesträume' or a Chopin nocturne; sometimes Matthew playing Mozart's graceful Piano Sonata in A Major while in the cellar next door Lucy worked with her friends Mary and Sally at her potter's wheel, a present given to her on her thirteenth birthday, turning out a variety of jugs, vases, and figurines. As for Mark and John, they were more than holding their own at junior school. After regular boxing lessons, they were now pretty good at defending themselves with their fists, much to Laura's disapproval.

'I don't see the point of teaching them these pugilistic skills, Billy,' she said. 'This is Didsbury, not Collyhurst. They're not likely to meet skenny-eyed bullies here.'

'Bullies are to be found everywhere, Laura. And if they

ever do meet one here or some other place in the future, they'll be able to give a good account of themselves.'

This particular morning Mark was playing goalkeeper in a school football match and John was helping Laura with her winter gardening chores. It was a funny thing, Billy thought, the way Laura seemed to begin tending her garden whenever he started work on his lathe. Maybe coincidence or maybe she thought she should be doing something useful too. Then again, it might have something to do with the racket and the vibrations caused by the machinery he was operating.

He turned his attention back to his lathe and gouged out the centre of the piece of mahogany he was working on. This would be the tenth bowl he'd turned out that week though he'd lost count of the number he'd produced in total. He only knew that everyone in both extended families had been given one and sometimes two of his creations to celebrate birthdays and festive occasions. He loved woodwork as an escape from the world of academia. Perhaps I'm in the wrong job, he often thought, and would have been more fulfilled in a manual occupation. There was no doubt that he was happiest in his workshop. He'd mastered the art of making coffee tables as well and had built around a dozen before Laura had called a halt, saying that twelve was plenty to be going on with. And that wasn't the only thing he'd turned his hand to. Using the book by C. J. Berry, he had begun making his own wine from a variety of natural fruits in one-gallon and five-gallon lots. His favourite was elderberry, a rich full-bodied wine, but he'd stored more than twenty gallons of different wines in the dark dummy cellar, which was ideal for the purpose. In a few years' time, he told himself, they should be beautifully mature wines that I'll be proud to offer friends and relatives when they come to visit.

If a stranger had walked into the cellar at that moment and viewed Billy's life situation, he could have been forgiven for concluding that he led an idyllic existence and was one of the luckiest men on earth. After all, wasn't his firstborn son upstairs playing Mozart, his daughter working at her pottery, his middle son out playing football, and his wife and youngest working in the garden? But the stranger wouldn't have been entirely correct in his judgement because Billy had problems. As Titch, his pessimistic friend, might have put it, every silver lining had a cloud and for Billy there was not one but two clouds and they were hanging over him like swords of Damocles.

Chapter Twenty-Four

Cloud number one was his mam's eyesight which had been getting steadily worse for some considerable time.

'The lights in the house keep going up and down,' she complained. 'One minute they're too bright, the next they're too dull. Everything looks foggy. Maybe we need new light bulbs.'

New bulbs were purchased but they made no difference.

Next, she put it down to the Electricity Board messing about with the current.

'I never did like this new-fangled electricity,' she declared. 'They shouldn't have changed us over from gas. We didn't have any problems when we had gas mantles. I blame the Conservative government for our troubles. They're one big clique and they've always had it in for us working class.'

It was her eldest daughter, Flo, who had suggested that it might have something to do with old age and failing eyesight.

'You've probably got cataracts,' she said.

'Cataracts! That's what the doctor said a long time ago. But aren't they some kind of waterfall?'

A visit to her GP had confirmed Flo's diagnosis. Mam had cataracts all right and in both eyes. Further investigation at the Manchester Eye Hospital on Nelson Street added yet further evidence and an appointment was made for an operation to remove them.

'There's a two-year waiting list,' the specialist told her.

'Two years! I'll be in my coffin by then.'

'In that case, you won't have need of your eyes,' he had replied laconically.

Now the two years had passed and her sight had deteriorated to the point where she was finding it hard to look after the house and to care for Dad. The operation meant a week in hospital and she became more and more worried as the day for her admission approached. Worried, yes. But not about the operation; she was concerned about Dad and who would look after him while she was away. Mam and the family had decided that it was inadvisable to let him visit as he was likely to become emotionally upset at seeing his wife in hospital and surrounded by medical paraphernalia.

'He'll have to be watched night and day,' she said before she was driven to hospital, 'or he'll get himself in trouble. Someone will have to make sure he takes his pills and that he gets something to eat.'

The family drew up a roster. In the mornings, Flo and Polly, Billy's elder sisters, would look after him and do the shopping as well. Les would take responsibility for the afternoons up to six o'clock. After that, Billy would take over and stay until the next morning and go straight to college from there.

'I'll leave the shaving of Dad to you, Billy,' Les grinned. 'You're obviously the expert in the Sweeney Todd department.'

On Mam's first afternoon in hospital, Billy went to visit her. It was the day before the operation and he found a wide representation of the extended family gathered round her bed, a scene, he thought, reminiscent of the famous painting 'The Death of Nelson'. He kissed Mam on the forehead and wished her the best of luck for the morrow, promising to get his family to say a prayer for a successful operation, but she seemed more anxious about the arrangements for looking after Dad than her own predicament.

'Don't worry about me,' she said. 'I'm in good hands here. Tomorrow I'll have my eyesight back. It's Dad I'm concerned about. He can't look after himself any more and you'll have to watch him like a hawk.'

That evening Billy drove up to Langley to relieve Les, taking with him a new Gillette safety razor, not wishing to use the dangerous open cut-throat on Dad's furrowed face. Les was already waiting when he got to the bungalow.

'He's all yours,' Les said. 'I've given him his tea and he likes a cup of cocoa and a biscuit at bedtime. The nerve pills are in the first drawer of the sideboard. The dose is two before going to bed. I mean for Dad, not you, though by the end of this evening I dare say you'll feel like taking the whole bottle yourself. Best of luck. Stay calm and take it easy.'

With that, Les was off like a shot to catch his bus.

Billy turned his attention to his father.

'Right, Dad,' he said. 'First thing we do is give you a shave. I'm getting so good at this, maybe I should take a second job as a barber.'

He went into the usual routine with shaving mug, hot water and brush, working up a healthy lather. With the safety razor, the job was much easier though navigating the numerous hills and valleys that constituted Dad's physiognomy was no easy task. He finished off with a little aftershave lotion. Dad sat quietly and passively throughout the operation.

'There, Dad,' Billy said when he had completed the job, 'you look so much better now. Fresh and alert.'

Poor old sod, he thought. There he sits having to have things done *for* him and *to* him. The man who used to terrify the life out of the family when he'd had one too many. But his mind nowadays is no longer on this planet. The result, I suppose, of all that heavy drinking every day after working like a donkey, portering in Smithfield Market. He must have drunk enough Boddington's bitter to float the Royal Navy.

Billy switched on the television to catch the news. Dad watched with unseeing eyes, unable to make sense of the flickering shadows on the screen. They sat quietly for a while, then it started. He leaned forward, looked at Billy anxiously and ever so gently asked, 'Excuse me, son, but where's your mother gone?'

'She's gone to the hospital to have cataracts removed, Dad. As soon as she's better, she'll come home to look after you again. That should be in about a week's time.' Billy turned back to the television which was now broadcasting some vacuous soap opera.

Five minutes ticked by. Then Dad leaned forward again and asked in the same dulcet tone, 'Where's your mother gone?'

Patiently Billy explained it to him once again. 'She's gone to the eye hospital . . .'

He accepted the explanation and nodded and went quiet again, absorbing the information. Or so Billy thought.

Three or four minutes later he asked the same question. Billy gave the same answer.

The question was repeated every few minutes for the next couple of hours and each time Billy gave him the same answer. When asked again for the umpteenth time, Billy's patience finally snapped.

'Look, Dad,' he said brusquely, 'I've already told you a hundred times. She's gone into hospital to have her cataracts removed. I can't keep saying the same thing over and over again.'

Five minutes passed slowly by. Then, nervously, Dad looked at Billy and asked, 'Excuse me. Now I don't want you to get angry with me but where's your mother gone?'

Once again, Billy told him. This was like the Chinese dripping-water torture or death by a thousand cuts. If it went on much longer, Billy thought, he too would begin to lose his mind. Then he thought of a possible solution. He found some pieces of white card in the sideboard and printed in large letters the answer he'd been giving repeatedly all evening.

'HERE IS A MESSAGE FOR MR THOMAS HOPKINS. YOUR WIFE, KATE, IS NOW IN THE MANCHESTER ROYAL INFIRMARY HAVING CATARACTS REMOVED. SHE WILL BE HOME AGAIN TO LOOK AFTER YOU IN A WEEK'S TIME.'

He didn't have to wait long for the question.

'Please, son, don't get mad with me, but tell me where your mother's gone?'

Billy thrust the piece of card in his hand and said, 'Read this, Dad. It's a message from the hospital.'

Painstakingly, Dad began to read it by following the words with his finger. Finally he looked up bewildered.

'You didn't tell me there'd been a message. When did this come?'

He read the card again slowly.

Billy looked at the pathetic figure of his dad puzzling over the piece of card. It's the beginning of the end for him, he thought.

He made his dad's supper, gave him his sleeping pill and watched him all the way into bed. This was necessary because Mam had told him that one night his dad had forgotten to get under the covers and had gone to sleep on top of the eiderdown despite the cold night. Billy tucked him into bed as if he were a baby before settling down himself on the bed settee. Next morning, he handed over the reins to his sister Polly and made ready to depart for college. Before he left, he prepared a small identification card to put on Dad's person in case he ever wandered off again and got himself lost. He printed in capital letters: 'THOMAS HOPKINS AGED 80. IF LOST, PLEASE PHONE MANCHESTER 668 4375.'

But where to place it was the problem. In his trouser pocket? No use. He might change his trousers and forget the card. His jacket? Also no use if he put on a different coat. There was only one piece of clothing that he was a hundred per cent sure to be wearing. His cap. Billy inserted the card in the lining of his headgear, confident that his dad would never go anywhere without it.

'See you tonight, Dad,' he called as he went through the door.

But Dad was once again reading the card that Billy had written.

191

The operation for the removal of the cataracts was successful and Mam was soon back to resume her roles of house manager and geriatric nurse. The family had been aware for some time that Dad's mind was slipping, but a week of caring for him brought home forcibly how far he had descended into the fog of oblivion.

Chapter Twenty-Five

The second major cloud or headache facing Billy concerned the knitting student, Beryl Benson. At first, the constant clicking of needles as she knitted all through his lectures had been merely irritating and a distraction. He was new to the college and didn't want to start off on the wrong foot by alienating one of his students so he'd tried to be tolerant and reasonable, but after a few weeks of the noisy needles and the constant staring, he could take no more. The time had come to tackle the subject with her and with this in mind he sent her a note asking her to see him in his office.

'I've asked to see you, Beryl,' he said, 'to discuss a small matter privately with you. I didn't want to embarrass you by raising it in public. It's about your knitting. I would like you to stop doing it in my lectures. I think you would be better occupied taking notes like the others.'

'Sorry, Mr Hopkins.' She smiled, crossing her legs and exposing a liberal amount of thigh. 'I think your lectures are wonderful but I find I can concentrate better if my hands are occupied. And there's no need for notes because not only do I have my mother's workbooks, I have a good memory and can remember everything said in lectures, especially yours.'

'But can you rely on memory? The other students seem to need to take notes.'

'I'm not like the other students. I'm a little older than the rest and . . .' she gave Billy a flirtatious smile, 'a little more experienced.'

Billy ignored this obvious coquetry.

'What made you come to college, Beryl?'

'The last three years of my life have been hell,' she told him. 'Three years ago I was jilted at the altar. At the last moment, my intended changed his mind and left me standing there in my bridal outfit. It was a distressing experience that's left me bitter and one I shall never get over. Then eighteen months ago, my father died. I felt that my life had come to an end and I couldn't see the point of going on. A family friend suggested that I apply to a teacher training college to try and make a new start. So here I am. That's my life story in a nutshell.'

'I'm so sorry to hear about these traumatic events in your life, Beryl, and you have my sympathy. I do hope that you make a success of your time here in college. I'm sure these tragedies will help you to become a mature and wise teacher one day.'

'Thank you for those kind words,' she said, 'and I'm sorry if my knitting has irritated you. You'll be pleased to know that I've finished the garment I've been working on so I won't be knitting in the next lecture.'

She opened her briefcase and produced a bright red sweater.

'I want you to have it,' she said with a smile and placed it on Billy's desk. 'After all, I knitted it during your lectures and I was thinking of you the whole time.'

Billy was embarrassed. There was no chance he would accept the gift but, he had to play his cards carefully so as not to offend her.

'That's most kind of you, Beryl, and I'm touched by your generosity but I'm afraid I can't accept. I'm not sure the college authorities would approve of lecturers accepting presents from students in case we're ever accused of favouritism, I suppose.'

'Oh, very well, Mr Hopkins. I understand. I'm sorry if I've done the wrong thing and put my foot in it. The trouble is, and I hope you don't mind me telling you this, but you remind me so much of my father. He, too, was patient and understanding.'

Billy felt he had handled a tricky situation pretty well. After the next lecture, he wasn't so sure. Instead of knitting, Beryl Benson sat in the front row gazing up at him, studying his every move. It was better when she knitted, he thought. At least then she took her eyes off him from time to time to measure the sweater she was producing. Now her attention was continuous.

Some considerable time after he had asked her to stop knitting, she asked to come and see him 'on a personal matter', and that was when things started to go really wrong.

She arrived wearing a very short skirt. The nuns would have disapproved strongly; they enforced a strict dress code for residential students although they tended to be more lenient with the day people. Billy wished the sisters would lay down the same rules for all. Some styles, especially the mini mini skirts, could embarrass the men on the staff.

'I've asked to see you, Mr Hopkins,' she began, 'because there's something I have to tell you.'

Uh-oh, Billy thought. He sensed trouble.

'I've attended every one of your lectures on my course and I want to tell you how much I've enjoyed them all.'

'That's nice of you to say so.' Where was this leading?

'Listening to you for a year, I feel as if I've got to know you intimately. The truth is I find I'm very attracted to you.'

Billy was nonplussed for a moment. Speechless. A rare situation for him.

'It's flattering, Beryl, that a personable young lady like you could be attracted to an old codger like me. It's not unknown for students to become infatuated with their teacher. It may happen to you one day when you begin work in a school. But this course you're on is pretty demanding and it'll require all your concentration if you're to succeed. The best thing you can do is ignore these feelings you speak of and get on with your work.'

'Say what you like, Mr Hopkins, but I know in my heart of hearts that you're attracted to me too. I can tell by the way

195

you look at me in lectures and seminars. I can sense it. It's called animal magnetism.'

'Let me assure you, Beryl, that you couldn't be more wrong. I'm a happily married man with four children and I don't hold such feelings for you. I respect you and I've a regard for you as a student but that's it. Forget these feelings you say you have. I shan't mention today's little episode to anyone. It shall remain our little secret.'

'I understand perfectly, Mr Hopkins. You're in denial but deep down I know only too well that you love me as much as I love you. You're just too afraid to admit it. At the end of my latest essay for you, I've given my home phone number in case you ever want to discuss things with me. Every night I shall wait by the phone for your call.'

'I shan't be phoning you, Beryl. Once again, I repeat, I do not reciprocate these feelings of yours. Go back to your classes and let that be an end to it.'

Billy stood up to signify that the meeting was concluded. Beryl got to her feet and went to the door. Before she departed, she put her hand on Billy's arm, looked into his eyes and said, 'There's no point in fighting it, Mr Hopkins. You fancy me and want me, and you know it.'

Billy was left deeply concerned about the matter. Thank God I have Titch and Gerry Flynn next door to talk it over with, he thought. He approached his two colleagues and told them about the situation that had developed.

'It's the wisest thing you could have done telling us about it,' Gerry commented. 'At least we're all forewarned. From what I've heard, this lady's unusual personality is well known amongst the other students and if she begins spreading stories, I don't think they'll take too much notice of her.'

' "Hell hath no fury like a woman scorned," ' Titch quoted. 'Somehow, I don't think you have heard the last of this lady.'

His friend was right. News seeped back to him, through Titch and a few of the more sensible students, that Beryl had begun gossiping amongst her fellow students, accusing Billy of making sexual advances to her in a tutorial, of having a roving eye that stared overlong at her legs and her breasts so that she felt she was being stripped naked under his scrutiny.

'Ludicrous', was Titch's reaction. 'Women wear skimpy skirts and see-through blouses with the express purpose of attracting male attention and as soon as they get it, they cry stinking fish. It beats me.'

Despite Titch's attempt to make light of the situation, Billy was deeply disturbed by these scandalous allegations. If any of the rumours got back to the college authorities, they might have serious repercussions for him; at the very least they could scupper his chances of having his job made permanent. The gossip had to be stopped and perhaps the only way to demolish the lies was to face his accuser head on.

At the end of a lecture, Billy looked straight at Beryl and said, 'Could I see Miss Benson immediately after this lecture on a private matter, please?'

Beryl looked triumphantly round at the rest of the class.

'Of course, Mr Hopkins,' she said in a tone of fake humility.

When they were alone, Billy turned on her angrily.

'Look, Beryl, I've been patient with you. I'm truly sorry for the lousy hand fate has dealt you but I must warn you that if this tittle-tattle that has reached my ears doesn't stop, I shall report you to the college authorities and I don't know what action they'll take. They could suspend you or even expel you if it was shown that you're acting maliciously to blacken the name of a teacher in this college. It would be such a great pity if that were to happen because you've suffered enough in the past and I think this college course means a lot to you. But you seem almost bent on self-destruction.'

'I don't see how anyone could accuse me of acting maliciously since there's no evidence against me. After all, I've broken no law,' she replied petulantly.

'True,' Billy said ruefully, 'but one of these days you'll go

197

too far and put your foot in it and that'll be the end of a promising career.'

Beryl was not prepared to leave it there. She began a campaign of harassment. Her behaviour became more and more brazen, and her presence ubiquitous. She seemed to be always there: on the train travelling to and from college; in the front row of his lectures, knitting once again, no doubt to annoy him, staring at him with that irritating, mocking smile on her face; standing opposite his home, watching the house; and even when he was out shopping with Laura – she'd suddenly appear in the same aisle in the supermarket. Once or twice at home he'd been called to the phone, only to find no one there when he answered.

'I should definitely report the matter to the Principal,' Titch advised, 'before it gets out of hand. The longer you leave it, the worse it'll get.'

Gerry Flynn agreed with him. 'You'd be well advised to cover yourself before any of it reaches the boss. At least you'll be able to defend yourself in advance. I think this student deserves everything she gets.'

'The difficulty,' Billy replied, 'is that she's been cunning enough to leave no evidence. It would be simply her word against mine. I feel that the more I try to defend myself, the more people will think "the gentleman doth protest too much" or "there's no smoke without fire". I'd prefer to tackle the problem myself without involving college authorities. One day she'll overstep the mark, write me a note or give some other evidence, and then you just watch me act.'

Billy told Laura about the problem. She was livid when she heard the details.

'I've never heard of anything so preposterous,' she exclaimed. 'We may not be able to do anything about her conduct at college but we can certainly put a stop to this young lady's prowling round our house. At college I think you should apprise the Principal immediately of all that's happened before things get any worse and the stories become more exaggerated as they're bandied about. Of all people, Sister Benedict should be able to call a halt to this malicious rumour-mongering.'

Billy loved the way Laura immediately took his side, never questioned him for a moment, and talked about taking action in the first person plural, 'we'. Not *his* problem but *ours*.

The following weekend, Beryl duly began her surveillance on the other side of the road.

'Right, kids,' Laura called in the hallway. 'Time for action! Everyone outside as we planned it!'

She, along with the four children and their numerous friends, formed a line in the front garden and stared back, waving cheerily at Beryl across the way.

'This is like one of those "Who'll blink first?" competitions,' Matthew laughed.

It was Beryl who did the blinking when she decided to call it a day and, turning on her heel, walked away swiftly down the road. That was the last they saw of her in the district.

At college, Billy went to see the Principal and outlined the sequence of events.

'A certain amount of this talk had reached my ears,' she said, 'but I want you to know, Mr Hopkins, that I don't believe a single word of it. I've heard nothing but glowing reports of your work and your relationships here in the college from both staff and students. I know that this particular student has her personal problems but she must not be permitted to continue maligning you in this way. This whispering must stop forthwith. I shall call her into my office and issue an official warning that if she doesn't cease this vindictive behaviour, serious consequences will follow.'

Billy felt gratified that Sister Benedict had shown such faith and trust in him. Whatever it was she said to Beryl Benson, it seemed to work. She became less conspicuous; she took a seat at the back of the class, her knitting activity ceased and he no longer saw her on the train journey to and from college. Billy concluded that she must have made alternative travel arrangements or taken another train.

There was another consequence, or so it seemed to Billy. It may have been his imagination but while skirts did not go back to the New Look fashions of the fifties, they became noticeably longer. Billy wondered if the Principal had perhaps delivered a little homily to the students on the need to adopt a more modest form of dress if they were to become teachers and models for the young.

'Well, that's the end of another fine mess,' Billy remarked to Titch over a cup of coffee in the staffroom.

'Don't be so sure,' his pessimistic friend replied. 'You may have merely scotched the snake, not killed it.'

Good old Titch. He could always be relied on to give a cheerful slant on things.

Chapter Twenty-Six

It was six thirty on a Thursday morning. Billy and Laura lay side by side in bed. Both wide awake. Both trying to summon up courage to get up and face another day. First there'd be the madcap rush for the bathroom, then the usual squabbles about someone being in there too long. Thank the Lord they had two toilets, for at least that took the pressure off a little. Billy had had a shower installed and he wondered sometimes if that hadn't been a mistake, for Matthew and Lucy always seemed to spend longer than the allotted ten minutes per person on schoolday mornings. Anytime now Billy expected to hear the whingeing of one or other of them. It was always: 'Dad, will you come and tell Matthew (or Lucy) he's gone over the agreed time? He's been in there twenty minutes. He'll make me dead late for school.'

This morning, however, there was no whining. Strange, Billy thought.

Mark and John were no problem in this department. They liked water about as much as Samantha the cat, and their lick and a promise took no more than two minutes flat, with the result that Laura usually had to go in after them to check that they'd included the neck in their ablutions.

'Well, Laura, who's it to be this morning?' Billy asked.

'I made the tea yesterday. It's your turn.'

'Tell you what. I'll give you a tongue-twister and if you say it without a mistake, I'll make the tea.'

'OK, you're on. But then I give *you* a tongue-twister in return and if you get it wrong, you make tea today and tomorrow.'

'Agreed. Here's mine for starters.

Moses supposes his toeses are roses,
But Moses supposes erroneously;
For nobody's toeses are posies of roses
As Moses supposes his toeses to be.'

Laura repeated it without error.

'Now it's my turn,' she laughed. 'If you can say correctly "It's a braw, bricht moonlicht nicht" then I'll make the tea.'

'OK, Laura, you win. But that was unfair, quoting a foreign language.'

Still complaining, he swung his legs out of bed and was about to put on his dressing gown when he heard the most blood-curdling screams. It was Lucy. Billy and Laura froze.

'Mum and Dad, please come quickly. It's Mark. There's been a terrible accident.'

'Good God!' Laura yelled. 'What on earth's happened?'

'We're on our way!' Billy shouted, rushing from the room, closely followed by Laura.

Mark lay at the foot of stairs quietly moaning. His face and head were covered in blood. His head was propped up against the newel post and his feet were pointing upwards to the top of the stairs.

'Oh, Lord above!' Laura cried. 'He must've fallen down the stairs and hit his head against the post.'

'Everyone stay calm,' Billy said, taking charge. 'Where does it hurt, Mark?'

'The top of my head,' Mark groaned. 'I think I must have banged it hard.'

'Be brave, son. We'll soon get help. Best not to move though.'

'I'll call an ambulance,' Laura wept.

'Yes. And in the meantime, we've got Dr Gillespie next door. I'll nip round there and get him before he sets off for his surgery.'

Billy ran to the front door but before he could open it, Mark suddenly got to his feet and, beaming all over, said,

'April Fool, Dad! April Fool!'

'We caught you out there, Dad,' Lucy laughed. 'You should have seen your face!'

'That's not in the least funny!' Laura said angrily. 'You might have given us both a heart attack with your tomfoolery.'

'I think I *am* having a heart attack,' Billy cried out, clutching his chest.

'Don't you start as well, Billy. One prank like that is enough for today. Anyway, aren't you supposed to be bringing me a cup of tea? And Mark, go and wash that tomato ketchup from your head and face. Now!'

'Sorry, Mum and Dad,' Lucy said. 'It was my idea. It was supposed to be a joke.'

'Well, it wasn't funny,' Laura retorted. 'Remember the boy who cried wolf. There may be a real accident one day, and we won't know whether you're acting the goat or not.'

At breakfast, Matthew finally put in an appearance. 'What was all the yelling and shouting about?' he asked. 'I was in the shower and everyone seemed to be bawling at once.'

'April Fool's Day,' Mark reminded him. 'You've missed the fun and so has John. Where is he, by the way?'

'He's still in the toilet upstairs. Can't you hear him? He's singing his head off as usual.'

The family cocked their ears to listen and caught strains of 'She loves me, yeah, yeah, yeah' sung at the top of his voice.

'I hope John doesn't have the trouble I've had in the toilet,' Matthew complained. 'First of all the bolt on the door is missing and it won't lock. Next the toilet seat won't stay up. I wanted to do a wee and I had to hold up the seat with my left hand and hold the door shut with my left leg.'

'You must have looked like one of those ancient Greek discus throwers,' Billy guffawed.

'Not funny, Dad,' Matthew complained. 'It was difficult holding that position, I can tell you. Did *you* fix things that way?'

'Me? Me?' Billy said, feigning innocence. 'How dare you! How could you even think of such a thing?'

'You know, Matthew, you could have simply sat down on the toilet,' Laura said.

'I never thought of that.'

'All this rumpus about April Fool's Day,' Billy said. 'Why, I'll bet no one here knows what it means or how it came about.'

'I'm sure you're going to tell us,' Laura sighed.

'And I'm sure you're all dying to know. Take out your scribble pads and start taking notes. There'll be questions afterwards.'

'This is not a lecture theatre and we're not your students, Dad,' Lucy said.

'Doesn't matter. Pin your ears back and learn something.'

'Somehow I think this is going to be boring,' Matthew exclaimed.

'Hundreds of years ago,' Billy said, ignoring him, 'April the first was New Year's Day. Then along came Pope Gregory the Great with his revised calendar and moved New Year's Day to January the first.'

'How many hundreds of years?' Mark asked mischievously, as Billy knew he would. 'And why was he called Great? Was he big and fat?'

'It was fifteen eighty-two if you want to be exact and the term "great" was reserved for kings and people like that to show that they were the most famous people in history to have that particular name.'

'You mean like Alfred the Great? We've been learning about him at school.'

'Right. Anyway, many peasants refused to accept the new date and went on celebrating April the first as New Year's Day. The other people thought they were daft and so they called them April Fools and sent them on stupid errands like asking them to go and find a book called *The History of Adam's Grandfather* or to bring back some "sweet vinegar". After that, April the first was adopted as April Fool's Day and all over the world people today play tricks on one another. The victim's usually called a noodle. In Scotland the fool was called April Gowk and he had a Kick-Me card stuck on his back. Finally, you're not supposed to play it after twelve o'clock noon but that's being strict about it. I hope you got all that down.'

From under the table, everyone in the family, including Laura, suddenly produced score cards like the ones used to judge gymnastic displays. Billy's little speech was accorded: 5.9, 5.7, 5.5, 5.3.

'No one ever takes anything seriously in this house,' Billy lamented. 'I try to educate you and this is the reward I get. You make fun of everything.'

At that moment, the doorbell rang.

'I'll get it,' Matthew said. 'It's probably Des ready to go to school.'

A minute later, he was back. He looked worried.

'It's the postman with a registered letter for Mum and Dad.'

'I hope this is not another of your tricks,' Billy said, getting up from the table.

'Hardly that, Dad. It's the postman and *he's* not fooling about.'

Billy returned with an official-looking registered letter.

'It's from Damian College addressed to Mr and Mrs W. Hopkins. I've no idea what it's about as I think I've forked out for all the bills I'm supposed to pay.'

'Why not open it and see?' Laura said.

Billy tore open the envelope and read it quietly to himself. He blanched.

'Not good news, Laura,' he said, handing the missive to her.

Damian College,
Regina Park
Manchester.
April 1st, 1965.
Dear Mr and Mrs Hopkins,
    I am deeply sorry to be the bearer of bad news about your

son Matthew. Up to the present date, he has proved a model
pupil in every way. He has worked hard at his studies and
has been a keen participant of numerous sporting activities,
football, cricket, swimming. This makes it all the more
difficult to tell you that it has been decided at a recent
Board of Governors' meeting that we must ask you to
remove him from the school.

Last week, Brother Felix, one of our lay brethren,
happened to go into the toilet to carry out an inspection
and he found a group of fourth formers smoking. Inquiries
have since revealed that your son was the leader of this
group which I believe is referred to as the Smoking Club.
We are a Catholic college and we cannot tolerate such
behaviour in our pupils and we have no alternative but to
expel him. It may be of some consolation to you to know
that a number of others have also been accorded the same
treatment, including his friend, Desmond Gillespie.

Any payments for College Sporting Societies will of
course be refunded to you.

With profound regrets,
Brother Dorian, CFD

Laura, too, had turned pale. 'Oh, Matthew! How could
you! After all our efforts and our hopes, to have let us down
in this way.

'I hardly know what to say,' Billy raged. 'Fancy doing such a
stupid thing as smoking in the toilets. We're deeply disappointed
in you, Matthew. What were you thinking of, you idiot?'

'You used to smoke when you were at school, Dad. Most of
the Upper Fifth do, mainly at dinnertime when we're off the
school premises. Anyway, I smoke only ten a day.'

'That's ten too many,' Billy snapped.

'We had such high hopes for you,' Laura sighed. 'We
could see you one day distinguishing yourself at college but
now it's all gone up in smoke, literally.'

'I think the college has been a trifle hard,' Billy said

solemnly. 'They could have first given you a warning about how serious they regarded the matter. I got away with it when I was at school so I've no room to talk. But it's no use crying over spilled milk. It's happened and we'll have to face up to it. What are you going to do with yourself now, Matthew? What are your options? You can't hang around at home doing nothing. You'll have to look for a job of some kind.'

'I don't know what you'll do with your life now, Matthew,' Laura said tearfully.

Matthew felt things had gone far enough.

'I thought I might take up an apprenticeship as a chicken sexer,' he said with a cheeky grin. 'I hear there's good money in that.'

'A what?' Laura exclaimed. 'Wait a minute! This *is* some kind of spoof. It's another April Fool gag!'

'Well, is it, Matthew?' Billy fumed.

'I don't know, Dad, but oddly enough seeing you read that letter has suddenly made me feel hungry.'

'Hungry? How do you mean hungry?' Laura demanded. 'Is this letter a bluff or not?'

'Let's say that I'm looking forward to my last lunch at school today. I believe noodles are on the menu, my favourite dish. That *was* the word you used before, Dad, wasn't it? Noodles?'

'Why, you, bl . . .'

But whatever Billy was going to say was lost in the laughter of the three children at the table.

'Sorry, Mum and Dad,' Matthew chuckled. 'Des Gillespie and I hatched the plan. It had to be pretty elaborate to deceive you. We sent a similar letter to his folks.'

'But how did you manage to produce such an official-looking letter?' Billy spluttered.

'With difficulty,' Matthew said. 'It was a group effort really and half a dozen of us composed the letter and inserted our names. Des has a typewriter and we swiped some college notepaper from the office when the secretary wasn't looking. We sent it out to several parents. It was a lot of trouble but

207

was well worth it to see the expressions on your faces.'

'OK, you got us there,' Billy said. 'Let's hope that's the last trick of the day. Now, it's time for all of us to get a move on. What's happened to John, by the way? He's been a long time up there in the bathroom.'

As if on cue, John walked in from the kitchen. He had a saucepan on his head with the handle pointing out from his forehead. 'I am a Dalek. I am a Dalek. I am from the planet Skaro. I am going to exterminate you,' he rasped in an uncannily accurate imitation of the TV robots.

The family collapsed in gales of laughter.

'That has to top the April Fool's Day celebrations,' Billy chortled. 'Full marks, John.'

'What's more, it's the kind of prank I approve of,' Laura added, 'not the sort that could give us a heart attack.' Then she looked at her watch. 'Goodness me! Look at the time! It's gone eight o'clock. All of us had better get a move on if we're not to be late this morning. Right, John, let's put the saucepan back in the kitchen.'

Taking hold of the pan in both hands, she tried to remove it. It wouldn't budge. She took a firmer grip and pulled. It didn't move. Not an inch.

'Here, let me have a go,' Matthew said, grasping the pan in his fists and tugging at it. In vain. The pan was determined to stay on John's head.

'This is like a Grimm fairy tale,' Billy chortled. 'Right! Enough wasting time. Leave it to Dad as usual.' When it came to twisting lids off recalcitrant pickle and jam jars and the like, he considered himself to be the last resort when everything else had failed.

He locked his hands round the obstinate pan and heaved. Same result. The cooking pot was well and truly stuck.

John began to whinge. 'I can't go to school with this on my head. Everyone'll laugh at me.'

'Don't get excited. Fetch some butter from the kitchen,' Laura ordered. 'That should do the trick.'

'I'll get margarine,' Billy replied. 'No sense in wasting butter.'

Liberal amounts of the grease were smeared round the edges of the saucepan until the stuff ran in rivulets down John's face. It had no effect. The pot had become a permanent adjunct of his head.

'Now you have some idea of how the man in the iron mask must have felt,' Mark told him. 'And no one at school will try to push you around as long as you're wearing a hard hat. You've only to lower your head and charge and watch 'em run. And at Christmas, you might even get a part in a *pan*tomime.'

These observations didn't do much for John's morale.

'I hope I don't have to wear this thing for the rest of my life,' he whined. 'How am I going to comb my hair? And what will the nit nurse say when she comes to inspect us at school?'

Despite his lamentations about personal grooming, he remained stoical throughout the various attempts to remove the metal from his head.

'It's no use,' Laura lamented after the tenth attempt. 'I think we're going to need the help of the medical services.'

'Please don't take me to hospital,' John pleaded. 'I don't want to stay there again. And please, Mum, don't let them prick me with those needles.'

'Don't worry, son,' Laura said. 'I won't let them do such things. Not this time.' Then turning to the other kids, she said, 'OK, the rest of you, off to school! Dad and I'll tackle this problem. And we'll have no more wisecracks. Can't you see how nervous John is about having to go to hospital?'

'He looks more than nervous,' Matthew grinned. 'He looks *pan*ic-stricken.'

'OK, that'll do,' Billy said sternly. 'Now off to school with the lot of you.'

Grumbling that they were going to miss the fun, the eldest three left for school, leaving Billy and Laura with the hapless John. Billy phoned the college to tell them he had an emergency at home and would be late, suggesting at the same time that Titch might take his morning classes. They bundled John into the car and drove over to the Manchester Royal Infirmary Casualty Department in Nelson Street.

They presented themselves at the reception desk.

'What is the nature of the trouble?' the secretary asked, inspecting them over the counter, as if children with saucepans on their heads were a normal, everyday sight. Billy explained that they had an obstinate pan stuck on their child's head and they were seeking help to remove it.

'Please go into the waiting room,' she said. 'A doctor will call you in due course.'

It had been over five years, Billy reflected, since he had last visited this particular Casualty Department, when Lucy broke her arm. They pushed through the plastic door and found that things seemed to be the same as ever. Here was the same derelict crowd, the detritus of Manchester's nightlife: wild-eyed alcoholics and meths drinkers cursing the medical staff, heavily-mascaraed prostitutes cackling like a coven of witches over some shared joke about punters, plus an assortment of bandaged and injured casualties sitting or lying around the place, waiting for their names to be called.

The appearance of a young lad with a metal container attached to his head attracted hardly a second glance from the waiting assembly, though a drunk with bloodshot eyes called out thickly, 'Hey up, lads! Here comes Peter Pan!' which caused one or two people to look up, shrug their shoulders and go back to staring vacantly at the walls. After all, this was the emergency room and in here anything was possible.

A musically inclined female inebriate, however, felt sufficiently inspired to treat the gathering to an off-key rendering of 'Come follow, follow, follow, the merry pipes of Pan'.

Two hours later, John's name was called and the trio trooped into the surgery to meet a heavy-eyed junior houseman who listened to their sad tale. Using an instrument not unlike a motor mechanic's grease gun, he managed to lubricate the inner edge of the pan with a little oil. Success! The pan moved ever such a little. More oil was applied and then, joy of joys, the young doctor was able to twist and remove the stubborn piece of aluminium headgear.

John's face lit up when his head was finally released from the encumbrance and he realized he was free to go home. Though they'd assured him several times that the hospital wouldn't be keeping him in and wouldn't be pricking him with a needle, he'd not really believed them. For several weeks afterwards, however, his forehead was marked with an interesting red indentation, which made him something of a hero at school and provided a topic of conversation at the dinner table and in the staffroom at Billy's college.

After taking Laura and John home and eating a quick sandwich, Billy drove across to college. He went straight into what should have been his second lecture of the day, and found his class already waiting. No sooner had he begun to get into his stride than a student came in and interrupted him.

'There's a phone call for you, Mr Hopkins,' she said, her eyes twinkling. 'The caller didn't give her name.'

'Thank you, Lisa,' Billy said, noticing the smirk on her face, 'but I think it'll have to wait till I've finished my lecture. It'd be foolish of me to leave the lecture theatre to take a call from some mysterious female, especially on a day like today.'

Lisa Cookson smiled broadly, winked at the rest of the class and went to her seat.

These students must think I was born yesterday, he thought. When it comes to playing April Fool tricks, they're amateurs given this morning's events.

After the lecture Billy walked over to his room and there received the biggest shock of the day. He opened the door and was confronted by a sight that made his hair stand on end. An open coffin! And in it lay what appeared to be the body of a little old nun. He let out a rare expletive. 'Bloody hell! What in the name of . . .!' His mind went into a flat spin and he sought a logical explanation. His first thought was that some elderly nun had died during the night and they'd had to act hastily. They'd chosen his room to place the body having

211

assumed that he'd be absent for the rest of the day and because St Joseph's Hall was in a remote part of the college.

Am I going mad? he asked himself. This can't be happening. Anguished, he yelled for Titch and Gerry to come quickly. They came running, hearing the note of desperation in his voice. When they saw the reason for Billy's panic, they too recoiled horror-stricken.

'God Almighty, Billy,' Titch exclaimed. 'What have you done?'

Billy scowled at him in reply.

Titch approached the body gingerly to investigate.

He pulled back the white sheet covering the cadaver, not knowing what to expect. He looked up with a troubled expression.

'It's a hoax,' he announced. 'And not in the least funny. Whoever did this has a sick mind. The coffin's a painted cardboard box, the face is a mask, and the body's made up of pillows.'

Much relieved, Billy approached and examined the dummy. It had been elaborately constructed and dressed in a nun's habit complete with wimple. Whoever had perpetrated the trickery had demonstrated not only a warped sense of humour but considerable skill in building the model.

'Look,' Gerry said. 'There's a note pinned to the shroud. It's addressed to Mr Hopkins.'

Billy took the note and read it out loud to his colleagues.

Dear Mr Hopkins,
Please take a look at this body. Perhaps it may give you some notion of what will happen to me if you continue to reject me. At the end of all my essays, I have added my home phone number and yet you have never given me a single call. Why do you go on denying your love for me? Please, please phone. I count the hours till I hear the sound of your voice for only that can save me from this fate.

'It's the knitting student,' Billy gasped. 'The stalker! I thought she'd put all that business behind her. But she's gone too far this time.'

'I warned you that you'd not heard the last of her,' Titch said. 'I should bring the Principal and head of department over to see this latest handiwork. Her behaviour's not the kind you'd expect of a future teacher.'

'I agree with Titch,' Gerry said. 'From what you've told us about this lady, she's been careful up to now to avoid giving concrete evidence of her obsession but this blatant piece of black humour has got to be the last straw.'

Billy followed the advice of his two colleagues and invited Sister Benedict along with Sisters Peter and Paul to view the 'cadaver'. When they saw the elaborate trickery, they were aghast that a student in their college could resort to such a sick joke. Beryl Benson was summoned to meet the Principal and reminded that she'd been warned that any future misbehaviour would result in serious consequences. At a formal meeting of the Board of Governors, she was suspended from the college for a period of one year.

As it turned out, Beryl chose never to return and some time later Billy heard on the grapevine that she'd got back with her former fiancé and they had set another wedding date. For everyone's sake, Billy prayed that the man, whoever he was, turned up at the altar this time.

Billy drove home that day thinking he'd had enough of April the first capers to last a lifetime. It'd be a great relief to get back home to family and normality, for surely even they must by now have exhausted their repertoire of monkey tricks.

The kids were watching television in the lounge when he reached home. Laura was out but she had left a note.

Dear Billy,
It's been a wonderful April First this year and there have
been so many great and imaginative pranks that I feel
worn out. I have taken John over to my mother's for the
rest of the day. Will be back later this evening. You'll find
dinner in the oven.
All my love,
Laura

Billy opened the oven door to see what gastronomic delight Laura had conjured up, only to find a recipe book entitled, *A Dozen Delicious Dinners Any Husband Can Make*.

He went into the lounge to announce the good news to the goggle-box watchers.

'Well, what'll it be, folks? I can offer the speciality of the house, eggs and cheese mashed up in a cup, or the latest addition to my menu, Heinz alphabet spaghetti in delicious tomato sauce, or baked beans on toast. Alternatively I could nip out to the chippy for fish and chips. What's it to be?' As if he didn't know.

The vote was immediate and unanimous. Billy's culinary skills were rejected.

Chapter Twenty-Seven

'Let's suppose,' Billy said, 'that we're doing a radio play and we want to tell the story of Jonah and the whale in a modern setting. Any suggestions as to how we might tackle it?'

Billy was teaching a course to a group of college students on how to use a tape recorder in the classroom.

The students looked blank.

'Come on,' he exhorted. 'Surely you have some ideas! Remember the story. Jonah's working in the fields when God appears to him and tells him to go to the city of Nineveh and tell the people there that, unless they mend their evil ways within forty days, He'll wipe them all out. Jonah isn't too keen on obeying God's instruction and tries to run away by boarding a ship to Tarsis. But when a storm breaks out, the crew blame it on Jonah and chuck him overboard, believing he brought them bad luck. Jonah is then eaten by a whale which transports him across the sea and casts him up on the shore near Nineveh where he eventually delivers the Lord's message. That's the story in a nutshell. Now, how can we bring it up to date?'

'How about changing Nineveh to Las Vegas?' one bright student suggested.

'Good,' Billy said. 'That's a start.'

'We could call Jonah John Jones and let him be, say, an ordinary office worker,' added another.

'Excellent,' Billy said. 'But how would God using modern technology get in touch with this Jones character to give him his orders?'

Suggestions came thick and fast.

'By courier.'

'Letter by Royal Mail.'

'Nah. Too slow. He'd never get it. Better by telegram.'

'Better still by telephone!' Lisa Cookson proposed.

'Good idea,' Billy said. 'By telephone. Imagine the scene and the dramatic impact that would make. The play opening with the ringing of a telephone. Jones picking it up and saying something like, "Hello. John Jones speaking." '

Lisa followed through with another brainwave. 'We could have the operator saying, "Hold the line, please, I have a long-distance call for you." And then we'd need someone to play the part of God.'

'It'd have to be a man, of course,' a student named Ulla Barton added.

'What about you, Mr Hopkins?' Lisa suggested. 'You'd be perfect for the role of God.'

'OK,' Billy replied, missing the irony, 'though I've never aspired to such an exalted position.'

'Well then,' Lisa continued excitedly, 'after the phone operator has said her piece, you, Mr Hopkins, could say something like, "Good Morning, Mr Jones. This is God speaking. I have an important mission for you." '

'What about Jonah's attempt to escape?' Billy asked. 'How would he do that?'

'He could board a jet aeroplane, which has to ditch in the sea,' Ulla offered. 'That would keep the whale in the story.'

'You know,' Billy said, 'I think we have the makings of a first-class radio play here. What do you say we get the dramatic opening onto tape. Lisa, you and Ulla take the tape recorder over to your hall of residence and wait by the phone. I'll ring you from the public phone in the main corridor, pretending to be God. When you've recorded it, come back to class and we'll play it back to see how it sounds.'

By this time, the class was bubbling with enthusiasm for the play they were creating together. Billy, too, had become caught up in the fervour. He waited for a few minutes to allow the two students time to get to their hall and then went out to the public phone on the main corridor.

He picked up the receiver and dialled the number. The student playing the operator spoke her part, 'Hold the line, please, I have a long distance call for you.' Then Billy took the phone from her and spoke the lines as agreed.

'Good morning, Mr Jones. This is God speaking. I have an important message for you.'

'Sorry, Mr Hopkins,' said Lisa on the other end, 'I missed that. Could you repeat it, please, a little louder?'

In a ringing John Gielgud tone of voice, Billy spoke his lines. 'Good morning, Mr Jones. This is God speaking. I have an important message for you.'

At that precise moment, the Principal walked past on her way to her office and heard Billy's words distinctly. She paused for a moment with a puzzled expression, shrugged her shoulders and hurried by.

If it had ended there, the matter might have blown over and been forgotten.

A few sessions later, the class encountered a sound effects problem: how to produce the hollow echo of the inside of a whale's belly. They tried everything: an empty church, the public swimming baths, an ordinary bathroom. It was no good, nothing seemed to achieve the effect they were looking for. Then by accident Billy found the answer in, of all places, an empty metal dustbin. On the same main corridor there was a brand-new bin with a coolie hat lid, and he found that by placing the microphone inside and lifting the lid ever so slightly, the exact sound of a large empty cavity was produced. Perfect, he thought. At last! He got down on his knees, lifted the bin lid and by way of experiment called into the interior of the bin. 'Hello! Is anybody in there? This is God speaking!'

Unbelievably, at that moment Sister Benedict once again passed by. This time she stopped and after a long, hard look at Billy who was still on his knees with his head in the bin, she said gently but with obvious concern in her voice, 'Good morning, Mr Hopkins. I hope you are well. I take it that this is one of the latest educational methods you are demonstrating.'

'Yes, thank you, Sister,' he mumbled, taking his head out of the dustbin. 'We're doing radio drama. I am God and this is the belly of a whale.'

'I see,' she said, bemused. 'Most interesting.' Frowning, she went on her way, shaking her head in disbelief.

Billy wondered if he should resign there and then.

Later that morning he met Titch and Gerry in the staffroom and over a coffee described the morning's events.

'I've blown my chances in this college,' he lamented. 'I'm sure the Principal thinks I'm round the bend, a schizo with delusions of grandeur.'

'I doubt it,' Titch said reassuringly, 'though talking into a rubbish container and claiming to be God *is* a trifle bizarre. And you must find being God stressful,' he grinned. 'It can't be easy looking after the universe.'

'It's not, Titch. The pressure gets to me sometimes but I've got the whole heavenly host to help out when the going gets tough. Seriously, though, what do you think I should do?'

'The only thing to do is to get yourself in her good books again.'

'Either of you got any suggestions?'

Gerry said, 'Write an article for an academic journal and get the name of the college on the map. That should please her.'

'You make it sound so easy,' Titch said. 'First you've got to have something to write about.'

'There *is* one subject that's always interested me,' Billy said slowly, putting down his coffee.

'And that is?' they asked together.

'Students' reading. I've noticed in seminar discussions that some are well-read and others appear to have read practically nothing. I've already done some preliminary work on the subject.'

Titch was sceptical. 'Why this obsession with books? So what if they've no interest in literature? What does it matter? They're going to be teachers not librarians.'

'My dear Titch,' Billy replied haughtily, 'education happens to be a matter of reading books and if we have no respect for the culture of our ancestors, the best that's been thought and said and all that, we might as well shut up shop. I want to know if students who like getting their noses stuck into books make the best teachers, that's all. I think it's a subject worth investigating.'

'OK, OK, Hoppy, keep your shirt on!' Titch said.

'I'd like to send out a questionnaire to a few hundred students with questions like, who wrote *Nineteen Eighty-Four*, *The Origin of Species*, *Mein Kampf*? And as a test of culture, who built St Paul's Cathedral, who painted the Mona Lisa? Stuff like that.'

'Just because someone can tell you who wrote a book doesn't mean that she's actually read it,' Titch objected.

'Don't be so awkward,' Billy laughed. 'Maybe she hasn't read the work but at least she's acquainted with the world of literature. That's got to mean something.'

'Fair enough,' Titch said, 'as long as you don't ask them trick questions like who wrote Shakespeare's plays?'

'Well, who *did* write Shakespeare's plays, Titch?'

'Search me. I'd guess it was Francis Bacon or Christopher Marlowe or a bloke called Billy Shakespeare.'

'If I do write an article about it, maybe I could earn some Brownie points with Sister Benedict.'

'You've got no hope,' Titch said, grimacing.

'Thanks, Titch, for your usual enthusiastic support.'

'Any time, Billy.'

It was on a Monday morning two months later that Billy heard from the *Education Journal*. He rushed into the dining room to show Laura a copy.

'Who'd a thought it, Laura? My name in print for the first

time! It may be in a publication that nobody reads but that doesn't matter. It's there in black and white! Recognition at last!'

A couple of hours later, he was sitting in his office looking over his notes for his next lecture when the phone rang.

'Mr Hopkins?' an official-sounding voice asked.

'Speaking,' Billy answered.

'Mr William Hopkins, Senior Lecturer in Education?'

'The same,' Billy replied, now concerned as to the identity of the speaker. Worrying thoughts flashed through his mind. Was he in trouble? Who was it? The Inland Revenue? H.M. Customs? The police?

'This is John Izbicki, Education Correspondent of the *Daily Telegraph*. I wonder if you'd like to add any comments to your article on general culture which is published today?'

Billy was flustered. How had the *Daily Telegraph* got hold of his article which was tucked away in an obscure research journal?

'The only thing I have to say,' he stammered, 'is that the article is the result of research among many hundreds of students, some of whom were brilliant and others less so.'

'Thank you, Mr Hopkins. May I quote you on that?'

'Certainly.' Bewildered, Billy put the phone down. What on earth was happening?

The phone continued to ring for the rest of the morning. Every national newspaper wanted a comment: the *Daily Express*, the *Daily Mail*, the *Guardian*, even the *Daily Mirror*.

Billy and the college were in the national spotlight for the rest of the day.

Titch and Gerry burst into his room at lunchtime.

'My, you're a dark horse and no mistake,' Titch exclaimed, flinging the morning newspapers onto his desk. 'You've put the cat among the pigeons this time. Secondary school heads are gunning for you and college lecturers want to award you a VC for putting up such a spirited defence on their behalf.'

'I can't help wondering,' Billy mused, 'why the press decided to give the article such prominence at this particular time.'

'I once worked on a newspaper,' Gerry said. 'This time of the year is the so-called "silly" season when newspapers are stuck for copy and interesting news. Your article was exactly what they were looking for to provide them with a few spectacular headlines.'

The newspapers, however, had not reported the research accurately but had concentrated on the howlers that Billy had described, especially the one where some misguided student had named the architect of St Paul's Cathedral as Christopher Robin. The *Morning Star* blamed the poor results on the corrupt capitalist system while an Oxford scholar writing to *The Times* said he was not surprised the students couldn't name the author of the *Odyssey* as classical scholars had been arguing about it for over forty years, to which another correspondent replied that everyone knew from Mark Twain that it had been written by a blind poet named Homer, or if not by him then by another blind poet of the same name. Giles of the *Daily Express* devoted the day's cartoon to the theme with a drawing of a classroom with one of the pupils turning round in his desk to say to his companions, 'And George Best invented the steam engine.'

For one day Billy became a celebrity and enjoyed Andy Warhol's fifteen minutes of fame.

But how had it gone down with Sister Benedict? That was the question that concerned Billy. It was hard to tell until the article was given respectability by no less a publication than the *Times Educational Supplement* when it described the work as 'significant'. One morning, Billy passed the Principal on the now infamous Jonah-and-the-whale corridor and she gave him a broad smile and said, 'Well done!' And he knew he was in again.

'There's one nutty nibble left,' Laura said. 'Who wants it?'

'BAGZZIT!' cried Mark, snatching it with cobra-like speed.

'Aw, that's not fair,' John wailed. 'He didn't give me a chance.'

It was Friday night and the family was sitting in the garden in deckchairs having tea and enjoying the evening air at the end of the week.

It's funny, Billy mused, the way kids establish their right to something by 'bagzzing' it before anyone else can say the word. Supposing the law adopted a similar procedure in establishing ownership. In his mind's eye, he saw the case being tried in a small claims court.

The prosecuting counsel would say something like, 'M'lud, my client young John Hopkins would claim ownership of the last nutty nibble by virtue of his tender age and need for sustenance.'

'But did he utter the expression "bagzzit" first?' the judge would ask testily.

'No, m'lud, but his need is greater than the accused's because of his weaker constitution.'

The judge would deliver his final word on the matter. 'If your client did not utter the word "bagzzit" before the accused, it's an open and shut case and he fails in his claim. The court finds for the defendant. Case dismissed.'

'It's been one heck of a week,' Billy heard Laura saying as he played out the litigation scene in his mind.

'Yes, it certainly has, Laura,' he agreed. 'I had no idea that my simple investigation would cause such a rumpus. But I must say I was disappointed at the poor showing of some of the students who couldn't answer even the easiest of questions. I thought everyone would know who wrote *Oliver Twist*. Why, I'll bet our own kids could have done better!'

'Why not try us out, Dad?' Matthew grinned, biting into a slice of Swiss roll.

'OK. Let's see how well you do. We'll start with you, Matthew. You should know this one. Who wrote *A Farewell to Arms*?'

'Easy. Jack the Ripper,' he said with a big grin.

'Very funny. Quit fooling about. We're checking out my research here. Try this one, Lucy. Who wrote *Gulliver's Travels*?'

'Was it Lily Putt, Dad?' she giggled.

'You're worse than the students,' Billy snapped. 'This was a serious piece of work. Maybe we can get more sense out of the junior members of the family. Here's an easy one for you, Mark. Who painted Mona Lisa?'

'No idea, Dad. But I know Lisa didn't like it. That's why she was a moaner.'

'I give up. Everyone in this family regards life as one big joke. Let's try the youngest. I'm sure our John won't let me down. OK, son, you show 'em. Here's one you're sure to know because I've seen it on your bookshelf. Who wrote *The Three Musketeers*?'

'Rag, Tag and Bobtail.' He too was infected with a fit of the giggles.

Billy's hackles rose. 'Doesn't anyone ever take things seriously? Your mother'll set you an example, I'm sure. Come on, Laura, let 'em see what's meant by general knowledge. Who wrote *Carmen*?'

'I thought everyone knew that,' she chortled. 'It was Henry Ford and Son.'

'Laura,' he barked. 'These kids of ours are forever acting the goat. Now I know where they get it from. It's from you.'

'Then you should rejoice. Maybe we'll produce a bunch of comedians, like Ken Dodd or Tommy Cooper.'

'We already have, Laura.'

Chapter Twenty-Eight

It was a Friday night in 1967, a year after Billy's moment of glory, and Billy was sitting with his four children watching television. Laura was in the kitchen cooking a special dinner to celebrate an important event. Although there had been some hairy moments in Billy's career at college, he had somehow kept a clean slate and had been rewarded at last with security of tenure. It meant that, if he wanted it, he had a job for life. To mark the occasion, Laura was preparing a family dinner and the smells wafting from the kitchen made the mouth water and set the gastric juices flowing.

They were watching a pretty imbecilic programme about a bunch of adolescent boys and girls cavorting to the raucous racket produced by spotty guitar-playing youths with long hair dyed in blindingly bright colours and gypsy clothing.

'That jangling noise,' Billy said, 'which goes by the name of pop music is like the sound of the Kellogg's corn flake factory when it's working flat out. Switch the damned thing off. I want to turn over to the news.'

'Dinner's ready,' Laura called through the doorway. 'My goodness,' she exclaimed catching a glimpse of the TV screen. 'They look like the Wild Men of Borneo. Who are they?'

'They're the number one pop group, Mum,' Matthew replied. 'They're called the Pretty Things!'

'I'm sure they are in your eyes,' she laughed, 'but if ever I see you looking like that, please stop the world for I shall want to get off. It'll be a case of "Beam me up, Scotty".'

'And I'll join you,' Billy said. 'We can book our passages to Mars.'

'It's a date. Anyway, dinner's ready!'

And what a dinner it was! Roast beef, Yorkshire pudding, peas, cauliflower with white sauce and, luxury of luxuries, not one roast potato, which had been Billy's normal ration in pre-marriage days, but several. The main course was to be followed by a special dessert of apple pie and custard.

'This is the main reason I married you,' Billy grinned mischievously. 'I took one look at you in your mother's kitchen, all those years ago in nineteen forty-eight, when your nose was smudged with flour, and I said to myself, that's the girl for me. I wasn't the type to be taken in by glamour and superficial beauty.'

'If you go on making that patronizing speech,' Laura said, 'I shall let fly with this roast potato.'

'Sorry, Laura,' Billy laughed. 'It's my peculiar way of expressing appreciation for your culinary wizardry.'

'You have a strange way of putting it but after seventeen years of marriage, I think I'm beginning to understand you.'

'Sorry, Mum,' Lucy now piped up, 'I know it's a lovely dinner and all that but I can't eat all this food you've put on my plate. Much too fattening. And please don't give me any meat as I don't believe in eating dead animals. I'll have the vegetables and one small potato.'

'Where *do* they get these mad ideas?' Laura exclaimed.

'From her friends at school, I should think,' Billy replied.

'Look, all of you,' Laura said. 'Eat what you can. Sometimes, I wonder why I bother.'

The men of the family had no such hang-ups and set to demolishing the dinner as if there was no tomorrow. There was solemn silence as they continued consuming the main meat course with concentrated dedication, savouring every morsel. It was Laura who broke the spell believing, as she did, that the business of eating should be accompanied by elevating conversation.

'This wood-turning that you're doing in the cellar, Billy,' she said, 'is making the whole house vibrate; it's as if we're having an earthquake. Not only that, it's depositing a thick layer of wood dust on everything in the house. Can't you find another hobby, something less messy?'

'But I love working down there, Laura,' Billy replied. 'Practical work gets me away from stuffy old education for a little while. And there's something hypnotic about watching wood whirring round and round on a lathe while you cut and shape it. Then there's the satisfaction of producing something beautiful in Brazilian mahogany.'

'We've been learning about ecology at school, Dad,' Lucy said, 'and you're exhausting the scarce resources of the earth. The hardwood you use is helping to destroy the Brazilian rainforests. It's a complete waste of resources.'

'Like your bra,' Matthew said through a mouthful of roast potato. 'Why, Dad's got a bigger bust than you.'

'Mum, please stop Matt from poking fun at me.'

'Matthew, don't speak with your mouth full and stop teasing Lucy,' Laura chided.

'Did you know that mini-dresses are subject to purchase tax,' Matthew continued, 'only if the bust size is over thirty-two inches? So that lets Lucy out!'

'Before you criticize others,' Lucy pouted, 'you should think about your own miserable name. Matt! That's something people walk all over and wipe their feet on. And in the art world "matt" means dull and colourless so there's one in the eye for you.'

'I may be dull and colourless but you and your friends simply contradict yourselves. The shoes you're wearing and that leather jacket Mary Feeney wears are all from dead animals.'

'He's at it again, Mum.'

'I'm an old cowhand, from the Rio Grande,' Matthew sang.

'OK, that's enough out of you two,' Billy admonished. 'Anyway, Laura, to get back to the wood-turning business, which everyone seems to be against, I don't only turn wood, I make furniture down there. High-quality stuff, as you know.'

226

'What I call Robin Hood furniture,' Laura said.

'Robin Hood furniture?'

'It's basic, rough-hewn. Looks as if it's been made by outlaws who've run away to the forest and only have rough axes to work with.'

'Thanks for all these compliments and after all the nice things I said about your cooking. That's it! I shan't touch another piece of wood as long as I live. But what about my wine-making? Surely you can't object to that? It's a nice, quiet hobby and it won't be long before I'm producing wine to rival the French and the Italians.'

'My friend Des and I have tasted some of it,' Matthew said, now joining in the discussion. 'It nearly took the top of our heads off. We reckon it should be called Rotgut and marketed as a paint remover.'

'And how can we ever forget your first bottles of wine?' Laura chuckled.

'I shall always be grateful to my family for its unfailing encouragement in my initial faltering steps into viniculture,' Billy said. His mind went back to the time he'd brought up the first six bottles of elderberry. He'd put them on top of the kitchen cupboard and looked forward to sampling them with dinner in the weeks to come. That night he and Laura had been woken up by the sound of gunshots.

'Billy! Billy!' she'd called, poking him in the ribs. 'There's someone downstairs in the kitchen.'

'Nonsense,' he said. 'You're dreaming.'

Then he, too, heard the crack of a firearm. He looked around the bedroom for some weapon to defend his family. There was nothing but a tennis racket. That'd have to do. Cautiously he crept downstairs ready to confront the intruder, switched on the kitchen light expecting to catch the burglar red-handed but there was nobody. But red was the right word because the kitchen had been transformed; it resembled the scene of the St Valentine's Day massacre after Al Capone's hoodlums had done their night's work. The

227

walls, once pale cream, were now crimson with elderberry wine.

'Well, what was it?' she asked anxiously when he got back. 'Was it a thief or Samantha knocking something over?'

'Nothing so dramatic. But you'll be pleased to learn that during the night little pixies have come into the house and given your kitchen a new bright décor. I think you'll like it.'

Billy had never been allowed to forget the episode. His mind came back to the present.

He cut himself a largish piece of beef and put it into his mouth ready to enjoy its succulent flavour when Matthew made a sensational announcement.

'I'm going to start a band.'

A vision of the long-haired Wild Men of Borneo flashed through Billy's brain and he guffawed so loudly that the chunk of meat slid down his throat with astonishing ease and lodged there. Quietly he began to choke.

Nobody noticed.

'You're going to form a band?' Laura laughed. 'What on earth does that mean? What sort of band? A rubber band? A band of robbers? A band of brothers? A Band of Hope? What?'

'No, a band of musicians. Des and I have got a bunch of pals at school together to play music. We're going to call ourselves the Aquarian Angels.'

'Aquarians! Sounds fishy to me,' Laura giggled.

'Me and my friends could be singers in it!' exclaimed Lucy. 'Mary, Sally and I could form your backing group.'

'No, me,' said John. 'I've got the best voice in this house.'

'Yeah, we've all heard it coming from the toilet,' Mark said. 'It makes all the windows rattle. But I could supply the clarinet parts,' he added. Mark had been learning the instrument for eighteen months and already fancied himself as Benny Goodman.

Billy got to his feet.

'Laura, I think I'm in trouble,' he said calmly. 'I have a lump of beef stuck in my gullet. What am I going to do?'

'Can't be. You're still talking. Are you sure the meat's still there and that you haven't swallowed it?'

'Positive.'

'I read somewhere that a fishbone can be moved with breadcrumbs,' she said. 'You could try that.'

'I think that might make it worse. This isn't a fishbone, it's meat.'

'If you were a baby, I could turn you upside down and slap your back but you're too big and heavy for any of us to lift you.'

'Laura, this is serious. Really serious.'

The family looked on silently and helplessly, not knowing what to do for the best.

Billy's only thought was: I've got about four minutes until brain damage sets in. He'd read about people suffocating on food obstructing the windpipe. Was this the end for him? What an ignominious way to go! Fancy arriving at the Pearly Gates with a lump of beef stuck in your gizzard. Why, St Peter might even accuse you of gluttony and send you down to the other place.

He went into the kitchen and swallowed hard. He felt acute pain as the meat moved past his Adam's apple. It was a critical and anxious moment.

Matthew, now sixteen, had grasped that the jesting was over and followed Billy through into the kitchen to see if there was anything he could do. Summoning up all his strength, he delivered a hefty thump to his dad's back. Something he'd often wanted to do but not in circumstances like this. All in vain. The meat was well and truly jammed in Billy's throat like a cork in a bottle. At least my windpipe is clear, he thought. If that had been blocked, I'd now be lying dead or at least fighting for breath. He thought he'd double-check to see if the obstacle was still there by sipping a little water. Any remaining doubt was now dispelled. The liquid remained right there bubbling in his throat. There was no getting away from it; he was in trouble.

'I think I'll skip dessert tonight, Laura, even though it looks delicious. You can share my apple pie and custard among the kids.'

'Good-oh. Thanks, Dad!' Mark and John chorused.

'I think you'd better phone Dr Travers immediately,' Laura said, now worried.

'But it's not an emergency, Laura. After all, I'm not choking, I'm breathing normally and so it can't be so serious that I should bother our GP on a Friday night when he's at home trying to relax. Supposing he's having dinner with his family and I interrupt it with my trivial complaint? That won't make me very popular, will it? From time immemorial in my family, there's always been an understanding that you never disturb the doctor at weekends unless it's a life-threatening situation. And it's hardly that.'

The truth was that Billy hated visiting his doctor at any time. And certainly not on a Friday night. It had been drummed into him from early childhood that calling out a doctor on a wild goose chase was the cardinal sin, a throwback to the old days when home visits had had to be paid for.

'In that case,' Laura said, 'why not take yourself straight down to casualty without bothering the doctor?'

'What? To join the derelicts and the down-and-outs? Not a chance. At weekends, the casualty department belongs to Manchester's lowlife with their black eyes and broken heads. I'm not dying or feeling ill. I'm hoping the obstruction will simply go down by itself.'

Nevertheless when Billy retired to bed later that evening, he was privately anxious. Throughout the night he remained sitting upright in case the obstruction moved and blocked his airway. There was no sleep to be had. If I'm going to snuff it, he thought, I want to be awake when the grim reaper comes to call.

In the bathroom next morning, he tried a few sips of water but the position was unchanged: the liquid could not get past the blockage and he had to spit the water out into the washbasin.

'*Now* will you go to casualty, Billy?' Laura pleaded.

'I think the meat is bound to move of its own accord,' he replied. 'There's no danger as it's gone past my windpipe. I have to be patient.'

Saturday went by slowly. A football match on the television provided a distraction and helped to pass the time but not much. His hunger pangs were becoming acute. He was still convinced that the obstacle would move without intervention, especially after he'd read in the medical encyclopedia how the gullet worked. As chewed food passes into the pharynx at the back of the throat, it said, the upper sphincter opens and the muscular contractions carry it into the oesophagus and into the stomach. The movement had nothing to do with gravity. There's absolutely nothing to worry about, he told himself. Good old nature will come to the rescue. No need for hospitals and medics. I have simply to wait and the problem will be resolved by a series of involuntary muscular spasms.

On Sunday, though he was famished, he went with the family to Mass as usual and prayed that God might break up the logjam and allow him to swallow but at Communion he decided not to tempt providence or the Lord by taking the sacrament.

Laura watched him anxiously out of the corner of her eye in case he keeled over.

'Stop worrying, Laura,' he said. 'I'll be at the doctor's first thing tomorrow morning.'

Throughout the ordeal, the enforced abstinence from food and drink had sharpened his olfactory sense to the highest degree. The odour of cooking emanating from the kitchen after church became sheer torture and his taste buds screamed for satisfaction. At breakfast, he had to go into the lounge away from the sight of the family tucking into bacon, egg, tomato and toast but even there his tongue was hanging out as the delicious smells floated in to him. And what would he have given for a cup of tea? His soul, that's all!

The rest of the day crawled by oh so slowly, hour by hour, minute by minute: the Sunday newspapers remained unread, and he could only half watch the afternoon programmes on television. By evening, he was faint with hunger and dehydrated into the bargain. I don't think I can take much more of this, he said to himself.

Another night of sitting up followed and the hours ticked painfully by as he waited for dawn. His fitful sleep was filled with wild, crazy dreams of Christmas turkey dinners and pints of ice-cold lager.

Next morning, weak though he was, he staggered over to the doctor's surgery. He'd found from past experience that no matter how bright and early he got there, he was invariably at the back of the line. Some of them must camp outside the surgery all night, he thought. This particular morning was no different. He arrived at eight thirty but there was no use his thinking he'd be first because the waiting room was already full. As he entered the room, everyone looked up expectantly, hoping it was the frosty-faced receptionist come to admit the next patient into the inner sanctum. When they saw it was yet another old crock like themselves come to pollute the air with his germs, they looked angrily at him for a moment then went back to scanning the dog-eared magazines.

Billy sat down to wait his turn. The sallow-looking lady on the next chair shuffled up hastily to make room for him. It looked like an act of kindness but was really fear of contagion. He sensed an air of tension and hostility about the place and, like passengers on the London underground, they avoided eye contact, looking immediately away if by accident their gazes locked on. There was no sound in the room except for the snorting and the snuffling of a few sufferers and the riffling of pages as people browsed through the tatty journals. Billy pretended to be reading a copy of last year's *Country Life* but what he was doing was glancing surreptitiously at the other people, wondering what they'd got. He guessed his immediate neighbour had jaundice or maybe yellow fever. Was that infectious? To be on the safe side he edged a little further away. And what about the man with the graveyard cough? How many germs was *he* transmitting? I'm probably the healthiest person in this room, he thought. Merely an inconvenient chunk of roast stuck in my oesophagus, that's all that's wrong with *me*. I'll be lucky to get out of here without picking up some serious disease. But even in that waiting room, time passed and after an hour of melancholy meditation, he found himself at the front of the line and immediately began to feel well again. Typical, he thought. It was always the case. As your turn to see the doctor approaches, your ailment begins to clear up miraculously. I'm here on false pretences, wasting the doctor's time. I'm sure the blockage has gone. Then he heard his name being called at last. He snapped out of his reverie and went into the surgery.

Dr Travers nodded and waited expectantly for Billy to say something.

'On Friday evening, Doctor,' he began. I sound like a real whinger, he thought. 'I inadvertently swallowed a large piece of roast beef and I think it may be still stuck in my throat.'

Dr Travers smiled indulgently. 'I doubt it,' he said, 'but I'll take a look. Good dinner, was it?'

The doctor held Billy's tongue down with a spatula and looked into his mouth.

'There's no meat down there as far as I can see. Mind you, I'd be surprised if there was. The roast beef will have gone down by now. Why, last week I had a patient in who'd swallowed his denture and that slipped through his system without any trouble. It's most unlikely a piece of meat would get jammed there.'

I knew it, I knew it, Billy thought. I'm here bothering the doctor when there's nothing wrong with me. Thank heavens I didn't call him out on Friday night. I've been so long here in the waiting room I've not had a chance to check my throat for an hour or so. So, as I suspected it would, my gullet has cleared up automatically, thank the Lord.

'But I'll give you a note for the casualty department,' he heard the doctor saying. 'Better go down to the infirmary this afternoon to be on the safe side.'

After lunch, other people's lunch that is, Billy went down to the now familiar Nelson Street casualty department. I have been here so often, he thought, they'll soon be inviting me to their staff dances. He introduced himself at reception and was given a long form to fill in. In the old days, he mused, they wanted to know about childhood illnesses like measles, mumps, chickenpox, but now they're interested in knowing all about my personal history: present and former addresses and for how long? Place of employment and how long? Am I married, divorced or living with another person? If so, sex and racial background of my cohabitant? And it was no easy matter filling it in because the blunt pencil was secured to the pad by a short piece of string.

'That's a very detailed questionnaire,' Billy remarked to the receptionist. 'I'm here for my throat not for a job in your office.'

He went into the main waiting room and was greeted by the prostitutes, the alcoholics, and the vagrants as an old friend and one of the family.

'So how's that young lad of yours getting on?' a stubble-chinned tramp inquired. 'The Dalek kid with the tin helmet?'

'Did they ever get that bloody pan off his head?' a harlot bawled. 'He was such a lovely boy. It'd be such a shame if he'd to spend the rest of his life with that stuck on his head. Give him my love and tell him to use a non-stick pan next time.'

Billy felt a warm glow knowing that he was accepted as one of the regulars and in some small way it compensated for the long wait he knew was coming. And why not a long wait? After all, that was why it was called the waiting room. It was a room specially made and furnished for waiting. Come to think of it, we spend most of our lives waiting for something new to happen. We begin life in the womb waiting to get born and then as kids we can't wait to be grown-up. After that we wait for marriage, for promotion, for the cheque in the mail, for the winning line on the pools. It's always a lovely day tomorrow. There's even a play by Samuel Beckett entitled *Waiting for Godot*. The only person who doesn't wait is the waiter who makes his customers wait.

He picked up a copy of the *London Gazette* and went into his usual trance. Several hours later, he was jolted into consciousness by hearing his name called. He put down the magazine and went forward. To see the doctor? Not a chance. It was to waiting room Number 2, which was much smaller and had no reading material. It was an act of wanton cruelty to raise hopes in this way. All they'd been queuing for was the next waiting room. At least, he supposed, it was a sign of progress. Maybe each waiting room led to yet other smaller waiting rooms like one of those Russian dolls or box puzzles with a smaller box inside another box, which went on until you reach the final box which is a tiny cube. Maybe the last waiting room is the size of a telephone kiosk with a dwarf-like surgeon waiting to examine you. Another catnap followed until he was finally ushered into the presence of the same weary young houseman who'd removed the pan from John's head.

Once more Billy explained his predicament, his account having acquired an impressive fluency through frequent repetition. The same routine followed except that the young doctor looked deeper into the recesses of his throat by means of a torch and a miner's lamp attached to his forehead. Billy waited to hear the familiar 'there's nothing there' diagnosis but was surprised to hear the medic say, 'Go home quickly and come back with your night things. You've got a blockage down there. Delay could be dangerous.'

It was good news and bad news. Good in that he'd been proved right all along, bad in that it now meant a stay in hospital.

Billy took a taxi home and was back within the hour, having explained to Laura that at last help was on the way. Supervised by a nurse in the ward, he got into his pyjamas, settled into bed, and waited for someone to make the next move. Fellow patients, like convicts, were interested to know what he was in for but by this time he was so weak he could only manage to mumble the briefest account. As usual the surgeons had been run off their feet that day and it was late into the night before they got round to Billy. Towards midnight, he was wheeled down to theatre and given a general anaesthetic. He knew no more until he was back in the ward and felt a hand shaking his shoulder. It was 2 a.m.

'Are you OK?' asked a doctor, still masked and robed.

'Fine,' Billy said sleepily. 'Did you find anything down there in my throat?'

'We did indeed,' he chuckled, 'half a pound of best sirloin steak.'

'It was roast beef,' Billy managed to grin.

In the bedside cabinet, he had reserved a bottle of Ribena in anticipation of this moment. Now he mixed himself a glass of the cordial and drank. In his life, he had once tasted champagne and on one memorable occasion a rare French claret but nothing on this planet then or in the future would ever equal the ecstasy of that sip of blackcurrant. He had been eighty hours without food or water. It had been a close run thing.

A month after the operation, Billy was invited to attend the hospital for an X-ray to investigate what they considered a defective swallowing reflex though he could have told them his difficulty had been caused not by any physical or muscular failing but by Matthew's bolt from the blue with his dramatic announcement that he was going to start a band. Billy arrived bright and early at the outpatients' department and found a large crowd of people dressed in floral shorty nighties. He'd been through this routine before and had learned that it was

236

wisest not to put up resistance or arguments about having to dress up in this piece of feminine apparel. It was back to waiting again but on this occasion there were lots of diversions to help while away the time. A pinstriped bowler-hatted City gent arrived with his wife and it was obvious from the start that he was a rookie because he began objecting to the senior sister about the nightie being an affront to his dignity and did they know who he was and how important a person he happened to be? Billy was thoroughly entertained by the verbal battle that followed because he knew only too well the inevitable outcome.

'I'm only here to have a sprained wrist checked,' the man complained. 'Surely I don't need to wear a nightgown for that.'

He'll learn, Billy thought.

Prevailed upon by his wife, the man eventually caved in, went into the cubicle and emerged in the flowery dress but still wearing the bowler.

'It doesn't suit you at all,' his wife commented. 'That bluebell pattern doesn't go with the colour of your eyes. And I think those gowns are supposed to tie round the back.'

'What do you mean?' the man said, twirling round and giving the waiting assembly a generous view of his derrière.

'Now I understand what is meant by those letters ICU,' Billy chuckled.

'It stands for intensive care unit, surely?' the man said.

'Not if you say it slowly. I-C-U,' replied Billy.

Next patient was a spotty-faced adolescent with his mother. He was adamant and refused point blank to wear the garment.

'It's either that,' the nurse told him, 'or no medical treatment for your fractured collarbone. Please yourself.'

'Come on, Wayne,' his mother coaxed, 'don't be such a baby. Look at all these nice gentlemen. They're not in the least embarrassed.'

Reluctantly, the youth went into the cubicle with his gown but would not come out.

'Everyone'll laugh at me,' he whined.

'Nonsense,' his mother said. 'Everyone's the same and they all look equally stupid.'

The boy was unmoved and there he remained until it was time for his visit to the radiology room.

Hospital authorities claim that it's essential to don these outlandish garments, Billy reflected, but sometimes I can't help wondering if it's part of a power struggle and there's an element of wanting to humiliate the patient into submission.

Eventually, it was Billy's turn to be X-rayed and for the best part of half an hour, he swallowed and reswallowed some unnamed but noxious substance as X-rays were taken of the movement of his epiglottis. It was a relief to get back into his civilian clothes and all he had to do now was wait for the results. But before he left the building, there was a general announcement to the waiting assembly that the X-ray machines had been faulty and the whole afternoon's work was therefore invalid. Would patients please make new appointments to return so that fresh plates could be made?

Billy decided to call it a day and take a chance on his oesophagus system being OK. He never went back and he'd have been willing to bet a month's salary that neither did the VIP businessman.

The original cause of the trouble, Matthew, went on to organize his band. As Billy worked on his 'Robin Hood' furniture in the cellar, he was only too aware of the rehearsals of the Aquarian Angels. From the lounge above, the music Billy loved had changed. Beethoven was out. The Beatles were in. Mozart was taken over by Manfred Mann, and strains of 'Do Wah Diddy Diddy' accompanied by loud foot-thumping on the floor floated down to him below as he produced his thirteenth coffee table. The piano recitals were now augmented by Des Gillespie's trumpet, somebody's double bass, a set of drums and last but not least Lucy's trio backing group. The noise of Billy's wood-turning activities which had so rattled the house previously was as a hamster turning on its wheel compared to the thunderous din coming from the 'Angels'. For some strange reason, Laura did not object.

'We must encourage them,' she said. 'You never know, we might have another Hollies or Herman's Hermits. And they have to have some place to rehearse.'

'What do you think of our backing group, Dad?' Lucy asked. 'It's far out, don't you think?'

'Not far out enough for me,' Billy replied. 'It's a cacophony.'

'Is that good, Dad, like polyphony?'

'Maybe you should look it up in the dictionary.'

A month later, the Angels had their first gig in Cheshire. When the group drummer, Tom Stephens, arrived at the house, Billy was in the lounge listening to a record of a Bach toccata being played on the harpsichord.

'Now that's what I call really boring music,' Tom remarked to Matthew as he waited in the hall. 'There's no oomph to it.'

Billy, along with Dr Gillespie, had the honour of driving the group with its heavy gear to its venue in Handforth in Cheshire, promising to collect them at 11 p.m. At ten forty-five, the two fathers were there to collect their musical prodigies and their entourage. It was a chance to see and hear the band in action.

The dance hall was well-nigh deserted except for one or two couples who were trying in vain to dance to the tuneless sound and the unrhythmic beat.

'Do you know if the band is ready to go home yet?' Billy asked the doorman.

'As far as I'm concerned,' he said, 'they can go any time they like.'

'Well, that was our first gig,' Matthew said as he loaded the gear into the car for the trip home. 'I think it went well, don't you?'

Tom Stephens and the backing group girls agreed whole-heartedly.

'Fantastic,' they chorused.

'What did our two fathers think?' Des asked, looking at the two dads for support.

'We arrived too late to hear much,' Billy lied. 'Maybe you should seek out the opinion of the doorman on these gigs as he will have heard the whole performance. But that was an unusual modern piece you were playing at the end. Modern and avant-garde. What was it?'

'That was Jimi Hendrix's "Purple Haze",' Matthew said.

'An appropriate title,' Dr Gillespie observed. 'It certainly made a deep impression on me.'

'Not only has it been a great night,' Tom Stephens declared, 'we also made five pounds. That's ten bob each, leaving thirty bob for us to celebrate our first gig with a trough at the chippy on the way back.'

The two cars pulled in at the Cheadle Heath Supper Bar where fish and chips plus a bottle of Tizer and a bottle of dandelion and burdock were on the menu for everyone.

'So this is what living in the fast lane is like,' Billy remarked.

'Let history take note of this date,' Matthew announced portentously in a President Kennedy voice. 'Nineteen sixty-seven. The year the Aquarian Angels had their first gig. We always knew we'd make it big one day,' he grinned, 'but we didn't expect it to come so early in our careers.'

Chapter Twenty-Nine

'You're going to be late this morning, Billy, if you don't get a move on,' Laura said when she saw Billy pouring himself a second cup of tea.

'No hurry today, Laura. I've got teaching practice supervision this morning. I've got a school to visit and I don't have to be there till half past nine.'

'Lucky old you! The kids left for school over half an hour ago.'

'You don't have to tell me how lucky I am, Laura. I've been at this college for over three years now and I've come to like the job more and more with each passing day.'

'You wouldn't think so to hear you moaning about it when you've got a pile of essays to mark.'

'Ah, you've picked on the one thing I find heavy going but I love the rest of it: the lectures, the seminars, the tutorials. But most of all I love teaching practice supervision because it gets me away from the academic stuff and back into the classroom where I feel most at home.'

'From what you've told me, Billy, the students don't sound too fond of TP. Understandable, I suppose, since you're the one handing out the assessments and they're on the receiving end. Are you still using the old five-point scale?'

'That's one thing that hasn't changed, Laura. It's still A for distinction, B for very good, C for average, D for adequate, and E for failure.'

'And the grades you award are still a matter of your opinion. A student's grade doesn't depend on you alone, I hope.'

'Not at all. There's a whole raft of people involved. There are the teachers in the school, the personal supervisors, the subject tutors, and maybe external examiners. Personally I put most trust in the class teachers' judgements as they see the students in action every day. Today I'll be taking a look at two of Titch's students to see if I agree with his assessments.'

'It all seems pretty arbitrary to me, Billy. Who can tell the difference between good and bad teaching? And how can you be sure how they'll teach when they're not being observed?'

Billy laughed. 'It's like the driving test, I suppose. If you can demonstrate to the examiner on a given day that you can drive satisfactorily, you pass. If you make a hash of it, you fail.' He looked at his watch. 'I'd better get going.'

He put on his hat and coat and collected his briefcase.

'See you tonight, Laura,' he said, giving her a peck on the cheek.

'Drive safely,' she said as he went through the door.

Billy's port of call was a secondary school in one of the poorer districts of St Helens. He found the school easily enough but wasted ten minutes walking round its perimeter trying to find the entrance. Always the same, he thought. Some of these schools are like fortresses with all the doors locked. As he circumnavigated the building, he noted the absence of litter and graffiti, which were often evident in some inner city schools. In his experience, he'd found that neat and tidy surroundings usually indicated that the place was well run with good standards of discipline.

Eventually with the help of a late-arriving pupil, he found an unlocked door at the back of the building. Billy presented himself at the school office to make sure the head teacher was aware of his presence – necessary protocol, he'd found from bitter experience; he'd once gone straight to the classroom without going through the accepted channels and been reprimanded like a naughty schoolboy.

Miss Debrett, the head, gave him a warm welcome and ushered him into her office where he found the students' form mistress and the modern languages teacher waiting for him.

'You have two of your students here,' the head said, 'and they're as different as chalk and cheese. In the case of Sybil Thornley, the history student, we've been extremely pleased and found her to be absolutely first-rate. In fact, we think so highly of her that, if she were ever to apply for a job here, we'd have no hesitation in appointing her. But with Miss Maria Medina, the other student, it's a different story, I'm afraid.'

'I agree wholeheartedly with the head,' Mrs Anderson, the form teacher, said. 'Miss Thornley is an outstanding student. Her lessons are beautifully prepared and her presentation in class has been exemplary. In fact,' she chuckled, 'Miss Thornley is so popular with the girls that I don't think they'll want me back when she returns to college.'

'When it comes to Miss Medina,' Miss Godley, the language teacher said, 'it's not good news, I'm sorry to say. I was so thrilled and delighted when I heard we were to get a Spanish-speaking student as it was so unusual and I thought she'd be a great asset in our Spanish class but she's got problems, as you'll see for yourself after break.'

Billy was conducted to the classroom of Form 3, and before he'd even entered the room, he detected the quiet hum of purposeful activity, a sound he'd come to recognize after twenty years in the teaching profession.

Sybil Thornley was a neatly dressed student of small stature, no more than five feet tall. She came forward to greet him with a slightly nervous smile, and it was obvious that she was a little tense. Who wouldn't be? he thought. After all, who likes another person sitting at the back of your classroom observing your every move and listening to every word you utter?

'Good morning, Mr Hopkins,' she said, handing him her practice file. 'I've reserved a place at the back of the class for you, if that's OK.'

'Thank you, Miss Thornley,' he answered. 'That's fine. I look forward to seeing you teach. I've heard good reports of you.'

'Thank you, Mr Hopkins. I hope I don't let you down,' she answered anxiously.

The class of thirty girls were now on their feet. 'Say good morning to our visitor,' Miss Thornley said.

'Good morning, sir,' they chorused.

'Good morning, girls,' Billy replied as he settled down in the seat reserved for him, trying, as far as possible, to make himself inconspicuous.

Billy examined the file. Miss Anderson was right. It had been immaculately kept. He noted, too, the numerous visual aids on the walls relating to 'Transport Through the Ages', the project she'd been studying with her class. Billy sat back to watch, sensing that he was going to enjoy it. She opened the lesson by recapping her previous lessons with a stream of brisk, lively questions.

'Let's go back two hundred years in time,' she said. 'Imagine a world without the modern transport we have today. How did people move themselves or their goods from place to place?'

'They walked, miss,' a girl called out.

'No calling out,' Miss Thornley said sternly. 'Raise your hand if you want to answer.'

Billy noticed the ring of quiet authority behind her admonition. Her pupils noted it too.

There was a forest of hands.

'Please, miss,' said one pupil, 'my dad calls walking Shanks's pony. What does that mean?'

Miss Thornley joined in the laughter which the question had caused. 'Shanks is another way of saying legs.'

She glanced anxiously in Billy's direction, wondering if it was OK to laugh like this in class. Her ready sense of humour, however, was a point in her favour and Billy made a note of it.

It wasn't long before the class was answering her question

about modes of transport with enthusiasm.

'By stagecoach, by scooter, by penny-farthing, by sailing ship, by barge, by hot-air balloon, by using animals.'

'Good!' she said warmly. Miss Thornley soon had them eating out of her hand.

She went on to give a vivid account of the success of George Stephenson's 'Rocket' at the locomotive trials held at Rainhill ('not a stone's throw from this school') in September 1829, the building of the first railways, and the excitement and fear of the first passengers. Throughout she illustrated her points with pictures and cartoons from *Punch* which she had enlarged on the college epidiascope. Finally she set the class an activity requiring them to imagine they were amongst the first railway passengers and to describe their experiences as if writing a newspaper report. As they worked, she walked among them answering questions, encouraging and rewarding them.

At the end of the lesson, Billy thanked her and came away. Sometimes he felt that being able to watch a talented student like the one today was one of the chief rewards of his job.

He was not looking forward to observing the second student, Miss Medina. From what Titch had told him, she had everything going for her since she was bilingual, her father being assistant lecturer in Spanish at the University of Liverpool, and she was fairly good at her academic work. Her problems lay in the classroom. By all reports she simply could not teach. At break, he sought her out to reassure her that he was no ogre but had simply come along to see if he could offer advice and help. She was a tall, thin girl with pale complexion and seemed withdrawn, which Billy put down to shyness. He looked over her TP file and noted the lack of planning and substance to her lessons. She seemed unclear about her aims and what the pupils were expected to learn in a particular lesson.

'What's the subject of your next lesson, Miss Medina?' he asked gently.

'Miss Godley gave me the idea of teaching the girls numbers by playing Bingo in Spanish.'

'That seems like a good suggestion. Do you have the numbered cards et cetera?'

'Oh, yes, Mr Hopkins.'

Billy waited ten minutes to give her the opportunity to settle her class before making his way to the same Form 3 he'd observed in the history lesson. As he walked along the corridor, he heard an unholy row coming from the room. It sounded like bedlam. He could hardly believe it was the same form. As he opened the door, he was met by a noisy, bawling, shouting, gesticulating gaggle of girls. Chaos reigned. Some of the pupils were kneeling on their desks and yelling 'Bingo' while one or two were screeching profanities at each other; others were pushing and scuffling to get to the front of the scrimmage. In the middle of the room, surrounded by a crowd of jostling pupils stood Miss Medina, a fixed smile on her face.

'How's it going, Miss Medina?' he asked her gently.

'Oh, I think it's going well, Mr Hopkins,' she simpered.

'What's happening now? Where did the Bingo-in-Spanish idea get to?'

'The girls refused to play it in Spanish and would only play it in English.'

'Why didn't you insist on Spanish?'

'Oh, I did, I did, Mr Hopkins, but they simply ignored me and I had no choice but to go along with them. Otherwise, I think they'd have broken the place up.'

Billy sat at the back of the room to watch. He was sorely tempted to take over and restore order but realized that would have been fatal and a sure way of destroying the student's confidence once and for all. His main cause for concern with her was that she seemed unable to assert any authority and instead was resigned to letting the pupils set the agenda. She'd lost control and was being swept along by her charges. Sometimes a classroom, he reflected, could become like a den of lions unless firm control was established from the beginning. School kids were forever trying it on to see what they could and could not get away with.

He sat it out to the bitter end and then returned to college for the afternoon session. It had been a strange morning, he reflected. From an A student to an E; from the heights to the depths.

In the afternoon, he reported back to Titch.

'I think your assessments are spot on, Titch. Sybil Thornley's a clear distinction and a joy to watch while Maria Medina's teaching was painful to behold. She's a weak personality and I think it'd be merciful to suggest that she find some other profession. If she took up teaching, her life would be hell. It's not the end of the world for her though; she'll have no difficulty finding a job as a translator or an interpreter.'

In the last week of the teaching practice, external examiners came to the college to visit and observe the teaching of selected students as a check on the accuracy of tutors' assessments. After four days going around schools, a final meeting with the college staff was held to standardize assessments, reconcile differences and to award final teaching marks. The nuns always prepared a magnificent lunch for the visitors, staff and students on these occasions. The sisters knew what they were doing all right, Billy mused. Soften the examiners up, get them into a mellow mood by providing a cordon bleu lunch in the hope they'd be generous in their evaluations.

After the meal, the college staff assembled in a spacious wing of the dining hall awaiting the appearance of the examiners who had been in private discussion with the Principal. There was an air of tense expectation when the five academics, one elderly male professor not unlike Neville Chamberlain, and four ladies in large hats, filed into the room. The staff rose to their feet. After a preamble praising

247

the work of the college and a few words of introduction, the chairman said, 'I should like to call on our first examiner, Miss Vanessa Frankland, to give her report on the students she's been to see.'

At the end of the table, Miss Frankland adjusted her pince-nez and consulted her notes and stood up to address the meeting.

'Well, yes,' she said pompously. 'I went to see your Miss Debrett early this week. I agree with your assessment. Her teaching was extremely poor and ill prepared. It'd be a disaster if we were to allow her to enter the teaching profession. I have no hesitation in awarding a failure.'

Throughout this little speech, Titch who was sitting immediately behind Billy, was jumping about and waving frantically. Hello, I wonder what's got into him? Billy thought. Must be the wine at lunchtime gone to his head.

Titch at last caught the eye of the chairman.

'Yes, you want to make a comment?' the silver-haired professor inquired.

'Yes, I do,' Titch said. 'Miss Debrett is the headmistress of the school.'

There was consternation at the examiners' table as they cleared their throats and hurriedly rechecked their notes.

'Ah, yes, now I see,' Miss Frankland stammered. 'That's the head of the school. The student in question is Miss Medina. Sorry, sorry. My mistake. And as for the other student, a Miss Sybil Thornton, brilliant teaching. A clear A if ever I saw one.'

At least she nearly got that right, Billy smiled to himself. It was Thornley who was the distinction. Let's hope they give the right mark to the right student.

The meeting continued smoothly without further mishap until the chairman himself gave his assessments.

'I accept the mark for Margaret Brown,' he said. 'Below average. Not up to standard. Definitely a D.'

Now it was Gerry's turn to fidget and to wave from the back of the room.

'Yes, what is it?' the chairman said testily. 'I believe I got the name right, didn't I?'

'You got the name all right,' Gerry said. 'But we've got Margaret Brown down as a B, not a D.'

The aged professor looked flummoxed. But not for long.

'Yes, I can see that. I suppose looked at from another angle she could be a B. Very well, put her down as a B.'

Goes to show how pointless this exercise is, Billy chuckled quietly to himself. Surely that must be the end of the misunderstandings now. Wrong! There was one more tricky situation to resolve. The last lady examiner gave her reports and everything was fine until she reached the final mark she had awarded.

'I watched Miss Armstrong teaching art and there's not a shadow of doubt in my mind that she is outstanding. A clear A in my book.'

'Agreed,' the art lecturer called out. 'Our best student this year.'

Nice to see such ready agreement, Billy reflected. Now, maybe we can all go home. No such luck. The head of the English Department was on his feet.

'Miss Armstrong is probably the worst teacher it has been our misfortune to meet,' he said. 'We cannot accept any mark but an E, a failure.'

Uh-oh, Billy thought. This dispute could go on all night. I hope Laura remembers to put my dinner in the oven.

'I see, I see,' said the professor, meaning that he didn't. 'We must compromise. Would you accept a C for overall performance?'

'Under no circumstances,' the head of art snapped. 'She's a distinction student. An A and nothing else will do.'

'If she gets an A,' the English tutor snorted, 'I resign here and now.'

It looked as if the two departments which had locked

horns had reached an impasse over the innocent Miss Armstrong. Perhaps the only way to resolve the deadlock, Billy thought, is by having an arm wrestling contest between the two men, in which case the art man would have prevailed as he was sixteen stone of solid muscle.

It was Sister Benedict who came to the rescue.

'Why not give the student qualified teacher status but include on her certificate a rider that she's not qualified to teach English?'

This was accepted, if ungraciously, by both parties.

'Thank the Lord that's over,' Billy whispered to Titch as they came away from the meeting. 'I wouldn't mind but, except for the failures, we don't even tell the students their teaching mark; it's a secret locked away in the files at the Ministry of Education. Well, anyway, that's the TP meeting over for another year. And now, show me the way home. Thank God it's Friday. How I'm looking forward to the weekend. I'm planning on taking the kids for a hike on Saturday in the Peak District. That should help blow away some of the mental cobwebs.'

'OK, Billy. See you on Monday morning.'

Chapter Thirty

Billy was having a nightmare. In his dream, the house was ablaze and he was standing with the family on the little bedroom balcony at the front of the house. He was panic-stricken and the family clung to him. Then came blessed relief when he heard the clanging sound of the fire engine as it tore down Wilmslow Road. He became aware of someone digging him in the back. It was Laura lying by his side.

'Billy!' she said urgently. 'The telephone! The telephone! You'd better go and see who it is!'

He looked at the electric clock on the bedside cabinet. It was 5 a.m.

'Who in heaven's name is ringing us at this time of the morning?' he groaned.

In this world there is nothing more distressing than the strident ringing of a telephone in the early hours of the morning. It can mean only one thing. Bad news.

Quickly he put on his dressing gown and went down to the hall.

'Hello,' he said thickly into the mouthpiece.

'Oh, Billy! Billy!' the voice cried. 'Thank God I've got you. It's about your dad!'

Billy's mouth went dry and the thump of his heart began pounding in his ears.

'What is it, Mam? What's happened?'

'I've had a call from the police. Your father's at Willett Street police station. They found his name and phone number in his cap. They want me to go and collect him. Oh, Billy, I don't know what to do. He's gone off wandering in the middle of the night and got himself lost again.'

'First of all, Mam, stop worrying, if you can. I'll put on some clothes this instant and go down and get him.'

'Please, Billy. Bring him straight home to me. I don't want him put in the cells.'

'Leave it to me, Mam. I'll have him back home in a jiffy.'

He put the phone down and went to tell Laura what had happened.

'The police?' she gasped. 'What's he doing with the police? I do hope he's not in trouble.'

'I'll call the station to find out what's going on, Laura,' he said, 'and then I'll have to go over to Collyhurst to get him.'

'Right, Billy. While you're on the phone, I'll make you a coffee before you go.'

Billy found the number in the directory and got through to Willett Street and asked if they had a Thomas Hopkins there.

The voice on the other end was careful not to say that they actually had such a man there but they did have a gentleman who had a card in his cap which bore the name that he had mentioned. The card was not proof of his identity as the man they were holding did not seem to know who he was. He was mixed up. The person they'd taken into custody had been found prowling about the district and knocking on people's doors at four o'clock in the morning, asking for directions to Smithfield Market. The people he'd disturbed had been terrified out of their wits and one of them had rung the police. Billy asked to speak to his dad but the officer refused, insisting that he should come and collect him and bring some form of identity to prove that he was indeed his son. 'We can't be too careful these days,' the policeman said.

Billy dressed quickly and drank a hurried cup of coffee to help him shake off his slumber.

'Sorting things out may take some time, and I may be late getting back,' he explained to Laura as he opened the front door.

Before he could step out, Matthew caught him on the threshold.

'It's Saturday, Dad. You won't forget our spends, will you? And I thought we were going for a hike in the Peak District later.'

'Sorry, Matthew. A family emergency has come up and so the hike's off for this weekend at least. I've left your spends together with the housekeeping on the dressing-room table.'

'Thanks, Dad.'

'You're a good man,' Laura said, giving him a kiss. 'And you're a good provider.'

'Thanks, Laura.' He smiled ruefully. 'I can see it now. I'm on my deathbed and the kids'll be saying, "Before you fall off your perch, Dad, where did you leave the chequebook?" '

'If I didn't know your sense of humour, Billy, I'd say you were a cynic,' she smiled. 'You get off and help your dad. Any idea when you might be back?'

'Not a clue.'

'OK, Billy, we'll see you when we see you. I hope everything turns out all right.'

At Willett Street police station, Billy went up to the desk sergeant and explained the purpose of his visit, namely to collect his father who'd been troubling people in the early hours of the morning by ringing doorbells and knocking on doors.

'He was trying to get to Smithfield Market where he used to work,' Billy told the sergeant.

'Well, I can tell you he's frightened a hell of a lot of people who were not expecting callers at such an early hour of the morning,' the officer said.

'Sorry about that,' Billy said. 'He thinks he's still a porter in the market.'

Billy showed his proof of identity then signed release documents before he was allowed to see his father.

Billy was taken aback when he saw him. He was sitting on

a wooden chair in an empty room staring into space, a feeble, shrivelled-up old man. He seemed crushed. He was unkempt and unshaven and was still wearing that perennial cloth cap of his. And this was the father who'd been so fastidious about his appearance in his younger days. His eyes were red-rimmed, he looked scared and completely washed out. He'd told people he was lost and he looked it. A stranger would have been forgiven for mistaking him for a meths drinker. He turned to face Billy when he opened the door but there was no immediate smile of welcome or recognition.

'Thank God, Jim. I thought you were never coming,' he mumbled, 'but I knew you'd come to get me out of here in the end.'

Billy wondered about being called Jim but let it pass.

'I hope you can prevent him wandering off again,' the sergeant said, addressing Billy as if Dad wasn't there. 'We'd hate to see him back here and I'm sure the people he troubled won't want to see him again either.'

In the car on the way back, Dad sat for a good twenty minutes without saying a word but when he did speak, it gave Billy a jolt.

'You know, Jim,' he said, 'it's good to see you. We never thought we'd see you again when you went off to sea on the *Empire Light*.'

'I'm not Jim, Dad,' Billy protested. 'I'm your youngest son, Billy. Jim was killed in the war.'

Dad looked bewildered for a moment.

'You're wrong there,' he said. 'Our Jim's not dead. I saw him this morning when I was on my way to work.'

Billy thought it might be best to change the subject.

'Dad, you're eighty years of age. Much too old to be thinking of portering in Smithfield Market.'

'I'm as strong as any of these layabouts I've seen down there in the market. And I don't trust any of 'em. If I don't get down there one of them'll pinch my cart.'

Billy knew it was a waste of time arguing. Dad was

convinced that he could still do a murderously hard eight hours' work pulling a cart. No use disagreeing.

'How did you get yourself lost today, Dad? You've been going to the market every day for over seventy years. I thought you'd know the way by now.'

Dad continued staring out of the window as if looking for someone.

'I caught the bus all right but on the way, I saw Danny and young Mary standing with our Jim at the bus stop. They waved for me to get off and it was then I got lost.'

Billy's dad seemed to be living in some parallel universe. Danny was Mam's brother who died in the trenches and young Mary was his daughter who died of diphtheria at the age of five in 1916. As for Jim, that was his son who'd been lost at sea in the merchant navy in 1943. Was it best to humour him and accept his hallucinations as reality? Billy was no psychiatrist but decided this was probably the best course.

'Were they still there when you got off the bus, Dad?'

His dad looked at him as if he were mad. 'Of course they were bloody well there. They walked some of the way with me talking to me and then they had to get back to wherever they came from. When they'd gone, I looked round and I didn't know where I was. So I knocked on a few doors to see if they could direct me. I don't know what all the bloody fuss is about.'

Billy reached across the car and put a hand on his shoulder. 'Anyway, I'm here now, Dad, to take care of you and get you back home.'

Still gazing out of the window, he grasped Billy's wrist with his hand; it was icy cold with fear.

When Billy pulled up outside the bungalow in Martindale Crescent, Dad asked, 'Why am I in this car and where've we just come from?'

Billy reminded him of the events and the visit to the police station but they didn't seem to register.

Billy was relieved when they got inside the bungalow.

Maybe Mam would know what to do. He'd been shocked when he saw his dad at the police station but if anything he was even more appalled when he saw his mother. She looked distraught and completely worn out.

'Thank God you got him back,' she wept. 'When he doesn't take his pills, he doesn't know what he's doing. I was so tired, I fell into a deep sleep on the bed settee in the living room and he must have sneaked out without me hearing him.'

She made Quaker Oats and a pot of tea for them both. His dad spooned the porridge down voraciously. Then she made Dad take his medication and tucked him into bed. He was asleep in seconds.

Billy phoned round the family and told them what had been happening and suggested they hold one of Mam's 'conflagrations' to discuss what should be done. Sam in Belfast was most upset when he heard the news, especially since he could not get over to visit. Les recognized the seriousness of the situation and undertook to drop everything and catch the bus to Langley immediately. His sisters Flo and Polly said they were not surprised to hear of Dad's escapade as they'd seen it coming. When they'd done Mam's shopping on Friday, they'd noticed his utter confusion. They promised to come at once to talk it over.

By two o'clock, everyone was there.

'We've seen him getting gradually worse from one week to the next,' Billy's eldest sister, Flo, said. 'When he started seeing people who have been long dead, I thought his mind had gone.'

Mam said, 'He's been losing his memory for a long time. First he kept losing things like his pension book, his keys and the thing he treasures most, his little racing diary, which he's been keeping since nineteen thirty-six. He used to enter up all the family events like births, marriages and deaths but all that's stopped now. I never know what he's going to do next. The other day, he came out wearing his underpants over his trousers. Some days, he doesn't even know who he is or who I am.'

'I'm worried about you, Mam,' Polly said. 'All this trouble must be affecting your own health. You look absolutely whacked. Are you getting enough sleep with all this disturbance?'

'It's not easy, Polly,' she lamented. 'I have to sleep on the bed settee because Dad keeps wandering about during the night. I have to stay awake in case he walks into the wrong place. A couple of nights ago, he walked into the wardrobe, and the night before that he went into the pantry. But last night I was in such a deep sleep I didn't hear him slip out of the house.'

'What we have to decide today,' Les said, 'is what we're going to do about him. These hallucinations he's having must mean that he's suffering from dementia and I think he needs professional help.'

Dementia. The word was out. Everyone had been avoiding saying it. But Les was right. Dad did need help.

'I don't want him to go into a home,' Mam sobbed. 'That'd break his heart. And mine as well,' she added. 'Besides, there are times when he's his old self and he's sensible. Maybe he's going to get better.'

'Nobody's putting him in a home, Mam,' Flo said, 'but you're going to make yourself ill if you don't take care of yourself. Then there'll be nobody to take care of him.'

'I think we should ask Social Services to examine him,' Billy said, 'and advise us as to the best course of action. They may take him to a home for a temporary period until he's better. One thing is sure, Mam. We're all going to need endless patience. This dementia Les talks about is like the lights in his brain being gradually switched off. Dad is unhappy and confused. It's as if he's groping his way in a mental fog. A doctor might be able to think of something that'll give him some relief.'

It was agreed that Billy would arrange for a doctor to

examine Dad and report back. Meanwhile, the family would keep an eye on things and if the situation became much worse, Dad might have to be hospitalized for his own good and for the sake of Mam's health.

The sound of voices brought Dad out of the bedroom. Dementia was a strange illness that could blow hot and cold. One moment he'd be completely disorientated, the next, thinking clearly again. Confusion interspersed with moments of clarity, like the sun coming from behind a dark cloud and then slipping back again.

'What's going on?' he inquired suspiciously. 'Why's everyone here? It's not about me, is it?'

'Now, Tommy,' Mam said. 'Don't go jumping to conclusions. Come on, you've had a good sleep and it's time for a nice cup of tea.'

Dad sat quietly in the armchair near the fire.

The conversation turned to normal subjects, like the children and how they were doing.

'I don't know where we went wrong,' Les chuckled. 'We've tried to bring our kids up as decent socialists and look at 'em. They've turned out to be Tories. And they've nicknamed me Pinko and our Tony who's a little to the right of Genghis Khan will insist on singing "Hinky Pinky Parlez-Vous" on every conceivable occasion.'

'Ours are just as awkward,' Billy laughed. 'Our two eldest look on Ho Chi Minh and Mao Tse-tung as the new Messiahs and their bible is the Little Red Book.'

'Kids today just want to be contrary,' Polly said. 'It's exactly the same with our lot. Anything to wind us up.'

The discussion continued along these lines until Billy's two sisters announced it was time for them to depart.

'My kids'll be going mad for their tea,' Flo said. 'We'll be in touch, Mam. Don't forget to phone if you need us.'

After they'd gone, Dad spoke up.

'Who were them two ladies? Were they nurses from the welfare?'

'They're your two daughters, you daft bugger,' Mam said.

'I didn't know I had any daughters,' he muttered. 'And who are these two big fellas? They've not come to take me away, have they?'

'They're your two sons, Tommy. They've come round to help.'

Billy stood up to go. He offered to give Les a lift home, which he gladly accepted.

They drove for a while in silence, deep in thought, still trying to come to terms with Dad's dramatic escapade. It was Billy who spoke first.

'You know, Les, I'm supposed to have had an education and all that. A fat lot of good that's been when it comes to dealing with Dad's problems – his loss of memory, his mood swings, his repetitions like a stuck gramophone record, and his panic attacks, especially when you remember what a fearless tyrant he used to be. I think he's going to get worse, and if he goes into a geriatric home, I don't think he'll be coming out. I told Mam it'd be a temporary stay so as not to frighten her and to get her used to the idea gradually.'

'It goes to show,' Les said. 'We never know how old age is going to hit us. It gets you thinking about how it'll come to you and the possibility that one day you too might lose your mind. I often wonder whether dementia is inherited and if we're going to go the same way as Dad.'

'I doubt it, Les. I think Dad's mental state is probably due to his heavy drinking after work. I read somewhere that alcohol abuse over a long period can shrink the brain, in which case you can dismiss the notion that it's a family gene.'

'Thank God for that,' Les said.

'Though they do say,' Billy laughed, 'that the first sign is loss of short-term memory. Like the fellah who went to the doctor's surgery.

'Patient: "Doctor, doctor, I think I'm losing my memory."

'Doctor: "When did this trouble begin?"

'Patient: "Which trouble?" '

'Big joke!' Les said. 'But it's not so funny when it happens to you. I often go into a room nowadays and forget what I went in for. And I'm forever losing my glasses.'

'That happens to all of us. That kind of forgetfulness is common. As for losing your glasses, it's when you find them and you can't remember what they're for that you're in big trouble. Fortunately, full-blown dementia is rare, it affects only about one in a thousand.'

'Try telling that to Dad,' he said mournfully.

As soon as he arrived home, Billy penned a letter to Mam's general practitioner in Langley. A week later, he had a polite reply telling him that he'd been to see Dad and confirmed what the family already knew, that he was suffering from senile dementia. The doctor said he'd contacted the local health authority who'd be organizing a geriatric consultant psychiatrist to visit Dad with a view to finding him a place in an appropriate nursing home. But, the GP continued, there was a long waiting list and it might be some considerable time before he heard anything more.

Billy had done all that he could for the time being. They would just have to sit tight and hope for the best now. Meanwhile, he and the family would organize a roster of visits and keep an eye on things to make sure that Mam was not overtaxed.

Chapter Thirty-One

It was a beautiful sunny morning when Billy set off for college on Monday morning at the start of the new week. Whenever he could, he travelled by train but it didn't always fit into his timetable. And on a day like today he didn't mind taking the car. His first lecture wasn't until ten o'clock and so he was able to drive at a leisurely pace along the East Lancs road. He pulled in at the staff car park, collected his briefcase, got out, and locked the Morris Oxford. As he turned to face the college, he was startled by the scene that met his eyes. Parading about the quadrangle were several students carrying banners which read: 'Reinstate Maria Medina'; 'Students Demand Their Rights'; 'Less Authority. More Liberty'; 'Berkeley '64: LSE '66: Now It's Our Turn. Sherdley '67'.

'What's all this about?' Billy asked one of the protestors.

'A demonstration,' she retorted, and continued her march round the close.

Billy opened the main door of the college and got his second shock of the day: sitting packed together on the stone steps leading to the main corridor was the whole student body of several hundred young women. They were crammed so tightly together there was no room for Billy to climb the stairs. They shifted reluctantly to give him just enough room to tiptoe his way through the mass. He asked again, 'What on earth's going on?' He was met with tight smiles but no answer.

The corridor, too, was jammed with students sitting with hardly an inch of space between them. This is reminiscent of my days in East Africa, he thought, when I had to tread warily through a line of safari ants. As he reached the

261

staffroom entrance, a student strumming a guitar struck up in Joan Baez style with 'We Shall Overcome'. The song was taken up by the rest of the demonstrators and their voices resounded through the college.

At last Billy reached the sanctuary of the staffroom where he found his colleagues sitting around, pale and drawn as if at a wake. Unusually, Sister Benedict was among them.

'Good morning, Mr Hopkins,' she said with a wan smile. 'Well, this is a fine kettle of fish, is it not?' Then, addressing the rest of the staff, she said, 'Apologies to you all for my intrusion in your staffroom but I'm afraid the students have occupied my office and I'm unable to gain entry. They have also taken over the lecture theatre and most of the classrooms. I know you're all wondering what this sit-in, as I believe these things are called, is all about. You must be as puzzled as I am. However, the president of the students' union, Eleanor Freeman, has agreed to meet with us along with two other student representatives at eleven o'clock. Then we should find out what has caused this rumpus.'

For the next hour, the room buzzed with conversation as various individuals aired their opinions.

'A damned disgrace,' said one. 'It's unknown for convent girls like ours to rebel like this. They're usually compliant and obedient. Someone's been getting at 'em.'

'It's this Eleanor Freeman character,' added another. 'I know her from one of my classes. She's a little older than the others. About twenty-five, I'd say. An agitator and a trouble-maker. A real rabble-rouser.'

'I've heard she's a regular soapbox orator,' said a third. 'A bit of a commie and a Beatnik as well.'

'It's a copycat protest like the one at the London School of Economics last year,' the head of history declared.

'I think they're trying to find meaning in their lives,' said Miss Whiston, head of religious studies.

At eleven o'clock, Eleanor Freeman accompanied by her two cohorts came into the staffroom. She was a stolidly built young woman who exuded confidence and self-assurance. Invited by the Principal to sit and state their case, she took her place at the long table and looking round the faces assembled there, said in a forceful tone of voice, 'The students in the college have for a long time felt a sense of injustice and they've elected me to speak on their behalf. We have a number of demands to present to you, the staff of the college, and I'm authorized to say that unless immediate attention is given to these just demands, we shall continue to occupy the college.

'First, we cannot accept the manner in which we're assessed in teaching practice. Important decisions are made about our future without us being present. This is like the Star Chamber court we read about in history, that is, being tried in absentia and found guilty without the chance to defend ourselves, as was the case with Maria Medina who recently failed her TP. We insist that she be given another chance to prove herself. Not only must justice be done, it must be seen to be done. We also demand the right to know what teaching mark we've been awarded. Why should this be kept hidden from us? In this respect, we also insist on access to confidential information kept about us.'

'You mean you wish to have access to your personal files?' Sister Benedict asked, hardly able to believe what she was hearing. She and the other nuns had turned a sickly pale colour.

'That seems only fair,' Eleanor replied. 'After all, we live in a democracy not a totalitarian state. We're demanding greater student participation in decision-making. The college is too autocratic and we want to see more opportunities for democracy because the decisions handed down to us affect us personally during our time here in college.'

'And suppose we find your demands insolent and decide to reject them,' Sister Peter snapped. 'What then?'

'I don't think I've made the position clear,' the student replied. 'We are occupying this building and shall continue to do so until our demands are met. We students in this college have been deprived of our rights. Decisions and rules affecting our lives are made without consulting us.'

'We must all live by rules,' Sister Benedict said. 'Which particular rules do you have in mind?'

One of the president's two companions now spoke up. 'The rules in the college are outdated and inappropriate for the sixties. The rules about hours of liberty are ludicrous. Requiring grown-up ladies to be back in college every night by nine o'clock is preposterous.'

'And the rules about dress code are medieval,' added the other representative. 'Wearing black and being forbidden to reveal arms and elbows is ridiculous. We also think that prohibiting boyfriends from the halls of residence is archaic and shows a lack of trust in us.'

'Very well, I shall put your points to a staff meeting and to the Board of Governors,' the Principal said. 'In the meanwhile, I suggest the students now return to their lectures and to their studies.'

'We shall do no such thing,' Eleanor Freeman replied. 'We shall consider returning to our work only after you have considered and replied to our demands.'

The three students rose from their chairs and left the room. By this time, the staff, especially the sisters, were looking shell-shocked.

When they'd gone, the Principal called for opinions and these were soon forthcoming in no uncertain terms. One or two older members advocated bringing in the police to clear the college; others saw the students' demands as blackmail and recommended refusing point blank to consider them.

'I object to ultimata,' said the head of music, 'and I don't think we should give in to them. If we accede to their threats, we'll appear weak.'

'They'll soon cave in when it's lunchtime and they get hungry,' added Sister Peter. 'I don't know what the world's coming to when inexperienced, immature young women begin telling us how we must run things. We should reject their claims out of hand.'

The younger members of staff, however, were in favour of listening to the students' petitions.

Titch said, 'If their demands are reasonable, I propose that we should at least give them a hearing. I think the demand to see their personal files and to attend teaching practice meetings is not on as it would inhibit free expression of tutors. But I can see no harm in their attending staff meetings or even the Board of Governors' meetings to take part in decisions that affect their lives.'

'I'm inclined to agree with Titch, er, Mr Smalley,' Billy said, putting in his two cents' worth. 'Whatever we do, we must avoid precipitate action, like bringing in the law, as that can only make things worse. This is what happened last year at the London School of Economics when the police were brought in and there was near riot, resulting in the death of a porter.'

'Thank you all for expressing your honest views on this tense situation,' the Principal said. 'I have called an emergency meeting of the Board of Governors for this evening and they must decide on what steps we should take. I shall report back to you tomorrow morning at a staff meeting.'

There was nothing to be done and many of the staff, including Titch, Gerry, and Billy, called it a day and went home.

Next morning when Billy arrived at college he found the students still in occupation and awaiting the outcome of the governors' meeting.

There was a strained, anxious atmosphere in the staffroom as they awaited the arrival of Sister Benedict. When she came into the room, the staff rose to their feet and looked nervously in her direction. What she was about to tell them could change the whole ethos of the college.

'Please sit down,' she said. 'I shan't keep you in suspense

a moment longer as I know how worried you are and eager to know what was decided. Last night, I had a three-hour meeting with the board and we agreed to put the following recommendations before you for your consideration.' She consulted her file. 'First, in the case of Maria Medina, the board recommended that she be given a second chance next year to improve her teaching performance.'

There was a gasp of surprise and several senior members shook their heads incredulously.

'I am prepared to offer Miss Medina extra tuition in teaching methods,' said the head of religious studies. 'I think with personal coaching she could possibly make the grade.'

'Second,' the Principal continued, 'students will be allowed to attend and participate at staff and governors' meetings but only to discuss subjects which directly affect residence and boarding matters. They will not be allowed to attend discussions about staff appointments or about student assessments. And they will not have access to personal files or teaching marks, which shall remain confidential.'

One or two veterans on the staff muttered about Orwell's *Animal Farm* and lunatics taking over the asylum. A vote was taken and the majority were in favour of the recommendations – anything that would help end this unpleasant business and let them get back to work.

Eleanor Freeman and her companions were called into the meeting and the decisions communicated to them. There was no need to ask if they accepted. Their answer was apparent in the broad smiles which lit up their faces. They nodded curtly to the staff and left quickly to tell the students who were still outside occupying the building.

Five minutes later there was tremendous cheering which echoed through the college for a good ten minutes.

'It's the beginning of a new era,' Billy remarked to Titch and Gerry as they came away.

'And about time too,' Titch chuckled.

Together, the trio marched over to their offices singing Bob Dylan's 'Times they are a-changing'.

As for Maria Medina, she decided that teaching was not her bag after all. She obtained an appointment as translator with a Spanish book publishing company in Madrid at a higher salary than she could possibly have earned in the classroom.

So all the fuss about her, Billy thought, had been for nothing but the news didn't faze Eleanor Freeman one bit.

'That's not important,' she said. 'We won our argument and it's the principle of the thing that matters.'

Chapter Thirty-Two

'Why are we waiting? Why are we waiting?' sang the Hopkins children as they sat in the lounge waiting for Dad to come in with their weekly allowance.

Billy knew that it was his duty to give them spends but he always made sure they'd squirm first by telling them the story of his life: how he'd had to get up at six thirty in the morning to serve seven o'clock Mass, how he'd had to earn his own spending money. The kids regarded it as part of the price they had to pay for their allowance.

'Here we go again,' Billy said, jingling coins in his hands. 'Same old routine every Saturday morning. Sometimes I feel like an old bird feeding worms to its young in the nest.'

'You may catch the worms,' Laura laughed, 'but I'm the one who has to cook 'em.'

'Any chance of a bit extra, Dad, this weekend?' Lucy wheedled. 'It's half-term and I could do with a little more. Ten shillings a week doesn't buy much nowadays. A couple of bars of chocolate, two magazines, and a trip to the flicks and it's gone.'

'And my pal, Spud Murphy, gets more than me,' Mark added.

'So does his brother Charlie,' John whined.

'Same goes for me,' Matthew said. 'I'll be seventeen next birthday, Dad, and a pound doesn't go far for someone my age.'

'Then you should give up smoking like I did,' Billy said.

'How did you know I smoke, Dad?'

'Do you think your dad and I were born yesterday, Matthew?' Laura said. 'We can smell it on your clothes and in your room and you have yellow, nicotine-stained fingers.'

'Dad smoked at my age, Mum. He's always telling us about the smokers' club at school and how they puffed away on their Woodbines at dinnertime in the alley.'

'Never mind what I did, Matthew,' Billy said. 'That's ancient history. If you go on smoking, it's your funeral, but right now it's costing us a bomb to keep you supplied with spending money. Have you ever added up how much it comes to? Eight shillings to John, ten to Mark, and thirty-two shillings to you two older ones. That's fifty shillings a week. That comes to ten pounds a month, which amounts to a hundred and twenty a year, which equals—'

'OK, OK, Dad, we get the picture,' Matthew said. 'What you're saying is, no pay increase.'

'That's right, Matthew. No pay increase without improved productivity, as Harold Wilson's always telling us.'

'How can *we* raise productivity?' Lucy asked petulantly.

'You could help more around the house by washing dishes or keeping your rooms cleaner for a start,' Laura said.

'But my room is already reasonably clean,' Matthew protested. 'What more am I expected to do?'

'Clean?' Laura exclaimed. 'Sometimes you leave a mess on top of a mess. It's more a job for a geologist to dig through the layers. And you shouldn't take food into your room. You might attract vermin.'

'By vermin, do you mean Mark and John?' Matthew grinned. 'As for food in my room, I ate one meat pie, once!'

'So that's what it was! When I found it, it looked like penicillin.'

It was Billy's turn to add to the complaints. 'Then there's the noise coming from that damned Dansette record player of yours, Lucy, plus the row from Radio Caroline. The racket's loud enough to loosen all my fillings. Can't you keep the volume down?'

'Anything else, Dad?' Matthew pouted. 'Or is that the lot?'

'That magazine you have in your room. *Oz*, I think it's called. Three and six a copy and it's not only pornographic, it preaches revolution as well. That plus your fags must use up a sizeable chunk of your spends.'

'So what do you suggest?' Matthew asked sulkily.

'When I was a kid in Collyhurst, we didn't get any spends as such. And there's no need for that eye-rolling, Lucy. By the time I was eight, I had to earn my money selling firewood or lighting fires for Jewish people in the Cheetham Hill district.'

'There's no call for firewood any more, Dad,' Lucy said. 'Everyone round here has central heating. And I don't know anyone who needs their fire lighting.'

'Use your imagination. Why not get together with your friends and see if you can come up with some ways for earning money of your own? It's time you all learned to be independent and to stand on your own two feet. As soon as you have a brainwave, come and tell me about it. If I think it's got possibilities and needs cash, I'll back you with stake money to get you started.'

'I hope you don't expect us to earn money straightaway, Dad,' Lucy said. 'It may take us some time to get things going. You'll be giving us pocket money meanwhile until we do, won't you?'

'Of course I will. I'm a reasonable man,' Billy said.

Matthew was the first to come up with a money-making scheme, though in his case it was in the plural because he had more than one. At Matthew's request, Billy went up to his room where he found him seated at his desk with his pal, Des, at his side. There was a typewriter on the desk and they'd been typing some document or other. The air was so thick with tobacco smoke that Billy could hardly breathe.

'Have you two ever thought of opening a window? It's stifling in here. You could cut the atmosphere with a knife. It's like the fug of a nightclub at three o'clock in the morning with all the air vents blocked up.'

'We've never been in a nightclub at that time in the morning, Dad, but it sounds exciting.'

'OK. So what are these brilliant ideas you've been hinting at?'

'Two ideas, Dad. First of all, Des and I have landed jobs playing in a Chinese restaurant on Friday nights. Twenty-five shillings each for a few hours' work.'

'Sounds good as long as you don't let it interfere with your studies. I suppose you'll be playing selections from *Chu Chin Chow*.'

'Very funny, Dad. We'll be giving the diners more up-to-date numbers, like Dave Brubeck's "Take Five" or maybe the Animals' "House of the Rising Sun". That should go down well with the Chinese!'

'I'm sure the management will want their music played prestissimo for a fast turnover,' Billy chuckled. 'Still, I'm glad to see your enterprise. But you said you had other plans?'

'Plan number two, Dad, is a "How To Give Up Smoking" course which we're at present designing.'

Billy was so overcome with laughter when he heard this, he had to sit down. 'What kind of course?' he asked through his tears.

'With the recent health report proving that smoking causes lung cancer, there's bound to be tremendous demand for such a course. We reckon a smoker derives great pleasure from a cigarette,' he said, drawing deeply on his fag. 'The aim of our course is to make smoking as unpleasant as possible so that the smoker will be put off tobacco forever. And think of the money he'll save by giving up! Our course slogan is going to be: THIS COURSE WILL MAKE YOU RICH!'

'How do you propose to achieve this effect?' Billy grinned.

It was Des who answered. 'We have to assume, Mr Hopkins,' he said lighting up a Park Drive, 'that the punters, I mean the clients, genuinely want to give up and will do anything to get rid of the habit. Otherwise, they wouldn't have applied to us for the course, would they?'

271

'I'm with you so far,' Billy said. 'So what do you give them for their money?'

'First, we give them a set of rules they must follow and a special chemical which will make them sick every time they smoke a cigarette.'

'You can't be serious,' Billy said, hardly able to restrain his mirth.

'It's not funny, Dad,' Matthew said, frowning and tapping the ash of his cigarette into the overflowing ashtray. 'We've put a lot of work into this. The cure is an astringent gargle and whenever a smoker gets the craving, he has only to wash his mouth and throat with our mixture. Then, on lighting up, the contact of the smoke with the impregnated saliva is so disgusting that the cigarette will be abandoned immediately.'

'Why not try self-hypnosis?' Billy asked, adopting a serious expression. 'It worked for me.'

'Nah,' Matthew said. 'Most people would find that too difficult. Walking about reciting "I am an abstainer" a thousand times a day. Our approach is simpler and has quicker results.'

'Our method is also a form of conditioning, Mr Hopkins,' Des added. 'The client will come to associate smoking with something unpleasant and will pack it in. It's like the way Pavlov's dogs linked food with a bell. Our customers will link cigarettes with vomit.'

'Have you ever heard that saying from the Bible?' Billy chuckled. 'Physician, heal thyself. Surely you should give it up yourself before you start advising others on how to do it. It's a case of practise what you preach.'

'No, Dad. You've got it wrong. We're not the dogs; we're Pavlov.'

'OK, OK,' Billy chortled. 'I'll be on tenterhooks to see how it goes.'

Lucy and her friends were next to present their big plans for making their fortune.

'I hope you don't have any hare-brained schemes like Matthew's,' Billy said when the three girls met him one afternoon.

'*Our* ideas are sensible and realistic,' Lucy said peevishly. 'We need about sixty pounds in stake money to get it off the ground.'

'That's quite a lot of money, Lucy, but I'm intrigued. Pitch it to me.'

'We've found the name of a fine arts studio in Hong Kong that paints on canvas and their charges are reasonable. It works like this: we send them a colour slide of a subject and they send back a beautiful oil painting within a few weeks. And the cost is only twenty pounds. We sell it to our customer for forty pounds, say, giving us a profit of twenty on each order, less the cost of postage.'

'Sounds promising but who would want such a painting?'

'My parents have already agreed to have their portrait done,' Mary Feeney said.

'And mine have promised to order one after they've seen the first results,' Sally Simpson gushed.

'Looks as if you've got it all worked out,' Billy said. 'And the idea sounds a lot more sensible than your brother's.'

'Naturally,' Lucy said haughtily. 'We've also got an Italian restaurant called Pirandello's interested in having their building done though Mr Spoletti, the manager, wants a balcony that isn't there to be added on "to impress Mamma and Papa back at home".'

'You know, the more you tell me,' Billy said, 'the more I like this idea. I've always fancied an oil painting of your mum and me. Put us down for one as well.'

'That gives us three commissions, Mr Hopkins,' Mary said, 'and that's without trying. I think we're going to make our fortune.'

'We shall require capital,' Lucy continued, ever the business woman, 'not only for the studio but also for stretchers and frames. We shall also need to borrow your Pentax camera to make colour slides.'

'The three of you have obviously done your homework,' Billy said warmly. 'I shall draw out the cash first thing on Monday morning.'

The trio glowed under his praise.

Given the ingenuity shown by the senior children, Billy wondered what the two youngest would come up with.

It was at the dinner table the next day that Mark and John pitched their money-making venture.

'Siamese cats,' Mark announced.

'Sorry, Mark,' Laura said. 'We're not with you.'

'Breeding them, Mum. We buy a male Siamese and get Samantha to start producing.'

'We can sell the kittens,' John added. 'How much did you pay for Samantha, Dad?'

'As far as I remember, it was fifteen pounds.'

'There you are then. How much would a male Siamese cost?'

'I suppose around fifteen to twenty pounds at the present time.'

'We've worked it out,' John said. 'If there are three to six in a litter, we stand to make thirty to sixty pounds each time Samantha has kittens.'

'We looked it up,' Mark enthused, 'and according to the book, a mother cat can produce about nine weeks after mating.'

'And another thing,' said John, equally fervent, 'a mother cat can have kittens twice or even three times a year.'

'Poor old Samantha,' Laura said.

'That means,' Mark continued, 'that we could sell maybe eighteen kittens a year at fifteen pounds each. That's two hundred and seventy pounds! What I like best about this idea is that it could lead to a life of luxury with the cats doing all the work.'

'You're a regular little capitalist, Mark' Billy laughed, 'and one day you're going to make a great lawyer with your dreams of an easy life and a fast buck. But I think your calculations may be a trifle optimistic. Have you forgotten the cost of buying a pedigree male, feeding it and all those kittens. There may also be vet bills to take into account.'

'Aw, come on, Dad,' Mark said. 'Don't spoil it. We're sure it'll work out.'

'If we go along with it,' Laura said, 'you two will have to do all the work feeding the cats and cleaning up after them.'

'With that proviso,' Billy sighed, 'we'll take a chance on it.'

'You're a great mum and dad,' the boys chanted.

'You mean a couple of loonies,' Billy said.

'It might also be an opportunity to teach them about sex and reproduction,' Laura said to Billy afterwards. 'I know how much you've always loved that job.'

A week later, Billy took the two young boys to a farm near Accrington and bought a handsome, muscular, cross-eyed, one-year-old Siamese of the chocolate variety. He was the Clark Gable of the cat world and cost £20.

'Is your Queen calling?' the lady breeder asked.

'Queen? Which Queen? Calling who?' Billy said puzzled.

'You know. Is the mother-to-be on heat?'

'Dunno. But she makes one heck of a row every two or three weeks.'

'Don't talk to me about "heck of a row",' she smiled. 'Not until you've heard the cat you've bought. He's the feline equivalent of Enrico Caruso.'

It wasn't until they got the cat home that they understood the full implications of what she'd said. They put Clark Gable/Enrico Caruso into his specially prepared box in the warmest cellar to let him get used to his new surroundings. A couple of hours later he treated the family to his first cry. Billy was hazy as to what a banshee actually was but he'd read somewhere about its legendary wail. There was also the howl of the coyote in cowboy movies but Billy would have willingly wagered a month's salary that in any competition for the most horrific howl, the sound that issued from their new Siamese would have won hands down. It was the yowl of someone being tortured on the rack and enough to have the neighbourhood ringing the police to prevent Billy from murdering his wife. No need for a discussion as to what to call him. It was a foregone conclusion and it was unanimous. Satchmo! For the first week in his new home, he prowled round the rooms marking his territory by spraying the place.

'This wasn't something you had in your plans,' Laura complained. 'We'll never get rid of the smell.'

When Satchmo began sharpening his claws by scratching the furniture, she'd had enough. 'Something must be done about it!' she commanded.

Billy tried to remedy the situation by buying a scratching post impregnated with catnip but neither cat could get the hang of it even though Billy demonstrated its use a thousand times by getting down on all fours, crawling up to the post and grating his fingernails on the material. No use. The cats simply watched him wonderingly, probably thinking, 'Ah, so the human has *his* scratch pad and we have *ours*, the furniture!'

Laura blew her top. 'From now on the cats are confined to the kitchen area and the basement,' she fumed. 'They can't complain as the boiler room's the warmest place in the house.'

'If the cats spend all their time down there,' Mark complained, 'they won't get enough exercise or fresh air.'

'Nonsense. The cats can have the complete run of both cellars and even the dummy cellar, if need be.'

As for giving the cats fresh air, Billy came up with the answer. For exercise, they were given lots of toys like imitation mice, table tennis balls, string, cotton reels, balls of paper. Preventing them from breaking loose from the house was a constant worry in case they got lost or were stolen. Every precaution was taken. First, collars and leads. Mark and John could be seen taking their investments for a walk every day, surprising the neighbours who were half expecting to see poodles at the ends of the leashes.

Next, a cat flap was built into the cellar door to let the pussies out into the garden but only to a restricted enclosure that Billy had moggy-proofed with wire netting. Samantha soon got the idea of going out and coming back but for Satchmo it was a problem. He knew how to get out all right but coming back flummoxed him.

'He's a feather-brained feline,' Billy declared.

'On the contrary,' Matthew said, 'I think Satchmo's a genius because he's observed that doors normally open only one way. He has assumed that the flap has the same properties.'

When it came to the mating bit of the enterprise, things didn't look too hopeful. They were given time to get to know each other. Their privacy was respected and they were left alone in the boiler room to get on with their courting but a spyhole bored in the door gave Billy an opportunity to observe the proceedings. I feel like one of those voyeurs hoping to see some action, he thought, a peeping Tom who gets his kicks by watching others on the job. However, if he'd been paying, he'd have demanded his money back for there was nothing doing. Maybe it was because Satchmo was inexperienced and clumsy in his chat-up line, or maybe he had halitosis or BO. It was more likely that Samantha resented him muscling in on her territory. After all, she'd been there first and this interloper had moved into her domain without permission or a visa. What was more, this gatecrasher was expecting a spot of how's-your-father into the bargain. Whatever it was, she didn't fancy him. He circled round Samantha several times sniffing and talking to her but she'd have none of it. She spat and growled whenever he came near and landed a couple of quick socks on his nose.

'Give them time,' Laura said. 'Perhaps he's not her type but in time she'll get used to him.'

Laura seemed to be right because three weeks later, Samantha started to show the first signs of a successful mating when she gave loud vocal indications that she needed more food.

Mark and John began counting their profits.

Chapter Thirty-Three

Matthew soon reported back the results of his joint venture with Des. The Chinese restaurant dispensed with their services after three sessions. Customers complained that they'd been given indigestion by the duo's interpretation of Pink Floyd's 'Interstellar Overdrive'. The management paid them off after deducting the cost of the food they'd eaten and switched to taped background music with an oriental theme.

Their give-up-smoking course attracted six customers, all of whom demanded a complete refund when they found that the cure was worse than the disease. One subscriber declared that he'd prefer to take his chances with Lady Nicotine than spend the rest of his life with his head over the lavatory bowl 'vomiting his guts up' as he put it.

'The one thing you forgot in your plan,' Billy laughed, 'was that Pavlov's dogs had no choice in the matter of being conditioned whereas your customers have free will. Why should they pay good money to make themselves sick? And I'd suggest that a better slogan for your course would have been: THIS COURSE WILL MAKE YOU RETCH!'

Total profits from the two businesses. Nil.

Two months after the girls had sent off the colour slides, a large parcel post-marked Hong Kong was delivered to the Hopkins address, causing great excitement, but Lucy refused absolutely to touch the package until her two companions were present.

Billy and Laura hoped to be invited to the opening of the parcels but there was nothing doing. The suspense was unbearable.

'We want to stretch the canvases,' Lucy explained, 'and hang them in their beautiful gilt frames before you view them so that you'll get the full effect.'

The girls came round immediately after Lucy's phone call and the three of them retired to the lounge to savour the moment. The family could hear the squeals of delight coming through as they ripped off the brown paper. It was a good hour before they were called in to look at the finished portraits. Billy and Laura were champing at the bit with impatience to see what the oriental artists had wrought in oils. They had waited over eight weeks for this day and, apart from that, Billy had a sizeable amount of capital riding on the enterprise.

'OK, Mum and Dad,' Lucy called. 'You can come in now.'

In a state of feverish expectation, they opened the door of the lounge and went in. The girls were smiling broadly as they invited the parents to sit down before the painting.

Lucy knew how to extract the maximum drama from a situation like this for she had covered the portrait with a piece of red curtain material. A roll on the drums and a fanfare of trumpets were the only things missing from the ritual.

'Are you ready?' she asked histrionically. 'Then voilà!' and she removed the red fabric with a flourish.

With wide, expectant grins, they looked at the picture. The smiles froze on their faces.

The clothes the sitters had been wearing were reproduced beautifully and with great accuracy as to detail. It was the faces that didn't look quite right for they had a distinctly Eastern appearance. The complexions had a faint saffron hue and the eyes were almond-shaped. Laura's lovely dark hair was there all right and she looked exquisite but it was a cross between Her Royal Majesty Queen Elizabeth and Anna May Wong, the film actress, they were looking at, not Laura. As for Billy, it wasn't Billy at all. It was the Duke of Edinburgh disguised as Charlie Chan, but without moustache and little beard, that stared out inscrutably from the canvas. Billy wondered if the Hong Kong artist had based it on an old colonial calendar they perhaps had hanging in their studio.

The two subjects of the painting were stuck for words. At last Laura broke the silence.

'In some ways, this painting's a true work of art,' she said diplomatically. 'Obviously the artist who created it has interpreted his subject in his own individual and subjective way. After all, it's not supposed to be a photograph. It's a portrait in oils and represents the subject as seen through the eyes of the artist.'

Billy was thinking that the artist responsible should be boiled in his own oil but instead he said, 'Exactly, Laura. We have only to think of Graham Sutherland's painting of Winston Churchill. It wasn't meant to look like him. It was Churchill as seen by the painter. It was looking into his soul. As Winston said at the presentation, "This can be described as a remarkable example of modern art." '

They didn't reveal that it was rumoured that Winston's wife, Clementine, had had the portrait consigned to the flames.

'So glad you both like it,' Lucy said. 'We were worried that you might think it too oriental.'

'We love it,' Laura fibbed. 'We shall hang it in our bedroom.'

'The painting of my own mother and father is as good as yours,' Mary Feeney now told them, unveiling the other portrait.

The second painting was not unlike their own. Anna May Wong and Charlie Chan were represented there also but it was Mary's dad who had the face of Miss Wong while her mam had that of Charlie Chan.

'I think my mam and dad are going to love it,' Mary said.

Do they have a choice? Billy asked himself.

'The personal portraits have come out well,' Lucy said, 'but we're not sure how the owner of the Pirandello will like the painting of his restaurant.'

She took the cover off the picture and they could see why she was concerned. The restaurateur had asked for a balcony to be added to the façade of his premises but what he'd got was a pagoda.

'Somehow, I don't think a pagoda is right for an Italian restaurant,' Billy told the girls. 'I doubt if Mr Spoletti will be willing to pay up, not unless he changes the name of his establishment to something like Teahouse of the August Moon.'

But Billy was wrong. Again. The Italian loved the curly-wurly architecture of its roof, and said it would impress the old people back in his home village even more than a balcony.

Everyone paid their dues to Lucy and her team but when Sally's parents decided not to commission a portrait, the three girls decided to call a halt, much to everyone's relief. When all bills were paid, they found they had a profit of £6 to share between them. Not a fortune, but better than nothing.

It was three months before Mark and John had any indication that their venture might pay off. Samantha showed signs of wanting to make a nest. Laura helped the two boys to prepare a large box for her by lining it with newspapers and placing it near a radiator in the kitchen. She rejected it, preferring a place near the boiler in the cellar. A second box was made ready to suit her wishes. The whole house was agog with anticipation as if it was a human baby that was about to be born. Satchmo wisely kept out of the way.

It was early one morning that the news was brought to Billy as he lay in bed suspended somewhere between slumber and consciousness.

'Which do you want first?' Laura asked, shaking his shoulder. 'The good news or the bad news?'

'At this time in the morning, I'll take the good first.'

'Samantha's had four kittens!'

'Fantastic! The boys will be pleased!'

'I'm not so sure,' she said dolefully. 'You see. Three of them are ginger and only one looks like a Siamese. At the moment, it's white all over but maybe it'll turn out to be chocolate pointed.'

'Impossible! We took such great precautions to keep the ginger tom at bay.'

'Obviously they weren't enough.'

'Maybe Samantha fancied a bit of rough in the alley. She never seemed to take to Lord Satchmo.'

'Maybe. But he must have managed it at least once because he's got himself a son. We'll have to find homes for the ginger kittens but the Siamese should fetch a decent price.'

And so it was. Friends and relatives had to be pressed or cajoled into taking a red-haired moggy and the Siamese sold for £15 to Uncle Les who accused Billy of being a capitalist speculator. With Mark and John, Billy did a profit and loss account and found that on balance they had made a loss of around £40.

'In one respect, you've been successful,' Laura said with a twinkle in her eye. 'You've always wanted your kids to be like you and your wish has come true.'

'How do you make that out?'

'Everything they've put their hand to has turned out a minor flop. No doubt about it, they're chips off the old block all right.'

'Thanks, Laura. But remember the saying, "The man who never makes a mistake never makes anything." '

'Who said that?'

'I did. Just now.'

Chapter Thirty-Four

Almost three months had passed since Billy had first written to the Langley GP about Dad's mental condition. Eventually the wheels of the Health Service turned and things began to move. It was a piece of good luck that Billy happened to be at home on holiday when Mam phoned because he was able to get across to Langley with Les to meet the psychiatrist promised by her local doctor who'd arranged for Dad's check-up.

It was a task that neither Billy nor Les was looking forward to. They were nervous about what the outcome might be but most of all they were sad. It looked as if it might be the end of the line for their mam and dad after fifty-seven years of marriage. During the previous week, Dad's condition had gone downhill. Mam had told Billy on the phone that not only did he not recognize her but he'd been extremely restless, wandering about during the night opening and slamming doors to cupboards and rooms.

They arrived early in plenty of time to talk to Mam before the consultant was due. One look at her appearance convinced them that she needed relief urgently from the strain that Dad was putting her under. She looked exhausted and on the verge of a nervous breakdown. If something wasn't done immediately, there was a real danger that her own health would fail.

Dad sat by the fire staring vacantly into the flames, mumbling incoherently to some unseen person.

'I've been getting hardly any sleep,' she said. 'During the night, your dad doesn't stay still for more than an hour or two before wandering about, trying to go out the front door.

He has no idea where he is or who I am. He spends his time muttering and seems to think that our Jim and Mary are here in the room with him. Do you think the nursing home will be able to help?'

'I'm sure of it, Mam,' Billy said. 'For the sake of your own health and sanity, you must let him go, if that is what the consultant recommends.'

'I didn't want to at first but now I think it'll be best for him if he received professional treatment. He's in a bad way.'

'I think Dad's not only disturbed, he's unhappy,' Les added. 'In hospital, they have experts who are used to dealing with people in his condition.'

There was a knock at the front door and Billy went to answer it. On the doorstep he found a tall, well-built dark-haired man with a lady in nurse's uniform.

'Good morning,' he said. 'I am Dr Nathan Mandelberg and this is my nurse, Mrs Evans.'

Billy invited them in and they walked into the living room and introduced themselves and explained fully what they were about.

'We've come to examine your husband, Mrs Hopkins, with a view to finding him a place in the Silver Threads Nursing Home.'

Dad continued to stare into the embers, hardly aware of their presence.

Adopting a gentle tone, Dr Mandelberg asked Dad a few basic questions, like his name, which he answered satisfactorily as 'Tommy Hopkins', but on other questions his confusion became apparent. He was asked to count up to ten and then to count backwards. Next, to say the months of the year forwards and backwards. He couldn't manage either. This from a man who used to remember long complex orders for fruit and vegetables when he was a porter. Then Dad made a strange observation.

'I've done some bad things in my life,' he announced.

Maybe he imagines the doctor's a Catholic priest, Billy thought, who's come to hear his confession.

'What sort of things?' the doctor asked softly.

The answer was even more bizarre.

'I've killed thousands of people.'

'Now which people have you killed, Mr Hopkins?'

'The Jews. I've murdered thousands of Jews.'

Even the experienced Dr Mandelberg was stunned by this answer.

At the conclusion of the interview, he told Mam and her two sons that Dad was clearly suffering from dementia and that a place was available if they cared to bring him down that afternoon.

Mam was in tears when the doctor had gone. 'I suppose it's for the best,' she wept. 'I don't think we've any choice. I've been expecting this and I already have his suitcase packed.'

'Silver Threads Home is only a short bus ride away, Mam,' Billy told her sorrowfully. 'You'll be able to visit him every day and the family will come at weekends. It's for his good and your own that he gets help.'

She made a sandwich for everyone and over a cup of tea they tried to puzzle out what Dad had meant by his self-accusation of mass murder. It was Mam who came up with a possible answer.

'Years ago, when he came home from the pub, he was always a bit of a bully. We'd have a row and I used to answer him back by saying something like, "Don't you shout at me, Hitler!" And now he thinks he's Hitler and he's killed thousands of Jews.'

After lunch came the heartbreaking part. Mam dressed Dad in his old raincoat and cap and made him ready to go.

'Come on, Dad,' Les said encouragingly. 'Time for off. We're going for a little ride in Billy's car.'

'Are you the police come to take me away?' he asked.

'Not at all, Dad,' Les half laughed. 'We're your sons.'

'I don't want to go nowhere,' Dad cried. 'I want to stop where I am.'

'Come on, Dad,' Billy said. 'It's a short ride. You like going in the car, don't you?'

They managed to get him to the porch where he grabbed at the metal door knocker and clung to it for dear life. Les loosened his grip gently and, taking his arm, led him out to the car. Mam was distressed and wept piteously.

'It's all for the best, Tommy,' she sobbed. 'You're going to a place where they can look after you properly.'

They drove down to Middleton and parked outside the nursing home. It was then that Dad had one of his rare moments of lucidity.

'I know where you've brought me,' he said. 'You're putting me in the bloody loonybin.'

'No, Dad,' Billy said vehemently. 'This is a nursing home where they'll try to make you better.'

'You can't kid me,' he declared. 'It's the bloody loony bin.'

They succeeded in persuading him to get out of the car and went into the unit and met the superintendent, Mrs Ainsworth, a kindly, soft-spoken middle-aged woman. She greeted them warmly and, after entering up Dad's personal details, explained that Silver Threads was a home specializing in the treatment of dementia, with mainly elderly residents. She asked them to wait in the lounge until she was free.

The four of them sat at the table conversing quietly when Dad suddenly said, 'Have you ordered yet? They're a bloody long time bringing them beers.'

Good old Dad! He thought they were in the Hare and Hounds waiting for the waiter to bring the round of drinks.

Mrs Ainsworth came over eventually and conducted them through the unit to the room that Dad would be occupying. It was a cosy room with a large window, and contained a single bed, a dressing table, a wardrobe, and a small bathroom.

'This is a lovely room, Dad,' Les exclaimed. 'And look at the wonderful view of the gardens.'

'If you like it so much,' said Dad, 'you can bloody well stay here instead of me.'

They helped him unpack and settled him in.

'You can leave him here confidently,' Mrs Ainsworth said. 'We'll look after him and make him comfortable.'

'What do you do to stop patients wandering off?' Billy asked.

'Patients are under constant supervision at all times. During the day, they spend their time in the lounge which also doubles as the dining room. We keep the bedrooms locked to prevent residents from helping themselves to other people's stuff.'

'Don't worry, Tommy,' Mam said sadly. 'We're not far away and I'll be back to see you every day.'

Dad made no response but stared ahead vacantly.

It was a melancholy little party that drove back to Martindale Crescent.

Next day was Sunday and Dad had his first visitors, five in all: Mam, Flo, Polly, Les, and Billy who were able to gain some idea of the routine of the place. As they entered the building, they caught a slight whiff of urine and stale food. Billy set to work immediately, giving Dad a shave, at which he'd become adept. Lunch followed in the crowded dining room and Mam was able to feed Dad, much as she'd done at home. The meal gave the family an opportunity to observe the home and its residents in operation. They each had their own particular foibles. One female patient finished eating quickly and then wandered round the tables helping herself to others' food, while another was apparently reading a book which was upside down; and one old lady preferred throwing her food down the table to eating it. Another for no apparent reason called constantly, 'Will someone come and help me! Will someone come and help me!' A burly man who had once been a policeman stood in the middle of the floor directing imaginary traffic. The inmates ignored him and each other.

As the family sat there watching the proceedings, a wild-eyed woman approached and asked brusquely, 'Have you got a fag, love?' over and over again. The nurse on duty explained that Bella had never been heard to say anything other than 'Have you got a fag, love?' But Bella hadn't reckoned on Les's doggedness for he replied each and every time, 'Sorry, love, I don't smoke,' to which, after the twentieth time, she finally screeched, 'Then you can piss off!'

A victory of sorts.

On the way home, Billy remarked to Les, 'It's a good thing that Dad's not aware of where he is or what's happening to him. What we've witnessed was like a corner of Hades. If I ever end up in his position, please do me a favour and shoot me.'

As the weeks went by, Dad became gradually institutionalized and went even further down the slippery slope that was dementia. He looked somehow smaller and frailer than ever. One of the nurses, Eileen, took a particular interest in him and he became attached to her. She was in her early forties, a big woman with a friendly face. Each morning, she helped him dress, wash and shave and he came to depend on her even though he could never remember her name. On one occasion Billy and Les offered to take him for a walk but he said he didn't want to go anywhere with 'them two policemen', preferring to cling to Eileen for security.

As it turned out, Dad hadn't long to suffer because a month after he'd arrived in the nursing home, Mam had a phone call telling her that during the night, he'd died peacefully in his sleep. Billy felt deep sorrow on hearing the news. It was hard for him to take in, as it was for the rest of the family, that Dad was no longer around. He had always been there ever since Billy could remember, a constant figure in his social landscape. Such a strong character should not have gone the way he did. At the same time, Billy's grief was tinged with a feeling of relief that his dad's suffering had come to an end before full-blown dementia completely wrecked him and reduced him to a vegetative state. Really, he'd died when he'd lost his mind. And maybe dying peacefully in your sleep, Billy reflected later, was not a bad way to depart this life.

The requiem Mass was held at St Chad's on Cheetham Hill Road. It was a sad but quiet service attended mainly by members of the extended family and a few fellow market porters who still remembered him. Uncle Eddie gave a brief eulogy saying how he'd been a good family man who'd brought his children up strictly to be good and respectable people. Then he added, 'Tommy lived life to the full,' and Billy wondered if what he meant was that his dad could sink a pint of bitter faster than anyone else in Collyhurst or even in Smithfield Market, and that was saying something.

Mam was broken-hearted and inconsolable at the death of Tommy and never got over his loss. Overnight, in her eyes, he was canonized and became Saint Thomas of Collyhurst. He was remembered for his generosity and his reliability as a breadwinner while all the bad things about him, like his heavy drinking and his tyrannical nature, were conveniently forgotten. But time heals all wounds and Mam's health took a turn for the better when she started to get a good night's sleep, though her eyesight had never fully recovered after her cataract operation. Soon she was going for short walks to the shops with her friend, Mrs Reynolds, and in the summer they even went on a charabanc outing organized by the parish to the shrine of Our Lady at Walsingham. And no doubt they had a good time slagging off Mrs Binks ('er next door). Meanwhile, Flo and Polly continued to do her big weekly shopping and the rest of the family made sure she was never without visitors at the weekend. For Billy, his dad's death was the end of an era.

Chapter Thirty-Five

Grandad's funeral, apart from Jake the Gerbil's obsequies, was the only one Billy's kids had ever attended. It was their first acquaintance with death and in the week following, they thought and talked about little else. They seemed obsessed with the subject and at the dinner table the conversation revolved around dying, the afterlife, and the occult.

'Why do people have to die, Dad?' John asked.

'Because nothing on this planet lasts forever, son. Everyone and everything is here only for a time and then life comes to an end.'

'Why? That doesn't seem fair,' John said.

'You'll have to blame Adam and Eve in the Garden of Eden, John,' Laura answered. 'When they defied God, they brought sin and death into the world.'

'Besides,' Billy said, 'who wants to live for ever? Look at Methuselah, he's supposed to have lived for nine hundred and sixty-nine years, poor bloke.'

'Are you and Mum going to die?'

'Yes, one day we too shall pass away but not for a long time yet, I hope.'

'How long do you think you've got, Dad?'

Billy laughed. 'Only God knows the answer to that, John. About a hundred years ago, the average age of death was only about forty but nowadays people live into their seventies and eighties, provided they're healthy and avoid nasty accidents.'

'And we humans are lucky,' Lucy who'd been listening added. 'At school, we've been learning about things that last only one day, like the mayfly and the day lily. They're called

291

ephemera. They're born, they blossom, then they snuff it.'

'Did you know there's a thing called a deathbed?' Mark said, joining in. 'I saw one in Grandad Mackenzie's attic once when I looked through the keyhole and I thought that if you went to sleep in it, you were certain to die.'

John said, 'And I thought that a death rattle was a toy which a murderer gives to a baby when he wants to kill it.'

'Did Grandad leave you anything in his will?' Matthew asked suddenly.

'My dad didn't make a will,' Billy sighed. 'He and Grandma don't have enough to make it worthwhile.'

'Have you and Mum made a will?' Mark asked.

'No, we haven't got round to it yet,' Billy answered. 'Maybe we should.'

'Then bagzz the piano,' Mark said quickly.

'Too late, Mark,' Billy chuckled. 'Matthew's already bagzzed it.'

'Then bagzz the painting of the African market!' Mark snapped.

'John's already put his mark on that,' Billy grinned.

'That's not fair, Dad. No one told me you'd started the bagzzing.'

'You can blame Matthew. He was the one who said bagzz being the first to bagzz anything.'

'I want you to leave me something of sentimental value,' Lucy said. 'Something to remember you by. Like money.'

'I wonder where Grandad Hopkins is at this moment,' John said, changing the subject.

'He'll be in heaven or at least purgatory,' Laura replied. 'I'm sure he's happy now.'

'Heaven for my dad,' Billy said, 'would be a pub with an endless supply of Boddington's draught mild. I'm sure that when he got up there, his first question would be: "What time does the bar open?" '

'I read somewhere,' Matthew said, 'that Churchill reckoned that death was an eternity of black velvet. I don't fancy that, staring at velvet forever and ever. Not only boring but it'd be enough to make you go cross-eyed. This talk about the hereafter is a load of bunk. When you're dead, you're dead, that's it. Curtains. Oblivion. Zilch. I'm an atheist, thank God. I believe in science not superstitious mumbo-jumbo.'

'It's a funny thing,' Billy grinned, 'but G.K. Chesterton said that when people stop believing in God, they don't believe in nothing. They believe in anything.'

'I believe in the immortality of the soul,' Laura said. 'The body is no more than a sort of overcoat. The day will come when you've no more use for it. The body dies, but the spirit goes on. I firmly believe that.'

'I like the idea of reincarnation, of coming back for another go,' Lucy said fervently. 'I've read about cases of young Indian kids coming back. One was able to describe the village where he'd lived in another life as the wife of one of the villagers. In Eastern religions like Buddhism and Hinduism, they say your actions in one life determine your fate in the next. It's called karma.'

'You seem to know a lot about it for someone not quite fifteen,' Billy remarked. It was sometimes difficult to take in the fact that they were no longer children. He was often surprised how quickly they'd grown up and developed minds and opinions of their own. Here they were talking about death and reincarnation. As the song said, 'I don't remember getting older, when did they?'

'Mary, Sally and I have been reading all about it in this,' she said, taking a book down from the shelf. 'We're interested in it, that's all.'

'This karma thing,' Matthew chuckled, looking pointedly at Mark and John, 'means that if you misbehave in this life, you might come back in someone else's body.'

'Yuk,' Mark said. 'I hope I don't come back in John's.'

'If you've been bad,' Matthew continued, 'you might even come back as a fly or a snake, or even a vegetable.'

'Fancy coming back as a cabbage,' said Mark, frowning, 'and being eaten, and passing through somebody's stomach and then into the toilet.'

'Then you'd be able to say with truth,' laughed Matthew, 'that your life had been crap. You'd end up on a sewage farm.'

'I think that's enough of that rude talk,' Laura admonished, trying hard not to laugh herself.

'I don't want to come back as anything,' said John. 'I might come back as a pig or a tick on a dog.'

'That'd be tough on the pig!' Mark said. 'But being a tick wouldn't be so bad. You'd get a free ride everywhere.'

'How long is this reincarnation stuff supposed to go on?' Billy asked, looking at Lucy. 'I mean it must come to an end some time or does it go on forever?'

'No,' Lucy explained. 'It goes on and on till you reach perfection – nirvana.'

'Perfection!' Matthew laughed. 'But I've already achieved it in my music.'

'The way you talk,' Lucy said, 'anyone'd think there's only ever been two musicians. You and Mozart.'

'Why bring in Mozart?' he grinned.

'What exactly is this nirvana?' Billy asked. 'It sounds like a skin cream.'

'It means,' replied Lucy, ignoring the two males and reading from the book, 'the extinction of all desires and passions and attainment. A kind of non-existence and attainment of perfection where there are no desires and no passion.'

'It sounds tedious,' Matthew said. 'After death, this indestructible spirit sits on a cloud listening to celestial harps. Is that what it's all about? Is that the purpose of existence? According to you and this karma thing, it's all been decided beforehand anyway.'

'It has,' Lucy said. 'Our fate is in the stars. Have you never heard of astrology? Our personalities are shaped by the influence of the sun, the moon and the planets at the time of our birth.'

'Complete bunk,' Matthew scoffed.

'*You* may think it's bunk,' Lucy snapped, 'but astrologers have been using it for hundreds of years to understand people and to predict their future. You're always sneering at things, Matthew. Don't you believe in anything?'

'I've already told you. I believe in science. At school, we've been taught to look for evidence and not take things for granted. Astrologers are con-merchants taking advantage of people like you. How can planets millions of light years away have any influence on the lives of people on earth? There must be about half a billion people with the same birth sign. So according to these shysters, one horoscope chart is correct for every one of 'em, whether a big movie star or a starving kid in Biafra.'

'No matter what you say, Matthew, many famous people believe in it.'

'Name a few!'

'Vivien Leigh, John Lennon, Jackie Kennedy.'

'It didn't do Jackie Kennedy much good,' Matthew said. 'Otherwise she and her husband wouldn't have gone to Dallas in nineteen sixty-three. I'll say one thing for astrology though. It proves, in the immortal words of Phineas Barnum, "There's a sucker born every minute".'

'OK, Matthew,' Lucy said angrily, 'I'll prove to you how accurate astrology is. You were born under Taurus, right? Here's your horoscope for the week,' she said opening up a copy of her magazine, *Jackie*. 'You are strong-willed and proud, but intensely private and not easy to know well. You are stubborn and like to get your own way in an argument and don't mind ignoring others' points of view.

'My own horoscope,' she went on, 'warns me to avoid the company of Taureans as they can be treacherous and you never know what they're up to the minute your back's turned.'

'It's a load of old rubbish,' Matthew declared. 'That can't be true. We Taureans would never accept such nonsense.'

'This argument could go on forever,' Billy said. 'Time to call it a day.'

'That's fine by me, Dad,' Lucy said, 'but despite Matthew's pig-headedness, I still believe there's more to the things happening around us than he'll admit to. For example, I think that the history of a place is stored forever in the walls and brickwork of a building through the vibrations of the people who once lived there.'

'You mean ghosts and things like that?' gasped Mark who had been quiet throughout the row between brother and sister.

Lucy said, 'Dad told us that a famous writer named Miles Benison used to live here. Who knows? Maybe he's still around.'

'Vibrations in the bricks!' Matthew exclaimed. 'What next? I've never heard such tripe.'

'You're like some boys we met at the youth club, doubting Thomases we called them,' Lucy said. 'They too think it's a load of rubbish. One day you'll sneer on the other side of your face when you find out there are things out there that you and all your science can't explain.'

'You mean ghosties and ghouls and things that go bump in the night,' Matthew scoffed. 'It's a load of old cobblers, though Mrs Cohen, the previous owner, did say she'd heard strange noises from time to time. But I'll bet if any of you lot met a bogeyman, you'd jump out of your skin.'

'Mum, tell them to stop talking about bogeys and strange noises,' John wailed. 'They're scaring me.'

'I think that'll do for today,' Laura said. 'And this is a Gemini ordering an Aquarius to come and help wash the dishes.'

'We Aquarians are always open to reason,' Lucy replied, 'and we like peace and tranquillity.'

Chapter Thirty-Six

It was three weeks into January 1968 and Billy and Laura had at last got a chance to examine the apparatus they'd bought in a rash moment from a mail order catalogue before Christmas. They'd opened up the huge boxes along with vast quantities of wrapping paper, plastic bags, blocks of polystyrene, and Styrofoam. They'd put all this stuff in the garage together with masses of other unwanted Christmas packing and the bin men had been bribed to take the lot away. But one look at the complicated instructions had been enough to persuade them to put off trying to operate the equipment until after the holiday. Now Laura was in the kitchen trying to unravel the mysteries of how to operate her new pressure cooker. Billy was in his cellar workshop puzzling over the manual for his prized new band-saw. The brochure had assured him that assembling it was child's play but had omitted to mention that it meant a child with a Ph.D in engineering. The instruction manual was a little under the length of *War and Peace* and he'd waded through several hundred pages of guarantees, vouchers, disclaimers, warnings in six languages, until at last he'd found a section which looked like English, the kind of English which had come via Taiwan and Germany. He read:

Congratulations on buying this machine. You WILL be pleased with it.

Please not to operate this equipment in the bathing-room, next to a kitchen sinken or near a swimming pool. If difficulty assembling please to phone Gerda in Amsterdam who is there for you. IMPORTANT NOTICE; IF

MACHINE NEEDS REPAIR, IT MUST BE TRANS-
PORTED IN ORIGINAL PACKING MATERIALS OR
WARRANTY IS INVALIDED.

As he was up to his eyes in screws, nuts and bolts and
other mysterious mechanical parts, Lucy came into the
workshop and stood a while watching him.

'I came top in the art exam this week, Dad,' she said at
last.

'That's great, Lucy,' a distracted Billy mumbled. 'Fantastic.
I always suspected you were another Leonardo.'

'D-a-a-a-d,' she said in her silkiest, most wheedling tone of
voice. 'Can I ask you something?'

'What is it, Lucy? Only I'm a little busy here as you can
see.'

'Next week, Dad, it's my fifteenth birthday and I wonder
if I could have a party.'

'Party?' Billy stammered as he tried to fit the part marked
X to the part lettered Y. 'Parties are your mother's department. If she says OK, then it's all right with me.'

'Oh, thanks, Dad,' she said, giving him a hug and knocking
part X out of his hand and into a pile of sawdust. 'I'll go and
tell Mum.'

Upstairs, Lucy approached her mother.

'Mum, I'm fifteen next week and Dad says it's OK for me
to hold a party.'

'If your father agrees, then it must be OK,' Laura
murmured, her whole attention focused on reading about
the warnings and dangers of allowing the water in the
pressure cooker to evaporate.

'Oh, that's great, Mum. You and Dad are the best parents
in the world.'

For Lucy the days that followed were devoted to organizing
her party and Billy and Laura wondered what they'd let themselves in for and how they'd allowed themselves to be duped
into agreeing. First there was the menu to be decided on.

'Let's make it a buffet,' Laura suggested. 'It's quick and easy to organize and it's less formal. I shall expect you and your friends to help in setting it up.'

'Oh, yes, Mum, we'll be glad to do it. We three girls are vegetarian and so we could have those things on little sticks like pineapple and cheese, and for sandwiches egg and mayonnaise; for the others, cocktail sausages, canapés, and ham sandwiches.'

'I hope there's going to be chocolate gateau,' Matthew grinned.

'And ice cream,' John said, smacking his lips.

'And apple pie!' Mark added.

'Who said you lot are invited?' Lucy asked.

Matthew said, 'I thought me and Des Gillespie from next door could be the male attraction. We could supply the music.'

'No fear,' Lucy replied. 'This is my party not yours. For music, we'll play records, thank you very much.'

'We must lay down some rules though,' Billy said, interrupting this little spat between brother and sister. 'The family plus Des from next door and your friends will attend the buffet and then the rest of us will make ourselves scarce and leave you to it. Who are your guests and how are you going to entertain them?'

'My two friends Mary and Sally of course, but we haven't decided on anyone else yet. We thought we might ask three boys we met at St Bernadette's Youth Club. We plan to have dancing to records and then a treasure hunt in the cellar.'

'And which of these three lads is your particular boyfriend?' Billy asked her teasingly, though if the truth were known he was solicitous as to who amongst her male friends she would consider acceptable. Would he be handsome? Intelligent? Polite? Like her father? Or would he be a vulgar, inarticulate yob?

'Dad, you're embarrassing me,' Lucy said, flushing. 'None of them is my particular boyfriend. They're friends of the three of us.'

'I've heard that she fancies a boy called Adam Miller,' Matthew smirked.

'I do nothing of the sort,' she pouted.

'That's as may be,' Laura, ever the peacemaker, said, 'but the party sounds OK, I suppose. And since this is a special occasion, we'll allow you to stay up later than usual but we expect the party to finish around eleven o'clock and then I think it'll be time for everyone to go home.'

'Perfect, Mum,' she said, giving her mother a big hug. 'And thanks for being so understanding.'

Billy and Laura presented Lucy with a silver cross and chain in a presentation box as her birthday gift.

'You're the most wonderful mum and dad in the whole world,' she gushed, embracing each of them in turn. 'I thought allowing me to have this party was enough as a birthday present but this is the icing on the cake. I'll treasure it for the rest of my life.'

'That's OK, Lucy,' Laura said, 'but your dad and I are still trying to work out how we got talked into this.'

A couple of days later, Billy overheard Lucy finalizing arrangements and setting up the treasure hunt with her two friends in the dummy cellar underneath the lounge.

'We can ask those three boys that we met at St Bernadette's Youth Club, you know, the doubting Thomases. My family will be at the buffet, plus us six, makes twelve. That'll be enough, I think.'

'What about inviting Jilly Hughes?' Mary suggested.

'Nah. I've gone off her. First she invited me to her party and then changed her mind at the last minute because she thought I'd pinched her boyfriend. I was disinvited. And now I hate her. She's the pits.'

'Oh, I dunno,' Mary said. 'I didn't get disinvited. Jilly's not so bad.'

'Look, Mary, if you're my friend and you want to come to my party, you've got to hate the people I hate, right?'

'OK then. I hate Jilly as well.'

On the night of the party, the three girls came early to prepare the food. The trio was dressed up to the nines in the latest teenage fashions and this included mini skirts.

It had always amazed Billy how simple-minded young girls could be about their legs, whether fat like pork sausages or thin like matchsticks, in thinking they had the right to display them in public. Teenage girls appeared unaware that their generous exposure of thigh might disturb other people, both those who liked it and those who didn't. In their adolescent servility to the fashions demanded by the teenage magazines, they seemed indifferent and nonchalant about other people's feelings. Insistence on decent standards of dress was left to authority figures like head teachers or concerned parents.

'Surely you're not going to wear those minuscule skirts in public!' Billy exclaimed when the girls arrived. 'They're more like pelmets than skirts.'

'All the girls of our age wear them like this, Dad,' Lucy replied. 'They're not as short as all that.'

'Not short! They're about the size of table napkins. If Mother Superior sees you, she'll order you to say a hundred Hail Marys and to take a cold bath.'

'Our friends'd think we were square, Mr Hopkins,' Mary Feeney said diplomatically, 'if we didn't go along with what the rest of the gang was wearing. They'd say we were peculiar and that's the last thing we want.'

Mary was the confident, self-assured one of the trio and the leader. Sally, being a little more nervous than the others, was obviously a follower. Lucy was somewhere between the two, sometimes leader, sometimes follower.

Around seven o'clock the three male guests arrived together in a convoy, sticking close together for security. They walked up the garden path observed by half the family who'd been watching their approach from behind net curtains upstairs. Lucy anticipated the visitors by opening the door before they had a chance to ring the bell.

'Why, look at them!' exclaimed Matthew. 'They're pygmies.'

'Now, don't exaggerate, Matthew,' Billy said. 'They're not that small.'

Matthew had a point, though, because next to their willowy, spindly-legged hostesses they looked like scaled-down versions of adult males. Not dwarfs perhaps but miniature men.

The three boys were models of decorum in their greetings as if they'd been rehearsing their entrance for some time.

Lucy introduced them as Adam, Nigel, and Sid.

'Good evening, Mr and Mrs Hopkins,' the youths chorused. 'How are you?'

I'm sure they're not in the least interested in how we are, Billy thought. What they're trying to say is: look how we're going out of our way to be nice to Lucy's boring old parents. It's the price of our admission ticket.

Billy didn't know it at the time but it was virtually the last complete sentence he was to hear them speak. For the rest of the evening, their communications consisted, for the most part, of single words or short phrases.

'We're well, thank you,' Billy replied, 'and how are you?'

'Great,' said Adam.

So that's Lucy's possible suitor, Billy thought. Smartly dressed, good looking and appears to speak English.

'Super,' said Nigel.

'Urhnuh,' muttered Sid.

'Oh, what perfect manners!' Laura sighed. 'If only our own kids were as polite!'

'Did you find our place easily?' Billy asked.

'S'noproblem!' said Adam.

'Z'okay,' said Nigel.

The third boy, Sid, mumbled something that sounded like 'Urwzeazy' and they took this to mean he too had had no difficulty in finding the address.

The girls led them into the buffet where the Hopkins

crowd plus Des Gillespie were waiting impatiently for the off signal.

'Help yourself to a sandwich or a canapé,' Lucy gushed. 'I hope you like ham or cheese.'

'Z'okay,' from Nigel.

'Urhnuh', from Sid, which they interpreted as, 'Yes, thank you, I like ham and cheese. In fact I can eat anything.'

'Which one of you is our Lucy's boyfriend?' Mark asked, giving the boys the once-over, causing Lucy to blush to the roots.

'Mum,' Lucy said plaintively. 'Can't you stop him? He's embarrassing us.'

'Not to worry. They'll be going to their rooms soon,' Laura said ominously.

There was a pause in the conversation as the company set to eating the food. John, who'd been studying Adam's upper lip for some time, seized the opportunity to ask him if he was trying to grow a moustache.

'John!' Laura exclaimed. 'Don't be so bad mannered. You mustn't make personal remarks like that.'

'Isn't it time you lot were off to your room?' Lucy snapped. 'This is supposed to be *my* party.' Then turning to her guest, she said, 'Sorry, Adam. I must apologize for my little brothers.'

'S'noproblem,' said Adam.

The conversation continued along these lines. Billy was sure that the three young men that Lucy had invited were graduates from the Marlon Brando school of method acting since they appeared to suffer from blurred speech and a limited vocabulary and when they did volunteer an observation, it was difficult to follow the drift.

At long last, and much to the relief of the partygoers, the unwanted Hopkins contingent drifted off to their rooms, leaving them to their own devices. Matthew said he'd be going with Des to the Gillespies for the rest of the evening.

'Call us if you need us,' Billy said to Lucy as he and Laura retired to their bedroom.

'No chance of that, Dad.'

Five minutes later, the house began to oscillate as they switched the record player on to full volume. In time to a deafening thump-thump that reverberated through the house, bric-a-brac, crockery, and utensils started to vibrate and dance off the shelves.

'When we bought this house,' Billy declared, 'I didn't know Didsbury was located over a major geological fault. This earthquake must measure at least five on the Richter scale.'

'You'd better tell them to turn it down,' Laura said, 'before we lose half our ornaments.'

'Always me that has to do the unpleasant things,' he moaned.

'Are you having trouble carrying that cross, Billy, or do you need help?'

He did as he was told and the volume was reduced.

Then after a short interval, everything went deadly quiet.

'You'd better go down and see what's going on,' Laura said. 'It's much too quiet for my liking. But whatever you do, don't interfere unless you feel you have to.'

'Either it's too noisy or it's too quiet,' Billy muttered as he tiptoed downstairs once again.

Standing in the lounge, he could hear voices in the dummy cellar below but they were too indistinct to catch what they were saying. Ah, they're having their treasure hunt, he thought, and he reported it as such to Laura to put her mind at ease.

Unknown to Billy, it wasn't a treasure hunt they were holding down there. Earlier that day, at the request of his sister, Matthew, in an uncharacteristically co-operative mood, had rigged up an artificial flickering flame plugged into the mains. Prevailed upon by Mary and Sally, Lucy had reluct-antly agreed to hold a séance in an attempt to disabuse their three sceptical males of their doubts about an afterlife.

'It'll be fun,' Mary had said, 'and if we make any contact

304

with the other world, it'll be one in the eye for these doubting Thomases.'

Sally was a little nervous about the idea at first. 'I'm not so sure we should be dabbling in things like this. Suppose something weird happens. What then? But if you say it's OK, Mary, I suppose I could go along with it.'

'I dunno,' Lucy said. 'I'm scared. That stationmaster at Didsbury once scared the living daylight out of me with his talk of about the day being for the living and the night for the dead.'

But Mary persisted in saying that a séance would be 'only for a bit of a laugh'. In the end Lucy gave in, on the strict understanding that no mention was to be made to any of their parents and that Mary, being the bravest, would act as the medium and do all the talking if they did get an answer from the spirit world.

So the six young people had retired to the dummy cellar and now, holding hands, they sat in a circle round the pulsating flame which lit up their faces with an eerie hue and created spooky dark silhouettes in the gloom.

'If you're all ready,' Mary whispered portentously, 'I'll make a start.'

'OK, we're ready,' they murmured.

'Is there anyone there?' Mary asked in a doom-laden voice.

The six of them waited, straining their ears for a response. There was no sound except for their own breathing and the beating of their hearts.

'If we do make contact,' Adam chuckled, 'ask the ghosts if they know who's going to win the Cup Final this year.'

'Better still,' Nigel laughed, 'which horse will win the Grand National so we can put a bet on it.'

'Maybe we'll get to see a bloke with his head tucked under his arm,' Adam giggled.

Sid seemed reluctant to join in the banter. Lucy was holding his hand and she could feel him trembling.

They waited some more, the atmosphere becoming

seemingly more oppressive as the light glimmered, threatening to go out completely.

'This is stupid,' Adam whispered at last. 'There's no such thing as a spirit world. Let's go back to dancing upstairs.'

'I agree,' Sally said nervously. 'Let's pack it in. Nothing's going to happen.'

'Wait,' Mary hissed. 'Give the spirits time to find us. Remember they live on another plane beyond the grave and they're far, far away in the ether.'

'This isn't going to work, Mary,' Lucy sighed. 'I say we give up and get back to the music.'

'A few more minutes is all I ask,' Mary muttered, 'and then if there's no response, we'll call it a night.'

Once again silence. Then out of the shadows they heard a quiet humming like a swarm of bees.

The hair on the young men's heads stood on end. This was more than they'd bargained for.

Next, a strange, unearthly voice spoke.

'Yes. I'm here.'

'Good God!' Mary gasped. 'So there is someone there! Who are you? Identify yourself.'

'I am Mephistopholes,' said the ghostly voice. 'I am a spirit of the underworld.'

'Where are you at this moment?'

'My body is in this lonely place, buried under the Sahara Desert. But my spirit is present with you.'

'How long have you been there?'

'Many thousands of years,' said the spectral voice.

'That's it! I want out!' Sid gibbered. 'I've had enough of this.'

'Me too!' hissed Nigel. 'Where's the exit?'

'Calm down, you two,' Adam barked. 'You're letting the side down. Pull yourselves together!'

'I don't give a damn about that,' Nigel snapped. 'You were always sneering about ghosts and spooks and all of that.

Well, here's your proof. Now which way is out?'

'Stay!' Mary commanded. 'You can't walk out now. It would displease the master. Tell us, Mephistopholes, can you lead us to the spirits of the underworld?'

'I can. Wait a little while.'

There was a pause. More humming. Then a man's voice. The six listeners froze in terror.

'My name is Miles Benison. I once lived at the residence where you are now. I was a writer.'

The voice sounded hollow and echoing.

'Tell us about your time here,' Mary said.

'I died in the front bedroom of this house.'

'When did you die?'

'On the third of June, nineteen twenty-eight.'

'How did you die?'

'I lived with my friend, Reginald. He too was a writer but his books did not sell as mine did. He became jealous.'

'And what happened next?' Mary gasped.

'I suspect him of poisoning me slowly with strychnine. My death was put down to natural causes but I was murdered by my companion.'

'And where was your body laid to rest?'

They waited for the answer but it never came.

Even in the dim light, the girls could see that the boys had turned a funny colour and looked green around the gills.

Then without warning the flame went out and they were plunged into total darkness.

'We've bitten off more than we can chew here,' Mary yelled, her equanimity now gone. 'I say we call it a night.'

'Agreed!' Adam bawled. 'Let's bring this to an end. Now! It's gone too far. How the hell do we get out of here?'

Suddenly Sid let out a blood-curdling scream. 'Something warm and furry just brushed against me!' he screamed. 'It's an evil spirit!'

'And me! Something weird rubbed against my hand!' Nigel screeched.

There followed a flesh-creeping yowl that would have made the hardiest of souls cringe. The howl of a soul in pain.

Lucy recognized it at once.

'Why, it's Satchmo come to investigate.' She sighed with relief. 'And Samantha has joined us as well. Our Siamese love company.'

'All the same, I think we should end it,' Sally stuttered anxiously. 'I wasn't keen on this in the first place.'

They clambered out of the dummy cellar and climbed the wooden stairs leading to the kitchen.

They turned the knob of the door and pulled. It didn't budge! They were locked in! Even Mary's iron nerve gave way and she joined in the panic-stricken shrieks. Their screams of terror carried to the top of the house.

'I think it's the spirit of Miles Benison's poisoner,' Sally wailed. 'He's taking his revenge by locking us in.'

They hammered on the door and the ceiling, yelling for dear life.

'I don't want to spend the night down here in the dark,' Sid whimpered.

Only Lucy remained calm. She had her suspicions. 'Nonsense,' she said. 'My dad will hear us and come down and undo the bolts.'

And, indeed, Billy did hear the clamour and came running down, unable to understand how a simple treasure hunt had resulted in such hysteria.

Lucy's guests didn't hang about. They asked for their coats, put them on quickly, and with hurried goodnights were off like bats out of hell.

Lucy gave Billy a full account of what had happened. He was not pleased.

'A stupid thing to do,' he said. 'You already suffer from nightmares and tonight's experiences won't help. You should have remembered your penny catechism and the first commandment which warns against experimenting in the occult.'

'Sorry, Dad. I know it was silly. But I'm furious with

Matthew,' she fumed, 'because I'm sure he's behind it all. If I find out that he was, I'll never forgive him as long as I live. He's ruined my party.'

'You've no proof of that, Lucy.'

When Matthew came in later, Billy confronted him.

'Can't help you there, Dad. Sorry. I don't know what you're talking about. I've spent the evening with Des next door.'

Billy went back to bed that night not knowing who or what to believe.

Of one thing he was certain. Neither Lucy nor her friends would be holding any more séances.

Chapter Thirty-Seven

Five months had passed and Billy was sitting at his workshop bench in the cellar mulling over a book on wood-turning designs when Lucy popped her head round the door.

'Don't forget it's Mum's birthday next week, Dad.'

As if he could! It was more than his life was worth to forget. Why all this fuss about birthdays? he pondered. When I was a kid in Collyhurst no one ever took a blind bit of notice of *my* birthday. I can't remember ever receiving a single card or a single present and neither did anyone else in the family. Maybe we were too poor to have birthdays or maybe we couldn't see the point of 'em. For the working class in those days, birthdays were seen as a middle-class thing. It wasn't until after marriage that they became a big deal. Every time someone has a birthday, we're supposed to get in a lather of excitement about it. But what does it amount to? Year in and year out, for every person in our circle, we've got to rejoice that they not only got themselves born but have managed to survive another year. What are we saying? Congratulations, you didn't die this year and you've succeeded in adding another twelve months to your age? Some achievement!

Choosing the right card is always a problem. For the early stages in life, a card giving the actual age number is acceptable. 'Happy 22nd birthday!' or 'You're 23 today! Congratulations!' but after the age of twenty-five, such cards are taboo until, that is, an advanced age like seventy or eighty is reached when it becomes OK again. And you have to be careful about the kind of card you send. One with a picture of, say, a beautiful lady lounging in a punt being propelled by a handsome man in a blazer is out, mainly because the couple may look as if they're enjoying a better time than the recipient. It's probably safest to send a card with a picture of flowers and a blank page for a personal message.

Laura appeared with a cup of tea.

'I thought this might help to inspire a few ideas for your next wood-turning project.'

'That's thoughtful of you, Laura,' he murmured.

'There's nothing like a cuppa at *our age*,' she said.

Ah, so that was it. In her roundabout way she was reminding him that it would soon be birthday time.

'You know, Laura,' he said, looking at her earnestly, 'you look younger every day.'

'Why, thank you, kind sir.'

He thought, that wouldn't be a bad thing to write on her card. 'You look younger every day.' He made a mental note of it.

He went back to his musing. Sending out birthday greetings to all those in our circle is a major headache, mainly for Laura since she's the one who sends them out and she attaches such store by this kind of thing. And there are so many in the loop now, it's becoming harder and harder to keep track of who was born and when. It needs a mind like the Atlas computer to store the data. Luckily, Laura has such a mind for she remembers the dates of birth not only of our own little family, but also those of the extended families on both sides plus their numerous offspring. Sending out cards to mark these events is such a massive chore, maybe we should think about employing a full-time secretary.

And thinking of cards, not only do we have to send out cards for birthdays, there are all the other occasions that require acknowledgment: new babies, anniversaries, weddings, illnesses and convalescences, retirements, examination successes, deaths. And what about divorces? Shouldn't we send out a card congratulating someone on a successful divorce? After all, isn't it a cause for rejoicing for the happy couple? And there's such a high turnover in the wedding stakes, why not a card congratulating someone on their *first* marriage?

And I've not even mentioned Christmas cards, that legacy of the Victorian age which causes writer's cramp throughout the nation every year. Laura regards it as one of her Christmas chores like cooking the turkey and baking mince pies. She sends them out by the score and they come in like an avalanche during December. It's not long before we're knee deep in them and every vacant space, every ledge, is crowded with the pictures of robin redbreasts, stagecoaches, town criers, angels, and stars of Bethlehem. When every possible horizontal surface has been covered, she resorts to hanging surplus cards up on a line like Indian scalps recording the number of conquests. In some ways that's what they are, because it's difficult to resist counting the number received and comparing it with last year's total or those of friends, though the latter have to be counted surreptitiously when visiting them. We got sixty-three this year, Laura; that's three fewer than last year but at least it's ten more than Titch and Elaine. Nothing from Aunt Valerie or second cousin Kitty this year! Maybe they've taken the huff. Wonder what we've done to them? As for those family newsletters which are sometimes sent round, they're more like school reports than newsletters. And we feel so inadequate when we learn of the brilliant, breathtaking achievements of their prodigies and their examination results. Next year I'm going to send a similar report on our family's progress: 'Matthew has just completed a year's stretch in Strangeways for GBH in a pub brawl; Lucy is in remand for shoplifting; Mark is in an approved school for vandalism while young John has been honing his skills as a pickpocket, he can now remove your wallet without you feeling a thing. But Laura is the one I am most proud of. She can now drink me under the table any time, any place. We are still in rehab, by the way, and hope to be out by Christmas to have a family knees-up in our local hostelry.'

Then there's the matter of the birthday gift. I never seem to get it right when I buy a gift for Laura. I've got to avoid getting something she doesn't want. I'm certainly not going to make the mistake Titch made with Elaine by buying her a vacuum cleaner. That was stupid and unimaginative; I don't know what he was thinking of. Money or a cheque are also prohibited for similar reasons and in addition they're considered too commercial. A gift certificate comes into the same category as it lacks the affectionate, romantic touch. Whatever I do, I must avoid anything that reminds her that she's getting older, like Phyllosan that claims to fortify the over forties or a bottle of Wincarnis tonic wine or a corn remover set. The easiest thing is to ask her. Or so I used to think.

'What kind of present would you like, Laura?'

'Something personal, something I wouldn't ordinarily buy myself.'

This places a severe limit on my choices for it excludes items like gloves, scarves, umbrellas since she usually buys these things for herself. But this birthday is her fortieth and I want to get her something extra special. But what exactly?

With these embargoes running through his mind, Billy was stuck. How to get round all these dos and dont's? The solution was to consult another woman, a lady who was bound to know the answer. Who was it he always went to when he had a problem? Why his mam of course! Her eyesight may have been becoming weaker but not so her mind; that was still as sharp as a needle.

That weekend when he and Laura were paying their usual Saturday afternoon visit to Langley, he managed to get Mam on her own in the kitchen when Laura had gone to do some shopping for her.

313

'This is no ordinary birthday, Mam,' he said. 'It's import-ant and I don't mind spending more than usual. What would you recommend I buy?'

'For an occasion like this,' she said, 'why not buy her not one but a few things to be on the safe side? Get her a pot plant like the one I have in the hallway; next, some-thing to make her life easier; third, a lovely piece of jewellery that she'll be proud to wear when you take her out; and last, what about a nice item of clothing, something bright, that will make her stand out in a crowd. Do you know her size?'

'I'm not sure of her exact size but I can make a rough guess.'

Mam was most helpful and she went on to detail the things that she herself would have liked. Good old Mam, always helpful with advice when he needed it. He made notes and went into town on Monday on his way home from college.

On Friday, 30 May 1968, Billy rose early and was soon down in the kitchen making Laura an early cup of tea. He'd been planning the day for some time and he wanted to make it memorable.

'Laura,' he said as he put the tea down on the bedside cabinet, 'this is indeed a red letter day. One that we should never forget as long as we live.'

Laura's face lit up. Ah, so he's remembered after all, she thought.

'I'm glad you think that, Billy.' She smiled happily. 'It's one I've been looking forward to for some time.'

'I didn't think you would have attached as much signifi-cance to it as I have.'

'Of course I did. It's only once in a lifetime that we can celebrate an event like this.'

'I'm surprised, Laura, as I never thought you would have noticed the date and how important it is.'

Laura was now looking puzzled. 'I presume we're talking about the same thing.'

'But of course. Later today, Matthew will get the results of the Oxford entrance exam he took at school last month and also his mock A-levels.'

'I'm aware of that, Billy. I hadn't forgotten. It's a big day for Matthew.'

'And there's something else, Laura,' he said with a wide grin.

'Yes, and that is?' She beamed.

'Manchester United's won the European Cup, the first English club to do so. What a match it was! They beat Benfica four goals to one in extra time. At full-time the score was one all. Let me read what it says in the newspaper:

'Within three minutes of extra time, Busby's team had shown us how magnificent is the pride that has taken this club to the top through frustration and even tragedy.

Best, hustled and bustled out of the game for most of the 93 minutes of normal time, picked up a header from Bryan Kidd, then dribbled past a vicious tackle. Then as cool and calm as you like, he sauntered round Henrique before tapping the ball in the net with the composure of a dad playing football with his lads on Blackpool sands.'

'I'm glad it makes you so happy, Billy.' Laura couldn't hide the disappointment in her voice.

'But that's not the only reason to be joyful,' he said. 'There's something else for us to look forward to.'

'What's that?' She smiled hopefully.

'Tonight there's going to be a bus parade through the city centre and the whole team will be there holding up the cup for everyone to see. I think we should all go down as a family to cheer them on. It's truly a great day for Manchester. I've arranged for us to go with your folks. You know what an avid fan your father is.'

'But of course we must go into town to celebrate,' she sighed, 'and I'm so glad we'll be meeting Mammy and Daddy.'

Downstairs the doorbell rang.

'I'd better go and see who that is,' he grinned. 'Probably the postman.'

He was soon back with a pot plant covered with a plastic bag and a sheaf of envelopes.

'A couple of bills for me,' he said as he riffled through the mail. 'The other ten look like greeting cards for you. But of course, I nearly forgot, it's your birthday! How old are you? Is it thirty-nine?'

'Quit fooling about, Billy. You know perfectly well I'm forty today. An old lady.'

'Happy birthday, Laura,' he said, kissing her. 'And being married to a youngster doesn't mean you're old.'

'You're five weeks younger, which doesn't exactly make you a youngster. But I've reached the big four-o and I feel as if I'm over the hill. Middle-aged in fact. I can hear the siren voices chanting on the wind. "Come and join us," they sing.'

'You don't mean you're going to join the Salvation Army?'

'No, these voices are in an old people's nursing home in Southport and they're inviting me to their Bingo session.'

'Then, my old dutch, here are my presents, specially chosen for you on this momentous occasion. First, a pot plant. I thought you might like this aspidistra,' he said removing the plastic bag with a flourish. 'It's not called the cast-iron plant for nothing; it'll grow anywhere and under any conditions.'

'I think it's nice, Billy,' she said carefully. 'And what a surprise! What made you think of an aspidistra, of all things? My old grandma used to have one in her room and didn't Gracie Fields have a song about one?'

'Glad you like it, Laura. Now, didn't you say I was to get you something that you wouldn't think of buying yourself? Well, here's hoping I made the right choice,' he said with a broad grin as he handed her a gift-wrapped package.

With a coy smile, she carefully removed the shiny paper. The smile froze a little when she saw what it contained. 'Why, it's an electric iron!' There was a slight pause before she said, 'How thoughtful of you. An electric iron!'

'State of the art,' Billy said enthusiastically. 'That should make that particular chore less irksome. It's the latest model. I wasn't sure about it at first. I thought you might consider it too utilitarian but it's not the only thing I've got you. And now for the highlight, a piece of jewellery I know you'll like,' he said handing her a small decorated box tied with a red ribbon.

'Oh, you shouldn't have, Billy. Wasting your money. I wonder what on earth it can be.'

Her expression remained fixed when she saw it was a mother-of-pearl brooch bearing the title MOTHER.

'It's . . .' once again a slight pause, 'quite lovely,' she murmured slowly. 'What made you think of a brooch like this?'

'It was my mother,' he said proudly. 'She said she's always been delighted with the one she's had for over forty years. She wears it on every festive occasion. And there's more. Since you now have a brooch, I thought you might like a cardigan you can pin it on.'

So saying, he produced the bright lime-green cardigan he'd purchased from Marks and Spencer's.

'I didn't know your size but I remembered it had a four in it and I thought it might be best to go for the bigger size rather than one that was too tight. It's size twenty-four. The lady in the store told me that cardigans are often worn loose nowadays.'

'Billy, I'll never be able to thank you for all your wonderfully kind gifts. You and your mother have really gone to town this time. When you were going on about Manchester United, I said to myself, ah, he's forgotten. But now I see that you hadn't. And it's the thought that counts.'

'We can celebrate it tonight by taking the family into town

to welcome the team back from Wembley. It'll be a big cavalcade and there'll be huge crowds there.'

'I suppose so,' she said, 'if that's the way you think we should celebrate my birthday.'

'You must think I'm a complete moron, Laura. I've also booked a candlelit dinner for two at the Casa España for tomorrow night.'

'I knew you would do something romantic in the end, despite the football distraction. And thank you for your lovely presents.'

'Do you like them?'

'I love them. Such imaginative choices.'

'If you don't like them, Laura, I have the receipts right here and you can take them back and exchange 'em.'

'No, I love them. Honestly, Billy.'

'I can tell by your face, Laura, that you're not that keen.'

'You're wrong, Billy. I'm quite taken by them all.'

'I'm so relieved. Though when my mam and I talked about it, we knew you'd go for them somehow.'

'They're exactly what I wanted. And they're certainly things I wouldn't normally have bought for myself. Incidentally, did I hear you say you had the receipts?'

Billy was gratified to know that she truly liked the gifts, as she did every year. Nevertheless he couldn't help wondering how she would have fared on a lie detector test. Had she been faking it all these years?

After breakfast, the kids brought their gifts. From Matthew, a manicure set; from Lucy a moulded vase which she had made in her art class; from Mark a box of Cadbury's Lucky Numbers (they were his favourite); and from John a box of Bassett's Jelly Babies (they were *his* favourite).

'You couldn't have got me better gifts,' Laura enthused. 'I'm lucky to have such a generous family.'

'I'm off to school,' Matthew said. 'This afternoon, we should get our exam results. Let's hope they're good enough for a further reason to celebrate.'

* * *

At four o'clock the family sat down to tea.

'We'd better get into town early if we're to get decent places,' Billy said. 'Matthew isn't in yet and I do hope he isn't too long getting back home.'

As if he'd overheard them, there was the sound of the key turning in the front door and shortly after that Matthew came into the dining room.

'Sorry to be late, folks,' he said, 'but I was held up at school. The sixth form was having a little shindig.'

'To celebrate the Manchester United victory, I suppose,' Billy said, still fooling around.

'No, Dad. As you know we got our results,' he said gravely. 'I think you'd better sit down for this.'

Uh-oh, Billy thought. Bad news coming. And on Laura's birthday of all days!

'You didn't fail, surely?' Laura asked anxiously.

'No, no, not quite. But the results were totally unexpected.'

'Don't keep us in suspense, Matthew,' Billy said. 'Come on, tell us. We can take it.'

'OK then. I took five subjects, you remember. Physics, chemistry, maths, additional maths, and general studies.'

'And, and . . .'

'I was awarded five As.'

'Impossible!' Billy gasped. 'No one ever gets five As, not even in the mock exams!'

'I did, Dad,' he said quietly. 'I'm sure I can repeat them when I do the actual exams next week.'

'That's the best birthday present you could have ever given me, Matthew.'

'Wait, Mum, there's more. I passed the first part of the Oxford entrance exam and I'm to be interviewed for Balliol. If successful, I'll start next year.'

'Balliol? Surely not!' Laura exclaimed. 'Why, only royalty and the upper classes go there! I do hope your tutor isn't aiming too high.'

'Some of our greatest leaders and statesmen went there!' Billy cried. 'Why, you couldn't count the number of great writers, poets, cabinet ministers, scientists that were educated there. Anybody who's anybody went there. And if you're accepted, you won't be the first Hopkins either. Gerard Manley was once a student there.'

'Whoa! Hold your horses,' Matthew replied. 'It's by no means certain that they'll accept me. Competition is fierce.'

But once Billy's hopes had been raised, there was no going back. He could already see his son there.

'What a great day this has been!' Billy said to Laura as he drove the family to town for the parade. 'First, a huge Manchester football success, then your birthday, and finally Matthew's magnificent results and a chance for Balliol! It's too much in one day.'

'I don't want to be a damper on all this excitement,' Laura said, 'but my Scottish upbringing has taught me to be cautious and not to count my chickens. Remember there's many a slip 'twixt the cup and lip. The time to rejoice is when the dream comes true.'

That evening they met Duncan and Louise in Piccadilly to welcome the Reds home. The Mackenzies were getting on in years but both seemed as lively and active as ever. When Duncan heard about Matthew's promising success, he almost did the sword dance right there in the street.

'Well done, young man,' he said, pumping Matthew's hand vigorously. 'You'll make a distinguished scientist one day. That's the Mackenzie brain coming to the fore.'

Huh, Billy thought.

Chapter Thirty-Eight

Some time later, Matthew travelled to Oxford for his interview and the second part of the entrance exam. Laura made sure he was immaculately turned out. Balliol had reserved a room within the college precincts for him.

'I can see it and smell it now,' Billy said. 'An oak-panelled room at the top of a narrow spiral staircase, at the end of a long winding corridor which is steeped in history and tradition.'

There had been little or nothing Damian College could do to coach him for the examination as the school had little or no experience of training their students for Balliol. Billy worried a great deal about how well Matthew was prepared since he was going into the unknown. His examination results were impeccable and Billy doubted if anyone from a public or state school would better them. Would they examine his general knowledge, his reading, his personal experiences, his background? It was anybody's guess. If they talked to Matthew about his knowledge of the sciences, he could more than hold his own but it was other fields that gave more cause for concern.

'You can but do your best, lad,' Billy said as he saw him off at Manchester's Piccadilly Station. 'But if you do get a place, it will be a feather in your cap. Remember you're a Mancunian and be proud of your background.'

'I think in many ways, Dad, I'd rather go to a red-brick university as I've got the impression from what I've heard that Oxford and Cambridge are strongholds of the upper classes. I should have a better idea after I've visited the place.'

For the four days that Matthew was away, Billy and Laura were on tenterhooks.

'I do hope he remembers to speak up and answer clearly,' Billy said. 'His experiences and education in Kenya might hold him in good stead.'

When Matthew did get back, the family crowded round him to hear how he'd got on amongst the 'eggheads', as Lucy liked to refer to them.

'Give Matthew a chance to catch his breath,' Laura said, as she handed him a cup of tea and a large piece of her celebratory apple pie. 'He's only just stepped off the train.'

'Oxford's one of the most beautiful cities I've ever seen,' he reported. 'It simply reeks of history and tradition and I found it awesome. As for my entrance examination, I don't think I stand a chance as the kinds of questions they set were beyond my ken.'

'For example?' Billy asked.

'There were so many I can't remember them all but stuff like, what did I think a university was for? What did I expect it would do for me? Had I read Newman's *Idea of a University*? What were my views on ethics in science. Stuff like that.'

'That's the kind of thing I'd expect you to be able to discuss *after* university, not before,' Billy remarked.

'One thing I did notice though. Many of the other candidates were from independent schools like Eton and Harrow, and others whose names I forget. Judging from their accents, I don't think somehow they're my type. I'm not at all sure how I'd get on with them. I definitely didn't feel at home in their company.'

'You had a public school accent when we came home from Kenya,' Laura remarked. 'A pity in many ways that you lost it.'

In August, Matthew received the stupendous news that he had achieved the five As that the mock exams had predicted. Next day, the *Manchester Evening News* sent a journalist round to the house to report on Matthew's results. He had achieved the best A-level results in the North of England and Matthew was the subject of a special news feature. Billy's pride in his son knew no bounds.

The news which came from Oxford later that year, however, was not so good, being just as Matthew had anticipated. He received a polite letter from Balliol regretting that they were unable to offer him a place.

The sixth form tutor at Damian College hit the roof when he heard the news, leaving no doubt as to where his political sympathies lay.

'Matthew was the ideal candidate to study science at Oxford,' he raged. 'They couldn't have found a better applicant. But without doubt there's class bias at work there. Oxbridge is like a finishing school for the British Establishment and they prefer to select their own. They don't take external examination results into account at all but prefer to rely on their own internal assessments. The headmaster of Harrow lodged a strong complaint when he heard that future candidates might be evaluated on their A-level results. You have only to look at the figures to see they're elitist. Relatively few successful candidates come from the north. Their intake overwhelmingly favours London and the south-east and nearly half their students are from private schools. Matthew probably had the wrong accent. I asked Balliol for a reason for his rejection and they told me that, despite his being highly intelligent, he lacked confidence. Have you ever heard such rubbish?'

Matthew was more conciliatory towards Balliol. 'In many ways I'm glad I was not accepted. It wasn't my scene. This isn't sour grapes but I'd have turned it down even if they had offered me a place. I didn't altogether like the look of the accommodation for a start. I felt stifled in the poky little room they put me in. As for the place reeking of history and all that, it was more like a fusty smell of boiled cabbage and beeswax. When I found out that the men's colleges in Oxford outnumbered the women's by something like five to one, that was it. I definitely did not want to go there. It'd have been the sexual segregation of Damian College all over again.'

Billy and Laura, too, were philosophical about Matthew's rejection. Laura in particular was fatalistic.

'If God had intended Matthew to go to Oxford, He'd have arranged it that way. Something better will turn up, you'll see.'

Somehow, Billy thought, it wasn't God but the snooty interviewers at Balliol who had fixed it that way. But Laura proved to be right. Again! Soon after the Oxford rejection, the offers of university places came pouring in from Manchester, Newcastle, Essex, Nottingham, Sheffield, and Sussex. Matthew had the pick of the crop. He was tempted to join his friend at the University of Essex but decided to choose the one that was considered to be the 'in' place to go.

'You two certainly picked the sexiest universities,' Billy remarked. 'Essex and Sussex.'

Chapter Thirty-Nine

'Sussex has a lot going for it,' Matthew explained, as he completed the forms of acceptance at the dining-room table. 'It's one of the newest universities, and at my interview in Brighton last month, I liked the atmosphere, the warm welcome, and the applied sciences buildings are fantastically well equipped. It's right up my street and I can hardly wait to get there.'

Billy drove him to Brighton at the beginning of term and he, too, was impressed by the place. After taking in the bustling holiday atmosphere along the seafront, they arrived at the rural campus situated near the East Sussex village of Falmer, on the edge of the South Downs.

'It's everything the brochure says it is,' Billy said, reading from the introductory booklet. ' "The only university in England entirely located in an area of outstanding natural beauty and it runs entirely from renewable energy sources. Founded in August 1961, one of several universities to be built in the sixties." '

'Thank God, Dad, that I didn't get accepted by Oxford. This is much better. I've heard that many students who *were* accepted at Oxbridge have opted to go for this place instead. Also there are loads of other students here because of the art college and teacher training college.'

'Mind you,' Billy laughed, 'I've read that it also has a reputation for having a radical and avant-garde student population. I hope you don't go joining any revolutionary movements while you're here.'

'That's news to me, Dad. First I've heard of it.'

'I was joking, Matthew. I'm impressed by this university,

especially now that the eminent historian, Asa Briggs, has been appointed as Vice-Chancellor. It has a tremendous reputation for its teaching and research. Your mother and I are so happy that you decided to come here. We know you're going to do well.'

The rest of the day was spent searching out suitable digs. They found lodgings near the Palace Pier in Kemp Town with a motherly landlady who promised to look after Matthew as if he were her own.

'Yes,' she bubbled, 'I'll see to it that he eats sensible, wholesome food, starts the day on a good breakfast, and goes to bed early with a nice cup of cocoa.'

Like home from home, Billy thought.

He drove back to Manchester later that day in a joyful frame of mind. To see Matthew happy and set up at a good university had been so important a part of Billy's dream and here at last it had come true. On the way home, he sang every song he knew that contained the word 'happy': 'Happy Days Are Here Again', 'It's a Hap-Hap-Happy Day', 'I Wanna Be Happy But I Can't Be Happy Till I Make You Happy Too'.

At home, he gave a full report to Laura who had stayed behind to look after the fort. She rejoiced to hear how things had worked out. For all that, there was an air of sadness in the house with Matthew gone. No deafening band rehearsals, no more pranks, no more disputations about politics or religion. Lucy in particular missed him at the dinner table as she had no one to bicker with. There was Mark and John but it wasn't the same. Everyone looked forward to Matthew's first letter giving details of his first few weeks. When it finally came, Billy commandeered it and found there were two letters in the envelope. One to Laura and the family and one specifically for him.

Laura read her letter voraciously. 'What a relief,' she said when she'd finished reading, 'to know that he's managing OK and seems to be enjoying life to the full there in Brighton.

I wonder when he gets time to do any work as most of his energies appear to be taken up with the social round. He says it's like London by the sea as there's something on every night. What does your letter say?'

'It's mainly about his digs and his fussy landlady and the walks he and his friend have been on. I suspect there is a hidden message behind his words.'

'I do hope he's managing his money all right. You hear so many tales of students running short of cash and not being able to cope.'

'I'm sure Matthew is more than holding his own. Perhaps you should read his letter and my reply. Here they are.'

5.10.68
Dear Dad,

Most of my news is contained in the letter to Mum and the family. This letter is specially for you to say thanks for driving me down here last week. I shall be forever IN YOUR DEBT and I'LL NEVER BE ABLE TO REPAY YOU for all you've done for me.

As you know my room is spacIOUS though the digs I'M IN are located in a QUEER little STREET in the suburb of Kemp Town. The landlady whom you met is a motherly sort who tends to overfeed me and I OFTEN HAVE TO decline the offer of second helpings, like the fish she cooked with French dressING FOR MY SUPPER the other night. All her meals are huge and I don't think I NEED all the BEANS, CABBAGE, SAUSAGE AND MASH, POTATOES, LETTUCE, and BREAD she is forever feeding us.

You'll be glad to know that I have made a good friend of the other student resident here, Paul Friedlander. We are planning to set up in our own FLAT next term. It may be a little more expensive but we thought we might splash out and go for BROKE. Brighton is a pretty town that caters for all NEEDs if you have the MONEY of course. On Sunday, Paul and I CLEANED OUT our rooms in the morning and

went for a walk in the afternoon on the <u>DOWNS</u> <u>AND</u> it was
good to get <u>OUT</u> for a while. The road up was <u>STONY</u> but we
enjoyed climbing <u>ON THE ROCKS</u>. Surprisingly on the top, it
was <u>AS FLAT AS A PANCAKE</u>. In many ways, the walk was a
mistake as I found the new shoes I bought in Manchester
were too <u>TIGHT</u> and <u>I REALLY FELT THE PINCH</u>, especially on
the <u>HARD UP</u>ward ascent. To make matters worse, I twisted
my ankle on the way down and when I took my sock off, I
found the <u>SKIN T</u>orn but a spot of <u>BORACIC</u> powder should
put things right. To be on the safe side though <u>I'M</u> going to
get it <u>STRAPPED</u> up.

*   <u>I'M</u> still waiting for my grant to arrive but I don't like*
<u>ASKING YOU FOR BOODLE</u>. But with my ankle the way it is I
think <u>I SHALL NEED A PONY</u> to get around.
That's all £or now
£ove,
Matthew.

'Do you think he's asking for money?' Laura said.

'That's Matthew's funny way of asking for help. Now read my reply which is also in code.'

10.10.68
To a <u>VERY DEAR</u> son
Dear Matthew,
Many thanks for your <u>NO</u>te. It was good to hear from you
and to k<u>NO</u>w that everything is going well. Driving you to
Brighton was <u>NOTHING. DOING</u> my duty as a father is
reward e<u>NO</u>ugh. But <u>NO</u>w for a spot of advice:<u>NOT A</u>
<u>BENE</u> Avoid distractions of which in Brighton there must
be ma<u>NY I.E.</u> Ten-pin-bowling and the like. If people try
to tempt you, stand for <u>NO</u> <u>NON</u>sense because being a
student is fi<u>NE IN</u> so many ways and the pursuit of
k<u>NO</u>wledge is a <u>NO</u>ble thing. With regard to your delayed
grant, <u>YOU MUST</u> write and complain to the Education
Authority and if they won't <u>BUDGE T</u>ry phoning them.

I CANNOT SEND YOU A PONY BUT AM ENCLOSING INSTEAD A COUPLE OF COCK AND HENS.
Love from your
£ather

Chapter Forty

Mark was expecting his pal, Spud Murphy, and was looking out through the front room window for him.

'Mum,' he called, 'there's a strange bloke coming to the front door. He's either a tinker or a tramp after money or odd jobs. He's dressed in an old army overcoat with a piece of string for a belt and he's wearing a tie but no shirt.'

'Leave it to me, Mark,' his mother said. 'I'll deal with him.'

Laura opened the door and stared uncomprehendingly at the man who stood on the threshold. 'Yes, can I help you?' Then the penny dropped. It was her son, home from Brighton for the long summer vacation.

'Matthew!' she gasped, embracing him immediately. 'For a brief moment I didn't recognize you. You've changed so much since you were home at Christmas.'

'I suppose I have,' he grinned.

'Billy, Billy!' Laura called down to the basement where Billy was producing yet another coffee table. 'Your long-lost son is here!'

Billy came bounding up the cellar steps two at a time. 'Well, I never,' he panted, taking Matthew's hand in a firm handshake. 'Home is the sailor, home from sea.'

'And the hunter home from the hill,' Matthew laughed, completing the Robert Louis Stevenson quotation.

'And the hobo home from the brick yard.' Billy grimaced. 'What happened to the Weaver-to-Wearer suit you went off in?'

'Had to pawn it, Dad, for some dosh.' Matthew grinned. 'Tell you about it later.'

By now, the rest of the family had come down to the hall and surrounded him, plying him with a thousand questions.

Billy: Did you come by train or bus? Was it a good journey?

John: Did you bring anything for me?

Lucy: When are you going back?

Mark: Why is your hair like a girl's?

Laura: Are you hungry? Would you like some food?

'Hold it, everybody!' Billy exclaimed. 'Give the lad a chance to get in. Plenty of time for questions later.'

'I'll bet you'd like to get out of those dirty old travelling clothes,' Laura said, 'and change into your best.'

'These are my best,' Matthew laughed. 'University students from Brighton don't exactly go in for sartorial elegance.'

Helped by Mark and John, Matthew carried his luggage to his old room at the top of the house. Minutes later he was back. 'Now what was it you were saying about food, Mum?'

Watched by the family, Matthew made short work of the plate of egg and chips set before him.

'Do you realize it's seven whole months since we last saw you, Matthew?' Laura said.

'Sorry about that, Mum,' he said as he tucked in. 'But as I wrote to you at the time, Des wanted to show me around the University of Essex and so I spent part of Easter vac with him at Southend. We took a couple of bar jobs to earn some money. Then I had to return his hospitality and he came to visit me at Brighton for a few days.'

'Anyway, it's good to see you back at last,' Billy said warmly. 'So tell us how things have been going. Have you settled in at Brighton? Hasn't the money I've been sending been enough?'

'Not quite, Dad, but I've managed to get by. As for settling in, things are fine now. At first, I felt like a small fish in a big pond, the other students seemed so much more worldly-wise and self assured, some of them posh and well heeled, with parents who were diplomats and aristocrats. Coming from an ordinary northern grammar school, at times I felt inferior but a bunch of us have formed a northerners' group and I'm much more comfortable with them because we speak the same language and try to be less pretentious.'

'Good for you, Matthew,' Billy said. 'And what about your academic work? How are you getting on in that department?'

'Quite well, Dad. I've been given a huge assignment for the vac. Got to write a dissertation.'

'Maybe I can help you with it,' Billy said.

'The subject is the philosophy of mathematics. I've got to write around twenty thousand words saying what we mean when we say that one matchstick AND another matchstick make TWO matchsticks.'

'I think I shall have to pass on that one.'

'Oh, and I forgot to tell you. At the end of the session, I was awarded the prize for best student of the year in mathematical and physical sciences.'

'So now he tells us!' Laura exclaimed. 'Drops it in our laps as a throwaway line. Prize for being best student! As if it were a mere nothing!'

'Congratulations, son!' Billy said, slapping him on the back just as Matthew had placed a few chips in his mouth. 'I always knew you had it in you. A true Hopkins!'

'Don't you mean a Mackenzie?' Laura said. 'We Scots are the ones with the brains.'

'What about my success?' Lucy asked sulkily. 'The whizz-kid there isn't the only one in this family, you know.'

'Sorry, Lucy,' Billy said. 'We got carried away as it's such a long time since we saw this young man. You should know, Matthew, that Lucy got herself three As at A-level this year. Tell him yourself, Lucy.'

'I got A for art, A for English and A for British Constitution,' she announced proudly.

'That's great, Lucy,' Matthew enthused. 'Congratulations! But I never had you down for British Constitution unless you mean dietetics.'

'I see your standard of wit has not improved. No, it was that or history or geography and I didn't fancy either of them. Anyway the three subjects are enough to get me into the College of Art in All Saints. With luck, I could have a Diploma in Art and be a qualified teacher earning a good salary in a few years' time.'

'And what about me?' Mark said. 'Have you forgotten that I'm now at Damian College and was second in class in the term exams and it won't be long before I'm studying for O-levels?'

'And me!' John piped up. 'I've sat for secondary school entrance exam and if I pass, I might be going to Damian College, like all the boys in this house.'

'By that time,' Billy commented, 'Manchester will have gone over to comprehensive with the eleven-plus exam abolished and so you'll probably go anyway without exams.'

'Wow! I'd forgotten what the rest of you were doing,' Matthew laughed. 'Everyone's growing up so fast.'

'And some of us are growing old,' Laura said ruefully.

'Just grow along with me!' Billy chuckled, putting his arm round her. 'The best is yet to be.'

A little later when they were alone, Billy said, 'You know, Laura, I'm so happy the way things are turning out. All my long-term plans for them are coming to fruition. Take Matthew. He and Des have taken holiday jobs in a Stockport bottling plant to earn their keep. I admire them for that. Who cares that they both look like a couple of Old Testament prophets with their straggly hair hanging round their collars? When I see Matthew today, I can see myself when I was his age. He's a chip off the old block all right.'

'Isn't that what you always wanted? To produce a carbon copy of yourself?'

'So what's wrong with that? Not quite a carbon copy though. Matthew isn't as good looking. Seriously, Laura, he's doing so well, he could be anything he wants to be. The possibilities are endless. I can see him now with a big job in research, electronics, nuclear power, aerospace, optics, engineering, you name it; the sky's the limit. He could even make university professor.'

'Fine, Billy, but as I'm always warning you, it's never wise to build up your hopes too high.'

For the rest of the holiday, Matthew and Des worked at the bottling plant. 'Soul-destroying' work they called it. As the vacation drew to a close, though, Billy wondered about Matthew's dissertation on the philosophy of mathematics as he didn't appear to be doing any studying. It was a case of work all day and clubbing with his friends all night. Billy couldn't understand where they got the energy from.

'No problem, Dad,' he said when Billy asked him about his assignment. 'I've got it well in hand.'

'But there's only a few days of the holiday left! How are you going to do it in that time?'

'You worry too much, Dad. I've got a whole week. In student time, that's forever.'

In the last seven days, Matthew got down to work with a vengeance. He retired to his room, sat at his desk and wrote and wrote for thirty-six hours without stopping.

'I pity the poor devil who has to mark this stuff,' he remarked when he emerged from the marathon.

'You know, Laura,' Billy said, 'this routine Matthew has adopted of working during the day, living it up at night, and at the same time writing a demanding dissertation must be murderously difficult. Matthew appears to keep going without sleep. It reminds me of the time when I held down two jobs at the same time. You remember? Teaching during the day and working at Kellogg's at night. But at least I got a little sleep each night. Matthew appears to be going without sleep. How *does* he do it?'

'Search me,' she said, 'but I'm concerned about his health. He looks so pale.'

'I don't want to worry you, Laura, but I can't help wondering if he's on some sort of drug to keep him going. I read recently in the *Telegraph* that drugs called Purple Hearts can keep a person awake and alert for up to forty-eight hours.

Some housewives use them as anti-depressants and for slimming.'

'Not this housewife, I can assure you, Billy, but I do hope Matthew's not jeopardizing his health.'

Billy broached the subject and asked Matthew outright the next time he saw him.

'I give you my word of honour, Dad,' Matthew said, 'that I'm not taking Purple Hearts, never have and never will. It's only the Mods who use 'em. I wouldn't even know where to get 'em.'

That was good enough for Billy.

At the end of September, Matthew returned to Brighton with his dissertation finished, ready for his second year. Lucy began her art course, and at Damian College Mark went into the Lower Fourth while John started his first year. Billy's long-cherished hopes and dreams for his children were falling neatly into place. His cup overflowed.

Chapter Forty-One

Nineteen seventy-one was a significant year in many ways. Uppermost in many British people's minds was the question of whether or not Britain should join the European Common Market. For months the government of Edward Heath had prepared the nation for life without pounds, shillings and pence and had introduced the people to pounds and new pence only. The Decimal Currency Board spent huge sums persuading everyone that not only was the change logical, it would make life simpler and bring the country into line with the rest of Europe. During the changeover there was a great deal of confusion, especially among the elderly, many of whom had to go back to school to be taught by their grandchildren. A few diehards resisted the changes but they fought a losing battle. They did succeed, however, in keeping the measure of temperature in Fahrenheit rather than Centigrade, and managed to postpone 'going metric' to an indefinite time in the future.

The name of Margaret Thatcher became better known when, as Minister of Education, she abolished free school milk and was dubbed 'Thatcher the milk snatcher'. In the world of fashion, platform shoes and hot pants took over from the mini skirt, while the Mohican hairstyle found favour among daring young men. The video cassette recorder (VCR) was introduced and in the same year the 140-year-old London Bridge was transported to the USA and rebuilt as a tourist attraction in Lake Havasu City in the Arizona Desert. Finally, after a three-year disastrous experiment with British Standard Time the country returned to GMT and British Summer Time, and the nation thankfully put their clocks back by one hour in October and enjoyed an extra sixty minutes in bed.

It was just before Easter and eight months after Matthew had gone back to Brighton. Billy was driving back home from college and looking forward to the weekend. As he negotiated the traffic down the East Lancs road, he thought about the interview he'd had with Sister Benedict that afternoon. She'd asked to see him in her office. At first he'd wondered if he'd unwittingly put his foot in it again but it was nothing like that. On the contrary, he'd found it flattering.

'Mr Hopkins, I've asked to see you to put an idea to you for your consideration. Our affiliated brother college just outside Kilmarnock in Scotland has a vacancy for the post of Head of Education. They've advertised it nationally and, while they've received a number of applications, they don't consider them suitable for this important appointment in a Catholic college. I hope you don't mind, but I've put your name forward and Brother Eugene, the Principal, was particularly interested when he learned of your qualifications and wide experience. Obviously nobody expects you to make an instant decision but we wonder if you and your wife would talk it over and let us know your reactions. The post means considerable promotion for you along with a commensurate salary to compensate for the upheaval it would entail.'

He'd replied that he was deeply honoured to have been thought about in this way but his initial reaction was to decline as it would involve uprooting himself and his family. Still it was nice to think that Sister Benedict had such a high opinion of him. He had been at the college for more than six years and perhaps it *was* time to think about applying for a more senior post but things were going too well at home to consider such a big move. Matthew had glittering prospects at university, Lucy was excelling in her art teacher course, and Mark and John were settled in at his old school, Damian College. Most important, Laura loved her home and the locality. No, a move was out of the question.

How the years have gone by, he thought. Time really does fly. Well, at least it does for me nowadays. When I was a boy, it seemed to drag and a year was like eternity. I suppose that's understandable since for a kid ten years old, a year represents one-tenth of his existence and that's a big slice out of his life. But for a forty-plus-year-old like me, a year is only one-fortieth. No wonder they say time appears to accelerate the older you get. For an eighty-year-old like Mam, a year must seem like a month and a week like a day. And to think, half a year has gone by since Matthew returned to university. Pity he couldn't make it home at Christmas, Laura and I were so disappointed but I suppose it's a sign that Matthew's become independent and is no longer tied to his mother's apron strings. In many ways, I can well understand his wanting to visit Des in Southend again. A better chance of getting holiday jobs there, he'd reckoned. But he's doing so well at Sussex, I can forgive him anything. One day he'll make his mark, I'm sure, and go on to a distinguished career in science.

Same with Lucy, she's well into her art course and is obviously enjoying it. I admire the way she's taken up part-time evening work for the last few months at that craft and book centre in town though I can't help thinking it's got a peculiar name for a bookstore: On the Eighth Day. The day after God rested, He created something better, they claim. And I'm not sure I approve of the kind of books exchanged there. There are some strange-sounding volumes on her shelves, like *The Tibetan Book of the Dead*. And what was it she was reading the other night? *The Zodiac and the Soul* by Charles Carter. What's that all about, for goodness sake? But I approve strongly of students working their way through college as long as they don't let it interfere with their studies.

His reverie was brought to a sudden end when he found he'd arrived home. He parked the car in the garage, turned his key in the front door, put his briefcase on the hallstand and went into the kitchen.

'Hello, Billy,' Laura said, pecking him on the cheek. 'I'll put the kettle on.'

There was something about her demeanour that wasn't right. She looked too serious, too solemn. Something was wrong. He could feel it in his bones.

'Where are the kids?' he asked.

'As usual, watching television.'

'Why are you looking so sad, Laura? What's up?'

She waited until he had a mug of tea in his hand before she told him.

'Matthew's home. He's in his room.'

'What? Matthew, home? But it's the middle of term! What's happened? Is he ill? Is it something serious?'

'I think I'd better let him tell you about it himself.' She went to the foot of the stairs and called, 'Matthew! Dad's home!'

A few minutes later, Matthew appeared and Billy was staggered when he saw him. It wasn't the long hair or his unkempt appearance as it had been when he came home for the summer holiday. It was his facial expression or, to be more precise, his lack of it. He looked tired and heavy-eyed. Billy had seen that look somewhere else but he couldn't place it. Then it came back to him in a flash. The geriatric nursing home! That's where he'd seen that vacant stare before. But surely not on his son! Where was the bright-eyed, intelligent youth who had departed from home last September?

Billy embraced him in a bear hug. 'Good to see you back, son. But what on earth's brought you home at this time? Is there some special reason?'

'Before you begin, Billy,' Laura said, 'I want Lucy in on this too. For the past few weeks she's had something on her mind and I think she may want to tell us something too.'

She went to the lounge to summon Lucy who had been watching TV with the two younger boys, leaving father and son gazing at each other. Billy was perplexed. Matthew looked drained but calm, a little smile playing about his lips.

'Right,' Laura said on her return with Lucy. 'We've all had our tea except you, Billy. I'll get it for you in a little while. I've settled Mark and John down with the TV, so we can talk.'

Something serious has happened, Billy thought, his heart pounding. 'Why are you home, Matthew? You haven't been sent down for doing something wrong, I hope.'

'I heard his news earlier this afternoon, Billy,' Laura said gravely. 'I'm deeply shocked and I don't know what to say, I'm so disappointed. It came like a bolt out of the blue.'

'I've done nothing wrong, Dad. It's nothing like that but I've given up the course at Sussex,' he mumbled, glancing up nervously at Billy. 'I'm finished with it and I shan't be going back. That's definite.'

Billy was thunderstruck and couldn't believe what he was hearing. It was like a bad dream.

'You can't be serious, Matthew,' he gasped. 'Give up your studies? It's preposterous! You're doing so well. You're not thinking straight.'

'On the contrary, Dad, for the first time in my life I am thinking straight. At last, I've seen the light. This year I came to realize that I've been trapped. I looked at myself and asked: what the hell am I doing here in Brighton? Why am I trying to become something I don't want to be? I feel as if my personal life has been mapped out for me. I'm like a hamster in a cage going round and round on a wheel. I'm supposed to jump through a lot of hoops in order to conform to the demands of a bourgeois society. I look into the future and can see exactly what's planned for me. I get my physics degree, then a job in weapons research or in dull soap-powder manufacture. Next I find a nice respectable girl and marry her, get myself a mortgage, and furnish my home on hire purchase. I spawn a couple of kids and educate them to wear a suit, like me. I get old and finally I snuff it and am buried after a refined church service when folk will say what an interesting and full life I led. End of story. It's not for me. I'm opting out of this rat race once and for all.'

Billy had turned pale and felt queasy. 'What's brought all this on?' he asked. 'And anyway, what's wrong with leading a fruitful and purposeful life? What's the alternative?'

'During the last vac, I visited Des in Essex and he introduced me to a substance called LSD. It stands for lysergic acid diethylamide, or acid for short.'

'You mean you took the LSD?' As he asked the question, Billy was hurting badly inside. 'That's not only a hazardous drug that can blow your mind, it's also illegal. You could have been prosecuted.'

'It's more than a drug, Dad. It's a new way of life and a means of opening the doors of perception in a way you wouldn't believe possible. LSD not only opened the doors but blew them off their hinges. I stepped from the shell of my body into another universe, an ecstatic nirvana. I had a number of experiences that have completely changed my outlook.'

'I've read something about this LSD,' Billy said slowly. 'If I'm not mistaken, it's promoted by that American academic, Timothy Leary, with the slogan "Turn on, tune in, and drop out". Hailed as the new Messiah. Isn't he the one?'

'Yes, but LSD is something else. It gave me the deepest religious experience I've ever had. I felt a profound inner peace which I cannot begin to describe. After an experience like that, it's impossible to go back to ordinary humdrum routine. LSD has completely changed my life. I think eventually it's going to change the world. It's the dawn of a New Age.'

Billy said, 'It sounds like the experience of Handel when he composed *The Messiah*. He said he saw the whole of heaven before him and the great God himself. But he wasn't on drugs at the time.'

'What happened to your Catholic faith?' Laura asked, hardly able to hold back the tears. 'Has that gone by the board?'

'Sorry, Mum, but that went years ago. That's a religion meaningful for only after you're dead. What we're doing is about the here and now. But LSD is not anti-religious in itself. Did you know that a Catholic priest in Vancouver was a strong advocate of it and even advised his parishioners to make use of it? Then think of all the great mystics of the Church, like St Teresa of Avila and St John of the Cross. What I experienced was similar to what they described.'

Billy sighed heavily. 'You know, Laura, you and I are a couple of babes in the wood. All this stuff is beyond our comprehension. And Lucy, you've been quiet up to now, what do you think about it all?'

'I don't agree with Matthew one little bit,' she declared.

'Thank God for that,' Laura exclaimed. 'When it comes to drugs, at least our daughter has common sense.'

'No,' Lucy continued. 'I don't believe for a moment that it's necessary to take any substance in order to have a mystical experience. LSD is highly dangerous and can result in a bad trip when, I'm told, it's a nightmare. I wouldn't touch the stuff. As you know, I've become involved with working at On The Eighth Day and a friend there by the name of Zven has introduced me to a movement called Krishna Kumaris of the Golden Dawn. Our Teacher and Master is the Baghwan Sherpa Sanyassi, and his disciples are called sanyassins. We have taken a vow to abstain from alcohol, tobacco, drugs, meat, tea, coffee and sex.'

'Wow!' Billy exclaimed. 'That's one heck of a list! It's as strict as an enclosed order of nuns. I do hope you're not required to shave your head, wear bright orange robes and prance about the place with a little bell chanting "Hare Krishna".'

'Nothing like that, Dad. That's the Krishna Consciousness movement. We're not the same.'

'Didn't the Beatles go to India to sit at one of these gurus' feet a couple of years ago?' Laura asked. 'I remember that they're supposed to have given him a lot of money.'

'Ours is a different movement, Mum. The Beatles went to

see the Maharishi Mahesh Yogi. Our Master is the Baghwan Sherpa Sanyassi and he teaches that we all exist in many different universes and live many different lives. My first phase of existence is over and I'm ready to begin a new cycle. I've experienced all that Matthew has described but without the use of chemicals. I have learned to meditate at the deepest level.'

'That's fine, Lucy,' a bemused Laura said, 'as long as you don't let it interfere with your studies.'

'Look, Mum and Dad, seeing Matthew here today has given me the courage to tell you what's been in my mind for some time now and I've been afraid to say for fear of hurting you. I'm sorry to lay this on you at this time but we may as well get all the bad news over and done with in one go. Mary, Sally and I had already decided that we're going to leave college and we don't want to go back under any circumstances. It's been hard to come to this decision but our minds are made up.'

Billy winced when he heard these words as if someone had struck him in the face. 'This is a nightmare, it isn't happening,' he groaned, shaking his head gloomily. 'My world is collapsing about my ears. Perhaps it's a temporary thing and you'll both change your minds. You'll both come to your senses and go back to college?'

There was no need to wait for an answer, their faces said it all. They were not going back.

'You haven't lost your faith in God as well, Lucy?' Laura asked.

'No, nothing like that, Mum, but I'm no longer a Catholic. Traditional religions teach us that if we lead a good life, we'll find our reward by seeing God in heaven when we die. But yesterday, when I was meditating, I saw God within me in the form of a beautiful mystical light that brought inner peace and bliss. I found an inner core of stillness deep within and was in tune with the cosmos. It was an enlightenment that cannot be described in words. It'd be like trying to describe the taste of an orange or the colour red. God is not somewhere out there; he's everywhere, in everything, every part of life is in communion with God. Knowing this has made the world of modern life and the business of making money seem shallow and irrelevant. Like Matthew, my life has been transformed.'

'So, what's new?' Laura said. 'If I remember my religious education lessons aright, we were always taught that God is within you. I think it's in St Luke's Gospel somewhere that Christ said, "Don't look for God here or there because the kingdom of God is within you."'

'The difference, Mum,' Lucy replied, 'is that through deep contemplation we have instant access to Him.'

'Why can't you wait till you die like the rest of us?' Billy said. 'That's the trouble with the young today. Everything's got to be immediate; it's got to be now! Now! Instant gratification and now instant mysticism. G. K. Chesterton said that if you want to start a new religion, the first thing you must do is get yourself crucified. These Indian gurus ride about in Rolls-Royces and have private aeroplanes. But surely this meditation thing you're into doesn't rule out studying art. Why not do both?'

'Dad,' Lucy said, 'I went to college with high hopes, expecting to be inspired. Most of the lectures were dull and uninspiring; some lecturers were completely inaudible; one simply sat behind a desk and read out notes to us, mumbling in a monotonous tone of voice. As for art, they didn't teach us a thing and my friends and I found it a complete waste of time. We wanted to learn technique but the tutors believed in free expression. So instead of learning to paint or draw, say, a room, we were encouraged to paint the vibrations of a wall.'

'Surely that was right up your street,' Matthew said, 'painting vibrations.'

'Look, this is serious, Matthew. We rolled in paint, cycled in it, slung it against the wall, dropped it from a great height, but didn't learn a thing about how to paint with it. The thought of four years of that fills me with horror. Not only that, I spent a few weeks in a school and saw how brutalized many teachers have become. They spent much of their time screaming and screeching, ranting and raving at the kids. That's not how I want to spend my life.'

Billy stood up from the table. 'I'm going out for a walk,' he announced. 'I feel absolutely confused. I can't take any more of this.'

'But, Billy,' Laura wept, 'it's started raining and you've had no food. At least wait until I make you something.'

'Food is the last thing on my mind, Laura. I feel sick to the stomach.'

He put on his coat and went out into the night, into the drizzle. Crestfallen, he walked along Wilmslow Road, not knowing where he was going. He felt traumatized and didn't know how to come to terms with what his two eldest children had told him. Without warning, all his hopes and dreams had disintegrated in the space of an hour. From the moment they were born, he said to himself, I had ambitions for my kids, for their success and for the kind of people they'd become; they were my whole raison d'être. I put my whole life into them and they've thrown it right back in my face. I never worked a day except for their benefit. As these thoughts revolved round his mind, tears of self-pity rolled down his cheeks. My family is the reason for my existence. My work at college, the hard graft getting extra qualifications, breaking my back to pay the mortgage and all the other bills to give them a home. And look at the result. A complete waste! They've simply dropped out of their colleges on a whim and made my efforts and my life seem utterly pointless.

Despondently he stumbled on and found himself in Albert Square. He had already come several miles. Where to go? Who might begin to understand? His mam? No, this was something outside her experience and understanding. The same went for his sisters. What about his old chum, Titch? His kids were too young for him to appreciate his pain. The only person who might have some inkling and sympathy for his predicament was his older brother. He turned down John Dalton Street towards Salford. Another hour brought him to Pendleton and to Les's house. He rang the bell and a few moments later Les came to answer the door. One look at Billy told him that he was distressed.

'Billy, what in the name of heaven brings you to this neighbourhood? You look a sorry sight. You're soaked through. Come in and dry off and tell me what's happened.'

Billy went into the house and found Annette with her children around her. They were watching television and they paused in their viewing to say hello.

'Long time, no see,' Annette said, 'but always nice to have you round.'

Les ushered him into the bathroom and gave him a change of clothes.

'Good job we're about the same size,' he said.

'Sorry to intrude on your happy family scene like this, Les,' Billy said, 'but I need to talk to someone.'

'Say no more, Billy,' Les said. 'We can stroll over to the Royal Oak for a pint. A pub is probably the best place for a chinwag.'

'I hope I'm not dragging you away from the television.'

'No problem, Billy. It was a load of rubbish anyway.'

Good old Les, Billy thought. No fuss, no questions. He simply accepted that his kid brother needed to get something off his chest.

In the lounge of the Royal Oak they kicked off with a couple of whiskies, and then with a couple of pints set before them, Billy told him the whole story.

'Four or five universities were begging for Matthew,' he said. 'And what does he do? He gets into Sussex and next thing I know he throws the lot into our face. Same with Lucy, she's going to walk out of college, just like that,' he added, snapping his fingers.

Les grinned mischievously. 'To misquote Oscar Wilde, "To have one child walk out is a misfortune; to have two walk out looks like carelessness." '

'It's no joke, Les, believe me. It keeps going through my mind that maybe it was something I did. I didn't bring them up right. I've tried to raise them along liberal lines so that they'd be free to be themselves, to be independent beings who could think for themselves, make their own decisions, and live with the consequences.'

'But that's exactly what they *have* done,' Les chuckled. 'They thought for themselves and made their own decisions. You just don't like what they decided.'

'Maybe so but I had such great hopes for them and what they could become. Their actions have made me feel that my whole life has been a ridiculous lie. I've been living a stupid dream for the last twenty years.'

'Don't take it so hard, Billy. England is undergoing a social upheaval; all values have been thrown into the melting pot. It's a case of anything goes. Wherever you look, authority is being challenged: in books, in the theatre, on television. It's a social revolution, make no mistake, and your kids are simply part of it, that's all.

'The kids of today,' Les continued, getting agitated, 'are ungrateful buggers. They don't know they're born, half of 'em. Don't give a damn about their parents' wishes. It's a matter of me, me, what *they* want and never mind the consequences. If other people's notions happen to clash with their own selfish wishes, it's too bad. We're too soft with them today, Billy. Things have come too easy for them, not like us who had to struggle to survive in Collyhurst and in Red Bank. Today, it's all laid on the line for them. They should be made to fend for themselves and learn to stand on their own two feet. Then they'll learn what life is all about and how tough it can be.'

Billy could see how his brother had gone into politics.

'But I thought you were a socialist, Les,' he protested.

'Doesn't that mean making things easy for people?'

'That's a misunderstanding many people have. Socialists believe in providing help for those who need it, not in mollycoddling people who take advantage of the welfare state and think it means something for nothing.'

'What about these two renegades of mine, Les?'

'They should be made acquainted with reality, stop wrapping them up in cotton wool. Let them feel a few rough winds on their backs.'

The conversation continued along these lines for an hour or two, becoming more condemnatory of the younger generation as the drink took hold. Billy's sorrow had now turned to anger and by the time the landlord called time, he'd become incensed by the rebelliousness of his two children and their insensitive behaviour.

He said goodnight to his brother and ordered a taxi home. By the time he reached his house, he was as mad as hell. He opened the front door and slammed it behind him, making the whole house shake. Laura came to meet him.

'What's all the noise about?' she cried. Then she saw the state of him. 'You've been drinking, and on an empty stomach,' she said. 'You'll make yourself ill.'

'Never mind about that now, Laura,' he rasped. 'I want those two renegades of mine down here, now!'

'Please, Billy,' she appealed. 'Calm down. You don't know what you're doing.'

'We'll soon see about that,' he said drunkenly.

He went to the foot of the stairs and yelled, 'Matthew! Lucy! Down here! Both of you! Now!'

Ashen-faced, they descended the stairs.

'What is it, Dad?' Matthew cried, bewildered.

'I want you two out of this house, right now, this minute!' he bawled. 'Get out and stay out! Don't come back! I don't want to see either of you again. I don't want you around here hurting your mother and me any more. Get your things together and sling your hook!'

'But where can we go?' Lucy wailed. 'There's nowhere, Dad. Please. Be reasonable.'

'This is stupid, Dad,' Matthew shouted defiantly. 'You can't throw us out at this time of night. We've no place to go.'

'Oh, stupid am I?' Billy bawled, raising his hand. 'I'll soon show you who's . . .'

Matthew squared up to him, saying with a zealous and triumphant stare, 'Oh, hitting now, is it? And which cheek would you like first? This one?' proffering his face for a slap.

Distraught, Laura got between the two of them. 'Stop this at once! No one's going anywhere. Now, you two,' she ordered, addressing the two children, 'go back to your rooms and stay there! As for you, Billy, I'm ashamed to see you like this. Go to bed and we'll talk in the morning.'

These words did the trick. The two children went quickly back upstairs. Through his drunken haze, Billy saw how furious and distressed Laura was and the sight of her angry face seemed to bring him to his senses.

'OK for now, Laura,' he muttered as he stumbled his way up to the bedroom. 'But tomorrow they go,' he said, determined to have the last word.

The next day was Saturday and a very different scene. Billy had slept off his drunken anger and next morning he appeared with a hangdog expression, like his own father used to be after one of his heavy drinking sessions.

My God, he said to himself, I hope I'm not getting like my father in that respect. I remember only too well how we despised him on those occasions and how terrified of him we were. Another thing that reminds me of my father is the way the kids always seem to confide in Laura and cut me out. I hope they're not as scared of me as I was of my own dad but I suppose that's the lot of us fathers everywhere. Being a father is a lousy role and it's hard to know sometimes what to do for the best, there's no manual to guide you.

At breakfast, still feeling confused and sullen, he was quiet and apologetic.

'I'm sorry, everyone,' he said sheepishly, 'for my behaviour last night. I don't know what got into me. But you're both making a big mistake. Possibly the biggest mistake of your lives.'

'Well, I know what got into you,' Laura said emphatically, 'it was several pints of Chester's, the fighting beer, I suspect. Let's put last night behind us and decide what we're all going to do.'

Billy restrained himself from retorting, 'Don't blame me for all this trouble. I didn't cause this.'

'Anyway, last night I went into a deep sleep,' he said thickly with a lopsided grin, 'more like a coma maybe, and in my dreams I saw the solution to the secrets of the universe. Unfortunately this morning I can't remember what it was.'

At least he could still manage a sense of humour.

'Do we still have to leave, Dad?' Lucy asked, half smiling but still tearful. Her eyes were red-rimmed and she had obviously spent the night weeping.

'I think we can forget all that nonsense,' Laura said, answering for him. 'This is your home and you'll stay here as long as you like.'

'We'll have to give that some thought,' countered Billy quickly, recalling what Les had said about mollycoddling. 'The question is, what are you going to do with yourselves if you're not going to college?'

'As long as I can stay here,' Lucy said, 'I'm sure I can work and earn my keep at the Eighth Day centre; it has plans to become a clothes shop and maybe later a vegetarian restaurant.'

'As for me, Mum and Dad,' Matthew said, 'don't worry. I'll find something, you'll see. Des has also left his degree course and we reckon we can make good in the field of music. It's what we've always wanted to do anyway. So, don't worry about a thing.' There were tears in his eyes as he said these words. 'I'm so sorry, Mum and Dad, that I've given you two so much pain. And I want to assure you that I shan't be dropping acid again. Before I left Brighton to come home, I had a bad trip, the worst nightmare I've ever had. This time it was a trip not to heaven but to hell. Despite that, the first experience of joy has had a deep effect on me and changed the direction of my life.'

Billy wasn't ready to hear these sordid details. He interrupted impatiently, 'Well, at least you've learned something. I suppose it's your life and you'll make your own road.'

In his mind he was still wondering if there was any way for him to turn the clock back a few months and get everybody back on track.

'So, that's all settled,' Laura said in a businesslike tone. 'I'm sure that, as a family, we'll survive, no matter what. We'll get by.'

All settled? Billy thought to himself. If only. As far as I'm concerned, it's one bloody big mess.

'I wish someone would tell me what's going on,' Mark complained, looking round at everyone at the breakfast table. 'Why's everyone crying? And why's everyone apologizing?'

'I know,' John said darkly. 'Matthew wanted a hamster and he pinched some money to buy one.'

'How do you know that, clever clogs?' Mark scoffed.

'Because I heard him saying to Dad, "I'd like a hamster in a cage going round and round on a wheel." And then he said he'd taken some LSD, and that means pounds, shillings and pence. So it must have been so he could buy a hamster, what else?'

Chapter Forty-Two

Next day when they were alone, a contrite Billy told Laura about the offer of a job in Scotland.

'It would mean a big step up the educational ladder for me,' he told her. 'The prospect of staying here with Matthew and Lucy hanging about the place with their numerous weird friends doesn't appeal to me one bit. Then there's Mark and John to think about. We don't want them following the same path, dropping out and drifting aimlessly as our two eldest seem to want to do.'

At first Laura wasn't too keen but the more she thought about the idea, the more attractive it became.

'This may be the answer to our prayers. It would be so easy to become estranged from our two oldest children. We could order them out of the house and we'd all end up as strangers no longer on speaking terms. I've seen it happen to other families and it's not going to happen to ours. No matter what, I want to keep this family together so that we can still have an influence over them. I think this is a temporary rebellious phase they're going through and they'll see common sense one day.'

'We could leave Matthew and Lucy in charge of the house. It may be the ideal way for them to learn responsibility.'

'Do you think we could trust them to look after the place, Billy?' she said, frowning. 'After all, it's our home and they might let it go to rack and ruin.'

'I can't see that happening,' he replied. 'Surely we can trust them to act responsibly. After all, Lucy's eighteen and Matthew'll soon be twenty. If you're still worried though, we could ask your father to keep an eye on them by calling in on them from time to time and sending us a report on their progress.'

'Do you really think it might work, Billy?'

'I'm sure it will, Laura. This is a big house and we could insist that they run things on a commercial basis and pay all the household bills by renting off some of the rooms.'

'Maybe we could take a chance that things will work out.' Then she smiled. 'I must admit, too, that deep down the idea of returning to the land of my birth does have a certain appeal.'

The following day, they went over to see Duncan to canvass his views on the subject. There was little doubt where his opinion lay.

'As a young tax officer, I used to travel widely about that particular district and it's a beautiful part of the world. Furthermore, the education your two youngest will receive there will be second to none. As you know,' he added proudly, 'Scotland's noted for its traditional education and its high standards. I think they'll both do well there. There are one or two good Catholic schools in the area.'

'Our first home was in Cumnock in the early days of our marriage,' Louise added warmly. 'It's a lovely spot to live. There are some beautiful walks around Afton Glen; you'll perhaps recall the poem, "Flow gently, sweet Afton, among thy green braes." Kilmarnock is a wonderful shopping centre and you're also within easy reach of the coast and there's a good train service to Glasgow if you want the big city.'

After hearing her parents, Laura became even more keen on the move. 'Billy, let's go for it, if we can. I'm sure Matthew and Lucy can run the house in our absence. I'll miss them terribly but we're not going abroad or anything like that.'

Mark and John took a little persuading at the beginning and they were not happy about leaving their friends but Laura painted a glowing picture of life there: rambles and picnics in the countryside, trips to the seaside, fishing for trout in the lochs and rivers, angling for sea bass at the coast.

Besides, they weren't going too far away. At holiday times, they could perhaps come back to Manchester to see Matthew and Lucy. And no, they wouldn't have to wear kilts in Scotland as part of the school uniform.

'You missed your way, Laura,' Billy remarked, 'you should have been in sales. You'd have made a fortune.'

On Monday morning, Billy went to see Sister Benedict and expressed his interest. A few phone calls were made and an interview arranged. He travelled to Kilmarnock by train to meet the Principal of the college, Brother Eugene McCarthy, and a small appointments committee. The interview seemed a formality as Billy came highly recommended by Sister Benedict. A week later, he heard that he had been appointed Head of the Education Department and would be in charge of six lecturers. Billy the Collyhurst kid was in town.

Billy had one worry on his mind before he finalized his decision: his mam. He paid her a visit and was encouraged to see that, although her eyesight was still not good, her friendship with Mrs Reynolds had flourished. They were a great help to each other and went shopping together in Langley. A home help called twice a week in the mornings. Les and his two sisters Flo and Polly promised to continue their regular weekend visits. Encouraged by these developments, Billy felt confident that he could go to Scotland knowing that his mam would be well looked after.

Chapter Forty-Three

The move to Scotland took place in August 1971. Once their minds were made up, they went all out to adopt a Caledonian lifestyle. They didn't go so far as to begin learning to play the bagpipes, but Billy went out and bought a wide range of records of Scottish singers and it wasn't long before the voices of Andy Stewart, Kenneth McKellar, and Moira Stewart filled the air. Laura taught Billy how to dance the eightsome reel and the music of Jimmy Shand rang through the house. Billy wondered if he should learn the Scottish dialect and if the television lessons given by Stanley Baxter's *Parliamo Glasgow* might come in handy. That summer term he could be heard reciting phrases like 'Gizza pair o' haddock' and 'Hey you, Jimmy, gizza pint o'heavy an' a bridie'. He thought the phrases suggested as useful for the dance hall were particularly interesting: 'Jiwanni dance?' But the retort of the girl who rejected the bald-headed suitor seemed cruel: 'Awa' an' polish your heid!'

'They're not all Rob Roys in Scotland,' Laura laughed. 'They understand English perfectly well.'

In the term before they moved, Billy drove Laura and the two young ones up to Scotland to look at houses. After Carlisle, they passed over the border and rejoiced to see a sign saying WELCOME TO SCOTLAND, which prompted them to sing out lustily,

> *O ye'll tak' the high road, and I'll tak' the low road*
> *And I'll be in Scotland afore ye,*
> *But me and my true love will never meet again,*
> *On the bonnie, bonnie banks o' Loch Lomon'.*

As they got further into Scotland along the A74, the graffiti painted on the bridges they passed under were less cordial.

HANDS OFF SCOTTISH OIL!
SCOTLAND FOR THE SCOTS!
AWA' HAME SASSENACHS!

'What's all this about, Laura?' Billy asked. 'I thought hostilities between our two countries were ended when we all signed the Act of Union back in the eighteenth century.'

'Take no notice, Billy. These graffiti were daubed by hotheads.'

In Kilmarnock, they found an estate agent who handled properties in East Ayrshire. Billy worried about getting another mortgage since he already had one on the Manchester house, and house prices had risen exponentially since 1963.

'No problem,' the agent assured him. 'In view of your position and high salary, we will have no difficulty finding you a mortgage, especially if you take an endowment policy to secure it. Furthermore, there's lots of spare equity in your Manchester house.'

It was double Dutch to Billy and Laura but if it got them a house, that was good enough for them. They particularly liked the Cumnock area where Duncan and Louise had had their first home. It was an area of great natural beauty, a delightful mixture of open countryside and heritage sites, many connected with Robert Burns.

When a house is put up for sale in England, the price suggested is usually the opening figure for negotiation; it means 'or nearest offer' and the vendor expects it to be reduced. But buying a house in Scotland, they discovered, was the other way round: the vendor expected his price to be raised. Billy found it a bizarre procedure. The estate agent was most helpful and suggested that, to save coming back several times, they should choose two or three properties and put in a bid for the one they liked best. Selecting a house was straightforward enough but deciding how much to offer proved to be a headache. They missed the first house they tried for. The advertisement had said, 'Offers around £14,000 to be submitted by noon next Friday.' It was a blind auction since they didn't know how much other people, if any, would be offering. The starting figure, Duncan had told them, was the 'upset' price – the lowest sum the sellers would be prepared to accept although they would be upset if that was all they got. Naively, Billy and Laura offered £14,500. Such a low offer didn't have a prayer. The house sold for £17,500, probably more than the buyer had needed to pay. The advantage of the system, Duncan explained, was that there was no gazumping as was common in England since once an offer had been accepted, it was legally binding.

'The Scottish system is much fairer,' Duncan claimed.

It would be of course, Billy thought.

For their second choice, they found a house at Dewarkirk to the north-east of Cumnock and about fifteen miles from the college and this time they were successful. It was a superb three-bedroom detached bungalow in a cul-de-sac called St Phillan's Court, with an upset price of £16,000. They offered £18,000 and Billy couldn't help wondering how much over the odds they'd paid. He would never know. The house was set in a good-sized, well-laid-out garden with two or three fruit trees and there was a glorious view of Cairntable. But what really sold the house for them was the small burn at the back, a tranquil little stream which had its origin in Lowther Hills some miles to the south.

'There may be trout in that water,' Billy remarked. 'If so, perhaps we'll get Mark and John interested in fishing.'

In the weeks before the move, Billy and Laura had gone over everything with Matthew and Lucy a couple of dozen times.

'We've split the furniture between us and so you should have more than you need to make yourselves comfortable. Are you sure you understand all that we've told you?' Billy asked. 'In the dummy cellar, I've left around twenty-five gallons of wine fermenting in five-gallon lots. Elderberry, peach, burgundy, piesporter, hock. It should be perfect in a couple of years' time.'

'And remember to keep the place tidy,' Laura said. 'Don't forget, a weekly clean, especially the bathroom and toilets.'

Matthew sighed. 'We're not kids any more. We'll look after the place as well as you did.'

'I suppose as soon as we've gone,' Billy grinned, 'you'll be calling in all your mates for a big party.'

'Trust us,' Lucy said earnestly. 'No partying and we'll keep the place spotless and there'll be no shenanigans.'

Reassured by these promises and accompanied by Mark and John, they drove up to Dewarkirk, the pantechnicon van with their furniture having already gone ahead.

It was beginning to turn dark when they arrived at their new home in the late afternoon. They opened up the bungalow and the removers unloaded and stacked their belongings into the house.

A friendly middle-aged couple came across to greet them.

'Welcome to Dewarkirk,' the man said, holding out his hand. 'I'm James McHarg and this is my wife, Mary. We're your next-door neighbours and if there's anything we can do to help, call out. As soon as you've finished unpacking, perhaps you'd like to come over for a cup of tea.'

'That's good of you,' Laura said. 'A little later a cup of tea'll be most welcome.'

They returned to the task of moving their belongings into the house. There was a snag. The lights didn't work.

'That's odd,' Billy remarked. 'I organized for the electricity people to turn on the power.'

Then he spotted the trouble. The previous owner had removed all the light fixtures, leaving behind bare wires sticking out from the ceiling. That's an odd thing to do, he thought. They could have at least left simple bulb-holders in place. There was nothing for it but to seek help and advice from their neighbours who rang the local electrician who came quickly and worked for a couple of hours to get their lights working.

'Thank the Lord,' Laura said. 'I thought we were going to have to spend our first night in Scotland in the dark.'

Later in the evening after their tea with the McHargs, they returned to their new home and began settling in. The first thing the boys did was decide who was having which room.

'Now what we need,' Laura declared, 'is hot water. I'll switch on the immersion heater.'

As she did so, a strange thing happened. The lights in all three bedrooms went on. They switched the lights off and the immersion heater went off. Turning on the hall light triggered the burglar alarm.

'I wonder if there are any other bizarre connections,' Billy said.

There were. The television would only work if the cooker in the kitchen was switched on. The porch light was linked to the kettle, and the bedside lamp in the main bedroom functioned only if the bathroom light was off. The difficulty was compounded when the electricians presented a bill of £50 for 'repairing the electrical system' and Billy refused to pay it until the Heath-Robinson wiring system was rectified.

'I do hope these signs are not omens of things to come,' Billy remarked.

Their first day in Dewarkirk was a busy one. The first part of the morning was devoted to unpacking and soon the house was a confusion of tea chests, wrapping paper, straw, ornaments, furniture and bedding all mixed up higgledy-piggledy. Billy's first priority was to assemble the beds, the family having spent the first night on mattresses on the floor; Laura's to put up the curtains. Next, the family turned its attention to putting things in their ordained places: crockery and pans into kitchen cupboards, clothes hung in bedroom wardrobes; pictures and clocks on the walls; Billy's numberless books on to the built-in bookshelves in the upper lounge. When chaos was at its highest, the electricians arrived to repair their repairs and get the various electrical appliances working: kitchen equipment for Laura, hi-fi for Billy and the ubiquitous television for the boys.

'I wonder if we'll be able to understand the Scottish language up here,' Mark remarked.

After lunch, the two boys explored the garden in a frenzy of excitement.

'Mum! Dad! We've got our own river! We can go fishing for trout,' Mark yelled.

'And it's not very deep and maybe we could go paddling!' John shouted. 'Not only that, we've got fruit trees as well: apples, pears, and cherries.'

'And one day,' Mark said, 'we could go walking up those mountains we can see from the garden.'

'There's lots of things to do and see in this region,' Billy enthused.

'All in good time,' Laura said. 'The first thing we must do is go into Cumnock and get in some food supplies.'

'And maybe a couple of fishing rods for these two aspiring anglers,' Billy added. 'We could also buy them some stationery materials for school, like pens, pencils and that sort of thing.'

The rest of that first week was given over to settling in and finding their feet. Billy and the boys tried their hand at fishing but caught nothing.

'Maybe we're using the wrong kind of worm,' Mark remarked.

'Could be,' Billy said. 'There's more to it than simply dangling your line in the water and hoping that the fish will find your bait irresistible. I've read somewhere that trout prefer to come out at night when things are quiet. Perhaps we should leave a few lines out and see what happens.'

They tried it and nothing happened.

'The fish round here are brainier than we thought,' Billy

said. 'We shall have to ask some local expert when we get the chance.'

He went to join Laura in the garden. 'Your mother was right, Laura,' he said 'This really is a lovely part of the world and I'm glad we came. Look at that view of the Lowther Hills and the wooded valleys.'

'True, Billy, but at the same time I can't help wondering how our other two are getting on down there in Manchester. I hope they haven't set the place on fire.'

'They'll be OK, Laura. And maybe they can come up here for a holiday.'

'I think the locals round here would get a shock if they saw them,' she laughed.

A week after their arrival came D-day. D for dreading. Billy and Laura were due to take their sons to their new school, St Bruno's Academy. The boys looked pale and wan.

'Supposing we don't speak their language,' John moaned. 'What do we do?'

'You'll have to buy an English-Scottish dictionary,' Mark jeered though he was as scared as his younger brother. As it was the boys' first day, Billy and Laura went to school with them to give them confidence and support. The two lads, dressed in hooded duffle coats making them look like a couple of miniature Franciscan friars, proudly carried their new briefcases and the pencil boxes with the sliding tops containing ruler, pencils, and sundry geometrical instruments, which they had bought in Cumnock the previous week.

They had to wait a long time to see the headmaster Mr Ferguson as it was the first day of term and he was run off his feet. Somewhere in the school, children were chanting spellings in a sing-song voice.

'There's the traditional education for you,' Billy whispered. 'That's what we came here for.'

When the head finally got round to them, he couldn't spare much time and he was curt and businesslike. Their two sons stood in front of his desk. They looked petrified.

'I've arranged to put these boys in Forms Two and Four,' he said, addressing Billy directly, not giving Laura or either boy so much as a glance. 'The school secretary will take them up to their classrooms. The form teachers are expecting them. We'll record all their details later when we've more time.' He stood up, signalling that the interview was over.

'I believe that's called short shrift,' Billy muttered to Laura as they went with the secretary to the Form 4 classroom. Mark looked as if he was going to face the firing squad. The form master came to the door of the room.

'Yes, what is it, Mrs Murray?' he snapped irritably.

'A new boy for you, Mr Hardie.'

'Not another! Oh, very well. Come along in then,' he said, inspecting Mark over his glasses as if he were a nasty insect. 'You can leave him with me now,' he added, addressing Billy and Laura. 'I'll deal with him now. Have no fear. He'll be quite safe.'

It sounded ominous.

They mumbled a few comforting words to Mark but he didn't notice. The colour had drained from his face and his whole attention was focused on the thirty pairs of eyes that had now turned in his direction as he went into the classroom.

'See you tonight, Mark. You'll be fine,' Laura said encouragingly.

John was next. He had turned deathly white. The secretary knocked on the door of Form 2 and the form mistress, a motherly-looking character, came to answer it.

'Good morning, Miss Craig,' the secretary said. 'A new pupil for you.'

'Ah, yes, the new boy,' she said. 'Thank you, Mrs Murray. We'll look after him now.' John looked ready to throw up.

'Chin up, John,' Billy said, patting him on the shoulder.

'See you tonight, John,' Laura said, looking almost as unhappy as her son.

John hardly heard their words; he was too intent on assessing the agony he was about to face in his new form.

'Don't worry, Laura, they'll be OK,' Billy said as they came away from the school. 'It's a matter of readjustment for all of us now we're here in bonnie Scotland.'

He had his own ordeal to face that day. A new job. A new set of faces. New responsibilities. How would the staff react to him, their new boss and an Englishman to boot? He grinned ruefully when he thought about those last words 'an Englishman to boot'. He hoped the new staff wouldn't take it literally. To say he was nervous about the new post was an understatement. Panic-stricken might be a better expression. He'd slept hardly a wink the night before. Starting a new job was always a cause for collywobbles but this new appointment was the most frightening of all. He was to lead a group of lecturers. Would they accept him, a southerner? Or would they tell him to get lost? He'd find out that day for he'd called his first staff meeting in order to introduce himself.

Chapter Forty-Four

Later in the morning, before the meeting with his own staff scheduled for the afternoon, there was a conference of heads of departments, a college cabinet of the bigwigs, and now Billy was one of them. He was introduced all round. 'This is Mrs McCartney, head of arts and crafts, Mr MacDonald, head of history, Miss McKerney, head of English.' The list went on and on. The names were announced so quickly, they became a blur and he knew he'd never remember them. Many smiled encouragingly in his direction but a few could only manage a curt nod of the head. As far as they were concerned he was a newcomer and, as such, was a rival for the limited college resources being allocated by the Principal that morning. The exception was the man sitting next to him for he proved to be most friendly and forthcoming.

'Welcome to the college,' he said, taking Billy's hand and pumping it vigorously. 'I'm Sandy Selkirk, head of educational technology. Call me Sandy.'

'Thank you, Sandy. I'm William Hopkins but friends call me Billy.'

'Then Billy it is. I hope you didn't find those introductions back there too confusing. There were rather a lot of them, weren't there?'

'Quite a few, Sandy, and they came at me so fast, they were beginning to fuse and sound the same: Mac-this and Mac-that. At one point, I wondered if I should change my own name to MacHopkins. Why, even the Principal is a Mac. McCarthy.'

Sandy laughed heartily. 'True, except he's an Irishman through and through. If the names hadn't come at you so fast, you'd have noticed we have also a Baird, a Campbell, a

Stewart, and a Whyte. Some of them are a gloomy bunch though. *Les misérables*, I call them. Don't let them put you off the place too much.'

Billy saw what he meant, for discussion at the meeting consisted of bickering and bargaining as the heads fought fiercely for a bigger piece of the financial cake being shared out by Brother Eugene. At times, the debate sounded like a foreign language, especially when one departmental head complained that a matter was 'outwith his remit", which Billy took to mean that it was not his responsibility. This wasn't the first time he'd found Scottish language incomprehensible. He'd once listened to a conversation between his father-in-law, Duncan, and his brother Bernard in Ayrshire dialect, the authentic language of Robbie Burns, and he hadn't understood a single word. Apart from that, to his English ears the tone of their voices as they argued their case carried a note of abrasiveness that suggested they might resort to fisticuffs to prove their point. He didn't remember any of his Scottish in-laws sounding like this though they could become quite heated in debate about the relative merits of Celtic and Rangers football players.

'The heads of departments in this college are a bunch of sycophantic Uriah Heeps, currying for the Principal's favours,' Sandy scoffed as they came away from the meeting at lunchtime. 'Did you notice how they held out their begging bowls and began their requests by whining: "If I may make so bold as to suggest and I hope you don't mind me saying, Brother, but my department needs an extra member of staff this term as we're so hard-pressed." It's the same each term. Not only that, they hate each other's guts. Mind you, I think the Principal encourages it. Divide and rule and all that. He's something of a petty dictator as well and is inclined to send round nasty notes when he thinks we've done something wrong. He rarely emerges from his office and gives no example of leadership whatsoever. Anyway, come on to the staff dining room and I'll show you the ropes.'

Billy took an immediate liking to this outspoken man for he had the quality that Billy most admired. Honesty.

In the dining room, Sandy led him to a drawer containing a heap of linen napkins.

'Each member of staff has a napkin ring. You have to bring your own from home but you can borrow one as it's your first day.'

The meals they collected from the kitchen assistant consisted of soup, fish and a selection of vegetables, all beautifully cooked and presented. They found a table for two and sat down.

'As you can see,' he said, 'the staff at this college eat well. It's the best feature of the place.'

'Tell me about the Education Department,' Billy said, as he tucked in. 'What have I let myself in for?'

Sandy grinned from ear to ear. 'A poisoned chalice if ever I saw one. Your two predecessors left for that reason. You're the third head in two years.'

'I'm getting used to poisoned chalices,' Billy grinned. 'This will be the second that I've drunk from in my career. The first was my initial teaching appointment when they gave me a top class of rebellious adolescents. Give me the bad news, Sandy.'

'You have six staff and five of them are fine, Robbie Logan in particular is a friendly chap, but one of them, McGonagall, applied for your job. As he didn't get it, he's mighty disgruntled and resented you even before you got here, especially since he regards you as a foreigner, an intruder.'

These words made Billy feel even more nervous. Two department heads had preceded him! What chance did he stand? Still he was grateful to Sandy for forewarning him.

'Watch out for Monty McGonagall,' Sandy said. 'He was sure he'd get the post. To make things more interesting still, he's a rabid member of the Scottish National Party and believes in Scotland for the Scots. If he can, he'll go behind your back, right in front of your face, then stab you between the shoulder blades.'

'That would take some doing. Can you give me some examples?'

'He'll sabotage your efforts as he did with your predecessor. He'll forget to deliver marks to you on time. He'll ignore your requests for schemes of work and syllabuses, teach his own individual syllabus and ignore yours, start a whispering campaign to undermine you, and he'll turn up late for lectures, sometimes not at all. When it reaches the ears of Brother Eugene, he'll send you one of his nasty notes and you'll take the rap. The last bloke before you got fed up to the teeth and left in high dudgeon, as they say.'

'There's usually a pain-in-the-neck character in every organization. There was one called Grundy in my first school and so McGonagall comes as no surprise. I shall take him in my stride.'

'As for the students you'll be teaching,' Sandy continued, 'you'll find the Diploma and B.Ed students a pleasure to work with. They're keen, alert and eager to please but . . .'

There's always a 'but', Billy thought.

'Be on your guard when you take the postgraduates, especially the science specialists. They've nothing but contempt for the so-called social sciences, which they consider a contradiction in terms. They're resentful because they have to pass the postgrad Certificate in Education to be accepted as qualified teachers. Which means wasting a whole year studying what they call non-subjects like sociology and psychology. All the staff find them a Bolshie lot, the college's awkward squad. Whatever you do, avoid confrontation with them if you can, though sometimes it can't be avoided.'

Billy wondered if he and his family should catch the next train back to Manchester.

After lunch, Billy made his way to the room where he had arranged to meet his staff for the first time. As he got near, he overheard a man's voice declare: 'What does a bloody Sassenach know about Scottish education, I'd like to know?'

Uh-oh, Billy thought. Here I go. Daniel in the lion's den.

Despite his apprehensions, that first conference went surprisingly smoothly: a discussion of duties, who was to teach what, content of courses, routines to be adopted, such as all requests for secretarial services to be countersigned by him. There were no problems. At the end of the meeting, Monty McGonagall approached him and addressed him in that faintly belligerent manner Billy had detected in the morning's 'cabinet' meeting.

'I've been asked to give you apologies from Ian McClusky for his absence. He was taking delivery of a gas cooker at home and so couldn't be here. He'll also be missing his lecture with the postgrads. And a word of advice in your ear. Never call staff meetings on a Monday as that's our day off, do you see? We like to make it a long weekend, you see.'

Day off? Billy saw red.

'Look,' he said addressing the staff, 'our working week is already short enough and I don't see how we can justify a day off. As for taking delivery of a gas cooker, I'd have thought a staff meeting took priority. After all, it's this job that supplies the wherewithal for buying gas cookers in the first place.'

One or two of the staff stared back at him defiantly. Obviously they weren't used to being spoken to in that way. Nevertheless, Billy felt he'd better establish his authority from the beginning even though he didn't like starting off in this manner. Let's hope things get better as we go along, he said to himself as he drove home that night.

At tea, the family reported back on their first experiences of life in Scotland.

'Not a good opening for the boys,' Laura said sadly. 'They've been having a hard time. I don't know what we can do about it, if anything.'

Billy was deeply disturbed when he saw Mark's face; he had a swollen lip and a red raw cheek.

'What happened, Mark?' Billy asked.

'It wasn't my fault, Dad. I got into a fight in the playground at lunchtime. This big kid named Duggie Savage called me a Sassenach bastard and said the English were a load of rubbish. Then he began pushing me around, so I pushed him back and a crowd got round us and began shouting "A fight! A fight!" until Mr Hardie, our teacher, came to stop it. He shook me and said, "What are you trying to do? Fight the Battle of Culloden all over again?" What *is* the Battle of Culloden, Dad?' he asked.

Laura answered. 'That was a battle between the Scottish Jacobites and the English army. Many brave Scots were killed.'

'They picked on me as well and mimicked the way I talked,' John said, holding back the tears, 'and someone put a drawing pin on my seat and when I sat on it, everyone in the class laughed at me. At playtime, they played a game of kung fu and they were all kick-boxing me and shouting, "Kick the bloody Sassenach!" ' John showed him his bruised legs. 'What's a Sassenach, Dad?' he asked, sniffling.

'I believe it's an old word for Saxon or English, John.'

Billy was both distressed and angry when he heard these tales of woe.

'I'll go to see the head immediately tomorrow and give him a piece of my mind,' he said. 'He should tell his teachers to protect new boys from the bullies in his school.'

'Whatever you do, please don't do that,' Mark said. 'It'll make matters worse. We'll fight our own battles, Dad, and I'll look after John tomorrow. Let anyone try anything,' he said, defiantly clenching his fist.

'Please, please, Mum and Dad,' John said, 'can't we go back to Manchester? I don't like this school. The other boys, and even one of the teachers, Mr Hardie, was making fun of us at dinnertime because we're English.'

'Look, kids,' Billy said. 'I'm sorry you've had such a rough time on your first day but it often happens to new boys in any school in any country. You're a natural target for bullies because you're different but in time the others'll get used to you and your accent and you'll get used to them.'

His sons looked at him doubtfully.

'I learned a long time ago,' Billy said, 'that the only way to deal with a bully is to give him a taste of his own medicine. Very often the bully's a coward and will only throw his weight around if he thinks he can get away with it. You haven't forgotten those boxing lessons I gave you back in Manchester when you were attending St Cuthbert's Primary School?'

'No, Dad,' Mark said. 'You always said that the best way to box was to slip under a punch and give two quick ones in return.'

'Right, Mark. I'm glad to see you haven't forgotten. Shakespeare said: "Beware of entrance to a quarrel, but being in, bear't that the opposed may beware of thee." '

'What does that mean in English?'

'It means don't fight unless you're forced to but if it can't be avoided, make sure you teach your opponent a lesson he'll never forget. It's the only law a bully under-stands. A good right cross on the chin is usually enough to make him see the error of his ways. Then dust yourself down and go home. Next time this Duggie Savage character tries it on, challenge him to a fight in the open, away from school where Mr Hardie can't pick on you, and give this Duggie a taste of his own medicine.'

'I don't think we should be encouraging Mark to fight,' Laura protested. 'Fighting never solves anything. Violence might frighten the bully but it doesn't necessarily teach him to think or mend his ways.'

'Maybe not, Laura, but at least it might nip the trouble in the bud. From the sound of it, Duggie Savage won't have a clue about boxing.'

'Look, boys,' Laura told them, 'it was your first day and I think the other lads were simply trying it on. It'll all turn out right in the end, you'll see. Be patient. But to change the subject for a moment. I went into Cumnock shopping with

Mrs McHarg. She introduced me to one or two other neighbours and I met nothing but friendliness everywhere we went. And the shopkeepers are so helpful and obliging. Not all Scots are like those you met at school, boys. Most of them are kind and courteous. When we've settled down, I think we'll all be happy here.'

'Tell you what'll we do,' Billy said to the two boys. 'If you put a full attendance in, we'll visit Manchester at half-term and see what's been going on there.'

That bucked them up no end and put the smile back on their faces.

Billy decided not to tell the family about his own experiences at college. His sons had their own problems and somehow his seemed small by comparison. At least Monty McGonagall would not, as far as he knew, be practising kung fu on him.

'Anyway,' Laura said cheerfully, 'while you've all been out, I thought we should celebrate our arrival in Scotland and I've bought some haggis for tea.'

'Haggis!' Billy said, his eyes twinkling, 'I always thought that was a coven of evil witches.'

'And I thought it was a musical instrument,' Mark added with a grin.

'You English ignoramuses,' Laura laughed. 'Don't you know that Robbie Burns honoured it with the title, "Great chieftain 'o the puddin' race"?'

For the two boys, the rest of that first week followed the same lines as their first day, their English origin continuing to be a subject for jeers and insults. They looked miserable as they were pushed out to school. John in particular complained of feeling sick and would have stayed home every day with a sore stomach if they'd let him. He became the epitome of Shakespeare's 'whining schoolboy, with his satchel, and shining morning face, creeping like snail unwillingly to school'.

On the third day, Mark's new pencil box of which he'd been so proud was broken into several pieces by some miscreant who'd jumped on it with both feet and then bent the compass, and snapped the ruler and pencils in two. And some person unknown had poured ink over his maths exercise book and he was given the strap by Mr Hardie who said, 'I don't know what they do down there in England but you must learn that here in Scotland we take pride in our possessions. Now hold out your hand.'

'Can we *please* go back to Manchester?' the boys kept asking. 'We don't like this school. Other kids shove us around and Mr Hardie sneers at us.'

'Do the other teachers sneer at you?' Laura asked.

'No, Mum, only that one. Most of the other teachers are very nice,' said Mark.

'And our form teacher, Miss Craig, is very kind,' John said. 'She tells the other kids off if they make fun of me.'

'It's just this Mr Hardie,' Mark said. 'He doesn't like the English but most of the other teachers are friendly and some of them have been asking me about Manchester and Manchester United. Sir Matt Busby's a Scotsman, you know, and he's their hero. They were amazed when I told them he lived in an ordinary semi-detached in Chorlton not far from us in Manchester and I'd talked to him once or twice.'

On the Thursday, things took a dramatic turn. The boys were late getting home but they both looked cheerful for a change. Mark had a bruise on his cheek but he was smiling broadly.

'It worked, Dad,' he said. 'Duggie Savage was shoving me and jostling me as usual, so I challenged him to a fight after school on a piece of waste ground. A little crowd came with us and formed a ring to watch and some of them were on my side. A lad called Andy Carswell and another called Bruce Crawford acted as my seconds.'

'So, come on, Mark, what happened next?' Billy said impatiently.

'He gave him a good thumping, Dad,' John enthused, 'and a lot of other kids cheered when Mark got him down on the ground and made him give in.'

'He was easy, Dad,' Mark said. 'He didn't know a thing about boxing. He kept losing his concentration and letting his attention wander.'

'How do you mean, Mark?'

'Whenever someone said, "Sock him, Duggie," he looked round to see who it was and lowered his guard. It was then that I gave him a couple of quick jabs. Another thing: his pants kept falling down and every time he hitched them up, he left himself open for another fourpenny one.'

'And a sixpenny one into the bargain,' added John gleefully.

'But it ended up more like a wrestling match in the end, Dad,' Mark went on. 'He grabbed me by the shoulders and tried to force me onto the ground but I got my legs behind him and twisted him down instead. Then I sat on his chest and knelt on his arms.'

'And Mark kept telling him to say "Give in" but he wouldn't,' John said breathlessly.

'So I pulled his ears till he said it for everyone to hear. Then some of the others cheered because we're not the only ones he's been pushing around.'

'And when we were coming home,' John said, 'lots of kids came with us and said they were glad he'd won. And Mark's got a girlfriend called Jeannie.'

'Oh no I haven't,' Mark retorted. 'And I told you not to tell, John. She's not my girlfriend just because she walked back with us. There were a lot of others.'

'But she was the only one linking you,' John said slyly. '*And* I saw her kiss you very quickly on the cheek before she ran off.'

'I still don't approve of fighting,' Laura said when she was alone with Billy. 'It doesn't solve anything.'

'But it did this time, Laura. I think the Savage lad'll think

373

twice before he tries it on again with Mark or John. That leaves only this Mr Hardie who doesn't seem too fond of us Sassenachs. Next week I'll phone Mr Ferguson, the head, and report him. I don't see why our boys have to suffer his anti-English jibes every day. Our college sometimes sends students on teaching practice to his school and I'll point out that this sort of behaviour from one of his teachers doesn't do much to promote good relationships.'

As the weeks went by, the situation improved for the boys when they found schoolfriends living in the next road: Jeannie, the 'girlfriend', who proved to be the sister of Andy Carswell who'd acted as Mark's second, and Bruce Crawford, the other second. They all met up each morning to walk to school together. Jeannie said how brave she thought Mark had been when Mr Hardie had given him the strap unfairly and said she wanted to be his regular girl. In the second week, she presented Mark with a new pencil and ruler to replace the ones Duggie Savage had broken.

A week later, Duggie himself apologized and he and Mark shook hands.

'I'm sorry I was so nasty,' he said. 'But last year we had another kid from England in the school. He was a real snob and thought he was better than anyone else. Always showing off and saying the Scots were a bunch of Picts who painted their faces with blue woad. I thought you might be the same and that's why I attacked you. If you like I'll take you and your brother fishing next Saturday in the burn. I'll show you how to catch trout using fishing flies.'

The following weekend, a group of six school friends, Andy and Jeannie, Bruce, Duggie, Mark and John made up a small party for a trip into the country. Armed with fishing tackle, they hiked over to Smallburn and fished for trout there. Duggie, it turned out, knew every pool, every eddy along the burn and where the bigger trout were likely to be lurking.

Later that evening, Mark and John came back triumphant.

They had caught their first fish: two trout weighing in at just over half a pound each. Nothing spectacular and not big enough to break any records but that wasn't the point. They ate them for supper and no food ever tasted better.

'Kids!' Laura exclaimed at the end of the day. 'I'll never understand them. One minute they're fighting and they're sworn enemies. Next day, they're bosom friends.'

'No different from adults,' Billy said. 'Look at us. Not so long ago Germany was our mortal enemy and Russia our ally. Now we have the Cold War, Germany's our friend and Russia's the enemy. It could change a few years from now.'

'You might enjoy a spot of sea fishing,' Billy's colleague, Robbie Logan, said one day in the staffroom when Billy told him about the size of the trout his sons had caught. 'We live in Stewarton but I have a small launch moored at Largs. You'd be welcome to come for tea. Bring your wife and the boys over next Sunday afternoon. Your wife could perhaps stay and have a chat with my wife, Meg, while we go over to Largs where I'll give you and the boys a few tips on fishing for bass.'

Billy took his family over to Stewarton and in Robbie's car they drove out to the little seaside town of Largs and spent a most enjoyable Sunday there. Laura was happy to remain behind with Robbie's wife whilst Billy and the boys tried their hand at sea angling. Robbie was an experienced fisherman and gave them a few hints and wrinkles.

'The secret,' he explained, 'lies in having the right tackle.'

'And a certain amount of skill, I should think,' Billy said.

Robbie showed them how to hook the bait and how to cast, with the result that they caught two fish, one two and a half pounds, the other three.

'Not very big,' Robbie chuckled, 'considering the biggest caught in deeper waters was over seventeen pounds, but not bad for a start.'

Billy and the boys were thrilled that at last they had

managed to catch something of reasonable size though most of the work and the skill came from their teacher.

Relaxing in this way with a colleague put a different complexion on things for a little while.

'Don't let McGonagall get you down,' Robbie told Billy as they sat waiting for the fish to bite. 'He can be a hard-nosed character and a bit of a headache at times; he's especially embittered that he's been passed over in the promotion stakes but Brother Eugene and he have never hit it off, I'm afraid. The Principal expects you to sort him out on his behalf. The trouble is that you're piggy-in-the-middle much of the time.'

It didn't solve the problem for Billy but it was good to know that at least a couple of people appreciated the difficulty of running a department with a potential saboteur on the staff.

Laura meanwhile had had a most friendly chat with Meg who'd reassured her that once they'd settled in, they'd be happy living in that part of Scotland.

On the drive home, Laura said, 'Meg has been telling me about all the things there are to do in these parts. Weekends could be pleasant, fishing at the seaside, walking in the Doon Valley, and there are lots of interesting boat trips from the coast. The *Waverley* paddle steamer calls at Largs in the summer months.'

Billy was not totally convinced. 'It's fine having a day out at the seaside like this, it's like a holiday. Weekends could be fine but for me, at least, it's the weekdays that are the problem. On Monday morning it's back to grim reality – college and McGonagall for me.'

Chapter Forty-Five

When it came to Billy's experiences at college, he found that the observations and warnings that Sandy Selkirk had made were totally accurate.

Teaching the Diploma students was a happy experience as they were a responsive and willing crowd, though he found it disconcerting that classes were organized in groups of one hundred and fifty. The mass lecture was the only teaching method possible and individual attention was out of the question. Marking essays from a crowd like this was a major headache for everyone but the task was made more onerous by Monty McGonagall's dilatory tactics in getting the results to Billy who needed them for reports on student progress. Teaching the B.Ed students was also as Sandy had predicted. They were alert, eager to learn and a joy to teach. Billy couldn't help but think of Matthew and Lucy and how their careers appeared to have foundered. Maybe the youth upheaval that appeared to be happening in England had not yet reached this part of the world. The size of the B.Ed groups, too, was a great help; at around thirty, it was reasonable, and intelligent discussion and participation were possible.

The postgrad students, however, were a different kettle of fish. Sandy Selkirk had been right. Going in to teach them was like entering a nest of rattlesnakes for they were argumentative and quarrelsome. The 'Glasgow Empire lot' Billy called them because they reminded him of the legendary tales told by actors who'd played there. The second-house shows on a Saturday night, when semi-drunken audiences would put the players on the rack with their merciless barracking, were a nightmare for visiting thespians. On the Moss theatre circuit, it was known as 'the graveyard of English comics'. 'Awa' an' catch your train back tae London!' they'd yell if they didn't like a particular performer. Acts which went down well in English theatres foundered at the Empire. Rumour had it that Des O'Connor was so nervous of going on, he pretended to faint on stage in order to escape the ruthless heckling and on one occasion hid himself in a cupboard and refused to come out.

I know what he must have gone through, Billy said to himself, because I feel exactly the same whenever I have to teach the postgrads. Before going in to face them on Friday afternoons, he had a sick feeling in his stomach. His sessions with them were not lectures or discussions but invariably the confrontations he'd been warned to avoid. On one occasion, thinking it might spark some interest, he had given a full account of the work of the husband-and-wife team of John and Elizabeth Newson who had devoted a lifetime to the study of social class and education in Nottingham.

'They showed that when it came to educational opportunity, working-class children were at a severe disadvantage,' Billy explained.

'Bilge!' bawled a student. 'I've never heard such crap. There's no such thing as social class.'

'It's an invention of sociologists to keep themselves in work,' yelled another.

There were a few sociology graduates in the class but they were diffident people who kept a low profile in order to avoid the sneers of the vociferous science students.

'I don't know how you can maintain that,' Billy said evenly. 'British society is rife with social class. It's to be found everywhere, even in the cemetery. Recently, *That Was The Week That Was* on the BBC perfectly described class attitudes. The tall aristocrat looked at the tubby middle-class gent and drawled, "I look down on him as my inferior." The middle-class man gazed up at the aristocrat and said, "And I look up to *him* but I looked down on *him*," indicating the little man in the muffler and the cloth cap, whereupon the little man simply said, "I know my place." ' One or two students grinned in response but the rest remained poker-faced. Billy tried to make light of it. 'Class, it has been said, is having grapes on the sideboard when nobody's ill. And of course you'll recall the infamous lines of the prosecuting counsel at the *Lady Chatterley's Lover* trial when he asked of the jury, "Is it a book that you would wish your wife or your servants to read?" '

The result of his efforts was stony silence. I'm dying the death of a thousand cuts here, Billy thought.

'Bilge!' pronounced the same student as before.

'You really are a man of few words,' Billy responded equably. 'While you're saying bilge, commercial interests exploit the differences between social groups and their lifestyles. Even the chance of getting into university as you yourselves have done is dependent to a large extent on social background.'

'Bilge!'

Billy persisted. 'If you give any sociologist worth his salt a few basic indices like occupation, level of education, age, religion, ethnic background, he'll be able to predict, within varying degrees of probability of course, lots of things about a person's lifestyle. For example, the kind of house he lives in and which part of town, how many children he probably has, which newspaper he reads, the music he likes, the state of his health and which illnesses he suffers from, the approximate age of his death, even whether or not he would fill in a questionnaire.'

'Bilge!'

It was difficult to know how to counter this argument and Billy expected the individual to bawl 'Awa' an' catch yer train' at any moment. He looked around for a Des O'Connor cupboard but there wasn't one. As for catching his train back to England, if only!

'Do you have any nautical connections?' Billy asked the scientist.

'No, I don't. What makes you ask?'

'I wondered, since your mind seems filled with the foul and dirty water that collects in the broadest part of a ship's bottom.'

Coping with the bloody-mindedness of Monty McGonagall was equally tiresome.

Getting work out of him was like drawing teeth, and it usually required several demands before anything was forthcoming.

'He'll get details of my new course when I'm good and ready,' Billy overheard him say to a colleague. 'Let the bloody Sassenach wait.'

It's annoying to be constantly accused of being a Saxon, Billy thought, because if anything, I'm Celtic, being of Irish extraction. He remained patient, however, and bided his time.

It was towards half-term that things came to a head. The Diploma students were due to take an assessment exam in McGonagall's subject, educational psychology. The students were seated in the examination hall, their pens at the ready. Billy was in his office marking essays when one of the assistant examiners burst in on him.

'We have a crisis on our hands,' he cried. 'We have a hundred and fifty students sitting in the hall but no question paper! What do we do?'

The chief invigilator, McGonagall, along with his test paper, was absent, and the candidates were twiddling their thumbs.

They phoned McGonagall's home but there was no reply. Billy had to think fast. He went to the hall and informed the students that there'd be a thirty-minute delay before the exam would begin. He rushed to the office and had the secretaries photocopy the previous year's exam paper, using all three office photocopiers at once. Thirty minutes later, the postponed exam began. No doubt news of the muck-up would reach the ears of the Principal and Billy would receive one of his customary nasty notes but he was past caring.

An hour later, McGonagall strolled in.

'Sorry,' he drawled, 'the exam completely slipped my mind.'

Billy blew a fuse for the first time.

'McGonagall,' he seethed, 'you're nothing but a bloody pain in the neck. You have set out to undermine all my efforts ever since I got here but this exam foul-up is the last straw. I've had it up to here with you and as far as I'm concerned you can take a running jump in a bloody lake.'

Fuming, he stalked back to his office and sat down with a deep sigh of anger. Then he suddenly got up from his chair and marched right back.

'McGonagall!' he raged. 'I take that back about jumping in a bloody lake. Correction. Make that a bloody loch instead!'

Chapter Forty-Six

Half-term came and Billy honoured his promise to the two boys that they would visit Manchester for a few days.

Apart from the promise, Billy and Laura's desire to take a trip home for a holiday after only six weeks away had been reinforced by two letters. One from Billy's brother, Les, who had reported that Mam's rapidly failing eyesight had been giving the family grave concern. The other from Duncan who'd told about a visit he'd made to their old house in Didsbury. 'I'm not too sure you'd approve of the changes they've been making,' he wrote. 'I think it advisable that you come and take a look for yourselves to see what's going on.'

Mark and John were not a hundred per cent sure that they wanted to go back now that they had made friends, particularly Mark who had a constant companion in the person of his freckle-faced girlfriend Jeannie Carswell.

Nevertheless, what bliss it was for them to see their beloved city once again! They arranged to stay with Laura's parents as all the rooms of their own home were well and truly occupied, as they were soon to find out.

It was good to talk with Laura's parents and it went a long way to bolster their confidence and regard for Scotland and the Scots.

'You'll find hare-brained, spiteful people in every society, not only Scotland,' Duncan said. 'Don't let this character McGonagall get to you.'

Easier said than done, Billy reflected.

The day after their arrival in Manchester, they went over to their own house. They were apprehensive about the visit as they didn't know what to expect. Even so, they were totally unprepared for the changes their two eldest children had wrought. Open-mouthed and with a growing sense of dismay, they viewed the transformation. It was every parent's nightmare.

For a start, Matthew and Des Gillespie were more hirsute than ever, though Billy and Laura had not thought that possible. They looked like a couple of subterranean troglodytes.

'Remember the Wild Men of Borneo, and the Pretty Things, Laura?' Billy said.

'How could I forget!'

'You said that if Matthew ever looked like that, you wanted the world stopped so you could get off.'

'And you said we'd book our passage to Mars.'

'Right, the time has now come. So, Beam us up, Scotty.'

After the obligatory cups of tea in the now communal kitchen (complete with a sack of brown rice and picture of Che Guevara) and some stilted, polite inquiries regarding each other's health, they embarked on a tour of the house, Laura screwing up her nose at the dirty mugs, Billy taking note of the strange burn marks on the ceiling.

The whole basement had been converted into what Matthew referred to as 'crash pads', including the boiler room and workshop, and looked as if it was normally occupied by hippies, with mattresses, cushions, clothes and records strewn about the floor. The workshop had received special treatment with a series of silken drapes giving it the appearance of the interior of a large tent like a Hollywood backdrop for *The Arabian Nights*.

Mark and John were entertained by it all and they grinned from ear to ear at everything they saw. This was their idea of the ideal home with its go-as-you-please lifestyle and the apparent absence of rules, order, and tidiness. Their house-proud parents, however, were shell-shocked by what they saw as anarchy and chaos.

Matthew knocked on the boiler-room door, from where

loud rock and roll was issuing. It opened to reveal, amidst clouds of smoke, a giant of a man with a menthol cigarette and a deck of cards in his hands.

'Hi, man,' Matthew said. 'Er, these are my parents . . .' He turned to Billy and Laura, 'Mum, Dad, this is Roger Lion, the DJ from the Enchanted Garden Nightclub.'

'Ah-ha, the landlord and landlady!' boomed Roger in perfect Oxford English and with a twinkle in his eye. 'Your fame precedes you. Are you into West Coast rock? Captain Beefheart? Hmmm, thought not. Well, ready for inspection!' he added, affecting a military salute.

Peering into the tobacco haze behind his six and a half foot frame, Billy wondered how he lived in the small space. At least half of it was occupied by a huge pair of loudspeakers and a stack of hundreds of LPs. The other half was covered by a single mattress on the floor, buried under papers and a typewriter. An office, in fact.

'Right, well, pleased to meet you. Must be getting on.' Roger closed the door and returned to his game of patience.

'Look, Dad, I don't expect you to understand the way we live, but the lodgers are all right on and they've all been paying their rent regularly,' Matthew said. 'You did say I was to make the enterprise pay and so I've hired out every available inch of space.'

Billy asked how many people lived in the house.

'Well, there's two students in each of the four large rooms, one in each of the small bedrooms, plus three in the cellar,' Matthew said, wrinkling his brow in concentration. 'That makes fifteen in all, and there's Vance and Alice in the garage, but they're only temporary.'

Dead right they're only temporary, Billy thought.

'Well, I suppose at least the house is getting used as it was in its Victorian heyday, with the servants in the cellars and attic,' Billy said, trying to make light of his growing discomfort, wondering nervously if this density of people was legal. 'But when I said you should cover the bills, I didn't have in mind a Californian-type commune of beatniks or for you to become the new Rachman.'

They had reached the dummy cellar and Billy peered into the shadowy interior.

'I presume you didn't rent off this part, Matthew; that would be going too far.'

'No, Dad. That's where I drew the line.'

Billy took a closer look into the recess. 'I presume the twenty-five gallons of wine I left maturing are still intact.'

'Dunno about that, Dad,' Matthew said evasively. 'I haven't checked on it for a while.'

Billy borrowed the torch Matthew was carrying and shone it into the darkness. There was no sign of any wine. He was about to flare up but thought better of it. What the heck! There were more important matters to get mad about.

'Surely you couldn't have drunk twenty-five gallons, Matthew! Not even you could have managed that.'

'Not me alone, Dad. It was the night of the party and they ran out of booze. Then I remembered the wine fermenting in the cellar. I thought we'd borrow maybe a gallon or two and replace it later. But like Topsy, the party just grew and grew. There were so many gatecrashers. Everyone got carried away and, well, I think it's all gone, I'm afraid. You are to be congratulated on the piesporter, by the way; it was particularly good and everyone said so.'

'I'm glad they liked it, and no wonder, considering it was free,' Billy fumed. 'You and your friends can damn well help replace it by buying the kits and setting to work. Or maybe they're only good at consuming and no good at creating. Have you any other surprises to impart to us or is that the lot?'

'No, I think that's everything, Dad.'

'Can we come back and live here with Matthew, Dad?' John asked innocently.

The scowl on Billy's face gave him his answer.

An attractive young woman in bare feet, blue jeans and

loose-fitting lumberjack shirt joined them. 'Hi, everyone,' she said.

Matthew flushed as he made the introduction. 'Er, Mum, Dad, this is Alison, she has one of the attic rooms.' He shuffled his feet, muttering, 'Er, shall we all go upstairs now,' before Billy and Laura had a chance to talk to her.

Upstairs was a different scene. Lucy had converted the upper floors to an ashram with every room painted a brilliant white. She was wearing a long, brightly coloured silk sari with a necklace of rosewood beads dangling round her neck, and her hair was combed straight back. She looked like an extra in a Hindi movie.

'Welcome to our ashram, everyone,' she said warmly.

'Why in heaven's name are you wearing a sari?' Laura asked.

'Because we're devotees of our Master, the Baghwan Sherpa Sanyassi. We think it's beautiful,' she smiled. 'And it cost hardly anything. Don't you like it, Mum?'

'I'd prefer it if you wore conventional Western dress,' Laura said. 'After all, we're British, not Indian.'

'When we're serving at the Eighth Day centre, we change into loose smocks as they're more convenient for working in.'

'And I see you've put on a lot of weight, Lucy, since we last saw you. What have you been eating?'

'We're all vegetarians in the ashram, Mum. We eat mainly nut roast, pasta, vegetables and salads.'

'Then you must be eating an awful lot of nut roast. And why the wooden beads? What happened to the silver cross and chain we gave you for your fifteenth birthday?'

'I sold that, Mum, and gave the proceeds to our movement. Same with all my other things. In order to enter the ashram, we have to give up all worldly possessions and turn our back on material goods which are a distraction from our true natures.'

'What's that funny pong?' Mark asked. 'It smells like Benediction at church.'

'That'll be our sandalwood joss sticks,' Lucy explained. 'We burn them next to the pictures of our Swami, the Baghwan, which are pinned up in every room.'

'Apart from the sandalwood, I detect another peculiar perfume as well,' Laura declared.

'That'll be the patchouli oil,' Lucy smiled. 'We're all wearing it.'

As they were talking, Lucy's old friends, Mary and Sally, appeared similarly attired in saris.

'Nice to see you, Mr and Mrs Hopkins,' they simpered.

'How's life treating you both?' Billy asked wonderingly. 'Do you like living in this house?'

'I absolutely adore it,' Sally said. 'As a sanyassin of the Baghwan, it's the happiest time of my life.'

'Same goes for me,' Mary echoed.

The parents thought they'd seen it all until Laura noticed the absence of her swallow-backed dining chairs.

'I suppose you've put them in the bedrooms, have you?' she asked.

Lucy blushed to the roots and looked evasive. 'No, Mum. Not exactly. We prefer bean bags to sit on when we meet for *satsang*. I think the chairs may be in the cellar.'

'Funny, I didn't notice them there,' Laura said suspiciously.

Before she could inquire further about the whereabouts of the chairs, they were disturbed by a male voice in the hallway intoning in a deep sonorous chant what sounded like, 'BOING! BOING! BOING!' over and over again.

'What the heck is that racket?' Billy asked, though feeling that nothing could faze him now. 'Sounds like one of those mantras I've been told about.'

'Who told you about mantras, Dad? Each sanyassin's given a different mantra but they're supposed to be secret.'

'Matthew once dabbled in it, then decided it wasn't for him. According to what he said, there are only about sixteen mantras all told, like "OM", "HU". And the one you're allocated depends on your age and sex. But I don't remember him mentioning BOING. That's a weird one and no mistake. Sounds like someone on one of those big bouncy space-hoppers.'

'I wouldn't take too much notice of what Matthew tells you, Dad . . .' Her voice trailed off as the door opened and a tall, thin fellow with a goatee beard and dressed in a Roman toga pranced into the room with both arms outstretched.

Lucy introduced him as Zven.

'I feel as light as a feather floating on the breeze,' he announced. 'I'm walking on a cloud and I'm at one with the whole universe.'

'These are my parents and my brothers,' Lucy said.

Before Billy or Laura could stutter 'How do you do', Zven said, 'You must excuse me, Mr and Mrs Hopkins. I'm so blissed out, I feel that I could fly off into the ether. I'm infused with the holy spirit. I feel animated and energized as if connected to some high-voltage cosmic electromagnetic force. I feel at one with all things bright and beautiful, with the birds and beasts of the field, with the flowers, with all living things on the planet and with some great astral power that our Master the Baghwan would call Prana.'

Billy and Laura exchanged looks. No need for words, they knew they were both thinking the same thing: what's happened to our children? They're living on another planet.

They toured the rest of the house, including three double rooms rented to other Sanyassi adherents and repainted from top to bottom in an eye-popping, brain-jarring Op Art style. Somehow, one of Billy's old history books had escaped the deluge and was still there gathering dust on top of a shelf, a sorry reminder of the days that used to be. After a tour of the house, they said their farewells, promising a return visit before they went back to Scotland. They left the house traumatized. How wonderful it was to get out into God's fresh air once again!

'Don't say anything, not a single word,' Laura said when they were outside. 'Let's talk it over tonight when we get back to my parents'. Something drastic has to be done to rescue our children from this Wizard of Oz world they're living in.'

'Agreed,' Billy said decisively. 'Right now, I fear for their future when it comes to surviving in this harsh world of economic reality. At this moment, I can't think straight. I feel bewitched, bothered and bewildered. Lucy says she's been eating a lot of nut roast and I think we should now give our house a new name. How about the Nuthouse?'

Later that night when they were alone, they reviewed the situation.

'Let's hope and pray,' Laura said, 'that what we witnessed this afternoon is merely a phase in the lives of our two eldest children and that eventually they'll come to their senses and return to reality.'

'Exactly my thoughts, Laura. I think our two eldest mean well and in many ways we've got to admire their courage and their zest for experimenting with different lifestyles but we live in different universes. We're operating on different wavelengths. There's an abyss between our points of view. What a contrast their lives are to my own upbringing in Collyhurst where life was a matter of survival and you had to pull yourself up by your own bootlaces. We were thrown in at the deep end and left to sink or swim. No time for choice or trying out different lifestyles, we had to get on with it or go under. Our children haven't had to struggle against adversity the way we had to. Everything's been laid on the line for them. I blame myself for the present predicament.'

'It's no use going over the past and looking for someone to blame, Billy. Right now, we must decide on our next course of action. First of all, I think we need to get our home back as soon as possible to restore normality.'

'So, what can we do?'

'We go back to Scotland and immediately after Christmas we reclaim our home here in Manchester and I come back with Mark and John.'

'That's our first priority, I agree. We put the house in Scotland up for sale and I begin looking for a job down here. I think in many ways the move to Scotland was a mistake though Mark and John are quite happy there now.'

The next day, Billy asked them, 'How do you feel about coming back to live in Manchester?'

It was obvious they were on the horns of a dilemma, torn between the two places.

'I'm beginning to like it in Scotland,' Mark said slowly, measuring his words, 'but I think if it came to the crunch, I'd like to come back. Most of my friends are here in Manchester and I definitely like Damian College better than St Bruno's Academy. But I'll miss Jeannie Carswell a lot,' he said, 'and also her brother Andy.'

'The same goes for me,' John said. 'I've made friends and I like fishing and all of that but I like it better in Manchester with my pal Charlie Murphy.'

'When we do come back,' Laura said, 'I shudder at the thought of the enormous cleaning and decorating job that'll be required to put the house back in order but we'll face that problem when we come to it.'

Before going back to Scotland, they told Matthew and Lucy of their plans to return and repossess the house. They accepted the situation with equanimity and gave notice to their innumerable tenants who began looking for other 'pads'. Billy was tempted to suggest the brick kilns on Barney's croft in Cheetham Hill. Matthew said that he and his fellow musicians had been thinking of trying their luck in London anyway and would be moving there as soon as their plans were finalized.

'I hope I'm not chasing you out,' Billy said to him. 'This is your home and you're welcome to stay as long as you like.'

'It's not that so much, Dad,' Matthew told him. 'I've talked things over with the rest of the guys and we think it's time to find pastures new.'

'What sort of pastures?' Laura asked. 'What will you do to earn your keep?'

'While you've been up in Scotland,' Matthew said, 'we've come on a lot since the Aquarian Angels days. Des, Tom Stephens and I have organized a quintet and have been playing gigs regularly at one or two places in town. We've been well received and have had good write-ups in the *New Musical Express*.'

'So why move?' Billy asked.

'We'd like to seek our fortune in London.' He grinned. 'Denmark Street! That's where it's at, where the best recording studios are. We reckon we could make it big down there if only we could get a lucky break.'

'OK, Matthew,' Billy said. 'It's your life and you must make your own decisions. I hope you'll reserve places on your yacht for your mother and me when you finally make the big time. What about you, Lucy? What are your plans?'

'I'd like to stay on here to keep Mum company until you're finally finished with Scotland. Mary, Sally and I have talked it over and we, too, hope to move eventually to an ashram in London.'

Billy grinned ruefully. 'I do hope you're not in a desperate hurry to move as it may be a while before I can land a job down here. I have yet to resign from my present post.'

Chapter Forty-Seven

On their return to Dewarkirk, they contacted the local estate agents and gave instructions for the sale of the house. A young smartly dressed executive came round the next day.

'It's a fine property,' he said, adopting estate-agent speak to tell them what they already knew. 'It's a detached bungalow in a quiet tree-lined cul-de-sac near shops, schools and train service. It should bring a good price. I'd suggest an asking price of twenty-three thousand.'

'Surely not!' Billy exclaimed incredulously. He couldn't believe his ears. He'd paid only £18,000 for it a mere six months ago.

The agent misunderstood. 'Well, we'd *start* at twenty-three thousand but we may reach twenty-four or even twenty-five thousand, depending on the market.'

This was too good to be true. But the agent knew the market better than Billy. An offer of £25,000 came in by the due date. It was the only offer submitted but the middle-aged couple making it didn't know that. When all expenses had been met, Billy and Laura found that they had realized a net profit of £6,000 which was considerably more than he had earned as head of education. I must be in the wrong business, he thought.

They spent Christmas at Dewarkirk packing their possessions and wrapping the glassware and crockery, making final preparations for Laura's move back down south with the kids.

It snowed heavily that December and the village became a glistening white fairyland. It was bitterly cold and everyone had to make sure they were well wrapped up if they dared to go outside into the garden to build a snowman or to pelt each other with snowballs.

'When I see Cairntable and the distant Lowther Hills shrouded in pristine white snow,' Laura sighed, 'I can't help but feel a twinge of regret that we're leaving. After all, this is my mother country and I've made some good friends here among the neighbours, especially the McHargs. It's been so disappointing the way things have turned out.'

'I can well understand your feelings, Laura, leaving this beautiful spot,' Billy said, 'but the happiness of the family is the most important thing in our lives, and it's imperative that we sort things out in Manchester. Also, I think Mark and John will be better off back at Damian College. To be perfectly honest, I'll be glad to get back to my home city myself.'

On balance Mark and John were happy to be going back to their beloved Manchester, although Mark was feeling blue at the thought of parting from Jeannie, his girlfriend.

'I'll write to you regularly every week,' Mark said.

'And I'll write back,' she said.

Billy wondered how long the promises would last.

In the first week of January, the removal people arrived, stacked the heavy furniture into the van, carefully placed their belongings into tea chests, and set off on the long journey south.

On reaching Manchester, Laura began putting the house back in order. It was a case of all hands to the pump and Billy and the four children joined in as the house was cleaned from top to bottom. What furniture remained was taken outside to be polished, new curtains hung, and the carpets professionally laundered. The whole place was repainted and papered by a firm of decorators with no expense spared, new furniture was ordered to replace the things that had mysteriously gone missing. The costs were considerable and it was a good job that they'd made a profit from the sale of the Dewarkirk house. As time went by, the Manchester home took on a new look, or perhaps it was truer to say it won back its old look as the rooms were gradually restored to their former condition.

During the Christmas holidays, Billy drove over to see his mam to see how she was managing. Her eyesight had deteriorated sharply and she was having difficulty seeing common objects about the place. One of her biggest problems was reading the numbers on the electric cooker knobs and she was having to guess how far to turn them and her guesses weren't always accurate. If it weren't for the help of her neighbour and friend, Mrs Reynolds, Billy doubted that she'd have been able to carry on. Though it must be said, Mrs Reynolds, too, was getting on in years and her vision was by no means a hundred per cent. A case of the blind leading the blind, Billy thought. In addition, Mam was still grieving for Tommy though it had been over three years since he'd died. The mourning had been replaced by a vague melancholy that something vital in her life was missing.

'I find myself still making his breakfast and his dinner,' she sighed. 'Then I suddenly remember that he's not here and I start weeping for him all over again as if he died only yesterday. We used to have lots of rows in our time, your dad and me, but just the same I miss him terrible. He was my friend and my companion. It's like losing a limb. You can't be married to someone for sixty years without it hurting when he's gone. I'm glad he died when he did though, for he was miserable when his memory was gone. A lost soul.'

As Billy saw his mam struggling to survive each day, he knew that the time was not far off when she would no longer be able to cope on her own.

'I don't know what we'll do then,' Les said when Billy broached the subject with him. 'Flo, Polly and I will look after her as long as we can but the present situation can't go on forever. As you know, Mam is fiercely independent and she won't accept the idea of giving up her own home so easily.'

'When the time comes, she may have no choice,' Billy said sadly. 'Perhaps we should be making plans for that day.'

And seeing his mam's plight gave further impetus to his search for another job. He simply had to find something nearer home but it was uphill work as he was soon to discover. He scoured the *Times Educational Supplement* every week looking for another post. There was no shortage of vacancies but the trouble was that they were in distant places like Devon or Durham, Sussex or Surrey. No use whatsoever. The next job had to be within striking distance of the Greater Manchester area.

The months went by but nothing suitable turned up.

Meanwhile, Billy drove home each weekend, leaving Scotland at 4.30 p.m. on Friday, arriving in Manchester five hours later. In the small hours of Monday morning, he had to drive back again, leaving at 4 a.m. Sometimes he felt sorry for himself but then recalled how his own father used to get up at that early hour for donkey's years to work in the fruit market. So what have I got to complain about? he asked himself. He usually reached college before nine o'clock. As colleagues greeted him, they little realized that he had driven through the night, often through snow and blizzards to get there on time. He came to know the M6 motorway, the A74 north of Carlisle, and the A71 through Darvel and Galston to Kilmarnock like the back of his hand; he became acquainted with every bump, every bend, every curve, every hill. During the week, he booked himself in at a bed and breakfast, preferring the privacy of a small hotel to lodgings, his experiences as a student in digs fighting off the demands of an amorous widow landlady in Leeds having left him disillusioned. It was a miserable existence but his one consolation was that his children were happy at school and making good progress. As for Matthew and Lucy, they followed their own plans and there was hope that they might eventually see the light, except, he thought ruefully, they'd already seen it, or so they claimed, and that had been the cause of all the headaches in the first place. When I think of our eldest two, he mused, my feelings fluctuate between

395

anger, frustration, sadness and deep affection. Maybe it's best not to see too much of them as we always end up at loggerheads.

At the college, little changed. Monty McGonagall was as awkward and bloody-minded as ever, maybe more so. Billy despaired of ever getting him to cooperate.

The annual written examinations for Diploma students were always held a few weeks before the Easter break and that year, 1972, McGonagall took it upon himself to fly off to Paris on holiday without sending the examination marks in for Billy to collate. The result was a crisis. Again! Billy had to find his phone number in France from one of his colleagues in order to discover what he had done with the results.

'They're in the right-hand drawer of my desk in my office,' McGonagall replied nonchalantly when Billy finally contacted him. 'What's the problem?'

'You left before the term had officially ended,' Billy said angrily. 'You were supposed to be in college until Friday.'

'Look, Hopkins, I had no more lectures after Tuesday and so I couldn't see the point in hanging around. You've got the results now so I don't see what you're beefing about.'

Brother Eugene got the students' collated marks late, prompting yet another of his nasty notes criticizing Billy for falling down on the job.

This was by no means the first of such messages Billy had received. I could almost wallpaper my office with these things, he chuckled to himself. Earlier that same month, he'd had a brush with Brother Eugene.

Billy had arranged to see two female students who'd made a habit of cutting lectures and were due to be enlightened as to the error of their ways. The time fixed was nine thirty on a Tuesday morning and Billy left his B & B in good time, hoping to cover the six miles to college in ten minutes. The engine started first time as soon as he turned the ignition key. Good old car, he said aloud to himself, never lets me down. He set off along the road and he'd covered a little less than a couple of miles when the engine started to splutter. Uh-oh, he thought, I spoke too soon. His pessimism proved justified. The car made a brave attempt to keep going but the effort was too much and, after a few asthmatic coughing noises, the engine gave up the ghost. Billy got out and tried to attract the attention of passing cars by waving and holding out both arms in a gesture of supplication. In vain. No one wanted to know. Everyone was in a hurry or didn't like the look of him. There was nothing for it but to walk to the nearest garage three miles distant. The Scottish mechanics were most obliging. Not only did they drive him back to his car but took him to college as well, promising to repair and deliver the vehicle later that afternoon. But it was ten thirty when he got to his room and the students had been and gone. Instead he found one of those notes on his desk.

> *Mr Hopkins,*
> *Two students have been to see me and reported that they*
> *had arranged to see you at 9.30 this morning about their*
> *lecture attendance but you didn't turn up. This is bad. If*
> *we cannot honour our arrangements with our students*
> *how can we expect them to honour theirs with us?*
> *Brother Eugene, Principal*

No explanation sought. No excuses accepted. Tried in absentia and found guilty. The brief communication was symptomatic of the closed college climate. The Principal rarely emerged from his room but ran things by diktat and didn't seem to treat the staff as real people. No wonder they were forever bickering and griping, Billy thought. An interesting sociological phenomenon, he reflected, that a whole institution could be sick.

The need to find another job was becoming more desperate with every passing day.

Chapter Forty-Eight

It was during the summer term that he saw it. A ray of hope. A head of education was required at a college of education in Crosby on Merseyside. It wasn't in the Manchester area but it was within reasonable travelling distance. He sent off his application right away and a few weeks later was invited for interview. At last, things were looking up.

The time set for the interview was 5 p.m. An odd hour to begin but he wasn't going to argue. The college went on to point out that candidates would be expected to stay overnight and a nearby hotel was recommended as suitable accommodation. Billy got to the hotel early at 3 p.m., intending to relax and prepare himself for the ordeal of a selection board. After a long hot bath and a close shave, and paying special attention to the silver streaks in his hair to bring out the mature look, he put on his best suit which Laura had pressed so carefully the night before, and started out on the two-mile walk to the college. As he strode along, he noticed five other smart-looking men walking in the same direction from the same hotel. They turned in at the college gates and he knew they were the other candidates on the short list. The Principal and Vice-Principal, both female, greeted them and ushered them into the lounge where tea and coffee were waiting. The conversation was desultory and cautious, being concerned mainly with the comparative advantages of the various routes people had taken to reach the place. Then Billy spotted a number of African carvings resting on the bookshelves.

'Are those carvings from Wamunyu in Kenya?' he asked.

'Why, yes,' the Principal answered. 'Do you know Kenya?'

'I spent several years there,' Billy answered, encouraged. Maybe I'm in here with a chance, he thought.

'Interesting,' she said. 'I used to be headmistress of a girls' secondary school in Nairobi.'

'I taught at an African boarding school in Marangu,' Billy said warmly.

The other candidates were now exchanging winks, raised eyebrows, and knowing looks. It's a fix, their faces said.

The Principal went on to explain how the college had expanded in the last few years.

'Originally we had only one or two houses and then we exchanged them for a hotel further up the coast. As we've expanded, we've acquired three more hotels and we're now looking at a fourth as our student numbers have increased yet again.'

'This exchanging of houses for hotels,' Billy observed with a grin, 'sounds like a game of Monopoly.'

It was the wrong thing to say as he soon realized when the Principal rewarded him with a painful grimace. 'Quite,' she said coldly.

The six candidates were next taken into the staff dining hall where they were joined by three governors, a Lady Jane Sefton and two military-looking gentlemen. This is like one of those War Office Selection Boards I've read about, Billy said to himself. Are we to be observed eating in order to check our table manners and to see if we know which knife or fork to use? He was tempted to try eating his peas with his knife to test their reactions. The meal passed without mishap, though once again the conversation was desultory and tentative – like a game of poker, no one giving anything away.

'We shall now go over to the admin block where we'll conduct interviews in strict alphabetical order,' the Principal announced after dinner. It was 7.30 p.m.

Ah, good, Billy thought. Being 'H' I should come some-where in the middle of the list. He hadn't reckoned on the other people's names: Brooks, Crowther, Campkin, Goldwyn, and Haslam. That put him to the back of the queue. For the next three and a half hours he sat glancing idly through sundry periodicals in the library, waiting his turn. I wish I'd brought *War and Peace* or *Gone with the Wind* with me to while away the time, he thought.

At last the Vice-Principal appeared.

'Mr Hopkins, please come this way.'

It was 11.15 p.m. and Billy was feeling tired and sleepy but nothing compared with the interviewing committee who'd been at it all evening.

A weary-looking Lady Jane asked him the usual questions about his qualifications, experience, and ideas on running a department. By this time, Billy was so sleepy he could hardly be bothered replying, just as the committee seemed hardly interested in his answers. The two military men yawned several times. In reply to their questions about his philosophy of life, Billy mumbled a few truisms about Plato's *Republic* and the Idea of the Good, and declared that his personal ethical stance wavered somewhere between relativism and nihilism, to which they nodded sagaciously as if concurring. The inquisition ended at eleven thirty and Billy sensed that he hadn't got the job, which was confirmed the next morning when, waiting in the library with the other hopefuls, the Vice-Principal entered and announced the verdict.

'Would Mr David Brooks please return to the committee.'

That was it. The unsuccessful candidates rose in one body and, without a word, marched swiftly out of the building. Billy drove home disconsolately, resigned to more months on the educational treadmill in Scotland.

It was 1974, two long years after Laura and the boys had returned to Manchester, before he saw anything that was remotely suitable and then in a part of the *Times Educational Supplement* where he didn't normally look. He'd combed through the usual columns in the educational press covering schools and colleges of education and once again had turned up a blank. Then by accident his eye was drawn to a notice in the technical colleges section: 'Applications are invited for the post of Staff Development Officer at the William Pitt Technology College. This is a key educational post in the North-West Regional Authority.'

His interest aroused, he read on. He didn't fully understand what the post entailed nor what a staff development officer did but there was no harm in applying. The important thing was that it was in the Manchester area and that was the clincher. If he didn't know what the job was about, so what! He'd soon find out. It was less pay than his present salary but that didn't matter either. To get a job nearer home, he'd try anything, do anything, preferably legal.

As soon as he had the forms, his application was in by the next post.

Once again, Billy was asked for interview, this time at the normal hour of 10 a.m. which, as far as he was concerned, was a point much in its favour. He turned up at the education offices a good fifteen minutes before proceedings were due to begin. At ten o'clock prompt, Billy was ushered into an anteroom to meet the retiring Head of Staff Development, Dr Fred Blunt, an outspoken man who didn't mince his words. Billy was the only applicant present, the other candidates' arrival times having been staggered.

'The place is a jungle,' Blunt told him, 'and to do the job, you have to have the hide of an elephant and the roar of a lion. Are you sure you've got what it takes? You'll meet opposition at every turn as I did: from the Principal, heads of departments, and even from some staff who ought to know better. You'll have to fight your corner every moment of every day. I've had to create this post from scratch, much to the annoyance of the Principal, Mr Forrester. It's more a job for a militant trade unionist than someone like you from a namby-pamby training college. You can lay on courses for the staff but the Principal won't give them time off to attend. You'll have to fight him on that one. The staff here are from industry and they're used to tough talking. Don't get the idea that you can handle them with kid gloves or you're in for a shock. If you think the job's too much for you, I'd advise you to turn round and go right back to Scotland.'

Not exactly encouraging, Billy thought, but this Fred Blunt didn't know how desperate he was to get back to home territory.

'Thanks for the warning, Dr Blunt,' he said equably. 'If I'm offered the job, I'll cross those particular bridges when I come to them.'

The interviewing board was more formal than the college of education, consisting as it did of the Principal, Vice-Principal, the Chief Education Officer of the Borough, several town councillors, staff representatives, heads of departments, and people from the university and other interested bodies. The Principal explained that the college was one of the largest technology colleges in the country, consisting of 450 full-time members of staff and 11,000 students, of whom 7,500 were part-time. The usual questions followed. Billy was becoming skilled in anticipating and responding to the kinds of things they wanted to know. Everything was flowing beautifully until the Vice-Principal bowled him a googly of a question.

'What would you do,' he asked, smirking and looking round the committee, 'if an old cantankerous member of staff with thirty-odd years' experience told you to get stuffed with your staff development ideas.'

Billy didn't have any staff development ideas to speak of but he wasn't going to let that stop him from answering. If the truth were known, he was also hazy as to what exactly staff development meant.

'If an old diehard stick-in-the-mud has come this far with such a negative attitude towards staff development, there's nothing that *can* be done except encourage him to seek early retirement.'

It seemed to be the right answer for everyone guffawed and nodded vigorously in agreement.

Later that evening, the Principal phoned Billy at home to tell him he'd got the job. He received the news with mixed emotions. Joy that he would be back in the Manchester area but a vague feeling of disquiet about what he'd taken on. Nevertheless, he accepted the offer. What bliss when he was able to arrange an interview with Brother Eugene to give him the good news. His final day at the college was typical of the painful years he had spent there.

The external examiner for the postgrad students was a professor from the University of Dundee who'd driven all the way down to Kilmarnock to present his report to a meeting with the Education staff. At the time scheduled, Billy and his staff were present ready to meet their important visitor. Only one person was missing and he'd sent in a note explaining his absence.

Dear Mr Hopkins,
I shall not be attending the meeting with the external
examiner as I am expecting the plumber to call to do
important repairs at my home and this is the only day
available for him. Please accept my apologies.
Monty McGonagall

At the end of the meeting, Billy thanked the professor and wished him a safe journey back to Dundee. Then Billy said farewell to his own staff and shook their hands, offering the hope that his successor would prove more to their liking. As a final gesture, he forwarded McGonagall's letter to Brother Eugene. It was time to give the Principal a taste of his own medicine. At the end of McGonagall's apology, Billy appended a short note.

Dear Brother Eugene,
I thought you might like to see the kind of thing I've had

to put up with during my time at this college. You may like to contact Mr McGonagall directly to discuss his priorities with him.
W. Hopkins

Billy never did find out what action, if any, was taken because he walked out of the college and climbed into his car which he'd already packed with his possessions ready for off. As he turned out of the college car park, he felt a shiver of ecstasy run down his spine as he realized that this would be the last time he'd be making this long journey home from Scotland. No more McGonagall. No more postgrads. No more nasty notes from Brother Eugene. All the way down the A74 and M6, he sang out for all he was worth the song that was playing on the radio, 'Home in Pasadena, home where grass is greener.'

The only thing that remained for him to do now was to find out what the new job entailed and what exactly they understood by 'staff development'. He'd worry about that later. Tomorrow was another day and who knew what was round the next corner?

Chapter Forty-Nine

For Billy, returning home to Manchester was heaven, like starting life all over again. He rolled up his sleeves, spat on his hands and the cellar soon echoed to the old familiar sounds of sawing, hammering and the wood-turning lathe. The local B & Q store was pleased to see him back as their balance sheet had taken a sharp dip during his absence.

Shortly after Billy's return, Lucy and her friends made their planned move to an ashram in the south.

'Mary, Sally and I feel in duty bound to go on living in an ashram,' she explained, 'in order to follow our Master, the Baghwan.'

'But doesn't it worry you, Lucy,' Laura asked, 'that you'll be giving up your freedom? And judging by the living conditions we found you in when we first came back, it looked like a pretty Spartan existence. Seven girl devotees bedding down on the floor in one room using sleeping bags. Not exactly comfortable.'

'No, Mum, but we're a mission with a purpose and for that we can put up with a little discomfort. Our movement can save the world by bringing inner peace to every individual and that's worth making sacrifices for. Besides, we're part of a new wider family, a commune. We're trying to encourage a different way of living, one not ruled by war, brutality and greed.'

'So what happens now, Lucy?' Billy asked, resigned to the fact that his views didn't count for much.

'My two friends go to London but initially my posting is to Cornwall where I've been asked to organize things. There are about a hundred people down there and we've been told it's chaotic. After that I've been asked to go to work in the head office in London but nowhere near Matthew, I hasten to add.'

'It sounds as if you've been singled out for promotion,' Billy said. 'That's a feather in your cap.' He couldn't keep the note of pride out of his voice.

'No, Dad. We don't have things like promotion in the movement. We're above petty achievements.'

'Oops, sorry,' Billy said, 'to bring in my bourgeois values of promotion but it does look as if they've recognized your leadership qualities.'

'What'll you do in London?' Laura asked. 'I mean, will you sit in an office organizing things?'

'Not entirely. I'll be working part-time in a mental hospital as occupational therapist teaching art and I've been told that there'll also be opportunities to study part-time for a degree if I so wish.'

This last piece of news cheered up Billy and Laura no end. Maybe the chances of Lucy working for a degree were slim but at least there was hope. Perhaps this oriental movement would achieve what they'd failed to do, namely get her back to studying once more.

It was a sad parting when she left. Laura was particularly sorrowful when the door closed behind her.

'The kids are finally flying the nest,' she sighed. 'I feel that this is an important milestone in our lives. Suddenly I feel old and I can definitely hear those Bingo players in Southport calling me.'

'But we still have the two youngest to think about,' Billy said. 'And when they've gone, you'll still have me.'

She laughed. 'What are you trying to do? Depress me?'

The two youngest were more than holding their own at school. That summer, Mark had achieved three good A-levels in English, History and British Constitution. John had achieved good grades in nine O-levels and was on course for success at A-level. If things hadn't worked out with the first two children, there was always hope with the last two. Ever since they'd been youngsters, Billy had had big ideas for them. From an early age, it had been obvious to him that Mark, the argumentative one with his dreams of luxury and a fast buck, was destined to enter the legal profession in some capacity while John had shown definite leanings towards medicine, his strongest subjects being biology, chemistry, physics, and botany. Ideal for a medical degree provided he got the necessary grades. Duncan, their grandfather, was enthusiastic about the possibilities.

'If you get your two sons into these professions, you'll have achieved something admirable,' he told Billy. 'Before I retired from taxes, we in the Inland Revenue always had the highest respect for gentlemen of the law. If Mark succeeds in this field, he'll not only earn a high salary but will perform a noble service for society. As for medicine, what higher profession can there be than devoting one's life to alleviating the suffering of one's fellow man? His uncle Hughie can give him lots of pointers.'

Billy couldn't help thinking that Duncan was a little over the top in his fulsome views about the legal profession. He wondered if he'd ever heard that Dickens's Mr Bumble had described the law as 'a ass – a idiot' or if he was acquainted with that infamous quotation from Shakespeare's *Henry VI*: 'The first thing we do, let's kill all the lawyers'?

Persuading Mark to take up law as a profession was no problem when he heard about the high fees that could be charged once qualified.

'You never hear of a poor lawyer,' Grandad Mackenzie told him. 'Your best bet is to get your feet wet by working as a pupil for a couple of years in a solicitor's office to see if the job suits you and if you suit the job. You'll get experience of the different kinds of court, like adult, family, criminal, private prosecutions, and the magistrates' service, and so on. It'll give you the chance to make up your mind whether you want to be a solicitor or a barrister. Then you go to university and study for a degree in law.'

'Sounds great,' Mark said, 'I'll do it. Will I need a wig and gown?'

'Not straightaway,' Duncan chuckled. 'First, in the immortal words of W. S Gilbert, you must clean the windows and sweep the floor and polish up the handle on the big front door. When you've qualified as a barrister and you're appearing in court, maybe then you get your wig and gown.'

'Be a barrister, Mark,' Billy pleaded. 'I can see it now. You in court like Lionel Barrymore strolling about the courtroom with your thumbs in your waistcoat and speaking to the jury. "Ladies and gentlemen of the jury. I am here to represent the plaintiff in the dock who is accused of murdering his business partner, Josiah Tintwistle. I shall prove his complete innocence in the matter." '

This appealed to Mark's imagination.

'I always had ambitions to be a lollipop man when I left school,' he grinned, 'because he doesn't start work till he's sixty-five. But you've persuaded me. I'll have a go at law. I'm eighteen now and I'll be twenty when I go to university, an old man ready to draw a pension.'

A few weeks later, Duncan pulled a few strings with his old acquaintances and got Mark a job in the offices of Broome, Broome, and Mistry in New Brown Street in Manchester city centre. Maybe things are going to work out for this son, Billy thought. And when he saw Mark go off for his first day at the office, dressed in a bespoke charcoal-grey suit, white shirt with tie and, most important, a traditional haircut, Billy's chest swelled with pride. And if friends and colleagues were to ask him what Mark was doing nowadays, he could affect an air of insouciance and nonchalantly examining his nails could answer, 'Oh, he's something in law.'

Chapter Fifty

The William Pitt Technical College (known to the locals as the Pit) was not difficult to find for it was the biggest edifice for miles around. It was enormous, consisting of nine floors and thousands of windows, and looked more like a factory than an educational institution. Billy looked up at the structure and an involuntary shiver ran down his spine. Was this where he was to spend the rest of his career?

He turned into the car park and looked for a space. It was impossible. The place was chock-a-block with vehicles of every size, make, and condition and he spent the first twenty minutes driving round and round in circles. He spotted a fair number of vacant bays but these were clearly marked as reserved for senior staff, their deputies and sundry personnel such as the college manager, nurse, and head janitor. He wondered if his own position as Staff Development Officer rated a parking space among this elite cadre. At last a vacancy was created when the ambulance and two police cars which had been occupying prime positions finally moved out with sirens wailing at full volume. He wondered what was going on. Perhaps the emergency services had been contributing to one of the college courses, like physiotherapy, chiropody, or radiology.

Billy got out of his car and climbed the stairs to the first floor and up to the wide, spacious concourse that wouldn't have been out of place in a five-star international hotel. As he walked across the terrazzo floor, he espied a heavily built woman waddling towards him eating a large meat pie. She looked like an earthy peasant from a Brueghel painting.

'Good morning,' Billy said with a friendly smile. 'I wonder

if you could direct me to the Vice-Principal's office.'

'Yis, I can,' she said, gravy running down her chin. 'Straight over there an' the first door on the right. But you're wastin' your time 'cos he won't see you. I've this minute tried an' 'e is much too busy. You 'ave to make an appointment with 'is secretary next door.'

'Thanks,' he said, wondering who this Pantagruelian lady might be. But he found that what she'd told him was accurate.

'Sorry,' the VP's secretary said. 'Mr Purdy's always run off his feet at this time of year with one meeting after another. The best I can do is book you in for an appointment for next week. Meanwhile, he suggests you go along to the Liberal Studies staffroom on the fifth floor and ask for John Quinlan who is one of your staff. He'll tell you what the score is.'

Billy took the lift as instructed and found a large room packed with lecturers two or three to a desk. He soon found the man he was looking for.

'Pleased to meetcha,' John said, greeting him with hand outstretched. 'We've been waiting for you. Let me get the rest of the education staff.'

The rest of the staff consisted of two female lecturers: a friendly woman with a generous smile indicative of a ready sense of humour, who introduced herself as Joan Upton, and a sharp-eyed lady named Sarah Shenkman. Billy was surprised to find that he had only three lecturers to work with.

'This is your education staff,' John said as if reading his thoughts, 'but you have responsibility also for the three technicians in the audio-visual aids unit on the ninth floor.'

'How did you find parking on your first morning?' Sarah Shenkman asked, eyeing him closely.

'Needle in a haystack stuff,' Billy replied. 'The car park was full.'

'You must demand a reserved bay from the VP,' she said. 'Our section needs to assert its standing. If you win status in the college, so do we because it reflects on us. At the

410

moment, we're treated like dirt. It's an insult that you should have to drive round in circles looking for a place to park. And we need to get our own staffroom as well. We shouldn't be in here living cheek by jowl with liberal studies riff-raff. You must take it up with Mr Purdy. Demand he give us the recognition due to us.'

'I'll do my best,' Billy said, 'as soon as I get in to see him. But I've only just arrived and I can't begin by making demands. I should've thought there'd be plenty of room in a college of this size.'

'It's the exact opposite,' John said. 'Rooms are at a premium and it's cut-throat competition for every inch of space by the four hundred and fifty on the staff. Well, four hundred and forty-nine now.'

'What makes you say that?' Billy asked, intrigued.

'Did you see the ambulance and police cars in the car park this morning?'

'I did and I wondered what they were doing here.'

'A science lecturer on the sixth floor topped himself. Swallowed cyanide in his laboratory. Couldn't face the thought of another year in this place, I suppose.'

'Good God! Does this happen often?'

'Not that often. A few years back somebody threw himself off the roof. He didn't half make a mess in the car park.'

'Talking of poisons and death,' Sarah Shenkman said menacingly, 'be on your guard if the VP offers you hospitality in the training restaurant. Politely decline or if you feel you must accept, choose a table nearest the exit so that you can get to the toilet quickly in case of emergency.'

'Remember the students are experimenting,' Joan Upton said with a grin. 'From the waiters who serve the meal to the apprentice chefs who cook it. Have a good supply of Alka-Seltzer handy.'

'Or maybe take a sick bag,' John chuckled.

'They're just joking,' Joan Upton laughed, 'though last year, one or two of the liberal studies staff went down with a bad case of the runs, which they blamed on one of these so-called banquets.'

'It's supposed to be one of the perks of the job,' Sarah Shenkman added, 'as if being a guinea pig is a fringe benefit. Food isn't the only perk, though. If you put your back out, call in a physiotherapist student who'll be more than willing to practise on you. A corn or an inflamed bunion? A learner chiropodist is waiting to get his hands on you.'

Their conversation was interrupted by a neurotic-looking young man flourishing a piece of paper.

'Sorry to break in. John, please take a look at this proposed title for a course and tell me what you think. It's urgent.'

John glanced at the paper. 'You're right, Sam, to try and spice up your titles if you want to attract students. The students read no more than the title before deciding if your course is for them. Try to get the words paranormal, sex offenders, drugs or rock and roll into it somewhere and you'll have a winner. And don't forget to add the words "and society" at the end. How about "Sex, Drugs, Rock'n' Roll and Society"? Or "Society and the Psychology of the Deranged and Perverted", or perhaps "Sex, the Paranormal and Society".'

'Thanks, John,' the young man said. 'You're a pal.'

'What was that all about?' Billy asked.

'The lecturers are worried about their jobs with all this talk of redundancies in the air. At the beginning of each year, they have to attract a decent number onto their courses or they're for the chop. It's a matter of market forces in operation. You've got to sell your courses to the butchers, bakers and candlestick-makers or you're out. That applies to us too, I'm afraid. We have to attract at least eighteen onto our FETC courses or we're out of a job. But you're the exception because it doesn't apply to you. Your post is unusual in that it doesn't need to be justified by numbers; you have a roving commission across the college. Lucky old you!'

412

'Since I'm supposed to be your boss, maybe I should know what this FETC course you teach is all about.'

'The lecturers on the staff of the college here are highly qualified in their specialist fields but they have no teaching qualifications. That's where we come in. We teach the Further Education Teaching Certificate to anyone willing to give up their precious free hours to attend our courses, which deal with the history, theory and practice of FE. Our main problem is that the Principal won't give them time off to come on our courses. Our trade union's fighting to change that.'

'If they have to give up their free time, why should they do the FETC? What's in it for them? Where's the incentive?'

'They do it for the certificate they get at the end, even though it doesn't make them qualified teachers but I suppose a piece of paper is better than nothing.'

'Maybe I could teach some parts of your course for you. Would you like me to?'

'With respect, Mr Hopkins, we'd rather you didn't. That would be like taking bread from our mouths. If you take away any of our precious hours, next thing we'd know we'd be given the chuck.'

'I'm not sure where I fit into all this,' Billy said.

'I think you're mainly concerned with improving the standard of teaching in the college. Some staff are lousy teachers and think a good lecture is simply reading from a book. The students often see no more than the top of their heads and that's not a pretty sight, especially if they have dandruff. Such staff need to learn how to present their stuff in a more interesting way and that's where you come in. You're also supposed to supervise us to see we're doing our job properly.'

Billy chuckled when he heard this last duty. 'He who can, does. He who can't, teaches. He who can't teach, teaches teachers. And he who can't teach teachers, supervises teachers of teachers. You can't get much further away from the classroom than that.'

413

'There's more to your job than that,' Joan Upton laughed. 'You're also at the beck and call of any departmental head who thinks a member of his staff needs remedial help with his teaching. You may be called in to help hopeless cases.'

'Meanwhile, where do I rest my head,' Billy asked, 'since I don't have a room?'

'You're best to work in the library until the VP finds you somewhere.'

'Fine,' Billy said. 'I'll speak to the librarian about it.'

'Whatever you do,' Miss Upton warned, 'don't call him "Librarian". He likes to be known as an "information management specialist". You'll find people in this college are prickly about their titles and like to be referred to by a fancy handle. For example, your head AVA technician, Jim Travis, calls himself "Advanced Technology Facilitator".'

'And I suppose,' Billy chuckled, 'a rubbish collector is a refuse disposal operative; a miner, a subterranean mineral extractor; and I suppose my wife is a "domestic duties coordinator". Who in heaven's name thinks up these glorified job titles?'

'I'm afraid I'm responsible for many of 'em," John said, grimacing. 'It's easy to invent them. Simply permutate titles from a three-column list and you get swanky job descriptions. Your job, for example, as Staff Development Officer would become Corporate Strategy Executive or Internal Operations Consultant.'

'Fine,' Billy said, 'but would it earn me a higher salary?'

'I doubt it,' John said.

Billy's next port of call was the audio-visual aid unit to meet the three technicians who were under his wing. The trio were busy on their various tasks but paused in their work to meet him. Head of the section was Jim Travis, a retired engineer and expert photographer; number two was Val Singleton whose specialization was audio-visual equipment, especially cine projectors; the third member was a young man named Phil Dexter who was in charge of video recorders and cameras. Billy was filled with admiration as he watched them at work, checking and servicing their apparatus.

'We supply a service to all departments throughout the college,' Jim Travis explained. 'If a member of staff requires equipment for his lecture, it's up to us to make sure it's set up when and where he wants it. We have to be careful though as some departments try to monopolize us and take us over. If we have problems, we're supposed to bring them to you. We work under your jurisdiction.'

'I shall remember it,' Billy laughed, 'when someone in authority tells me precisely what I'm supposed to be doing here.'

Billy spent his first week in the library – the 'information resources facility'. There wasn't a thing he could do until he met his immediate superior, the Vice-Principal, Mr Purdy. Billy filled in the time by reading the morning newspapers from cover to cover and then switching to solving the crosswords at which he was becoming quite good given the daily practice. Pretty soon, he thought, I'll be able to rival Laura and her mother.

The period of waiting finally came to an end and he made his way to the VP's secretary to confirm his appointment. He had been looking forward to this meeting for he'd built up a list of requests.

'Yes,' the secretary said, 'we have you down for ten thirty, immediately after the VP has seen Mr Pickup, the head janitor. Please make yourself comfortable in the waiting room.'

Billy went through and sat down next to a worried-looking gentleman.

'Good morning,' Billy said cheerfully. 'My name's Hopkins, I'm the new Staff Development Officer. You're Mr Pickup, the head janitor?'

'Yes. That's my job but I prefer the title Hygiene Maintenance Coordinator because that's a more accurate description of what I do as I'm in a charge of a large staff.'

'That's impressive, Mr Pickup. How many cleaners do you have under you?'

'You mean Floor Sanitation Service Operators. I have thirty. Most of them have attended an advanced course in the operation of sanitation equipment.'

'You mean a mop and a sweeping brush?' Billy grinned.

'There's more to it than that nowadays,' he said in a peeved tone. 'They work with sophisticated vacuum cleaners and mechanized polishers.'

'Sorry, sorry. I'll remember not to offend them by calling them cleaners. What are you here to see the VP about?'

'I don't know. I simply got a message that he wants to see me about storage facilities. Going in to see Mr Purdy is an ordeal, I can tell you. His office is like bloody Wall Street. He has three telephones and they're ringing all the time you're in there as he shouts his orders at some unlucky bugger at the other end of the line.'

The door of the office opened and the secretary beckoned Billy's companion to come in.

'Mr Purdy will see you now, Mr Pickup.'

Billy strained to hear what they were saying inside the inner office but couldn't make out any details. He had the impression, however, that there was a fierce argument taking place.

After ten minutes, Mr Pickup emerged red-faced and fuming.

'I knew it,' he said to Billy. 'He's taken away my storage room on the ninth floor. Says the operator on that floor can put her equipment on the eighth. I tell you, he doesn't live in the real world.'

It was Billy's turn to be summoned into the office. He strode in purposefully, list in hand.

'Come in, Mr Hopkins. Good to see you. Hope you're settling in OK. As usual, I'm run off my feet but I can spare you ten minutes.'

'Fine, Mr Purdy. I have one or two requests I'd like you to consider.'

'Sure, sure. Fire away.'

'First, what exactly are my duties? These were never made clear at my interview.'

'That one's easy. You are to be concerned with contingent management facilitation. You're the college consultant when it comes to departmental needs for improvement in staff performance and also a source of advice if a head of department feels a member of his staff is in need of remedial help. They'll call on you should your services be required. Next, I want you to give a series of induction talks to our new full-time students when they enrol in a fortnight's time.'

'What sort of talks?'

'Giving guidance as to the best way to study and make the best use of their time here. There are various groups, like the radiology students, the physios, the chefs, and so on. Now did you say you have other requests?'

'If I lay on talks for our regular lecturers on methods, for example, on how to lecture, how to take tutorials, and so on, would you give them time off to attend? At the moment, the staff, I'm told, have to sacrifice their own free time and I think that's unfair.'

'That's a hot potato, Mr Hopkins. It's a trade union matter and you'll have to speak to the Principal about it. I don't have the power to authorize that.'

'Right. I'll take it up with Mr Forrester. I have another request. Could I be given a reserved parking bay like the other senior personnel?'

'That also is a tricky one,' he said, pursing his lips and taking an inward breath. 'I'll have to think about it. Give me—'

The white phone on his desk rang.

'Yes, yes, what is it?' he barked down the mouthpiece. He listened for a moment than snapped angrily, 'Look, I've told you before, you've got a vote of five thousand for that

417

equipment. If you spend a penny more than that, you'll be surcharged personally.'

He slammed the phone down.

'Sorry, Mr Hopkins. What were you saying? Something about a reserved parking space. Can't be done yet. People are hypersensitive about their position in the hierarchy, you see—'

The phone rang again. This time the black one.

'Yes, what is it?' he snapped into the phone. 'No, you must not do that without consulting me! I've told you before. If you step out of line again, you'll be out of a job.' He slapped the phone back on its cradle.

'Sorry, Mr Hopkins. Now, about a reserved parking place. Tricky. It's a status symbol, you see. I'll have a dozen people on my neck if I gave you one. My hands are tied. I'm snookered, you—'

His secretary opened the outer door of his office.

'Director of North-West Regional Board on line one,' she said, indicating the red telephone.

'Sorry, Mr Hopkins, I'll have to take this call. Yes, yes, sir. I've arranged a meeting with Mr Forrester and the head of building for next Wednesday. That'll suit us fine. Leave it with me, sir.'

He put the phone down gently this time and turned to Billy. 'Now was there anything else, only I have another appointment in a few minutes?'

'Yes. I'd like a separate room for myself and my little staff who are at the moment lost in the Liberal Studies common room.'

'I've got good news for you on that front. Can't give you a room for four but I've found an office for you on the ninth floor. Room nine-twelve. It's being prepared for you as we speak and should be ready by this afternoon. Now, if you'll excuse me . . .'

He stood up to signify the interview was over.

'I hope you settle in here happily. One perk I forgot to

mention is that every fortnight, you and your staff are invited to a formal dinner served to you by our students from the Catering Department. It's part of their training but it's high-class stuff. Book it with my secretary if you're interested.'

Billy found himself outside the door and Purdy was already ushering the next visitor in. Some perk, he said to himself. Allowing ourselves to be poisoned by a bunch of apprentice cooks. What did I achieve in that interview? Not very much. I now have a rough idea of what my job is. Wait till I tell Laura I'm a consultant. No reserved parking space but at least I have my own room. That'll be a lot better than reading the newspapers in the library-cum-information facility.

In the afternoon, he took the lift to the ninth floor and soon located Room 912. It was the broom cupboard that Mr Pickup had been forced to vacate that morning. It was about six by six feet, the size of a small bathroom, without a window, and had barely enough room to accommodate a small table and chair. There was no telephone and anyone wishing to contact him would have to visit in person. To make matters worse, there was a powerful pong of disinfectant and floor polish. My God, he thought, is this where I'm to spend the next few years of my life? I shall suffocate.

Chapter Fifty-One

Billy occupied his first week delivering talks to new full-time students on how to make the best use of their time in the college. He gave the same advice to radiologists, physiotherapists, typists, chiropodists, and a whole host of 'ists', including maybe a few oboists, Maoists, and hypnotists. If only someone, he thought, would come along and offer me advice on how I might use *my* time wisely. He spent the next few days sitting in his broom cupboard with the door open to avoid being liquefied, waiting for customers but no one came. I took my harp to a party, he sang softly to himself, and no one asked me to play. After three weeks of claustrophobia, he felt it was time to do something about it. Instead of waiting for clients, he'd go out and get them. Or so he thought.

First he made appointments (only a two-day wait here) with all eight departmental heads in turn to discuss setting up programmes for their staffs. From each of them came the same answer. Nothing doing.

The head of science was typical. He had a superb office with a large window overlooking the college buildings and the surrounding area. His room contained a large oak desk with two telephones, fitted carpet, a large fish tank with aquatic plants and several beautiful goldfish.

'I have a staff of over eighty lecturers,' he explained. 'If I were to allow them two hours a week to attend your courses, it would cost me one hundred and sixty hours of teaching. That would require eight additional members of staff to cover their absences. It can't be done, old chap, unless we get more staff. The lecturers themselves are already up to their eyes and I doubt if they'll give up their free time. However, I've no objection to your putting up a notice on our board and if you can attract people onto your courses in their own time, well and good.'

Billy pinned up notices in all eight departments advertising his proposed courses.

ARE YOU HAPPY WITH THE STANDARD OF YOUR TEACHING?

IF NOT, WHY NOT TAKE A STAFF DEVELOPMENT COURSE? THE NEWLY APPOINTED STAFF DEVELOPMENT OFFICER IS PREPARED TO OFFER TEACHING METHOD COURSES ON A VOLUNTARY BASIS. LEARN HOW TO PRESENT YOUR LECTURES, HOW TO MAKE USE OF AUDIO-VISUAL AIDS, HOW TO CONDUCT YOUR SEMINAR DISCUSSIONS.

SIGN BELOW INDICATING WHEN YOU WOULD BE FREE.

A week later, he returned to collect his notices and to gauge staff response. The omens were not good. Many had scribbled replies to the effect that they were not prepared to attend courses unless they were released from teaching duties. In the Engineering Department, someone had scrawled a stark message: 'Who do you think you are? God?'

It looked as if Billy had been appointed to the job that never was, that of development officer in a college where no one wanted to be developed. He was caught at the friction point between the trade union on the one hand and the education authority on the other. There was nothing for it but to arrange an appointment with the big white chief himself, Mr Forrester, Principal of the establishment. There was a three-week waiting list to get in to see him. Almost as bad as getting to see a medical consultant, Billy thought. Nevertheless, he was willing to join the queue as his raison d'être at the college depended upon the outcome.

When the waiting period was finally over, Billy was

ushered into the Principal's office by his fusspot secretary.

'Mr Forrester can give you only five minutes,' she twittered as she opened the door into the office of the great man. 'He has an *important* appointment immediately after you.'

The Principal's room was palatial. No other word for it. The Managing Director of ICI or the Bank of England would not have been out of place there. It had everything: a huge picture window with a panoramic view of North Lancashire and the distant Pennines. It was equipped with wall-to-wall carpeting, a large L-shaped desk with four telephones, and the latest technology including an intercom system. On the wall behind his desk was a picture of L. S. Lowry's 'Coming From The Mill'. Billy assumed it was a reproduction but he could have been wrong.

'Well now, Mr Hopkins, what can we do for you?' Forrester said condescendingly, swinging his chair round ninety degrees to look out on the Lancashire panorama, and offering Billy a first-class view of his profile.

Billy had had weeks to prepare his little speech and he now put on his boldest expression. 'I want to discuss the role of the Staff Development Officer in this college,' he announced bravely. 'If we don't allow staff free time to attend methods courses, I don't see any purpose in my being here.'

'Good point, Hopkins,' he said warmly, addressing the picture window. 'A ticklish situation, that one. It's a matter between the North-West Regional Council and the trade unions. Look at it from my angle. We have four hundred and fifty staff. If I allow each of them one hour off, that translates into twenty-three staff required to cover them; if I allow two hours off, that means forty-six new staff. Can't be done. The Borough Council would never countenance it, d'you see? It always comes down to a question of money.'

'So what's the answer, Mr Forrester? What am I doing here? Why was this post created?'

'Second good point, Mr Hopkins. Your role here is a contingent one in case the dispute about hours is ended.

We'd look pretty foolish if the impasse was resolved and we'd no staff development officer in situ, wouldn't we? For the present, you must make your courses so attractive that lecturers are willing to give up their free time. Meanwhile, be on standby in case your services are ever needed for difficult cases, and—'

The intercom crackled with the secretary's voice. 'May I remind you, sir, that you have an appointment with the Chief Education Officer at the town hall in ten minutes.'

Forrester wheeled round in his chair to face Billy, at the same time making a steeple of his hands. 'Good talking to you, Mr Hopkins. Must do it again some time. Good points you made. Very good points indeed. Must give them consideration. Goodbye for the time being.' He held out his hand in dismissal and Billy shook it.

'Thank you for seeing me, Mr Forrester.'

Next thing, he found himself out of the office and on his way back to his cubbyhole to lick his wounds.

What did I achieve there? he asked himself. Zilch, the answer came back. Stalemate.

'It's all pretty depressing having a non-job,' he told Laura that evening. 'I don't know what I'm being paid for.'

'At least you're out of that awful job in Scotland, Billy. How would you fancy giving up your present post and going back there, driving north every weekend through the snow and the blizzards to deal with Monty McGonagall and Brother Eugene with his nasty notes? At least you're home every night. Here, you can visit your old mother more easily, and as for me, I like being near my own parents.'

'I suppose so but sometimes I feel as if I've jumped from the frying pan into the fire.'

'Count your blessings, Billy,' she said, determined to cheer him up. 'Things are looking up with the kids. Mark's well on his way to being a solicitor, and, judging from John's mock exam results, it looks as if he'll win a place in medicine at

Sheffield. From London, too, it's been good news as well. Matthew's band has now gone upmarket performing in West End restaurants while Lucy's still teaching her art therapy and at the same time studying for a degree in religious studies. So taken all round, everything's going well. We've got a lot to be thankful for.'

'You're right as usual, Laura. I've got to think positive, though at times it's difficult sitting in a broom cupboard.'

For the next few months, Billy occupied his time by visiting the audio-visual unit every day where Jim Travis introduced him to photographic skills, including developing and printing. Val taught him the niceties of the latest film projectors so that he could set up a film ready for projection in five minutes flat, and Phil showed him how to operate and make best use of a video camera. Occasionally he was invited to give a guest lecture, but apart from that, there was no call on his services. Through constant daily practice, he became skilful in solving crosswords in both the *Telegraph* and *The Times* versions. He embarked on a course of reading the classics and got through a series of hefty books, including Tolstoy's *War and Peace*, Dostoevsky's *Crime and Punishment*, Balzac's *Le Colonel Chabert*, Kafka's *The Trial* and most appropriately *The Castle* with its vision of lonely individuals trapped in bureaucratic labyrinths. Having nothing better to do, he began writing his autobiography for his family. How I wish I had the memoirs of my great-grandparents, he reflected. I'd love to know how they felt about things, what emotions they experienced, what made them laugh and what made them cry. At least I shall leave my own family in no doubt about matters like that.

Whenever he left his den, he pinned a note to his door:

THE STAFF DEVELOPMENT OFFICER IS OUT ON A COMMISSION AT THE MOMENT. MESSAGES AND REQUESTS FOR AN APPOINTMENT

SHOULD BE PUSHED UNDER THE DOOR. THEY
WILL RECEIVE IMMEDIATE ATTENTION ON HIS
RETURN.

Six months went by and not a single request was received.
No one checked on his whereabouts or what he was doing.
No one seemed interested. Some afternoons he took to
driving over to Langley to see if his mam needed any help.
At least there his services were in demand: he put up a new
curtain rail, fixed a light switch over her bed, mended a
door that was sticking, did shopping for her and her friend,
Mrs Reynolds.

One particular wet afternoon he called on her around
four o'clock and found her sitting by the kitchen window
looking out at the rain. She presented a sad, forlorn figure.

'It's me again, Mam,' he said as he kissed her on the
forehead. 'I've come to try and fix the knobs on your electric
cooker so that you can tell by touch how far you've turned
them.'

'You're very good, Billy. I don't know what I'd do without
you. You've done so many jobs around the house. I'm about
to make some tea. Would you like some?'

'Let me make it for you, Mam.'

'I can make it myself. I'm not an old cripple in a wheelchair
yet, you know.'

'All right, Mam. You make it.'

He watched her movements as she shuffled into the little
kitchen and groped her way around. She filled the kettle but
fumbled as she tried to connect the plug into the socket.
Next, she located the tea caddy and put in two heaped
teaspoonfuls and added a third.

'One for the pot,' she said.

Then came the pouring of the boiling water. It looked like
a risky business as she estimated where the teapot was. She
managed it, but only just. There was real danger that one
day she would miss and scald herself.

After tea, Billy glued small studs to the knobs on her electric cooker so that she could feel how far she had turned them.

'That's much better,' she exclaimed as she tried a switch. 'You're a good boy, Billy, and brainy with it as well.'

These are only temporary fixes, he reflected. The time is coming soon when it'll be unsafe to leave her on her own.

Billy was so worried about his mam that the following weekend he arranged a meeting at his home with Flo, Polly and Les to discuss the situation. He phoned Sam in Belfast to apprise him of the situation and he agreed that some action would soon become necessary.

'I've noticed for some time how bad things have become,' said Flo, the eldest sister, 'but Mam is independent and she won't want to give up her home.'

'I've done as much as I can to help her get by,' Billy said, 'but I think we ought to be looking at alternative accommodation.'

'If you mean a nursing home,' Polly said, 'you'll never get her to accept that. For her, the word "home" means poverty and the workhouse.'

'Maybe so,' Les said, 'but to leave her as she is, trying to cope with failing eyesight, has become dangerous. I'm afraid she'll have a bad accident one of these days.'

The little family conference ended with Billy and Les agreeing to look into the possibilities of a place in a geriatric nursing home for the blind. During the Easter break, they spent a few days driving round the Manchester and Salford district looking for suitable homes. The choice was limited. They found only two that seemed to fit the bill. The first one in Salford was near a general hospital and offered accommodation along with a resident nurse for blind and near-blind geriatrics. The matron took them on a tour of the facilities.

'This is the main lounge,' she said conducting them to a large room round which sat a large group of shrivelled-up elderly people in various stages of dementia and helplessness. Most stared vacantly into space, mouths open, one or two muttering gibberish to themselves, others shaking uncontrollably with palsied limbs. Billy and Les said nothing, did not even exchange glances but each knew without a word being spoken that they were thinking the same thing. Next, the matron showed them the bedrooms.

'There are three single beds to each room but residents have their own wardrobe.'

'How do they spend their leisure hours?' Billy asked.

'Mainly in the lounge with the other patients. There's a television but no one's interested since only a few can make out the images on the screen.'

Billy and Les came out of the home profoundly depressed by what they'd seen.

'There's absolutely no way we can put Mam in a place like that,' Billy said as they drove off. 'She may be losing her eyesight but not her mind.'

'I'm in full agreement, Billy. That'd be condemning her to purgatory. We must think of something else.'

They visited two more institutions but found a similar situation.

'It's no use,' Billy said. 'One of us must take Mam in when the time comes though that may be some way off yet. It's the least we can do after she's devoted her life to looking after us. The question is who?'

It soon became obvious who the 'who' was to be.

'We'd love to have her,' Flo said, 'but our house is that small, we wouldn't have room for her. We'd be living on top of each other and she'd be most unhappy. She needs her own space.'

'Same goes for us,' Polly said. 'Steve is very fond of Mam but the walls in our place are paper-thin. You can hear everything that's going on in the next room. She wouldn't like it. It'd be a big mistake if she came to us.'

'As you all know, we wouldn't hesitate for a minute to take her in,' Les said, 'but we still have the kids with us and she'd have to mix in. She'd never get any privacy.'

'And she definitely wouldn't want to go over to Belfast to live there,' Billy added. 'That leaves only one house, ours. It's all right with me but I'll have to talk it over with Laura first. It all depends on her reaction.'

That afternoon he approached her.

'Laura, I want to ask a big favour of you. You've done so much for me and our kids that I don't like asking you this. I want my mother to come and live here so that we can take care of her. What do you say?'

She didn't hesitate. Not for a minute.

'Of course she must come to us. Now the children are leaving us one by one, we have the space. In my own home before we were married, my mother and father took in old Grandma and Aunty. We have a duty to look after our old folk as the Africans in Kenya were always telling us. One day, we'll be old too and it's to be hoped that our own kids will look after us when we can no longer do so ourselves. We can set up the large bedroom at the front of the house as a granny flat. She'll have privacy and easy access to the bathroom, which is important at her age. Consider it done.'

Tears sparkled in Billy's eyes. 'When I hear you talk like that, Laura,' he said, 'I suddenly remember why I married you.'

'Because I'm a big softie, that's why.'

Billy phoned round his family and told them the good news.

'When the time comes and Mam is ready to move in with us, I'll put the plan into action. We'll call it Operation Flit.'

Chapter Fifty-Two

One Tuesday morning, towards the end of his first year at the Pit, Billy went to his broom cupboard-cum-office as usual. He opened the door to let in fresh air and there on the floor was a letter addressed to the Staff Development Officer. It was from the head of liberal studies asking him to go and see him regarding help for a member of his staff. At last! His first commission. He'd practically given up hope of anyone asking for his services and here it was in black and white. He could hardly believe his eyes as he'd waited a year for a letter like this. He phoned Mr Fairfax immediately and arranged to see him later that morning.

'I'd like you to take a look at one of my lecturers,' he told Billy. 'I'm not happy about her. It's not so much her teaching as her general demeanour and attitude which are lacking somehow in professional dignity. She's a figure of fun among the students. If you can help her become a little more decorous and polished, it'd be a great step forward in improving her image. Her name is Primrose Proudfoot and I've asked her to go to your office to see you this afternoon. You can't mistake her; you'll know her when you see her.'

'Leave it with me, Mr Fairfax. Robbie Burns had the answer to our problem when he wrote:

> *O wad some Power the giftie gie us*
> *To see oursels as ithers see us!*
> *It wad frae mony a blunder free us,*
> *An' foolish notion*

'I propose with her permission to film her lecture and play it back to her. When she sees the kind of image she's projecting to the world, she'll probably alter her behaviour accordingly. It's useless telling her where she's going astray. She must see it for herself.'

'Best of luck,' he said. He didn't sound too hopeful.

Billy was intrigued as to who the mysterious lady might be and didn't know what to expect and so when at 2 p.m. there was a knock at his door, it was with a certain amount of trepidation that he opened up. But there was no surprise for he'd already met her. It was the lady from the Brueghel painting, the one with a fondness for juicy meat pies.

'We'd better leave the door open,' Billy said. 'There's hardly room for two chairs in here.'

'As you like. Now, what can I do for you, Mr 'Opkins?'

'Mr Fairfax has asked me to attend one of your lectures, if that's OK with you, Primrose. With your permission, I'd like to film it.'

Far from looking suspicious as Billy had expected, her face lit up.

'But of course you can,' she gushed. 'I'm flattered. He's 'eard about 'ow good my lectures are, 'asn't he? Always glad to pass on my skill to others. I think I may be in line for a spot of promotion.'

'You think so? Anyway, thanks for allowing me to attend. When would you suggest?'

'What about next Monday afternoon at two? I've got the bricklayer apprentices on day release, Brickies Three we call 'em an' they're a right lively lot, I can tell you. I'm supposed to be teachin' the Shakespeare, 'Ollywood and Society course, if they'll let me. They've already watched videos of *Romeo and Juliet* and *West Side Story* and I'm hoping to get them to discuss a comparison between the two.'

'Sounds interesting. I look forward to it, Primrose. I'll book Phil and his video equipment for that time. See you then.'

I'm going to have my work cut out, he thought to himself when she'd gone. A more unprofessional character it would be hard to imagine. She'd sat throughout that little interview with her legs splayed like an uncouth peasant.

At the appointed time on Monday afternoon, Billy was in place with Phil all ready with his equipment. Primrose had made an effort to dress smartly in dark skirt and white satin blouse. It was a pity about the gravy stains.

At two o'clock, only five students were present.

'The others'll be here soon,' Primrose apologized. 'They usually go for a pub lunch in the local and what with one thing and another, they're always a bit late.'

At two fifteen, ten beefy, red-faced students came ambling in and lounged at the desks. One wearing a red Manchester United shirt stretched his legs across the desk in front of him.

'Where've you lot been, as if I didn't know?' Primrose bawled good-naturedly. 'The 'ead of department thinks you're so good in this class, he wants to videotape you. Anyroad, shurrup, 'urry up an' get sat down.'

'Jud'll be late,' said the United fan. 'He had a big win on the gee-gees at dinnertime and so we've been celebrating. He's in the gent's spewing his guts up but he'll be here in a few minutes.'

'Right,' Primrose said. 'Last week we watched the video of *Romeo and Juliet* by Zeffirelli. What did you think of it?'

'I thought you said Shakespeare wrote it,' protested one of the brickies. 'Who's this hi-tie bloke Zeffirelli?'

'He was the director, you ignorant git,' another brickie shouted. 'Get with it.'

'If this Shakespeare geezer's such a great writer, like you say,' the red-shirted youth exclaimed, 'why couldn't he write in proper English that we can all understand instead of that hey nonny nonny crap?'

' 'Cos that's the way they used to speak in them days,' said

431

a pimply-faced lad, rummaging into a bag of pork scratchings.

'Yeah, so what? I couldn't understand a bleedin' word of it,' the footballing aficionado said. 'I liked that bit when they were in bed though. Juliet was as starkers as the day she was born.'

'Yeah, but she had no tits,' said another.

'What did you expect, she was only just gone fourteen,' said Pimples. 'Isn't that right, Miss?'

'You're on the ball,' said Primrose warmly. 'Shakespeare said that Juliet "hath not seen the change of fourteen years" but Romeo was a bit older.'

'Then Romeo could have been done for rape as she was under sixteen,' said a youth with a cropped hairstyle that gave him the appearance of a Gestapo officer.

'They'd have been better getting someone like Diana Dors as Juliet,' said a pasty-faced boy, licking his lips.

'Piss off,' the Red Devils fan said. 'Diana Dors can't act for toffee.'

'No, but think of her leaning over a balcony,' pasty-face said lasciviously. 'She's got knockers like big water melons.'

'Anyway, Romeo should've been locked up for having it off with a young virgin of fourteen,' said Cropped Hair. 'I went out with a chick the other night – you'd have swore she was eighteen. Turned out she was only fourteen. How's a bloke supposed to know? Nowadays, the girls get dressed up so you can't tell their age. What's a bloke supposed to do if he scores with one of these birds? Ask to see her birth certificate before he gets on the job, or wha'?'

At this juncture, Jud, the punter, tottered in. He looked haggard and white as a sheet. He collapsed at a desk and proceeded to moan quietly, holding his head in both hands.

'What about that drug the holy Willie gave to Juliet?' a tall thin student asked.

'You mean Friar Laurence?' Primrose said.

'Yeah, that's the bloke. Were the priests in them days drug dealers, or wha'? I reckon it must've been a couple of downers like Valium he give her. I've tried them myself. They're great if you're looking for a good night's kip but you feel like shit next morning.'

'Yeah, and what about the poison shit Romeo bought at the chemist's?' added Pork Scratchings, ' 'E must've been pals with the chemist 'cos you couldn't buy smack like that today without a prescription. Even then the chemist would make you sign the poison register and all that. It must've been a lot easier in them days if you wanted to top somebody or even top yourself.'

'Goes to show, though, how you've got to watch it when you're taking drugs,' said a runt-faced brickie. 'Romeo must've bought an overdose from that chemist. You've got to be careful when you shoot up. Always best to get the good stuff and weigh it before you inject.'

'The pigs in the olden days must have been kept busy,' said the Gestapo haircut. 'What with rape and drugs going on all round them!'

Billy wondered if Primrose was going to make any attempt to direct and guide the discussion. She seemed to have read his thoughts for she now joined in.

'What did you think of *West Side Story*?' she asked. 'Did you notice how much the story was like *Romeo and Juliet*?'

'Yeah, I liked it better,' said Manchester United. 'It was great the way the gangs got into a rumble. But there was one thing about the fillum that really got on my wick.'

'Oh, you have a criticism?' Primrose exclaimed excitedly.

'Yeah. It was spoiled by all that bloody music. Can't you just see our United lads after a match having a punch-up with the Millwall lot and suddenly breaking off to sing and dance like a bunch of pansies. Didn't make any sense. But I liked it better than that Shakespeare crap. At least I understood a lot of what they were sayin'.'

'The best writer I've ever read,' Jud mumbled, suddenly

lifting his head from the desk, 'is Mickey Strang. Man, he's a way out, cool scribe. Check this out,' he rhapsodized, taking a cheap, tatty-looking paperback from his pocket.

' "All of a sudden Babyface slammed his knee hard up into Fatso's guts. Fatso's kisser came down with a jerk and Babyface whammed it with a haymaker thwack. The knuckle sandwich smashed the bone to smithereens, making blood and pulp splatter like an overripe tomato. Fatso collapsed on to the pavement, spitting dirty yellow teeth. He was gurgling quietly stretched out in the gutter, so just for the fun of it, Babyface kicked him in the balls with his Doc Marten. Then, for luck, he gouged out Fatso's right eye with his heel and stamped on to the pulsating mush that once was Fatso's face."

'Follow that if you can. Yeah. Mickey Strang. One real happening writer.'

That ended the debate on English literature. The class changed tactics and in order to avoid further discussion of *Romeo and Juliet* they questioned Primrose about her last holiday.

'Last year me and my 'Arry went to Ireland,' she responded, warming to the subject. 'We had a beltin' time. Took the ferry from Holyhead. The coach took us all round the shop from Dublin to Cork and over to Limerick . . .'

The remainder of the time was devoted to a Cook's tour of the Emerald Isle while several students took out their copies of the *Sun* and *Reveille*.

At the end of the afternoon, Billy arranged a private playback for Primrose in the audio-visual unit. Billy knew how important it was that he desisted from making any kind of comment. It was crucial that Primrose watched herself and made her own observations of how the discussion had gone. Self-criticism and insight were the essential features of the method.

'We'll now play the whole lecture back to you,' Billy told her. 'If, at any point, you want to stop the tape to say something, call out. Is there anything you'd like to say before we begin?'

'Nothing, except I thought it was bloody good. First class, I'd say. One of my best lectures ever. Tell Mr Fairfax he's got my permission to use it as an example to weaker members of staff. I expect he'll promote me to senior lecturer when he sees the tape.'

Bewildered by this bizarre notion of her own abilities, Billy told Phil to start the playback.

Primrose watched the whole thing in silence, nodding appreciatively from time to time. When it was over, Billy asked, 'Well, Primrose, what do you think?'

'I've one criticism I must make,' she said earnestly. 'It's so obvious.'

'Yes, yes,' Billy said enthusiastically. The method was working.

'I need to lose some bloody weight,' she said.

When he saw Primrose's reaction to the video-tape, Billy began to have doubts as to the effectiveness of the method. But somehow or other it must have sown a seed in her mind because later that term, he noticed, when passing her on the concourse, that she'd lost weight. Not only that, it was evident she'd begun to take pride in her appearance. No meat pie. No gravy stains. Instead she wore a smart two-piece suit and some genius had worked wonders with her hair. The improvements also seemed to carry over into her professional life because when Billy attended one of her classes as a follow-up, there was a newly found confidence about her. She established firmer control of the situation and was less inclined to let the students take over the proceedings. So, he reflected, Robbie Burns' 'giftie . . . to see oursels as ithers see us' paid off for Primrose Proudfoot in the end.

Chapter Fifty-Three

September and the start of the new academic year at the college came round. Billy was not looking forward to it particularly as it meant more of the same routine: sitting in a cubbyhole reading the largest volumes in the college library. Before taking up his duties, or non-duties, Laura and he paid a visit to his mam in Langley.

'The day can't be far off now, Laura,' Billy remarked as they drove up Rochdale Road, 'when she'll have to come to live with us.'

'She can come whenever she's ready,' Laura replied, 'but it'll be a traumatic experience for her giving up her home after so many years. I don't blame her wanting to hang on to her own place for as long as possible.'

Mam was peeling potatoes before the fire when they arrived. It was obvious that she was finding it hard to see for she was cutting away more potato than peel. Billy noticed the bandage round her wrist.

'Why the bandage, Mam?' he asked.

'I was doing some ironing and I accidentally caught my hand on the hot iron but it's nothing. I've known worse than that in my time. If you'd like to make a pot of tea, all the stuff's there in the kitchen.'

'I'll do it,' Laura said, filling the kettle and plugging it into the socket.

'You'll find a jug of milk in the fridge,' Mam called, 'and if you look in the bread bin, there should be a Madeira cake. Cut yourself a slice. Make a sandwich an' all if you want one.'

A few minutes later, Laura called from the kitchen. 'Billy, can you come here for a moment?'

'Is everything all right?' Mam called. 'Did you find everything?'

'No problem, Mrs Hopkins.' Then, turning to Billy, she whispered, 'Take a look in the bread bin.'

He did so. They exchanged concerned glances. There was a cake all right but it was stale. The loaf of bread had patches of green mould at the edges.

'How long have you had this cake and this bread, Mam?' Billy called.

'I can't remember. A couple of days, I think.'

'It's been there longer than that. Doesn't your home help look into the bread bin?'

'No, she sweeps and cleans the place but she doesn't go through my larder or the bread bin; that's not her job.'

'Mam,' Billy said, 'the cake and your bread have gone mouldy. Why don't you come and live with Laura and me before you have a serious accident or make yourself ill with bad food?'

'No, no, Billy. You and Laura are kind but—'

'Matthew and Lucy have left and we've plenty of room. We could convert the big front bedroom into a granny flat. It has a big bay window, catches the sun and you'll be able to look out and watch the world go by.'

'You are so thoughtful and don't think I don't appreciate it but—'

'Mam, the family had a meeting and we don't like the idea of you living up here all on your own.'

'I have a wonderful family. Every night I go down on my knees and thank God but I'm *not* here alone. I have Mrs Reynolds. I've been here fifteen years and I'm used to it. I don't know anyone in Didsbury.'

'We'd love to have you,' Laura said, taking her hand. 'We'll make you comfortable and your family can come and see you. You'll have more visitors than ever because they won't have so far to come.'

'Laura, you're a good daughter-in-law but I want to stay in

437

my own home. I have my pension and I get by. I don't want to be some old woman lodging with her children. If ever it comes to that, where I can't manage, I'd rather be put on top of Tommy in the cemetery. I don't want to be a burden to anybody.'

'But, Mam, your eyesight has nearly gone,' Billy said, 'and one of these days you'll have a nasty accident and there'll be no one here to help you.'

'Whatever happens, Billy, I won't be a burden on my kids. As long as I can keep going, I won't be a burden on anyone.'

They knew it was no use arguing. Before driving home, they went round to the local shops and did a little shopping to replenish her supplies. But when they left, they were troubled in their hearts.

'No matter how she protests,' Billy said, 'I think we'll be hearing from her soon.'

When they reached home, there was something unexpected waiting for them. More of a shock than a surprise. John was still out at college but on the sideboard there was a letter addressed to Mum and Dad which they recognized as Mark's handwriting.

'Hello, what's this?' Billy asked, slitting open the envelope. He read the contents and his heart skipped a beat. Dumbfounded, he handed the note across to Laura. She read it quietly and exclaimed, 'Oh, Lord, it's happened. I've been half expecting something like this but even so, it's a bombshell.'

Billy took the note back and stared at it in disbelief. He read it again to make sure he hadn't misunderstood. He hadn't.

Dear Mum and Dad,
I hope this doesn't come as too much of a jolt for you but I have decided to resign from the solicitor's office. I couldn't stand working there another day. I'm going down to Kent to help pick hops for the season. Don't worry about me.

Things will work out, you'll see. Will probably be back
around Christmas or the New Year.
Your loving son,
Mark

Billy was dazed as he took the news in. 'What the devil's
going on? Has the world gone mad? Gone to pick hops in Kent!
What about his career in law? Is there no end to it? First Matthew
and Lucy. Now Mark. I've helped raise a bunch of rebels. You
said you half expected it, Laura. What did you mean by that?'

'For some time now, Mark has been making noises about
not liking his job. Said it was boring and he never got to do
anything interesting. Spent most of his time photocopying
and writing up boring old documents about probate, conveyancing, and divorces.'

'But if you knew all this, why didn't you tell me instead of
letting it come as a bolt from the blue? Don't I count in this
family?'

'We saw how upset you were when Matthew and Lucy left
their courses and I didn't want a repeat of that scene. So I
kept it quiet but I didn't think for a minute that Mark would
suddenly walk out of his job like this.'

'I think our kids are too undisciplined to accept a regular
orderly routine. The idea of a steady job, putting in a forty-
hour week, is like purgatory for them.'

'You can only blame yourself for that, Billy. Taking them
out to Kenya and showing them the wide open spaces. The
free and easy lifestyle they saw there has put them off forever
from taking a tedious routine job.'

'I suppose there's nothing we can do, Laura, but grin and
bear it. As Mam always used to say, "When you've buttered
your bread, you just have to lie in it." '

'The one thing I'll say for our children, Billy. They're all
individuals.'

'True. Strangeways is full of 'em. Our hopes are now
pinned on John, our youngest. He's been accepted at

Sheffield and so he's well on his way to becoming a doctor and I don't think he'll let us down. He's too dedicated. Don't you think so?'

Laura didn't answer.

'What we must do is give John encouragement and support and strengthen his resolution.'

Billy invited Duncan, Louise and Hughie who had done his medical training at Sheffield over for tea and while Laura was engrossed in swapping news with her mother, he seized the opportunity to invite John to join his grandad and uncle for a drink at the Nag's Head. Hughie's experience in medicine would give invaluable support and if anyone could bolster any dithering on John's part, that man was Duncan. For was it not he who had inspired Billy to take a degree all those years ago, who had given him a thorough grounding in accounting and encouraged him at every stage of the hard grind? Over a glass of ale, Duncan began the process.

'So, young John, what makes you want to be a doctor?'

'Dad and I have talked about it a lot, Grandad, and I think I'd like to help people in need.'

'Then why not be a social worker or a priest or a policeman?' Hughie asked.

'When I was ill in Booth Hall as a youngster, I remember how Dr Hugh Jolly saved my life and I've had admiration for medics ever since. I'd like to save lives as he did.'

'Good answer, John!' Duncan exclaimed. 'Almost as if you'd rehearsed it.'

'I had, Grandad. It's the answer I gave at my interview for Sheffield.'

'Then you've displayed two important skills a doctor must have to succeed,' Hughie laughed. 'The ability to give a smooth answer and to sound sincere as you're giving it.'

'How do you feel about dealing with the sick and the diseased every day?' Duncan asked.

'I'm not sure, Grandad. At the moment, the sight of blood and guts makes me feel queasy but Dad tells me I'll get over that.'

'Most people do,' Hughie informed him. 'You become case-hardened and grow a skin like an elephant. To be a good doctor, you have to develop professional aloofness.'

'I'm sure you'll be a great doctor one day, John,' Billy said. 'One that we can be truly proud of. In many ways being the last son, you remind me of the story of Joseph and the Technicolor Dreamcoat in the Bible.'

'How do you make that out, Dad?'

'While you're telling Bible stories,' Duncan grinned, 'I'll get another drink in.'

'Jacob in the Bible had twelve sons but his favourite was Joseph because he'd been born to him in his old age and so he had a richly ornamented robe made for him. When the other brothers saw this, they hated him but Joseph turned out to be the most successful of them all. It turned out right in the end because they all became reconciled. Maybe that's your destiny, to succeed where the others failed. I'm relying on you, John, as the last of my sons. Be a doctor and set an example to them all. Make us proud of you.'

'That's a heavy load to lay on me, Dad. I'm not sure I'm the one to carry it.'

'Of course you are, son. You'll see.'

Chapter Fifty-Four

It was a month after Mark's unexpected departure and the visit to Billy's mam that they got the phone call. Billy picked up the receiver in the hall and was shocked when he heard the agitated voice of his mam at the other end. She sounded distraught, there was a note of desperation in her voice.

'Is that Billy? It is. Oh, Billy, Billy! You were right. Can you come and get me? I've done something stupid. I reached across the cooker and I've burned the back of my arm on the hotplate. I forgot it was still on. Billy, I don't know what to do. And another thing, the electric lights here keep going bright and then dull again. Up and down. I can't stand it any more. I don't want to be left alone any more. I don't want any more accidents.'

Billy was shaken to the core by the news but an inner calm took over his mind. Time for action.

'Right, Mam. Stay where you are and leave everything to me. I'm coming to get you. It'll take me about an hour to get over there. First, try to keep calm. I'm going to phone your friend Mrs Reynolds right away and ask her to go round and help till I get there. Tell her to bathe your arm gently in cold water and put some clean lint and a light bandage on the burn. Don't put ointment or anything like that on it. I'll be as quick as I can.'

He told Laura what had happened. She responded instantly.

'Her room has been ready for some time, so I'll make up a bed immediately. I'm glad she's coming, Billy. She'll be happier here where we can look after her and keep an eye on her.'

Billy phoned Mrs Reynolds who said she'd go round immediately and treat the burn as he'd advised her. Next he phoned the family and told them what had happened and that Mam would be moving into his house that day. 'Operation Flit' was on.

Worrying all the way, he drove over to Langley and found Mam had calmed down, having taken a couple of aspirin to ease the pain. His heart went out to her when he saw her. There she sat with her arm all bandaged up, a sad old lady having to give up her independence after all these years. It wasn't merely the bungalow she was leaving. In a sense, it was the home she'd first created in 1910 when she'd married Tommy. All the bits and pieces that made a home and which she'd loved and cherished over a lifetime were now to be broken up and dispersed.

Mrs Reynolds and he packed a few temporary things into a case and they were ready to leave. It was a sorrowful parting from her neighbour as they had become good friends in the past couple of years, providing comfort and support for each other.

'It's not forever,' Billy told the two old ladies in reassurance. 'There's no reason why you can't visit each other. I'll bring Mam up to see you and maybe your son can bring you over to Didsbury when she's settled in.'

That weekend, Les and he hired a large truck from Salford Van Hire and moved Mam's furniture and the rest of her things to Billy's house. Most of it was stored in the spacious basement but Billy and Laura used some of it to create a granny flat as similar to her own bungalow as they could humanly make it. She had her own bed, her own fireside chair and settee, her own wardrobe, her own ornaments, and things to make tea for visitors.

'What will you do with the rest of my furniture, Billy? Don't you want that big chest of drawers?'

'No, Mam, we haven't got room for it but I've stored it in the cellar.'

'It's such a fine piece of furniture. Then there's the dining room suite with the mahogany table. I've polished that every

443

day of my life since I got married. Get the rest of the family to come over and choose something. Don't let it all go to the furniture dealers. That was my home and I don't want it sold in a second-hand shop.'

'OK, Mam. I'll ask the family to choose something.'

On her first night in her granny flat, Mam reported a strange dream. She said that the ghost of Tommy had come to visit her.

'I could see him as clearly as I can see you,' she said.

And that's not clear, Billy thought, as you've got only twenty-five per cent vision.

'He was over there by the window,' she continued. 'He was a bright white light and I could see right through him. He was wearing gloves and his raincoat and he still had his cap on his head. "Kate," he said. "I've been looking all over for you. I searched up in Langley but you weren't there. Nobody told me you'd moved. Anyroad, I've found you now." He's happy now he knows where I am.'

It didn't take her long to become settled and Billy felt happier about her than he had in years for now he could see she was safe, secure and as snug as a bug. Laura provided her with first-class room service every day: morning tea, breakfast, morning coffee, lunch, afternoon tea, evening meal, and a late supper of Horlicks and a biscuit. Billy arranged for 'talking books' from the RNIB, the novels of Bruce Marshall, Maurice Walsh and Catherine Cookson being her favourites. Every morning before setting off for college, Billy made sure she had everything she needed. When the weather was fine, she was able to sit in the garden enjoying the sunshine and the singing of the numerous blackbirds nesting in the trees all round the district. She looked more content than he had seen her in years and the little lines of worry on her face seemed less evident though at first she was nervous about not putting her foot in it. It was as if she was starting in Swinton Industrial School all over again. One morning she left the tap in the bathroom running and the water overflowed onto the floor.

'I do hope I've not failed my test,' she said to Les who was visiting her.

Passing by Mam's room one morning, Laura heard her talking to herself. From the snippets of conversation she picked up, it soon became obvious that Mam was acting out some scene from her life.

'Oh, no,' she was saying. 'Don't you tell me that our Polly looks consumptive. It's your own kids you should be worried about. Your lot have seen more dinnertimes than dinners.'

Laura called Billy to come and listen at the door.

'Why,' Billy whispered to Laura, 'she's acting out her own life story. We've got to get this down on tape for the sake of posterity.'

Next day, Billy took in a portable tape recorder and placed the microphone on the coffee table.

'We heard you talking yesterday, Mam,' he said gently. 'It sounded really interesting. I'm sure the rest of the family would love to hear your life story. Why not tell it to me and I'll tape-record it for them and send them copies.'

'Do you think anyone would be interested in the ramblings of an old lady?'

'I'm sure they would, Mam. Your story sounds like something out of Charles Dickens. I'll interview you like they do on the wireless and you talk naturally and I'll get it all down. First of all, what was it like when you were a little girl?'

Kate started talking and she must have kissed the Blarney stone because the words came out so smoothly and effortlessly as she replayed the events in her life.

'I had a happy childhood,' she began, 'till my father got sick. He worked in a glassworks and his job was making fancy bells, lamp glasses. I used to take his supper when he was on nights. I used to say, "Daddy, make me a flip-flop." It was like a bottle when he blew it out, and when he turned it from side to side, it went flip-flop, flip-flop . . .'

For several days, she talked into the microphone until she'd filled four tapes telling her life story through the death of her father, her ordeal in the workhouse, her training at the Swinton Industrial School, through domestic service, her marriage, the heartbreak of the Great War, and the Spanish flu epidemic of 1918. Billy duplicated the tape and sent copies round the family who listened to it over and over again. The tape became a treasured family heirloom.

'You know, Mam,' Billy told her one day, 'your story is so well told, it's a shame more people don't get to hear it. You should be on the wireless.'

'That'll be the day,' she said.

At the end of October that same year, Billy had a phone call from Mark in Kent.

'The hop-picking season is over now, Dad,' he said. 'I'd like to come back home if that's OK with you.'

'Of course it is, Mark. You're our son and this is your home.'

'One other thing, Dad. I'll be bringing a friend with me. Someone I met when hop picking. Will you be able to put us both up?'

'No problem, son. There's only Grandma with us at the moment and so we've plenty of room.'

A week later, there he was at the front door, suitcase in his hand. With his friend. He hadn't mentioned the fact that the friend was a girl. And a pretty one at that with dark hair cut short, giving her a boyish look. Petite in stature, her nose retroussé and her blue eyes round and solemn.

'This is my friend Tiffany,' Mark said with a grin. 'Sorry, I forgot to tell you she was a girl.'

'I'm so pleased to meet you, Mr and Mrs Hopkins,' she said. 'Mark has told me so much about you and the family.'

Her open face and husky voice added to her attractions.

'Come in, both of you,' Laura said warmly. 'I'll put the kettle on.'

Billy took them into the lounge.

'So how did you two meet?' he asked in an attempt to break the ice.

'We were working side by side pulling the bines, Mr Hopkins,' Tiffany said. 'We got talking and we became very good friends.'

She laid stress on the 'very good' and threw Mark a meaningful glance. Billy was quite taken by this perky young lady with the faint Cockney accent and found himself trying to ingratiate himself with her, almost flirting with her.

'Obviously my son has shown good taste,' he replied.

Laura came in with the tea tray containing the best crockery and a selection of biscuits. She, too, was showing off because Mark by himself would never in a million years have merited the best china. The conversation flowed easily and Tiffany displayed a quick wit and a ready sense of humour.

'What I find difficult to understand,' Billy grinned, helping himself to a chocolate biscuit, 'is how you could possibly have been attracted to Mark there. You should see what he's like in the morning.'

'But I already have,' she smiled mischievously, 'and I still liked what I saw.' There was that impish look again. Mark grinned sheepishly; he was putty in her hands.

The subject inevitably turned to Mark's resignation from the solicitor's office.

'What made you do it, Mark?' Billy asked. 'Being bored is one thing but walking out is something else. And what about all the court cases? Surely they were interesting.'

'At the office, Dad,' Mark said, 'our clients were mainly Manchester's lowlife and we dealt mostly with petty criminals, pick-pockets, shoplifters, society's dregs. Apart from that, I didn't want to spend my life in a humdrum, musty old office, photocopying documents for conveyancing, probate, divorces, and the like.'

'I've got to know Mark well,' Tiffany added, 'and he definitely likes to be outdoors and mixing with ordinary people. He's so persuasive, he could talk the hind legs off a donkey. Daddy was impressed by him.'

'What does your father do, Tiffany?' Laura asked.

'He's an estate agent in Sittingbourne, Mrs Hopkins.'

'Glad to hear you think Mark is persuasive, Tiffany,' Billy said. 'I always thought his talents would have been put to good use as a solicitor or a barrister fighting big cases in the criminal courts. He'd need all his powers of persuasion there.'

'You've read too many novels, Dad. That stuff about being a famous barrister at the Old Bailey was pipe-dreaming. We can't all be Lord Carson or Lionel Barrymore. At my office, we dealt only with the drunk and disorderly or GBH cases, stuff like that.'

'Very well, Mark, but what are you going to do now you're back in Manchester?'

'I thought I'd first give Tiffany a tour of Manchester's highlights and then see what our city has to offer.'

'Mark would make a great salesman,' Tiffany enthused. 'Fridges to the Eskimos, sunray lamps to the Africans. You name it, he'd sell it.'

'On a more mundane note,' Laura said, 'I've made up your rooms. You, Mark, are in your old room and I've put Tiffany in Lucy's old room, if that's all right.'

Mark and Tiffany exchanged embarrassed looks.

'Tiffany and I are partners, Mum. We share the same room.'

'You mean you sleep together in the same room?' Billy gasped.

'We tried sleeping together in different rooms, Dad,' Mark laughed. 'It didn't work. We found it impossible.'

'It's no joke, Mark,' Billy said. 'You can't sleep together if you're not married. Not under my roof. That's living—'

'In sin, Dad?' Mark grinned, finishing it off for him. 'In this day and age, it's not regarded as such. We're what's known as an item and it's the accepted thing.'

'No, Mark, it isn't,' Tiffany said. 'We shouldn't embarrass

your parents in this way. I'm perfectly happy to have Lucy's room, Mrs Hopkins, and thank you so much.'

Laura thought it wise to defuse the situation by changing the subject.

'Grandma up there will be wondering what's happened to her afternoon tea. I'd better take it up to her before she thinks we've forgotten her.'

'Let us take it up for you,' Mark volunteered. 'It'll give me a chance to introduce Tiffany.'

'That's very good of you, Mark. I'll make up her tray. She always likes a chocolate biscuit with her tea.'

As soon as Mark and Tiffany had left the room, Billy said, 'I really like this girl. She could be the makings of Mark. I hope he appreciates what a find she is. He'd be a fool if he let her get away.'

'I like her too, Billy, but in our day, when two people shared a bed they usually got married. I wonder how serious they are. When they say they're an item, does that mean a temporary relationship or does it mean they're contemplating marriage?'

'No use asking me, Laura. I don't understand it when they say they're partners. If they did decide to marry, they'd need money and I have the impression that they're not too well off.' Then Billy had an idea. 'I think I know a way of resolving the situation,' he said.

'Another one of your cunning plans?' Laura laughed.

'This one will work and should make everyone happy.'

Fifteen minutes later, the young couple were back.

'By heavens,' Mark exclaimed. 'Grandma can't half talk.'

'She tells a good story,' Tiffany added. 'I could have listened to her all day. Now I know where Mark gets the gift of the gab.'

'While you were upstairs,' Billy said, 'we've been discussing your situation. If you're living together and you love each other, why not get married and settle down? We'd recommend the marriage state. Your mother and I have been married nearly twenty-six years and we've been very happy.'

'Eventually, I'm sure that's what we'll do,' Tiffany said,

glancing at Mark, 'but at present we can't entertain the idea as we don't have the financial resources.'

'Look, Mum and Dad,' Mark said, 'if our living together embarrasses you, then starting tomorrow we'll look for a little flat in Fallowfield until we make up our minds what we're going to do.'

'When you were taking the tea to Grandma,' Billy said, 'I had a brainwave. It's this: first, I'll help you find a flat and give some financial support towards a deposit. Second, if you decide to marry, I'll provide some capital to set you up in a little business.'

'So that's your idea! Another one of your little businesses!' Laura chuckled. 'You've not had much luck with them in the past.'

'With a brilliant salesman like Mark for a son and with a wife like Tiffany, how could they possibly go wrong?'

'We'll have to think about that one,' Mark said. 'If we do get married, we'll take you up on that offer.'

'It'll be one of those offers we can't refuse,' Tiffany laughed.

What a beautiful melodious laugh she has, Billy thought.

At eleven o'clock, they retired to their various rooms.

'Don't forget Grandma's in the room next door,' Laura said.

'She's a light sleeper,' Billy added slyly, 'so any noise or moving about in the middle of the night might waken her. Just as well to be aware.'

Mark and Tiffany had been in their Fallowfield flat only a fortnight when they came to see Billy and Laura.

'We'd like to take you up on your proposition, Dad,' Mark said. 'Tiffany and I have decided to get married.'

'Oh, I'm so relieved,' Laura said, 'but it's a trifle sudden, isn't it? I mean, when and how? There won't be time to make all the preparations. A church wedding, I hope. I do love a church wedding.'

'Not a church but as good,' Mark said. 'We had my friend

Spud Murphy and his girlfriend Maureen round to tea on Sunday. They're planning to tie the knot and we thought we might join them.'

'How do you mean?' Billy asked suspiciously. 'Arranging a wedding takes a lot of organization. There's a great deal of planning involved and it takes time. What sort of marriage do you have in mind?'

'Spud's a member of a movement called the Charismatic Fellowship which believes that we can be baptized and married in spirit. No need for churches or registrars. There's a weekly meeting in Birmingham when people can be both baptized and married at the same ceremony.'

'I don't understand,' Laura said, wrinkling her brow. 'Charismatic Fellowship? I've never heard of it.'

'It's experimental worship and it's been going for five years. Spud said there'll be about a hundred couples wed in a sports centre by the leader, the Reverend James Beddoes, all at the same time. Those who are wed in this way are called Bedfellows. There'll be rock music, laser lighting and dancing as part of the service. Couples profess their vows in public and that's it. They're married in spirit.'

'Married in spirit? What on earth's that supposed to mean?' Billy cried. He was about to explode but held himself in check. What the heck, he thought, it's no use arguing any more. As Mam likes to say, it's a mad, mad, mad world.

'Spud told us,' Tiffany said innocently, 'that sometimes those baptized and married in the ceremony are granted the gifts of the spirit, like the ability to heal and speak in foreign languages unknown to the speaker.'

'The mind boggles,' Billy said, shaking his head in disbelief. 'But this is the New Age everyone's going on about. However, if you've taken vows, I'll have to go along with it, I suppose. I'm not sure it counts as true marriage but it's better than nothing. It's pretty weird if you ask me and I doubt if it's legal.'

'Let's give them the benefit of the doubt,' Laura said quickly, anxious to keep the peace.

'Very well,' Billy muttered. 'I'll have to accept it and honour my promise to set you up in a small business on the strength of it but I'll never get used to this crazy new world.'

A week later, Mark and Tiffany took marital vows and became Bedfellows; Billy staked them to a small capital sum to start them off. Together the couple had the idea of a stall in Manchester's Corn Exchange to sell Christmas fancy goods.

'There's a big sale to be held at Eric Wagman's warehouse in Oldham,' Mark enthused. 'There'll be a wide range of brand new items going cheap. We'll be in time to catch the Christmas market and the fancy goods that are up for auction will be much in demand and should sell easily. We'll make a fortune.'

'Like father, like son,' Laura remarked when she heard this. 'I seem to have heard that song somewhere in a different life and sung by another person.'

Billy drove Mark and Tiffany up to Oldham to the huge warehouse where the auction was to take place. At the office, they filled in personal details, collected a card with a bidder's number, and went into the main hall. There was a large crowd and some were obviously dealers, judging by the confident and idiosyncratic way they responded to the auctioneer's spiel. The atmosphere was tense as the seller held the various objects up to the crowd for inspection and asked for offers.

'What am I bid for these fifty magnificent clock radios which were salvaged from a Chinese ship before it sank?'

Billy went into a hypnotic dream. At an auction he was like an alcoholic in a pub during happy hour. He was in his element and started bidding as if there was no tomorrow. For everything the auctioneer presented, Billy was in there with his numbered card. Clock radios at £4.50 for ten? That's only 45p each! Who could resist such a snip? Certainly not Billy! An endless stream of Yuletide gifts went under the hammer. Billy was there every time with his card held aloft. What bargains! What giveaway prices!

'I think we've got enough now, Dad,' Mark whispered.

'You can never have enough, son,' Billy retorted, as he put in a bid for five hundred 'Merry Christmas' decorations.

'What am I bid for seventy-two wind-up somersaulting dogs?' the salesman cried.

Billy found himself competing with a dealer and had to pay £1.80 each for them.

'They'll sell for at least a fiver,' he said in an aside to Tiffany. 'You two are going to make a bomb this Christmas. Should set you up for life.'

'Maybe the dog will sell,' Tiffany said hesitantly, 'but I'm not sure that we can move three thousand Christmas cards even though they were only eightpence each. Maybe we should call a halt, Mr Hopkins, and see how it goes before we buy any more goods.'

'Nothing ventured, nothing gained,' Billy said. 'We're here at the auction and we should strike while the iron's hot.'

Three hours later, the sale was over. Like a punch drunk emerging from the ring, Billy, accompanied by the two newlyweds, went to the office to settle the bill. It took a little while for the clerk to tot up the amount but when it was placed before Billy, it was a knock-out blow. He looked again. Then polished his reading glasses and looked for a third time. He checked the calculation. It was right: £2,211.80 including VAT. He didn't remember bidding for so many toys: trucks, trains, dolls, huggy bears, and wind-up dogs. And what on earth was he going to do with 700 balls of wool and 200 spice racks? There were only 7 packets of twisted red candles, thank the Lord, but then he discovered that each pack contained 200 candles.

He had the wherewithal to pay all right but he hadn't intended spending such an astronomical sum.

'Why didn't you stop me?' he said to Mark accusingly.

'Dad, it would have been easier to stop an express train.'

He paid the bill and drove the Morris Oxford to the collection point where several warehousemen had piled up his purchases.

'You've not got a cat in hell's chance of fitting them bloody goods into that little station wagon,' the foreman said laconically. 'You'll need more like a Luton box van.'

There was nothing for it but to hire a couple of Transits. It was fortunate that Tiffany was an experienced driver and that Mark had acquired his driving licence while in Kent. The Christmas gifts were unloaded into the basement to join his mam's furniture. The cellar was now so congested, it was difficult to close the outside door.

'How am I supposed to get to the washing machine down there?' Laura asked.

'It's only temporary,' Billy said. 'At Christmas, these things will sell like hot cakes and that'll clear the room.'

'Well, roll on Christmas then,' she said with a familiar resigned look.

On the first Saturday morning after the auction, Billy took Mark and Tiffany to Manchester's city centre and negotiated a lock-up stall with a couple of trestle tables at the Corn Exchange. The Exchange, known as the grand old lady of Hanging Ditch, was a beautiful Grade II listed Edwardian building where a hotchpotch of traders plied their wares and where it was possible to buy anything from tarot card readings to rare stamps, records, military medals, antique jewellery, and the services of a private detective. Pervading the atmosphere was the pungent smell of veggie sausages sizzling in the Greasy Spoon café beneath. It was not expensive to hire a stall in the Exchange for it was a little off the beaten track and, apart from the habitués patronizing their specialist traders, the only visitors were shoppers taking a short cut from Victoria Station to busy Market Street nearby.

Mark and Tiffany unpacked the goods on the first day and tried to set up an attractive display to catch the passing trade.

It was Tiffany who made the first discovery when she untied the first packet of the three thousand Christmas cards they had acquired. Nothing wrong with the top fifty, they

454

were fine. Normal cards with pictures of Santa Claus and snow and robins. It was the rest of the cards that were the problem. There were the usual Christmas greetings but they were addressed to specific members of the extended family, especially in-laws. 'Merry Christmas Sister-in-law'; 'Happy Yuletide Father-in-law'; 'Season's Greetings Daughter-in-law'. There were 2,950 in similar vein. Finding customers for such specialized cards would not be easy. As for the two hundred spice racks, not a single one had a lid.

'No problem,' said the ever-optimistic Billy when it was pointed out to him. 'Tell the customers they can buy corks at any Home Brew shop.'

'Maybe we should check that out, Mr Hopkins, before we tell them that,' Tiffany said slowly, her voice filled with doubt.

'At least the rest of the goods are OK,' Billy answered. 'There should be no problem moving them.'

Pete, the record seller in the stall next door, came over to offer a few tips.

'Before you sell any of your items,' he said, 'you'd be well advised to let the Trading Standards officer give them the once-over in case any of them are dangerous. Otherwise you could find yourselves being prosecuted.'

There was such an officer on site and he came over to examine their wares.

It didn't take him long to pronounce judgement. 'The wiring on the clock radios has rotted and is potentially lethal; the red candles are held together by means of a razor-sharp spike which any child could convert into a deadly sword; the fifty container trucks are constructed in metal with sharp corners and are dangerous, kids are likely to cut themselves to pieces on them. Apart from that, the other goods are safe.'

'Let me say it first,' Billy muttered, when Laura heard the results of the officer's assessments. 'That's another fine mess you got us into, Stanley.'

For the fortnight before Christmas, Mark and Tiffany

455

diligently tended the stall trying to unload the merchandise on to the occasional shopper hurrying through.

'How's it going?' Billy asked one day.

'Not too good, Dad,' Mark replied. 'Hardly anybody comes into the building, let alone to our stall. Only one person has come into the Exchange so far this morning and he thought it was the *Royal* Exchange. All the same, we sold him a Merry Christmas sign for seventy-five pence.'

'Better than nothing, Mark.'

At that moment a middle-aged lady with wild staring eyes stopped to examine the merchandise.

'Quick, Mark,' Billy hissed, 'a potential sale!'

'I can tell you this, for certain,' the strange lady remarked. 'You'll never sell this lot. Not in a month of Sundays!'

'Miserable old witch,' Billy said when she'd gone.

'Do you know who that was?' Pete, their neighbour, laughed. 'That was Chloe Clayton, the clairvoyant with the stall in the corner, the one with the long queues.'

Daily sales varied from two pounds to five pounds on a good day.

'Five pounds! Things are looking up,' Billy said when he got the news.

'Six Merry Christmas signs, four in-law-greeting cards and one huggy bear,' Tiffany said. 'At this rate, it will take us approximately twenty-five years to move this little lot.'

'You need to be a little more aggressive in your selling technique,' Billy told them one morning 'Here, let me show you how it's done.'

A mother with two little children was crossing the trading floor.

'Could I demonstrate this jumping dog to you and the kiddies, madam?' he said to her. 'Only five pounds for this amazing, stupendous jumping dog.'

He wound up the toy dog and its mechanism began to whirr. There was a slight pause and suddenly the dog leapt up and executed a series of jerky somersaults. It came as such a shock that the two kids set up a terrified howl that resounded round the building.

'People like you should be locked up, frightening little children like that,' the mum yelled as she hurried out with her two bawling infants.

'Must be something wrong with those kids,' Billy observed thoughtfully.

'Maybe so but we need to do something drastic, Mr Hopkins,' Tiffany said, 'if we're going to shift the rest of these goods. Come on, Mark, you're the one with the bright ideas. What do you suggest?'

Mark was not a man to sit still bemoaning his lot and the following week he sold all the greetings cards for a song to an unsuspecting newsagent in Fallowfield. The rest of the stuff he put into Isaacson's auctions in Salford.

The assistant at the salesroom recognized the items right away.

'You got these from the Wagman's sale, didn't you? And aren't those the spice racks with the missing lids?'

The goods sold in one day at Isaacson's sales but at knock-down prices. No doubt the purchasers would in turn put them back into the auction when they proved unsaleable. They could be doing the rounds for years, Billy reflected. After the auctioneers had deducted their commission, Billy totted up his bills for the whole venture and found he had made a loss of £1,300.

'We can put it down to experience,' he told Mark and Tiffany. 'At least you now have a good idea of how tough it is to earn a crust in this rotten old world.'

In the New Year, Tiffany's dad offered both Mark and Tiffany jobs in his estate agent's business, which they decided to accept. They returned to Sittingbourne in the New Year, found themselves a little flat there and settled down to life in Kent.

Chapter Fifty-Five

It was late September 1977 and the start of a new academic year at the William Pitt Tech. The huge staff was assembled in the small theatre of the college for the annual briefing by the Principal. At ten o'clock precisely, Mr Forrester accompanied by his senior team members comprising the Vice-Principal, Mr Purdy, and the eight heads of departments plus three administrators strode onto the stage. The whole staff rose to its feet. Mr Forrester in his familiar bow tie sat at the head of the long table whilst the others arranged themselves along the sides facing the audience. The scene, Billy thought, was not unlike Leonardo's painting of the Last Supper.

Every year there was the usual pep talk about the need to work harder, attract more students, and achieve better examination results. Billy had heard it all before, for three years running in fact, such that he could practically recite it with the Principal word for word. But this year it was different. What Mr Forrester had to say put Billy's head into a spin.

'Those of you who have been watching the national and international news,' he began, 'will be aware of the gloomy economic outlook. The Chancellor of the Exchequer recently unveiled his emergency crisis budget designed to cope with what he described as the gravest situation since the end of the war. Recent massive oil price increases have resulted in a multi-million trade gap. The International Monetary Fund has promised a loan to Britain provided that it excises rampant excess. The effect of all this has been the urgent need for drastic cuts in government expenditure in every field. In universities and technical colleges such as ours, there are going to be cuts, cuts and yet more cuts in everything.'

'What about Comic Cuts?' some wit from the building department yelled, to the applause and laughter of the assembly.

'We shall have to cut student intake and student accommodation,' the Principal continued, 'the number of courses, cleaners and porters, library books, and plans for building extension will have to be axed. Finally we shall have to cut teaching staff.'

'What about the hordes of administrators?' the trade union man called. 'They're top heavy and need to be trimmed down.'

'Agreed,' Mr Forrester conceded. 'They, too, will be reduced.'

'And about bloody time,' someone called.

'I have been ordered by the Borough Council,' Mr Forrester went on, 'to cut half a million pounds from the college budget. Apart from the things I've mentioned, that translates into reducing teaching staff by about forty lecturers. The council wishes to avoid compulsory redundancies if possible. I shall therefore be asking for voluntary retirements. The terms can be generous, involving a cash lump sum and enhanced pension.'

When Billy heard these last words, his mind raced. Voluntary retirement! Why not? If there was one job the college could well do without, it was that of Staff Development Officer!

That night when he got home, Billy was beside himself with excitement.

'Laura,' he exclaimed, 'it's what I've been waiting for these last three years. I have been cooped up in a broom cupboard in a job that nobody seems to want. I started teaching in nineteen forty-seven and that gives me thirty years' teaching under my belt: twenty-four years in Britain and six abroad. An enhancement of ten years added to that will give me almost a full pension. It's an offer being presented to me on a silver platter. What do you say?'

'It looks as if you've already made up your mind, Billy. But you're only forty-nine. Isn't that rather young to be thinking about early retirement? And what would you do with all that free time? I heard somewhere that retirement means twice as much husband on half as much money.'

'First of all, Laura, by the time the formalities are completed, I'll be nearer fifty than forty-nine and I wouldn't sit around twiddling my thumbs. I could spend more time looking after my mother, talking to her and listening to her stories. I could finish the autobiography I'm writing for the family. I could take up some practical pursuit that supplements our income, something that's a complete contrast to academic work.'

'Not more wood-turning, please, Billy.'

'Nothing like that. I've always fancied making elaborate doll's houses. Remember the one we saw at Ribchester, the one made for Queen Victoria. Making something like that would take real skill and would be a great challenge.'

'You'd need capital to set that up, Billy.'

'We still have some of the profit we made on the sale of the house in Scotland and I'll receive a lump sum on retirement. I reckon I could sell the doll's houses at Christmas and make a small profit. Add that to my pension and we'll get by easily. If I have to stay any longer in that stifling cleaning cupboard, I shall die or go mad.'

'You've obviously worked it all out, Billy. If that's what you want, go for it!'

Billy did. He put in his application, obtained and completed the forms, furnished all necessary detail, and signed his name in a hundred and one places. Three months later, he was granted early retirement with a pension. On the last day in college, he made a tour of the place, said goodbye to friends and colleagues, and collected his belongings. As he closed the door of his malodorous cubbyhole, he knew how an inmate being released from Strangeways must feel when he finally heard the great prison gate swing to behind him. He heaved a deep sigh of relief. Freedom and fresh air at last!

Mam had settled down well in her granny flat. The days went by quickly and winter turned to verdant spring. On most days, she had a stream of visitors from the immediate and extended family, including her numerous grandchildren, such that Billy was considering fitting a turnstile. Her old neighbour, Mrs Reynolds, managed to visit on a couple of occasions and once or twice Billy drove Mam up to Langley so she could reciprocate the trips down Memory Lane which they enjoyed so much together. And on one never-to-be-forgotten day, her younger sister Cissie accompanied by brother Eddie made the journey over from Salford to see her. Soon from her room there came gales of happy laughter and joyous weeping as they recalled their times together in Ancoats, in the workhouse, and in Swinton Industrial School.

Things didn't always go so smoothly though. Mam had been there for just over a year and had slipped into a comfortable routine. The crisis when she'd burned her arm and cried out for help had been forgotten and consigned to history. She started to look back on her old life in Langley through rose-coloured spectacles and to have misgivings about having moved.

'You know, our Billy,' she said one morning, 'you'd no right to get rid of my furniture the way you did. I'm sure I could've managed up there in Middleton by myself if you hadn't been in such a hurry to move me. Just because I burned my arm didn't mean that I wanted to flit. I do miss my own place, my independence, and my old friend, Mrs Reynolds. I want to go back to Langley.'

'That was over a year ago, Mam. Mrs Reynolds has moved now and gone to live with her own family. Have you forgotten how you kept having one accident after another?'

'Doesn't matter. You shouldn't have given my bits and pieces away.'

Les laughed when Billy told him about this. 'Now she's got used to living here, she regards you and Laura as warders in an institution. She's forgotten how bad things were when she was on her own.'

A few days later, Billy happened to overhear her talking to his sister Polly who was visiting.

'I don't know what 'er downstairs is giving me on my bread but it's not best butter, I can tell you that.'

Billy was most upset when he heard this as Laura was providing five-star service every day and to hear his wife being referred to in this offhand manner touched a nerve. When Polly had gone, he went in to collect the tray containing the tea things.

'You know, Mam,' he said gently, 'Laura does a lot for you, cooking all your meals and bringing them up to you, looking after you the way she does. You shouldn't refer to her as "'er downstairs" who doesn't give you best butter. You should be grateful for all she does for you.'

It was a mistake and Billy lived to regret it for the rest of his days. The old lady became deeply troubled that Billy had reproved her, no matter how gently. For several days after the incident, she could be heard bewailing the fact that he'd dared to imply that she'd said something amiss.

'He was such a lovely baby,' she mumbled to herself over and over again. 'Seven and a half pounds when he was born. Always smiling and laughing. A bonnie baby; everyone said so. Then he went to that there Damian College and it ruined him. Made him into a snob. He became stuck-up. Just because I said I liked best butter. I wish I were dead. They should bury me and put me on top of Tommy and have done with it.'

Billy tried to apologize a thousand times but it was no use. He'd dared to reproach her and there was no going back. In time, the incident faded into the background and Billy and his mother became reconciled. But in Billy's mind, his thoughtlessness and stupidity continued to trouble him.

Chapter Fifty-Six

A year after Billy's blunder, Mam developed flu-like symptoms. She had a harsh, dry cough and reported a pain in her chest. Laura phoned the surgery and Dr Travers came round that morning to examine her. He gave her a thorough examination, took her blood pressure and temperature, and listened to her chest with his stethoscope and then began tapping her gently on the back.

'A-ha,' he said at last. 'Listen to this,' he said to Billy and Laura.

On one side there was a clear hollow sound and on the other, what sounded like a dull thud.

'You've got lobar pneumonia,' he told Mam. 'You'll have to go into hospital for treatment, I'm afraid. I'll phone the hospital right away and ask them to reserve a bed this afternoon.'

'Well, you'll be in the right hands, Mam,' Billy said, trying to sound cheerful. 'You'll get the right treatment there. We'll pack a few things for you.'

Early in the afternoon, the ambulance called to collect her.

'Right-o, Mother,' one of the paramedics said chirpily. 'We've come to take you to Withington. We'll soon have you tucked up in bed, my little darlin'.'

They bundled her up in several blankets, sat her in a wheelchair, tilted it back as if she were a cabin trunk, and started to carry her down the stairs. It was taking place so fast that no one had time to think or react to what was happening.

When they reached the hallway, Mam called out. 'Stop for a minute. What's the hurry?' Then turning to Laura who was standing in the hall watching the sad parting, she said, 'I

463

want you to know, love, that I'll never forget your great kindness in taking me into your home and looking after me the way you did. You've worked so hard feeding me and taking care of me when you've had your own family to think of. I think you're an angel sent from God and you'll always be in my prayers. Our Billy was the luckiest man in this world to get you for his wife. And thanks to him as well for all he did for me. God bless you both.'

Laura was visibly moved by this little speech and was too choked to say much but in reply she squeezed Mam's hand and said, 'Thank you, Mrs Hopkins. That means a lot to Billy and me. We'll be along to see you in hospital first thing tomorrow.'

'I've ordered another talking book for you, Mam,' Billy said, 'and it should be here soon.'

'Keep it for me, Billy, and I'll listen it to it when I get back, if God spares me.'

Billy accompanied her in the ambulance and carried her little suitcase up to the ward where she was shown the bed she had been allocated. The nurses closed the curtains round it while she changed into her nightdress and dressing gown. Sitting up, she looked round the ward which contained twelve beds, six on each side.

The elderly lady in the next bed nodded in a friendly manner. Then she smiled weakly and, putting her hand on her heart, said plaintively, 'Angina.'

'Pleased to meet you, Ann,' Mam said warmly. 'I'm Kate.'

Billy wasn't sure whether his mam was being funny or whether she had genuinely misunderstood. There's going to be fun and games on this ward, he thought. They'll give the nurses a run for their money.

'See you tomorrow, Mam,' he said, kissing her on the forehead. 'You'll soon be out of here and back in your own room. I'll have your new talking book waiting for you.'

Billy returned with Laura to the hospital the next morning and found the scene had changed. When he'd left Mam the day before, she'd been bright, alert and sharp as a new pin.

Had she not made that little speech thanking Laura and him in easy, fluent language? Today, only a few hours later, she looked remote as if she'd been drugged. He'd read somewhere that it was not unknown for nursing homes and hospitals, when short-staffed, to resort to the use of neuroleptic medicines to subdue patients and keep them quiet. He hoped that this wasn't the case in this ward but it was hard to explain the sudden change of behaviour.

'I think I closed that window, Billy, but I can't remember,' she murmured dreamily.

'You're not at home now, Mam; you're in hospital, don't you remember?'

'Yes, I was forgetting. I came in an ambulance, didn't I?'

'I've brought you a new bedjacket,' Laura said. 'Let me put it on for you.'

Mam seemed hardly aware of what was happening as Laura helped to fit her arms through the garment.

'I've got new dentures,' Mam mumbled. 'The young nurse collected them all in yesterday to wash them but she's given us all the wrong teeth. Anyroad, they're not getting these back; I like 'em better than my old ones.'

The rest of the family came to visit: Flo with Barry, Polly with Steve, Les with Annette, and it became a little congested round the bed.

'I'm sorry,' the ward sister said, 'but I'll have to ask some of you to leave. On this ward, we have to take special care not to crowd and overexcite the patients.'

Billy and Laura departed, promising to return the next morning. For a week, they visited every day and it became obvious that Mam was getting weaker and wanted simply to close her eyes and rest.

At 7 a.m. one morning the phone rang. Billy answered it.

'Hello. Billy Hopkins speaking.'

'This is Father Earley, chaplain at Withington Hospital,' a voice said softly. 'I have some sad news for you. Your mother Catherine passed away in her sleep about two hours ago.'

Though Billy had been expecting it, the news hit him like a thump in the chest.

'Thank you, Father, for telling me,' he managed to say. 'I think all of us in my family have been half prepared for it but it still comes as a shock. I'll phone round and tell everyone the news. May I come in to see her this morning?'

'I'm so sorry for your loss and of course the hospital will allow you to come in to see her. They'll move her body to a quiet room within the mortuary. Come to me first and we'll go together.'

Billy relayed the message round the family, including Sam in Belfast. That done, Laura and he went to the hospital to meet the chaplain. In the mortuary quiet room, Mam lay there on a stretcher, her eyes dead and staring but on her face there was an expression of utter peace and tranquillity. She seemed to have shrunk and looked smaller than in real life.

'I think she must have sensed that the end was near,' Father Earley told them, 'for last night she sent for me to hear her confession and I was able to administer the Last Sacrament. She's with God now,' he whispered. 'I know this is a sorrowful time for you but in many ways it's also a cause for celebration of a wonderful life that was so complete and fulfilled.'

Billy heard his voice but it sounded far off. Everything around him seemed unreal. He found it hard to accept that she was no longer there. She should be sitting back in her room listening to a Bruce Marshall novel on tape. She couldn't be dead, surely. She was the bedrock of the family and shouldn't be allowed to slip away quietly in her sleep. She had always been there, a constant figure in his life, a permanent, unchangeable part of his world. Now she was gone. It was as if part of himself had died with her, as if a light in his life had been extinguished.

After the sorrow and the sadness came self-recrimination. Could he have done more? he asked himself. Was it his fault that she had contracted pneumonia? Had she been warm enough in that room? And why, oh why had he rebuked her for calling Laura "er downstairs'. It was only her simple way of referring to people and she'd meant no harm by it.

It was as if Laura read his thoughts, for she embraced him and said, 'We did everything we could for her, Billy. We couldn't have done more. She had a fruitful and meaningful life and brought up a wonderful family. That's about the highest accolade you can give a person.'

'And ninety-two years of age is not a bad run,' he smiled through his tears.

She had died at 5 a.m. and that morning there had been the most glorious dawn with the sun filling the sky in a blaze of golden light, a fitting tribute to a beautiful life but for Kate Hopkins, née Lally, there would be no more sunrises or sunsets.

When Billy and Laura got home from the mortuary, there was a postal package waiting. It was from the RNIB and contained the 'talking book' of Catherine Cookson's *Our Kate*. It had arrived too late for her to hear it.

'Maybe somebody in heaven will read it to her,' Laura said.

'No, Laura,' Billy said. 'In heaven she'll have perfect vision and she'll be able to read it herself.'

It was left to Billy to make the funeral arrangements as his house had been her last address. Without the leaflet 'What to Do When Someone Dies' he'd have been lost for there seemed to be hundreds of people who had to be notified: registrar, solicitor, social security officer, bank manager, insurance agent, funeral director; the list went on and on. From that moment on, she lost the title of 'mother' and became 'the deceased' while he was no longer referred to as the 'son' but the 'informant'.

At the registrar's office, he was required to supply every last detail of his mother's life and demise. The young registrar must have sensed his impatience for she said brightly, 'I'm so sorry that you have to go through this routine at such a time but the good news is that you will be entitled to a death grant of thirty pounds towards the cost of the funeral.'

Ten minutes later, she was back. 'Sorry. I got it wrong. Your mother won't be eligible for the death grant after all. She was born in eighteen eighty-six and the grant doesn't apply to anyone born before eighteen eighty-eight when the Burial Act came into force.'

Billy could almost hear his mam saying, 'Typical of this government; it's so mean, it won't even help to bury me.'

Mam's body was moved from the hospital to the funeral rest home where Billy found himself having to make macabre decisions with a mortician flicking through a coffin brochure as if browsing through a family album.

'This is our best line,' the director told him. 'It's a de-luxe model, solid mahogany with brass handles. It should last . . .' For a moment Billy thought he was going to say 'a lifetime' – 'and give good service for many years. Or you could go for something cheaper and biodegradable.'

Mam was taken to the Chapel of Rest within the funeral home where those who wished could view the body. Billy encouraged his own children to go.

'In my Collyhurst days,' he told his family, 'death was not an uncommon occurrence and, as children, we were used to being taken in to view the corpse. It served as a reminder of the inevitability of death.'

An insurance policy had been taken out on Mam's life just after she'd been born ninety-two years ago when it was common practice for working-class families to take out death cover as soon as a baby was born. Mam's policy paid out £107.74, not enough to cover the funeral expenses, which amounted to £350, but her life savings of £1,600 more than made up the balance. Billy shared out the surplus with the other four members of the family, giving them an inheritance of £271.40 each. The policy had been with the CIS and naturally the obsequies had to be conducted by the Co-op Funeral Services.

'She'd have approved of that,' Les smiled sadly. 'I hope you claimed the divi.'

There was a huge crowd of mourners at the requiem Mass at St Chad's. They came from near and far. The extended family itself was vast, consisting of every one of Kate's own children and grandchildren; her brother Eddie and sister Cissie along with their brood; her stepbrother John and stepsister Hetty plus their progeny. Innumerable friends and neighbours from Ancoats, Collyhurst, Red Bank, Cheetham Hill and Langley came to pay their respects. Every seat in the church was taken. When it came to the singing of Kate's favourite hymn, the congregation raised the rafters.

> *Soul of my Saviour,*
> *Sanctify my breast*
> *Body of Christ,*
> *Be Thou my saving guest;*
> *Blood of my Saviour,*
> *Bathe me in Thy tide,*
> *Wash me with water*
> *Flowing from Thy side.*

'Kate died peacefully after a full and fruitful life,' Father McGarry said in his eulogy. 'In her time, she knew both joy and sorrow which is the human lot of us all. Born in eighteen eighty-six, her life spanned many momentous events. She saw in her time six monarchs: Victoria, Edward the Seventh, George the Fifth, Edward the Eighth, George the Sixth and our present Queen Elizabeth; she survived two world wars and the Spanish flu epidemic of nineteen eighteen; she witnessed the General Strike of nineteen twenty-six and the Great Depression of the thirties. And most important of all, despite unbelievable hardships, she raised a wonderful family, many of whom are here today. In my time as parish priest, I have celebrated many requiem Masses for aged people like Kate but I cannot remember ever seeing an attendance as large as this because, sad to say, so often the deceased has outlived everybody in her circle and there are few people left to grieve. Your attendance here today is a sign of how much she was loved and respected by all who knew her: family, friends, neighbours. A funeral like this is indeed a sorrowful event but it's also a fundamental part of the human condition and reminds us all that we, too, will die one day. The most comforting words of hope I can offer on this day of sadness are taken from the gospel of St John. "I am the resurrection and the life: he that believeth in me, though he were dead, yet shall he live again. And whosoever liveth and believeth in me, shall never die." '

There was a reception after the ceremony at the Red Lion pub on Rochdale Road, not too far from Moston Cemetery. Funerals are like weddings in that they are occasions for the gathering of the clans. Long-lost family members appear from nowhere and make themselves known. Old aunts and ancient uncles shake out the mothballs from their mourning outfits and make their way to the requiem service and the reception afterwards. But once the deceased has been put into the ground, often he or she is hardly mentioned again and the reception becomes a social occasion, offering an opportunity for the extended family to catch up on each other's news – like a party but minus the main guest. Nevertheless, it was a joy to see old Aunt Cissie in earnest conversation with her younger brother Uncle Eddie and her half-brother and sister; to see brothers, sisters and in-laws in friendly discourse; to see the various cousins exchanging news and views though they barely knew each other.

'A pity Mam couldn't be here,' Les remarked to Billy. 'She'd have loved it.'

Chapter Fifty-Seven

The funeral was held on a Friday and Billy and Laura's family had arranged to stay until the Sunday. They were to have their own rooms back for a couple of nights. It would be a chance for everyone to bring each other up to date about their latest goings-on.

Laura laid on a superb meal, making sure her children's favourite food was on the menu, and soon delicious smells of roast beef and Yorkshire pudding emanated from the kitchen. Roast potatoes, garden peas, carrots plus rich 'Ah Bisto!' gravy were a sine qua non of the menu. Billy had never been able to understand how Laura managed to conjure up such a spread in so short a time and with the minimum of fuss. Whenever he'd volunteered to produce a main course, Hungarian goulash being the only one he was acquainted with, at least three hours' preparation was needed and the aftermath left in the kitchen resembled a bomb site with pans, plates, and cutlery scattered everywhere. Lucy offered to produce a concoction of cream and Angel Delight pudding, her favourite. Billy, as befitting the senior male present, cut up the roast with the electric carving knife. The family settled down to enjoy the feast.

The death of someone close always has the same effect on me, Billy thought to himself. Apart from the grief and the sorrow, I'm reminded of my own mortality. 'We are all in the waiting room,' Mam had been fond of saying at funerals. And what was it the Bible said? 'Man that is born of a woman is of few days, and full of trouble.' Then he thought, hey, wait a minute, I'm becoming morbid here. I must stop being so gloomy and start to think of cheerful things. Because

471

when all's said and done, Mam had a pretty good innings, though that's hardly an appropriate analogy since, as far as I know, she never played cricket.

Another thing about death, he pondered, is that it puts things into perspective. We spend much of our time worrying about this and that but will any of it matter a hundred years from now? On television the other day, I saw some old cine footage of people living around the year 1905 and they were going about their ordinary business: at home, at the factory, at the seaside or at the shops. And the thought occurred to me that here were all these ordinary people walking around with their hopes, fears, dreams, problems, and worries. Maybe one of them was in debt and couldn't pay his bills; another anxious about his job; still another afraid of being evicted from his home. But what does any of it matter now? Most of them will have passed on into the next world. And a hundred years from now, it'll be the same for us and our concerns won't matter either.

He gazed at his family sitting round the table. Now here's something to be cheerful about, he thought. It's a scene that never fails to move me and I'm always reminded of those wonderful lines from Walt Whitman's poem which we learned at school.

> *Why, who makes much of a miracle?*
> *As to me I know of nothing else but miracles,*
> *Whether I walk the streets of Manhattan,*
> *Or dart my sight over the roofs of houses toward the sky,*
> *Or wade with naked feet along the beach just in the edge of the water,*
> *Or stand under trees in the woods,*
> *Or talk by day with any one I love,*
> *Or sleep in the bed at night with any one I love,*
> *Or sit at table at dinner with the rest . . .*

That last line especially, he reflected, brings tears to my

eyes every time. It's certainly a cause for rejoicing for me to be here at this moment with the ones I love. That for me is the miracle.

He looked over at his children who were enjoying some joke or other and he wondered what on earth he'd been so worried about as they'd been growing up.

Sure, he told himself, they led us a merry dance as they kicked over the traces and 'did it their way'. Laura and I had to make some pretty major adjustments in our way of thinking. We worried ourselves sick about whether they'd be able to survive in this dog-eat-dog world of ours. How would they survive? Where would they live? Would they have jobs? Would they be able to pay their bills? Would they be able to support a family of their own? All needless torment because in the end everything had turned out all right.

Take Matthew there. He walked off his course at the University of Sussex and I thought it was the end of the world. What a fool I was! Look at him now. How he's changed!

For one thing, consider his turnout: smart blue suit, white silk shirt, black tie and, wonder of wonders, a 'traditional' hairstyle. It's hard to believe that this is the same person as the long-haired hippie of a few years back. Now an accomplished musician performing in West End restaurants and, what's more, about to take up studying again.

A similar story with Lucy. She left art college and joined an oriental religious group; travelled all over India and is maybe going to go to South Africa soon to recruit more followers. Quite a perk! She also acquired a degree in comparative religion and normally works doing art therapy in a mental hospital. So why did I cause myself all that needless distress?

As if echoing Billy's thoughts, Laura broke into his reverie and said to the family, 'It's like old times seeing you all sitting round the dining table like this.' She sighed happily. 'Almost as if you've never been away. But so much has been happening with everyone in the last few weeks, and I'm dying to hear the latest.'

'So am I!' Billy said. 'You've got to admit, Matthew, that you certainly led us a merry dance as you decided what to do with your life.'

Matthew looked up from his plate and affected a weary look. 'Glad to see you're still thumping the same old tub, Dad. Don't you old folk ever learn anything?' He grinned. 'Right, I suppose I'd better kick off with my latest doings.'

'Fine, Matthew,' Billy laughed, 'as long as you don't shock me and make me swallow my meat, as you did once.'

'No shocks, Dad. Nothing like that,' he said. 'As you know, the band's been doing well since we got the Ritz residency. We've left those smoky pub gigs behind. That scene was seriously overcrowded. Believe it or not, some of the best venues actually charge the bands to play! Those times were 'ard, as they say. Like me, all the guys love forties music, Nat King Cole and Sinatra and so on, the jazz harmonies are fantastic. So we worked up a jazz set to go upmarket, aim at the West End restaurants. We play Cole Porter tunes in white tie and tails under the name the Henry Irving Ensemble. Our agent, Harry Schwartz, soon had the work flowing in – mainly wedding jobs off the back of the residency. My stage name, by the way, is Rio Fortune.'

'That reminds me of the old days and Lou Preager's band at the Hammersmith Palais,' Billy chuckled. 'He used to have a singer by the name of Paul Rich. It all sounds promising.'

'Yeah, it worked out pretty well, Dad. Mind you, I'm really looking forward to getting back to full-time study at Imperial College. It'll seem a doddle after juggling gigs at night and study by day.'

'Will you study music there?' Laura asked.

'No, Mum. Just experimental studies of the physics of ultracold rubidium atoms, as it happens.'

'Sounds sinister but I'm delighted,' Billy exclaimed, unable to hide the emotion in his voice. 'But what about your gigs?'

'Hold it right there,' Lucy said. 'He's not the only one around here who's been doing things.'

'Uh-oh, I knew my dear sister wouldn't let me hold the floor for too long,' Matthew laughed. 'OK, sis. Over to you!'

'Gosh, it seems like *ages* since I finished my degree,' she said with a pointed look at Matthew, 'but my news is that I have been promoted to team leader of my group – still teaching art therapy in a mental institution, of course.'

'Wow!' John interrupted. 'That'll be a challenge! I thought your degree was in comparative religion.'

'And what about the Krishna Kumaris?' Laura asked. 'Are you still connected with the Baghwan Sanyassi?'

'Very much so, Mum. Recently I was chosen as an initiator and sent on a training course at a spiritual centre run by the Baghwan in Japalpur in India. We spent a wonderful month with him and after that went on the road to teach people here in Britain. Three days here, three weeks there, living out of a suitcase. There's a good chance that my South Africa trip will be in July.'

'Is this the little girl I used to know?' Billy asked. 'The little girl I used to tell bedtime stories to?'

Lucy frowned.

'Your little girl has grown up,' Laura said, swiftly changing the subject, 'and what's *your* latest, Mark?'

'My turn, is it?' Mark grinned. 'Not much change since I gave my Christmas report. I can't compete academically with either Matthew or Lucy, I'm afraid. But I think I've found my niche at last. I have a job that suits me down to the ground, working as an estate agent in Sittingbourne. Twenty thou a year and a company car.'

The mention of a company car triggered Billy's musings again. Mark nearly gave me a heart attack when he left that note announcing that he'd quit the solicitor's office and was off to Kent to pick hops. But he always had the gift of the gab. Married now too. Well, sort of married. To Tiffany. Should he call her his partner? Common-law wife? Bedfellow? Either way, a lovely girl who'll keep him on the straight and narrow. So there, too, our worries were unfounded.

Yes, they've all done their own thing though I've often thought they've done it the tough way, going round by Australia to get to Piccadilly. So what could we do? We could only stand and stare. They chose their own route and we had no choice but let them get on with it.

He heard Laura ask him something.

'What? Sorry, Laura, I was miles away.'

'Billy, you're in never-never land. I asked you if you'd like another roast potato. What were you thinking about?'

'I was thinking how wonderful it is to have everyone here sitting round the table, like the old days. I was remembering how we agonized about them all and how it was all for nothing in the end, and I was remembering Mark and his gift of the gab. He always had a tendency to exaggerate,' Billy chuckled. 'Ideal qualities for an estate agent.'

'There's a wee bit more to it than that, Dad, as I was just telling Mum. Tiffany's father, Jack, is encouraging me to study for National Association of Estate Agents exams. I'm specializing in residential sales.'

'Sounds impressive, Mark,' Laura said warmly. 'What does that involve?'

'First-time buyers are usually nervous because buying a house is the biggest purchase of their lives and they need bags of help. That's where I come in. You wouldn't believe how confused people are about what they're looking for. Like, do they want a sunny garden or a leafy neighbourhood? Repayment or endowment mortgage? Or to be near shops or a school? I talk it over with them and help them make up their minds. I love every moment of the job as I'm out of the office and half the time I'm in the open air.'

Billy said, 'I hope you make lots of money, Mark, like I did when I sold the house in Dewarkirk. Listening to you so far, one thing is obvious. You've all ignored me and done your own thing. And you seem to have fallen on your feet. The only one who's followed my advice is John there doing medicine at Sheffield.'

Everyone, including Laura, suddenly looked embarrassed. John lowered his head and seemed preoccupied in studying the willow pattern on his empty plate.

'What's up?' Billy asked. 'Have I said the wrong thing?'

'No, Dad,' John stammered, looking up. 'It's just that I . . .' He had difficulty getting the words out. 'I'm still at Sheffield but I'm not doing medicine. Haven't been doing it for the last eighteen months.'

'Not doing medicine?' Billy gasped. 'It's a good job I've finished dinner or I'd be choking on my food again. So what have you been doing then?'

'I switched to horticulture in my first year, Dad. Medicine was not for me. The thought of blood and guts turns my stomach even now. Even the sight of Mum cleaning out the turkey at Christmas used to make me feel queasy.'

Billy looked at the faces round the table. 'The rest of you knew about this, didn't you?' he said accusingly. 'You too, Laura. Why do you always leave me out of these things? Don't you think I have a right to know?'

'No need to get upset, Billy,' Laura said quietly. 'John did tell me about his intentions but I didn't inform you as I didn't want to distress you. I felt you had enough on your plate with your mother's illness and death. I saw how much you were hurt when Matthew and Lucy walked off their courses. But things are not as bad as all that. You remember how as a kid John had a flair for gardening, green fingers and all of that? Well, that's where his true aptitude lies.'

'I'm not finding this easy to take in,' Billy sighed wearily, 'but I suppose it's par for the course. This makes number four to walk away from the career I envisioned for him. But what made you change so suddenly, John?'

'Everything was going fine until we went into the dissecting room. I couldn't eat anything that morning. Even thinking about it made me feel ill.'

'But you saw the body of Grandma Hopkins when we went to view her in the Chapel of Rest,' Billy protested. 'So what was the problem?'

'Sure, Dad, but she was wearing clothes and we didn't have to dissect her. The first body allotted to me was a woman and I made the mistake of wondering about what she'd been like when alive. Did she have a family? Had she been married and did she have any children? You're not supposed to wonder who the corpse was. You've got to be dispassionate and detached. I'm not like that. Then when it came to making an incision, that was it, I fainted. I just couldn't do it.'

'Surely the other students found it just as hard,' Billy said.

'True, Dad. The difference was that they plucked up the courage to force themselves back in there but I couldn't. From the moment I was faced with having to cut up a body, I knew medicine was not for me. Instead I switched courses and I'm now doing something I really like.'

'So, all of a sudden you decided to pack up the medical course?' Billy said.

'It wasn't sudden, Dad. I've never really wanted to be a doctor.'

'Then why did you waste everyone's time by starting the medical course in the first place?' Billy snapped.

'I was doing it to please you and Grandad. You were both forever saying that it was best to join a profession and you wanted me to be a doctor. I didn't have the guts to tell you the truth.'

Billy's voice sank to a low pitch when he said, 'What's the use of arguing? It's a fait accompli. At least you're continuing your studies at the university. You are doing that, I hope.'

'Yes, Dad. I expect to finish my first degree this summer and after that I'm hoping to go to Kew to do an advanced diploma. My ultimate aim is to get a masters in horticulture

478

and become a landscape gardener at one of the stately homes like Chatsworth.'

Billy grinned ruefully. 'Maybe you'll be another Capability Brown. Who knows? Grandad Mackenzie and I had big plans for you all. We had it all mapped out for you. And look what's happened. All four of you rejected our ideas and did your own thing in the end.'

'Hark the thump of that tub again – such music to our ears,' retorted Matthew on behalf of all.

'As the saying goes,' Laura said, 'you can lead a horse to water but you can't make it drink.'

'Too true, Laura,' Billy said, 'and I've had to learn the truth of that saying the hard way. I was hoping all along that you children would achieve the things that I never managed to do. I suppose I was trying to relive my life through you. I was wrong to try to force my own ambitions on you.'

'Did I hear right?' Matthew grinned in mock surprise. 'You mean you're admitting you were wrong, Dad? That's new. As a kid I always thought you were never wrong. But hang about. Later, as a teenager, I always thought you were never right!'

'The first part's true, Matthew. I was never wrong. Wait a minute, though, I thought I was wrong once but then I found out later that I wasn't. So I was wrong about that.'

The laughter round the table relieved the tension.

'Come on, everybody,' Laura said cheerfully. 'We've got a lot to be grateful for and we should count our blessings.'

'Talking about counting our blessings, Mum,' Lucy said, 'isn't it time we had the Angel Delight? I consider it my masterpiece.'

'Oh, yeah, like adding powder to milk takes years to master,' chipped in John.

Soon, the whole family was engaged in checking that the taste of the butterscotch pudding still had its zing.

'We've been telling you about what we've been doing,' Lucy declared, 'but what about you, Mum and Dad? What have you been doing with yourselves?'

Laura said, 'Looking after this house, your dad and grandma when she was here have kept me well and truly occupied. I still practise the piano every day and now that I have more free time, I'll go back for lessons to my old teacher Mr Gregory at the College of Music in Albert Square.'

'As you know,' Billy said, 'I took early retirement and as a complete contrast from academic work, I now fill my time making doll's houses. At first they were small and unpretentious. But now I'm building elaborate mock-Tudor houses complete with lights and miniature furniture. I have my mind set on mansions and stately homes, like John there.'

'Typical Dad,' Mark said. 'Always gets carried away once he gets the bit between his teeth. Is there any money in it?'

'Not much, Mark. I make about twelve per year and sell them at Christmas for two hundred pounds each. I barely cover my costs but money isn't the point. It's creative and keeps me out of mischief. Oh, I've also been working on my memoirs but for the family only. You can all read them after I've fallen off my perch.'

'I'd love to read them now,' Lucy said, 'not after you're dead.'

'I shall place the handwritten copy in your hands this very day but so far I've only reached the age of seventeen.'

On Sunday afternoon, everyone left and Billy and Laura were left once more in the empty house.

'I don't know what it is,' Laura said, 'but after the party's over and the crowd's gone home, things seem unnaturally quiet and sad, especially when it's your own family. Well, what did you think of them, Billy? Aren't you pleased at the way they've turned out? Even though they didn't follow your plans to the letter.'

'I'm more than pleased, Laura. My concern all along has been that they wouldn't be able to support themselves when you and I are kicking up the daisies. It looks as if my worries

480

were needless because they seem to have landed up in fairly good jobs. In fact, I have only one reservation.'

'What's that, Billy?'

'I wonder, just wonder mind you, whether they're not too wrapped up in their own little worlds, their own little cocoons.'

'I don't see how you can say that, Billy, because aren't we all wrapped up in our own little worlds to a certain extent? You've got to accept that they have their own lives to lead now. You should rejoice that they've cut loose and are now self-reliant. Surely that's what you've always had in mind for them. What more do you want?'

'I dunno. Apart from Lucy who is doing such good work in a mental hospital, I'd like to have seen them involved a little more in caring for others. I wonder if they'd ever care for us the way you have for my mother, for example. Suppose one of us became ill, how would they respond then?'

Laura looked thoughtful. 'Billy, you're a hard bloke to please. We can't all be Albert Schweitzers or Florence Nightingales. Rejoice in your children's achievements. And in answer to your question, I'm sure they'd come to our aid if ever it was needed. I'm surprised you even have to ask it.'

Chapter Fifty-Eight

A year had passed since his mam's funeral and Billy had been visiting a shop in Bolton that specialized in miniature furniture and doll's house supplies. As he walked along Bradshawgate on his way back to the railway station, his nostrils were alerted to the mouth-watering, saliva-inducing smell of fish and chips coming from a nearby shop. He was drawn to the aroma as a wasp is to a pot of jam. Only a saint could have resisted the temptation and when it came to fish and chips, Billy was no saint.

He joined the small queue and soon emerged with a generous helping of deep-fried, crispy brown chips and battered cod, though there seemed to be more batter than cod. Blissfully he munched his feast as he strode along. Bolton Station was a long, draughty barn of a place through which the icy blast of a December wind howled each time a sleet-covered train made its thunderous entrance. This station, he reflected, as he turned up his coat collar and wrapped his muffler tightly about his neck, must be the nearest thing to Siberia we've got in this country.

When the slow train to Manchester eventually arrived, Billy had begun to feel distinctly queasy and was experiencing sharp pain in the upper part of his abdomen. Maybe the fish and chips were a mistake, he thought. By the time he reached home, he had a temperature and was experiencing intense pain.

'A hot drink and straight to bed!' Laura commanded as soon as she saw him. 'I'll call the doctor right away.'

'I think you may have gallstones,' Dr Travers said after his examination. 'The hospital will check it out with an X-ray or an ultrasound scan. I'll book an appointment for you for tomorrow morning.'

Next morning, the pain had faded but the scan confirmed the doctor's initial diagnosis.

'Gallstones,' the surgeon pronounced. 'And from what you've told me, it sounds as if the stone has already passed through the bile duct. If a stone ever became lodged there, it could block the flow of bile thus causing jaundice. You can get by perfectly well without a gall bladder and in your case I'd recommend its removal. The problem is that there is a waiting list of about a year for the operation but I can put your name down if you like.'

'Please do, Doctor.'

'Meanwhile,' he said, 'eat sensibly and avoid rich and fatty things.'

Goodbye fish and chips, Billy thought, as he drove away from the hospital.

A week after the hospital visit, Billy had settled down with Laura to enjoy a lunch of salad and cooked meat when the phone rang. It was the hospital.

A voice said, 'The surgeon attending you has asked me to tell you that owing to a sudden cancellation, he can fit in your operation for the removal of the gall bladder this coming Friday afternoon. If you turn this opportunity down, it may be a year or more before he can accommodate you again. Could you let me know in the next hour as we may offer the chance to another patient if you turn it down?'

Billy hesitated about accepting as the trouble seemed to have cleared up by itself and he lived by the axiom, 'If it ain't broke, don't fix it.'

'Might be best to take it,' a worried Laura advised. 'You never know, the trouble might flare up again. I'm told it's a fairly simple operation and you should be back home within ten days.'

Billy phoned back his acceptance and was told to attend at the hospital on Thursday morning at nine o'clock.

'I may have a long wait,' he said to Laura. 'No sense in both of us sitting there twiddling our thumbs. I'll contact you as soon as I know which ward I'm in.'

Maybe he should have guessed that things were going to go wrong when an Amazonian-type nurse strode into the waiting room where he'd been sitting for over four hours and said in a Lady Bracknell voice, 'Winifred Hopkins?'

'I think you may mean me,' he faltered.

'Follow me!' she commanded. 'What are you here for?'

'Apparently a sex change seeing as my name is William.'

She gave him a withering look. It was only later that he came to realize that it was unwise to make jokes in an NHS hospital. You were liable to get what you joked about.

'We have managed to find you a bed in Ward Seven,' the sour-faced nurse said, 'but you may have to move later as we're in the process of closing the ward down.'

She handed him over to a motherly auxiliary who took him to his bed.

'Now, sweetheart,' she gushed, 'shall we change into our pyjamas and get into bed?'

'I'll get into *my* pyjamas but I don't know about getting into bed with you. I'm not sure my wife would approve.'

The irony was lost on her. 'Do we want to do a wee, darling?' she asked.

'Don't know about you,' Billy replied evenly, 'but I wouldn't mind paying a visit, if you'll show me where the toilets are.'

Next to call was a student nurse who closed the curtains round the bed and in a loud voice that echoed through the ward asked a stream of personal questions: name, address, date of birth. Did he drink? If so, how much? Smoke? If so, how many? Any allergies, childhood illnesses? Was he constipated? When did he last go? Colour of stools? The list of questions seemed interminable. Fellow patients listened with interest as they became familiar with the workings of his digestive, urinary and other bodily systems.

That same evening he was taken down to theatre and as he lay on the trolley waiting to go in, he could hear that the main topic of conversation was about the exciting things nurses and surgeons were going to get up to at the weekend: golf at Sale, a caravanning weekend, walking in the Lake District, taking the wife out to dinner, and worming the cat. Around 6.30 p.m., the last on the list, Billy was wheeled into theatre. The next thing he remembered was awakening briefly to a scene like *Casualty* on TV as a crowd of medics pummelled him, slapped him, and shouted out esoteric numbers and medical jargon. 'He's coming round now,' one called. In a brief moment he had triple vision as they resuscitated him but then went under again.

Billy woke again next morning in his bed and found he was on a drip feed with a tube leading from the operation site. Only three other patients remained in the ward. The evacuation had begun. A little later, a different doctor examined his wound.

'Everything went well,' he smiled. 'Provided it continues so, there's no reason why you can't go home at the end of next week.'

'I'm grateful to you, Doctor,' Billy said. 'I should like to thank the surgeon too when he makes his rounds.'

'He's gone away on three weeks' holiday,' he explained, 'and so you won't be seeing him again.'

Later that day, Laura came to visit.

'According to the doctor,' he said, 'the operation was successful and I should be home again in just over a week.'

'The phone hasn't stopped ringing,' she said. 'All the family's asking about you. The children are wondering if they should come up to see you.'

'No need, Laura, I don't want to disturb them. It's not a serious ailment and I'll be out of here soon.'

'Very well, Billy. I'll be coming to see you every day of course.'

At the end of the following week, the tubes were removed.

Billy was the only patient left in the ward. Two doctors came to examine him.

'The wound is healing up nicely,' one of them said. 'I think we can release you tomorrow. The district nurse will attend to sutures and dressings at home. I dare say you'll be glad to go, as you're left here now in splendid isolation.'

Oh, what sweet relief when Laura came with Mark to take him home. It was all over. The operation was behind him and the troublesome gall bladder gone.

The following Monday morning while shaving, Billy saw himself in the mirror and had the shock of his life for the reflection gazing back at him was someone that looked like the portrait that had been painted in Hong Kong. Charlie Chan was back.

'Jaundice is perfectly normal,' the district nurse assured him when she came to visit. 'After all, the bile from your liver has to go somewhere now there's no gall bladder. It'll clear in good time.'

Two days later Billy resembled one of the chorus from the *Mikado*.

'All normal,' said the district nurse.

By Friday, Billy had become the Mikado himself with a luminous lemon complexion.

'Never mind what the district nurse says,' Laura announced, 'I'm calling in the doctor immediately.'

Dr Travers came round in the afternoon and, putting on his sunglasses to examine him, exclaimed, 'Wow!' or words to that effect. Within the hour Billy was back in hospital. The timing couldn't have been worse. It was the beginning of a Bank Holiday weekend when normal services ground to a halt! The operating surgeon was still on holiday.

Billy was fuming and his temper was not helped when a junior doctor told him he should resign himself to being in for at least the long weekend. So this was the simple operation he had been told about! As expected, nothing happened and he lay there beneath a huge clock ticking off the seconds. He was put on a drip but no one explained what it was they were feeding into his system.

On the Saturday morning, a consultant followed by his retinue of imprinted students called at each bed and, like a grand chessmaster, made one or two subtle moves, uttered a few erudite comments, and passed on. He hardly glanced at Billy.

'How did you know he was a consultant?' Laura asked him next day.

'He was wearing a suit, and student nurses were genuflecting and strewing rose petals along his path.'

Gradually Billy calmed down and resigned himself to the inevitable. The system had grabbed him in its tentacles.

'It's a chance for lots of rest, peace and quiet, Dad,' Matthew told him when he came up from London to visit.

'Huh! You've clearly never been inside nor met any of the inmates.'

Along the corridor in a private room there resided the nearest thing to a Barbary coast pirate Billy had ever seen. He was the evil villain from a James Bond movie, a mountain of a man with a huge paunch, gold teeth and earrings to match and a body covered from head to foot in tattoos, and he strutted around in itsy-bitsy swimming trunks. Every night at 6 p.m., a huge crowd of what looked like rugby players, or sumo wrestlers, descended on him en masse, with surplus guests flowing into the corridor. For two hours there followed roars of ribaldry and bawdy laughter. It was a scene far removed from the days of Sir Lancelot Spratt, when only two visitors per patient had been allowed. In the corner of the ward, an elderly patient had been admitted with a heart attack and it was hard to understand how he survived with such a racket going on around him.

There seemed to be no upper limit to the number of visitors allowed.

In the bed to the left of Billy was Ted, who'd had half his

stomach removed the previous week. He decided one evening to call a meeting of his extended family – seventeen people in all, three of whom sat on Billy's bed until he called for the nurse to explain to them that it was not the done thing.

'How many visitors are allowed nowadays?' Billy asked the sister.

'We're not too fussy about the number,' she answered.

Ted's eight-year-old granddaughter spent her ninety-minute visit staring at Billy as if he were a specimen in a zoo, which he was beginning to feel like.

Billy was soon made acquainted with the procedures by the other patients who never hesitated to express their opinions of the nurses and the hospital.

'Most of the sisters are OK,' said Joe who was in for diabetes, 'but watch out for Big Bertha. She's a tartar and no mistake. She regards us patients as bloody nuisances, always wanting something and asking too many questions.'

One night, Ted was in distress and rang his bell three times. It was over an hour before Bertha came.

'What if it had been a heart attack?' Billy protested.

'Then he wouldn't have been able to press the bell, would he?' she retorted.

Touché.

Around 10 p.m. after the various nurses had made their rounds, the last drinks trolley had trundled off, the blood pressure and temperature ladies had done their stuff, the noises of the night began. Snorting, snoring, moaning, occasional shrieks and hysterical screams for mother. And that was just the nursing staff.

Last caller of all was the drugs nurse who came round with her pills and potions between 11.30 p.m. and midnight. One night slightly before twelve o'clock, Billy was awakened from a deep slumber by someone shaking him by the shoulder. It was Bertha with the drugs wagon.

'Do you need a sleeping pill?' she asked.

'I didn't but I do now,' Billy mumbled.

One night on the ward, a couple of alcoholic patients kept up a stream of curses and imprecations into the early hours, ranting against doctors, nurses, and humanity in general. No one got more than two hours' sleep that night.

'You may be sick and feeling off colour when you come in here,' Joe remarked, 'but a week in here and you'll be at death's door.'

'If there are any diseases going the rounds,' Ted gasped, 'this is the place to pick 'em up. New patients are constantly bringing in their nasty bacteria from all over the world. Hospitals are storehouses for the latest viruses.'

'My sympathies go out to the medical staff,' Billy said. 'They're always short-staffed. At night, there are only three nurses on duty to look after the whole floor of four wards and three private rooms.'

After two weeks of this routine, Billy was climbing up the wall with boredom, frustration and jaundiced depression. No one seemed to know what was happening to him nor how long he would be in for. The various drains attached to him, saline drip and antibiotic stand that he had to push around, didn't help matters. At least things can't get any worse, he thought. O foolish thought! Later that day, they attached a tube to his liver to catch the bile and he now had a 'handbag' to deal with, plus a tube through his right nostril to catch the excess bile which had been leaking into his system.

'Is that it, God? Or is there more?' he asked. There was.

One morning Big Bertha approached and in a robot-like voice said, 'The registrar insists you have a catheter.'

'That's thoughtful of him,' Billy said innocently, thinking a catheter might be some sort of cappuccino coffee he hadn't heard of. She explained mechanically the nature of the procedure and Billy paled beneath his jaundice.

At that moment the family arrived for a visit.

'Couldn't it wait until my family's gone?' he pleaded.

'Sorry. The registrar insists on immediate insertion. And

would you mind if a student nurse does it under my supervision?'

Did he have a choice? 'And how long have you yourself been a nurse, Bertha?' he asked.

'Almost a year,' came the answer.

The family had to go for a walk while they carried out the operation. In excruciating pain, he had to talk to his family as if things were normal.

That was not the end of it. They attached an automatic blood pressure machine plugged into the electric socket. Moving became like the game of Twister that young people played at parties when they tried to move around squares, unravelling themselves and tying themselves into knots in the process. Now, he was completely immobilized.

That night as he lay there in the dark with his thoughts, he felt entombed and the notion struck him that perhaps bad luck floated around the universe, settling arbitrarily on one person or another. But why me? he asked himself. Then again, why not me?

It was the longest night of his life. He felt trapped in a Kafkaesque nightmare in which he'd been tried, found guilty in absentia and condemned to a term of imprisonment and torture though he couldn't recall having broken any particular law. Had he committed some unpardonable sin that had to be expiated? He remembered a prayer he'd learned at school. 'O Lord, send me here my purgatory.' Maybe that was it, his purgatory.

Next day, deliverance arrived in the form of the original consultant surgeon who had interrupted his long weekend to give him two minutes of his time. Billy told him all that had been happening.

'Catheter's completely unnecessary. Nurse, remove it at once!' he commanded.

Oh, what sweet relief! Now the other constraints were as nothing.

'In my career,' he informed Billy, 'I have removed over

490

four hundred gall bladders without a single problem. Yours is the first in my experience to have gone wrong.' Billy had momentary visions of a mention in *The Lancet*. 'Let me assure you, I removed all the stones. But perhaps the heat generated during the operation constricted the bile duct and bile is escaping into the blood stream. We might put in a stent but the trouble is that the scan has shown that your bile duct is not dilated.'

The consultant could have been speaking ancient Persian for all that Billy understood of it.

After that, every day was a repetition of the day before. Like being stuck in an NHS time warp. Scan after scan proved inconclusive. In Billy's interior, bile continued to leak into all the wrong places. The doctors were baffled. Billy begged them to open him up again and see what was going on inside, but they were adamant. They would go on with their ultrasound scans.

You're in here forever, chum, a little inner voice told him. You're never going to get out.

The weekend became six weeks and Billy watched other patients come and go until he began to feel like a permanent fixture and part of the ward furniture. How could a 'simple' operation become such a nightmare? he asked himself His urine was the colour of Guinness, he was more jaundiced than ever, he'd lost his appetite and sense of taste, was dehydrated despite innumerable glasses of water, and was becoming weaker by the day. The candle of his life force was gradually waning. Slowly and reluctantly he had to accept that he was seriously ill and unless somebody did something, and soon, they'd be ringing down the final curtain. Where was the cavalry when you needed it?

Help came from Laura and the family. Their mood had evolved from 'concerned' through 'extremely worried' to 'downright determined'. Lucy postponed her trip to South Africa, the three sons abandoned their various jobs and came north to stay at the family home.

'It's an unpleasant business having to question the competence of health professionals,' Matthew said to a meeting of the family, 'but there's no alternative. I've done some research and I have the names of the best specialists in gastrointestinal surgery in north-west Britain. Let's insist to the hospital authorities that Dad is seen by one of them.'

Armed with this information and in militant mood, Laura and the family marched into the hospital and demanded to see the registrar.

Laura was fuming. 'We have been extremely patient with the efforts of this hospital to diagnose the cause of my husband's serious illness, but enough is enough. No more scans, no more second-guessing. We'd like some action.'

Matthew took up the confrontation. 'We believe that in my father's first operation there was damage done to the bile duct and bile has been leaking into his abdominal cavity. We want an immediate second opinion from one of these specialists,' he said, placing a list on the desk. 'Either that or we'll take our complaint to the medical ombudsman this day.'

It worked. The next day, Billy was removed by ambulance to the university hospital and put into the care of a Mr Andrew Yan. Within twenty-four hours of admission, Billy was recovering in the intensive care unit from a five-hour operation in which the unfortunate accident that had occurred in the original operation had been corrected by reconstructive surgery. Mr Yan reported that he had replaced a small section of the bile duct with a piece taken from the small bowel. It had been an extremely delicate and tricky operation but it had been successful. The family were aghast to hear that, remarkably, he had removed over five litres of bile from the body cavities.

Despite the seriousness of the surgery, the family felt relief all round. At last Billy was in safe hands and had been granted the wish he'd expressed at the beginning, that he be opened up again and the problem sorted. On Laura's first visit she could see only a bed surrounded by a forest of drips, monitors and tubes that led, as all roads led to Rome, to Billy's drowsy body.

It had been a close run thing but slowly the road to recovery began. First, a tiny sip of water, then the gradual, day by day removal of the tubes, which came to symbolize his recovery: first the nasal feeding tube and oxygen mask, next two abdominal drains, the epidural drip, a further abdominal drain and at last the hated catheter which had been re-inserted. Once the internal plumbing had been repaired, Nature set about her miracle cure. Appetite and taste returned, complexion became normal and the urine changed from the colour of Guinness to a healthy Heineken lager. Next came his first faltering steps to the end of the ward and back. A fortnight after the operation, Billy was sent home to convalesce with the warning that he had to take things easy or else . . .

Chapter Fifty-Nine

It is said that a drowning man sees the whole of his life pass before him. Billy was not drowning; on the contrary he was recuperating but during his convalescence at home, a cavalcade of his past life seemed to parade before him in the form of the many visitors who came to wish him a speedy return to good health. Titch and his wife Elaine, accompanied by Oscar, made the journey across to Didsbury to spend a pleasant hour or two reminiscing about the days that used to be. Titch and Elaine were happily settled after their early marital troubles, their chief interest in life being the latest escapades of their twin sons. Oscar was head of English in a grammar school and was still sharing a house with the same partner, Derek.

Laura's younger sister Katie and brother Hughie came to visit. Katie was still a nurse but had moved with her new husband to Southport where she worked in the local hospital.

Hughie, now a general practitioner in Stoke, was still unmarried. 'Don't seem to be able to find the time,' he said.

From Edinburgh came Jenny with husband Hamish. Still the same, exchanging barbed comments, their unique way of expressing love for each other.

Billy's two older sisters, Flo and Polly, travelled over from north Manchester with their husbands Barry and Steve and fussed over their baby brother Billy as if he were five years old again.

Billy's big brother Les came with his wife Annette in their new Volvo. 'I can't let you get away with being the only one in the family with a car,' he laughed. 'And what's this I hear about you swinging the lead so as to get yourself a few days in bed being waited on hand and foot?'

'That's right, Les, and if you want to follow suit, I recommend a diet of fish and chips, preferably from Bolton. That way you could conjure up a gallstone or two.'

After Les, their long-lost brother Sam came over from Belfast. That worried Billy a little because Sam only ever travelled across the Irish Sea for weddings and funerals. I must be sicker than I feel, he thought. However it was OK on this occasion as Sam had come over simply to congratulate Billy on his survival of an NHS operation.

Laura's parents Duncan and Louise paid a visit. They were now a spry septuagenarian couple and still very much with it. Louise spent her time in the kitchen with Laura swapping recipes. 'I need a break from Duncan's pontificating,' she said. 'Ever since his retirement, he's been laying down the law. Anyone would think he was procurator fiscal the way he goes on.'

Duncan himself devoted his hour to advising Billy as to how he might have sued the NHS for a botched operation. 'If it had happened in America, you'd now be a millionaire,' he declared.

'But we're not in the States, Duncan, we're here in England, and who needs the hassle and worry of litigation? I'm perfectly happy with my life, thanks in large measure to you and your unfailing support over the years. I'll never be able to repay you for all that you've done for me.' Duncan was touched by these words, which was saying a lot considering he was a Scotsman and an Ayrshireman into the bargain.

A week after returning from hospital, Billy convened a meeting of his own little family before they departed for their various destinations.

'This is what my old mother would have called a family conflagration,' he said. 'As you know, I am a man of few words.'

'If only,' Laura said from the sidelines. 'I have a feeling there's a speech coming on.'

'I've had lots of time to think while in hospital,' Billy told them, 'and I want you all to know that I'm deeply proud of what you have achieved and the kind of people you have become. As you know, I was worried sick about you when you each decided to flout parental authority and go your own way. Would you be able to earn a living? I kept asking myself. And I tried to push you into jobs of *my* choosing, not yours. That was a huge mistake. What I've come to admire most about all of you is the way you decided for yourselves what you wanted to do with your lives. It's a sign of maturity that you've been able to make up your own minds and not let yourselves be pushed into doing what other people thought you should do. You've followed Shakespeare's dictum: "To thine own self be true." '

'Hey, Dad,' Lucy said. 'You'll have us all in tears if you go on like this.'

'Too late,' Laura said. 'I already am.'

'One last thing,' Billy said, 'and then I'm done. After Grandma's funeral when you told us what you'd been doing with your lives, I was profoundly moved when I realized that you'd become independent, autonomous individuals. I wondered, mistakenly I realize now, whether perhaps you were a little too wrapped up in your own little cocoons. How wrong you've proved me! The way you rallied round when I went into hospital put the lie to that misconception. At times my light was in danger of being extinguished but it was rekindled by your care and compassion. I'm still not sure if you realize how close I came to giving up the ghost.'

'God, Dad, don't say that,' interjected Lucy. 'OK, at first we thought, Dad's always been as strong as an ox, but as time went on we could literally see your life force fading away, and we knew we had to act fast. It was a nerve-wracking time.'

'It was for all of us, Lucy,' Billy said, continuing his little speech. 'Anyway, I think you've all become considerate, tender-hearted people and have developed what I consider to be the most important human attribute of all, namely kindness. For me, possession of this quality means more than achieving social status, professional success or a large bank balance. Now, I'm going to shut up before I break down.'

'Hearing you talk like that, Dad,' Matthew said, 'I almost wish we could rewind the tape and live life over so that we could show you how much we care about and love you. It wasn't always plain sailing but one thing's certain: we couldn't have asked for a better father.' He paused. 'Or mother.'

'In that case, on the playback, maybe you could omit the part where I go into hospital,' Billy grinned. 'I had my fill of 'em the first time round.'

'If ever you felt like moving to Kent,' Mark said, 'say the word and I'll find the house of your dreams.'

'And I'll create a garden that would make Capability Brown green,' added John.

'But could we afford it?' Laura smiled.

'Listening to you today, Dad,' Lucy said, 'I'm more and more convinced that you should write a book. I've read the memoirs you've written so far and think they have the makings of a novel. It's all there. The tears and the laughter.'

'The autobiography I've been writing,' Billy said, 'is for family consumption only. I can't see how anyone outside our own immediate circle would have the remotest interest.'

'As you're always telling us, Dad, nothing ventured, nothing gained.'

'What could we call it?' Laura wondered.

'What about *Growing Up in Collyhurst*?' Matthew proposed

'How about *Billy the Kid*?' Mark suggested.

'Or *The Kid from Collyhurst*?' from John. 'That has a nice ring to it.'

'What about *The Kid from Angel Meadow*?' Lucy said.

'I'll have to think about it as I've never written a novel before,' Billy said. 'Maybe I will and maybe I won't. I must admit, though, I've always had a hankering to write ever since I took my first job as copy boy on the *Manchester Guardian*. Somewhere along the road I got shunted into teaching.'

'Then maybe now's the time to take up your pen again,' Laura said.

The next day, the four children departed for their various destinations and whilst Billy and Laura were deeply sorry to see them go, they knew that they each had their own lives to live. And after all, that was what it was all about, wasn't it?

Chapter Sixty

Billy settled at his desk in the front room. He took out a pencil and the exercise book he had bought the previous day at W.H. Smith's. He sucked the end of the pencil for a little while and then started to write.

OUR KID

CHAPTER ONE. A MIXED INFANT.

Billy was six and he knew how to whistle . . .

Now you can buy any of these other bestselling
Headline books from your bookshop
or *direct from her publisher*.

FREE P&P AND UK DELIVERY
(Overseas and Ireland £3.50 per book)